His Eye *Is on the* Sparrow

God, Guns, and Grandma

M. L. Vaughn

His Eye is on the Sparrow: God, Guns and Grandma must be deemed a work of fiction, although many events in this novel were actually based upon real events.

Copyright © 2010 MaryLou Vaughn

This book was published on-demand in cooperation with CreateSpace.com. On-demand publishing is a unique process and service of making a book available for retail sale to the public, taking advantage of on-demand manufacturing and Internet Marketing. On-demand publishing includes promotions, retail sales, manufacturing and order fulfillment, accounting and collecting royalties on the behalf of the author.

ISBN 10: 1-45371-127-9
ISBN 13: 978-1-45371-127-9

Cover photo: © William Britten, Licensed through istockphoto.com.

Cover and interior design: Robert Dyer

Printed in U.S.A.

ACKNOWLEDGEMENTS

My appreciation to Robert Dyer for all he has done for me to make my manuscript into this book. I wanted a setting in Southern Illinois for the cover, and, to me, the "sparrow" is so special. Robert, I thank you.

I also want to thank a longtime friend and avid reader, Mrs. Carol Lubell that took time from her busy life's fun and work and traveling schedules to proofread my manuscript. I really appreciate her many notations, comments and encouragement.

I have turned the years back in my mind and revisited them and learned from them and feel a love for all of the many people and daily and seasonal events that have enriched my life's memories. Thomas Wolfe said "You can't go home again." How true. But, we can remember the good times, as well as the rocky roads.

There are so many Teachers, Professors and Ministers that I have admired and learned from. But, there are a few who touched my heart, and inspired me to do the best I possibly could, in whatever, I had to do.

I especially want to thank these Methodist Ministers and their wives from Southern Illinois; Reverend Oscar and Paulene Maerker, Reverend Tommy and Mrs. Harper, Reverend Roscoe and Wilma Rose, and Dr.and Mrs.C.C. Hall.

The Epworth Youth Fellowship, met every Sunday evening for an hour before the regular service, and had quarterly meetings with all of the youth within the designated districts. Music was an integral part of the services.

Four of the guys became known as "The Epworth Four", and they became a very popular quartet that sang in many churches and high school auditoriums throughout Southern Illinois.

They were Charlie Todd, who also played the guitar, mandolin, and ukulele, and sang tenor; Billy (Willis) Harlow, Baritone, also played the guitar; Cal Ryan and Wayne Artist, who each sang on different occasions, and Earl Vaughn, Bass, who always wore bow ties that would sometimes light up and drive the crowds crazy. The pianist was Mary Lou Kinison. Thanks to Glen Wall and Tom Osborn for taping.

I am especially indebted to these two fabulous, dedicated and caring teachers that I had in class at Mt.Vernon Township High School; Mrs. Ruby Sanders who taught Business Education and Commercial Subjects that helped me keep my feet on the ground when I needed to; and Leila E. Mudge, who was a most knowledgeable Speech and English teacher with a penchant for the ironic, surprising and often hilarious situations that one would always learn from and remember forever. She was an absolute walking "Thesaurus" of the American Language, and of the great books as well as the then current authors. She delighted in the folksiness of our peculiar dialect and our common usage; *usus loquend*, (it'll be on the next test). I admired her tremendously and still frequently think of something kind or funny or thought-provoking that she said or did that made the world a better place for me.

There were so many wonderful Professors in the Colleges and Universities that I attended in our many moves, but there are two who "challenged" and "inspired" me in their own ways.

Dr. F. Jay Taylor was the Chairman of the Dept of History at Louisiana College, when I attended there in Alexandria-Pineville. He had just edited a book, *Reluctant Rebel*. His classes were always full, fun, and demanding. He was the first to encourage me to write my "own manuscript."

Dr. Kasurni Teshigahara, was the President/Master of The Sogetsu School of Art. It was an honor and privilege to study with him. Many of my awards and blue ribbons were due to what I learned the two years I studied at Sogetsu in Tokyo.

CONTENTS

IN MEMORY OF

AND

IN TRIBUTE TO

MY FAMILY

1

🦃 AN ORANGE IN MEMORIAM

Southern Illinois bears little resemblance to the central or the northern sections of the state. Early settlers referred to it fondly as 'Little Egypt' because of the similarity to the Nile River Delta in Egypt. The great Mississippi River on the west and the Ohio River to the east and south borders this region that is comprised of the Ozark Plateau and the northernmost tip of the Gulf Coastal Plain. Orchards of apples, pears, peaches and nut-bearing trees thrive during the long growing seasons on the gently sloping, rolling hills. Rich deposits of coal and oil lie deep beneath the surface which is blanketed with woods and valleys and cultivated fields and forested hills with hundreds of varieties of deciduous trees that burst into green in the early spring and blaze in vibrant colors in the late autumn.

Illinois: Land of Lincoln, The Garden Spot of the Nation, The Prairie State, The Sucker State. And then there is Southern Illinois; Little Egypt, my home, where the setting is rural and the towns are small and the people are friendly and honest and hard-working with dispositions as changeable as the weather. Their dialect is peculiar to the area and their home-spun philosophy is rich in axioms and colorful phraseologies that bespeak a wisdom akin to Solomon's.

The Great Depression hit hard and there were honorable men who, stripped of their life's savings and working capital, paid their debts with deeds of acreage and thus retained their integrity and held their heads high while tightening their belts against the adversities that ravaged their life's savings, eroded their worldly accumulations and sapped their very strength.

My Grandpa was such a man and my world revolved around him when I was little. I would climb onto his lap and watch his mustache wobble and his dark blue eyes twinkle and crinkle as he talked and laughed. He smelled of tobacco and felt of warmth and security and strength. We would share an orange and he would laugh about all of his fruit trees bearing such luscious fruit, and yet he was partial to oranges from Florida. He would peel the orange so carefully with his pocket knife, unfurling it in one long thin curlicue and then slice off the white with bits of juicy orange for eating because, "The white part's good for you, too".

When I was first sent to Sunday School I did not understand what the God talk was all about until one time when the teacher used an analogy likening God to an old man. I envisioned Grandpa and thought; Gee, *if God's like Grandpa then He'll be alright.*

I had gone out to the garden early in the morning with Grandma and helped her gather the flowers. She kept sighing and wiping her eyes and seemed more annoyed than usual at the ants on the peonies. She would give them a vicious shake before wrapping the stems in wet newspaper.

"Your Grandpa loved these peonies and lilacs. You be sure they put them at his headstone."

"Will Grandpa know they are there?"

"He'll know." I looked up at Grandma. She always seemed to look the same and her voice was always soft and low and calm. Her blue eyes were sad and tearing but her face was smooth and free of wrinkles. Her long softly waved gray hair was always neatly gathered into a soft roll at the nape of her neck. She usually wore a bonnet and long apron and gloves when working in the garden, but not today. She was dressed for traveling in a black silk dress with lace at the collar and cuffs.

"Grandma? Is it very far to Aunt Katie's?"

"No, not far. You'll be there before dark."

"Will we stay there very long?"

"We'll see, Honey."

I followed Grandma as she carefully picked her way through the rows of peonies and looked sadly at the good promise of irises and roses. The four-o-clocks and zinnias that we had helped Grandpa sow had pushed up through the black soil and Grandma dirtied her hand pulling up some stray weeds from amongst them. She cut long stems of purple and white lilacs and I buried my face in them inhaling their sweet perfume.

"Grandma? May I have an orange?"

"An orange? Why—I don't think there are any oranges around here this time of the year, Honey. Your Grandpa used to special order them."

"I want to take Grandpa an orange. You said he'd see the flowers, so, he'd see the orange and he'd know it's from me."

Grandma's chin quivered and she stared off into the distance as tears rolled down her cheeks. Hard sobs welled up from deep inside me and my throat ached as they tore out into the early morning quiet. Tears were blinding me and I heard my voice screaming, "I want Grandpa. I want . . . to give . . . Grandpa . . . an orange!"

The back door banged as Dad came running from the house calling, "Mama? . . . Toot? What's the matter? Did a bee sting you? . . . Are you alright, Mama?"

I saw Mother, heavy with child, standing on the back porch shaking her head and talking to the wind. Dad tried to pick me up but I wouldn't let him. My arms were full of the lilacs for Grandpa's grave and I didn't want them to get crushed.

"Toot, what'sa matter? You're making a terrible racket. Here now! Tell me what's wrong."

I gasped between sobs, "Iwannaorange" as Dad's big hands held me by the shoulders. He looked incredulous. "You what? You want an orange?"

Grandma walked over to where Dad was kneeling beside me. Her face was crinkled and tears glistened in her eyes but she was smiling as she said, ever so softly,

"She wants to give an orange to her Grandpa."

Dad looked off into the distance and then took out his handkerchief and wiped my face dry saying, "We'll get you an orange, Toot. Now, hush your crying. I'll get you an orange if I have to go to Florida. Don't fret anymore now."

He took the lilacs from me, gathered up the peonies and carried them to the back porch where Mother was waiting with a barrage of questions.

"What's all of the commotion about? An orange? She threw a tantrum over an orange? Why, I don't believe it!"

Mother approached me in a flurry of hurried preoccupation, misunderstanding, and sincere concern.

"We've got some applesauce, Honey. Do you want some applesauce? You shouldn't cry and carry on like that over an orange. You ought to be thankful for what you have. Now you come in here and have some eggs and applesauce."

Mother ushered me on into the kitchen where Alf, Loralee and Marj were around the breakfast table. I could hear the movers upstairs taking down the beds and struggling down the stairs with the heavy furniture. There seemed to be strange men all over the house stripping it of everything that made it home. I still had a lump in my throat and was feeling a bit shy. Loralee was solicitous and filled my plate with scrambled eggs and lots of applesauce. She wiped my face and hands with a steaming hot washrag, smoothed my hair and urged me to eat my breakfast so I'd grow tall and pretty. We could hear Dad and Grandma explaining to Mother about why I wanted an orange.

Marj looked at me with disdain, "If Dad gets you an orange, he'd better get some for the rest of us, too. That's so dumb! You can't put an orange on a grave. It'll just shrivel up. Grandpa's dead. He can't eat it!"

Alf looked at me as he buttered another biscuit, "Toot, she's right. Oranges are hard to get. They cost a lot, too. If you put it on the grave you're just wasting it. Some squirrel or wild cat will get it."

Loralee saw the tears starting up in my eyes and patted me on the shoulder and said, "Don't you listen to them, Honey. I think it's a lovely thought. Besides, wild animals don't eat oranges."

Marj stood, crossed her arms with all of the authority of her fourteen years and said, "Oh, such a lovely thought! Well, if a wild cat doesn't eat it, then the ants will or it'll just shrivel up and rot!"

She tossed her long ash blond curls and flounced out.

Dad called Alf to help with something and Loralee patted me on my arm and told me to finish eating and hurried off to do some more packing herself. Since I was all alone I crumbled my biscuit in my applesauce and sprinkled more salt on the eggs. Their talk of the orange being wasted or eaten by wild animals nagged at me, but I wanted it for Grandpa, and Grandma had said he would see it. The food wouldn't go down over the lump in my throat. I jumped up to go get in the hallway hat tree, my secret place, but the foyer was empty except for boxes. I hated moving and I wanted Grandpa, my Grandpa.

I would follow him about the house and yard and sometimes he would take me with him when he went downtown. We would stop and watch the wooly worms on the sidewalk or the butterflies fluttering about the hedges. He knew how to find animal shapes in the clouds and after he got so he couldn't speak very well he would have me call a cheery "Good Morning" to the people we would meet and he would just smile and tip his hat.

On rainy days he would clean and oil the guns and tell me stories of how his great, great, great grandfather had come to America from Germany. He would show me the guns our ancestors had made and point to their names or symbols with pride. I would dust the powder horns and practice counting with the lead balls. When Grandpa would say it was nap time, we would wash up, he would get an orange from the sideboard and we would sit in the big rocking chair and share it and laugh about how oranges are so much better than cod liver oil.

One morning when I came downstairs for breakfast Mother told me they had taken Grandpa to the hospital. I asked, "When's he coming home?"

She busied herself about the kitchen and said, "Well, I can't say. We'll just have to wait and see."

It seemed he was gone a long time. Then one day an ambulance drove up our driveway and pulled over on the grass and drove right up to the front porch. Two men in white uniforms got out, opened the back doors of the ambulance and pulled out a cot that had Grandpa on it. From the porch, I could see his face; it was as white as the blanket they had over him. He tried to say something and grimaced in pain. I ran to the man nearest me and started kicking him and yelling, "What did you do to my Grandpa?"

Mother tried to pull me away from him but I hit him with my fists and yelled, "You're mean! You're bad! You hurt my Grandpa!"

Dad and Dr. Matthews pulled up in the driveway and as the doctor directed the attendants into the house, Dad sat down with me in the swing and lifted me up on his lap.

"Toot, that man is helping your Grandpa. They brought him home from the hospital in the ambulance because he isn't well enough to ride in the car."

"Why?"

"He's sick. He's very sick. He's had a stroke. That's why he can't talk very much. But he wanted to come home to be here with you and Grandma."

The men in white came out carrying the cot. Dad gave them some bills and they said something about understanding and too bad, mighty sad. I ran inside. I could hear Mother in the kitchen talking about me. "I don't know what got into that girl; kicking and fighting like that. Why, he looked like he was going to cry and I couldn't get her to stop. She was kicking and hitting and yelling like a wild girl. I'll bet he thinks we've never taught her anything."

I climbed up onto the seat of the hallway hat tree. I liked snuggling up in it with the big heavy coats hanging on either side and the hats on pegs above. It smelled warm and wooly and tobacco-e. The umbrellas stood on one side. I got Grandpa's big black one and opened it up and held it in front of me, shutting out the accusing voices, the strangeness and the frustrations of my changing world.

Dr. Matthews peeked around the edge of the umbrella. "Anybody home in there? You may go up and see your Grandpa for a minute, Toot!"

I had never seen Grandpa in bed before and I did not like it. Grandma was sitting in a chair beside the bed looking worried. He raised his head and motioned for me to come to him but then he went to sleep. Grandma held me beside her in the big blue reading chair, and we sat there slowly rocking back and forth with the silence punctuated by the creaking of the rocker. Dad moved the Victrola into the bedroom and we'd crank it up and play the big thick records of Alma Gluck or the 1929 big hit of Bing Crosby singing *Mary Lou*. That was my favorite, but there were other songs too with family names; *Margie, Lorena, Aurale, Ka-ka-ka-katy*, and *Peg Of My Heart*. There were records of arias and church songs and one about a train wreck that I did not like, but I always listened closely.

Grandpa regained enough strength that he could walk well with a cane and could speak clearly if he took a lot of time. We spent the long winter hours oiling the guns and he would retell the tales of our forefathers, of how they had come to this country, fought Indians and Redcoats, endured unimaginable hardships, established a village and made the best shooting, most dependable long guns of their time.

Grandpa had trouble opening his pocket knife so that became my job. I would fetch an orange so he would not have to get up, but he insisted on peeling it himself and he did it perfectly every time. He never left the house that winter but he did make a lot of phone calls. He would have me tell Miss Molly, the operator, who he wanted and then I'd sit on his lap and listen as he talked of money matters and the depression and Roosevelt and the old farm and orchards and coal mines. He was always tired and sometimes near exhaustion when he finished the calls.

One April morning, a neighbor lady, Mrs. Badgett, was fixing breakfast when I came downstairs. She was nervously cheerful as she stirred the oatmeal and buttered toast. Marj, Loralee and Alf were sitting quietly around the table. They were usually gone to school by the time I came down. I asked if they had taken Grandpa to the hospital again. Loralee was looking out the window. Alf was stirring his oatmeal intently and Mrs. Badgett was making little noises in her throat. Marj said, "Grandpa died in his sleep last night. They've all gone to the funeral home."

Mrs. Badgett hurried to my chair and hugged me tight, "Now, Honey, it's alright! Your Grandpa's gone to heaven! He won't be sick anymore."

I fought my way out of her suffocating embrace and ran to the library. I opened the draperies and a flood of sunlight bathed the book and gun lined room in blinding brightness. I opened the box under the library table and chose a heavy flannel rag that smelled strongly of boiled linseed oil. I could not get the guns out of their racks but I began rubbing the stocks of the ones I could reach. Alf came in and without saying anything, got another rag and together we 'dusted' them all.

Relatives, family friends and neighbors started coming to pay their respects. Dad and Mother and Grandma were preoccupied with 'arrangements'. A black wreath was hung on the front door and the funeral director transformed our comfortable, cheerful living room into a heavily draped vignette for the coffin with folding chairs lining the walls. I had stayed in my room during the preparations. I did not like any of it. I did not want to see what they had done to my Grandpa and I did not like what they were doing to our house. I did not like the people talking in hushed tones and clucking their tongues about how I would miss my Grandpa. I did not like the men handling Grandpa's guns and getting their fingerprints all over them. I did not like to see Grandma being so strangely quiet and weeping and I did not like my Mother's constant chatter. I especially resented the gloomy preacher in the black suit who talked on and on about heaven and a great reunion in the clouds. Grandma frowned slightly at his words and Dad looked embarrassed. Mother offered him a glass of sherry and everyone seemed relieved when he declined it and left. No one said anything about him but everyone talked about it being too bad that Reverend Alson was ill because he and Grandpa had been such good friends.

Later Loralee and I went outside and studied the clouds. She pointed to the white puffy shapes in the late afternoon sky and explained, "They're called cumulus clouds. They're the best kind for seeing funny shapes of animals. Lots of times I couldn't even see them until Grandpa would point them out."

The grass felt cool and damp and I moved closer to Loralee as we sat looking up at the clouds.

"Grandpa's not in the clouds—is he?"

"No, of course not. That preacher's dumb. There's only rain in the clouds. But Reverend Alson says there is a heaven; a place where your mind and soul lives on forever and you do happy things."

"Is Grandpa in heaven then?"

"Oh, yes, Toot. I'm sure he is."

There was a wet chill in the air and the puffy gray clouds and some darker blue ones were mingling with the white ones. They resembled a giant kaleidoscope as they intermingled into constantly changing shapes and forms. We watched the shadows grow and fade on the lawn as the clouds moved between the earth and the sun. I simply could not fathom how my Grandpa could be lying in there in the casket and be up in heaven, too.

"Grandpa used to say you can't be in two places at one time."

Loralee laughed and stood and stretched her arms wide. Her eyes were shining and twinkling and her dark brown hair was tousled and wind blown.

"Of course you can't be in two places at once. But, Honey, when a person dies that just means that the real person, the soul and heart and mind of that person, has moved on. The body is kinda like a house that the soul lives in. When the house wears out, why, then, the soul, the real person, moves on to a different place."

"You mean heaven?"

"Well, yes, we call it heaven."

I rubbed the goose bumps on my arms. The breeze was getting stronger and colder but I didn't want to go back in the house with all of those people. I liked being with Loralee. I thought she was the prettiest girl in the whole world, but it was more than just being pretty. Grandpa used to say that pretty is as pretty does. Loralee had a sweet, gracious way of making ordinary things seem extraordinary. I watched her as she gazed at some distant point lost in thought. She had her legs pulled up under her full skirt that billowed about her. I scooted nearer her. She looked at me, smiled, hugged me, smoothed my rumpled hair and solicitously asked, "What is it, Honey?"

"Do I have a soul inside me?"

She hugged me to her briefly. Then cupping my chin in her hand, she said in a reassuring voice, "What do you think I am? The Encyclopedia Britannica?"

I giggled self-consciously as Loralee pushed the dimple in my chin, and sing-songed, "Push the button and get a question." She sighed resignedly and began pulling at some blades of grass which she would hold aloft, letting the wind blow them away. "Everybody has a soul, Honey. But I can't explain it right. It's something like the wind; you can feel it and you can see where it's been but you can't actually see the wind itself. You wantta try something?" I nodded. "Take a real big breath and hold it."

I stood up as tall and straight as my five years would allow and took the deepest gulp of air possible, puffed my cheeks, and tensed myself for some great truth. I did as I was told: I held my breath. My chest felt heavy, my eyes were blurring and tearing, and my head was getting dizzy. Loralee gently cupped her hands around my face and said,

"You'd better let it go, Honey, 'fore you pop."

The breath exploded from me with a rude noise. I gasped several short breaths and felt myself reel for a step or two. Loralee put her arm around my shoulder to steady me and together we started walking toward the house as she explained,

"You see, Toot, you can't see the air you breath, but you can feel it. I think our souls must be something like that. Our bodies have to breathe and we just do it without thinking about it. When we get older, our bodies start to wear out, but the wonderful love and caring for each other that comes from our minds and souls goes on forever, even after we die, and nothing can ever change that special love that we have in our family."

The threat of the April shower was swirling last autumn's leaves about our feet. We could smell the wood smoke from the fireplace chimney and see strange figures bustling about in the kitchen and dining room. Cars were parked at odd angles all up and down the long driveway and to the side of the house nearly blocking our view of the back porch, where a group of men stood smoking and talking.

Loralee and I stood shivering on the back walk looking toward the house.

"And our souls live on in heaven when our bodies die?"

"Yes."

"Doing happy things?"

"Yes, doing happy things."

"Like, talking about funny stories and guns and eating oranges?"

Loralee laughed and tears welled in her eyes as she said, "Yes, Toot, yes. Like telling funny stories and talking about guns and eating oranges."

Dad emerged from the cluster of his friends on the porch and called to us, "What are you girls doing out there without your wraps on? You'd better get in the house and get warm before you catch your death of pneumonia."

Loralee gave him a wave and called, "We're going in now, Dad. We were just looking at the clouds."

Dad looked up at the sky and then gave us a searching, knowing, understanding glance with just a trace of a smile. Turning back to the men he said, "It sure looks like we're going to get more than just an April shower."

It seemed as though Grandpa had been gone a long time now: everything was changing. I helped Dad wrap the guns in flannel and soft wool cloths and I watched as he inventoried them and packed them in long heavy wooden boxes. Mother was fussing and talking about selling them so we wouldn't have to move. Dad tightened his mouth and said on a whisper, "I'm not going to sell a one of them. They're our heritage and our security."

He would not let the movers put them in storage with the furniture. He took them to the train depot for shipping to Uncle Ralph's and Aunt Katie's, and then came back to get Grandma. She was going to ride the train so she could keep an eye on them.

Grandma stood looking at our big brick house for a long time before she got into the car. Mother looked like she was going to cry, but she didn't. Dad had just stood there holding the car door open for Grandma. His forehead was creased and he looked worried and sad as he said, "I'm sorry, Mama. We've got to go if we're going to catch that train."

We were in the car nearly all afternoon. Dad had to stop several times to "see someone" and his "I'll just be a minute" was answered with sullen resignation until he was out of earshot. Mother rolled the window down all the way and began fanning herself with her handkerchief.

"If I had a nickel for every minute I've had to wait for your Dad, I'd be a wealthy woman."

Alf, Loralee and Marj were awkwardly half-sitting, half-lying on top of and amongst the luggage in the back seat. The excitement of the actual moving day experiences, the emotional trauma of leaving a comfortable home and close friends and good neighbors had blanketed them in retrospective quiet. Even the spasmodic scrambling for leg room and more comfortable seating was restrained and good natured for the most part.

Alf was holding Grandpa's gold pocket watch, calling out the minutes, ". . . four minutes . . . five minutes . . . six minutes . . ."

Marj's patience erupted and she snapped, "Oh, shut up! And put that watch up. I wish Grandpa hadn't given it to you. You're such a show-off! You'll just break it."

Mother sighed, shifted her weight and pointed a finger toward Alf. "Now, that's enough of that, young man. Your Grandpa carried that watch for many years and he wanted you to have it, but if you're too young to appreciate its worth, then, I guess, I'll just have to put it up for you until you can."

"Aww, Mom, I'll be careful with it." Alf slid the watch back into his pocket and gave Marj a cocky grin. She ignored him with practiced hauteur and complained, "It's so hot in here! Why doesn't he come on? We're never going to make it to Aunt Katie's before dark. Oh, I'm burning up!"

Loralee answered her with a condescending tone of patient endurance. "It's all in your mind, Marj. Think cool thoughts and then you won't notice the heat so much."

"That's dumb, Smartie. Anybody knows the temperature is the same irregardless of what you think!"

Mother shifted about again, and pointed her finger at Marj. "Regardless, Majorie. Not irregardless. There's no such word as irregardless. And, it wouldn't hurt you to experiment with thinking about something cool and refreshing. Why, just look at Loralee. Honey, I declare, you do look so cool—and here I am burning up!"

Mother began fanning herself vigorously. Dad came hurrying toward the car and grimaced as he got in to the admonition of, "Well! It's about time. We thought you'd decided to stay all day!"

Mother talked incessantly. Her tone was usually pleasant, her voice lilting, sometimes mimicking as she repeated conversations she had had with others. It was easy to fall asleep with the car in motion. The steady drone of the motor, the gentle whishing sounds of the breeze we stirred as we traveled through the seemingly deserted roads of Southern Illinois.

Mother's low-pitched, well-modulated, on-going voice citing familiar names and familiar tales lulled all of us children into light dozing.

The huge red and white peonies and purple and white lilacs were in a bucket of water that was sitting in the floor of the car between Mother's feet and the gear shift. I was sitting in the middle and had to keep my feet up on the seat. I clutched the big, round, thick-skinned orange tightly in my hands, fearful that I might somehow lose it, unaware of the time and effort it took Dad to get it for me, intent only on offering it as a memorial to my Grandpa.

It was getting late in the afternoon when we stopped at the cemetery out in the country from Oaksville. Dad had clippers to trim the grass around the graves and headstones. Mother placed the lilacs and peonies and we all agreed there had never been more beautiful ones. I laid the orange down on Grandpa's grave, feeling shy and a little doubtful after all of Alf's and Marj's teasing but still determined to give it to Grandpa. I solemnly whispered, "Grandpa? That's for you—from me."

Marj was acting mad and pouty and kept mumbling something about creepy and superstitious nonsense and spooks and wildcats and dumb kids and spoiled brats and wasting food. Mother told her to be quiet or go sit in the car.

Alf complained about there not being any pecans about and said he guessed the squirrels got them. Dad thumped him on the head and Loralee glared at him. Mother was talking about how nice it was, so pretty and peaceful; birds singing, beautiful old oak trees and so near the old farm home. Dad called, "Lookie here, Toot"

I joined him and Mother in front of a small marble headstone. He said, "That's where Billy is buried. My, the two of you were really somethin'. The way you would play and laugh and sleep and eat was really somethin' to watch."

"I'll never understand it." Mother said, wiping her eyes on a handkerchief.

"That baby was never sick a day of his life until he got that cold."

"Did he look like me, Mother?"

"Oh no, Honey. Why, you were exact opposites. He was fat and chubby with lots of black curly hair and big black eyes and he never cried or gave me a minute's bother. You were so skinny I could hardly hold you and you didn't have a hair on your head when you were born and you were colicky and cross and sick all the time. Why, when I weaned you, you couldn't even take cow's milk. That's why we had to get the nanny goat since goat's milk was all you could keep down. Never been twins in either of our families before. I just don't understand it. God gives and God takes away, but there just isn't any rhyme or reason for a perfectly healthy baby to just get sick and die without warning. Dr. Mathews says if only we had had penicillin then he could have saved him. But, now, your Grandpa was up in years and had had a stroke and would never have been himself again and it's sad that he had to go but that's life and there's nothing we can do about it. But, poor Billy, such a perfect baby, didn't even have a chance."

Dad put his arms around her and cautioned, "Now, Martha, don't get upset. Maybe you'll have twins, again. Looks like you're big enough to."

"Humph! Having them is hard enough but having to nurse two doesn't leave time or energy for anything else. And here we are now without a home and you with no work."

Dad spoke sharply. "Now, don't worry about it! I was inquiring about a job while ago and I think I've got it. I've got two or three other possibilities if this one doesn't work out. But, I thought we'd go ahead and stay at Katie's a few days. It'll be a nice change for you and her both, and it will give the children a chance to learn about farm life. Katie said you could help her supervise the women in the kitchen. All that juicy gossip ought to more than season the cooking."

Mother's charming coquettishness soothed us all and with Dad's arm about her shoulders we all meandered toward the car. I looked back to the big tombstone over Grandpa's grave and the beautiful flowers that Grandma had gathered and, of course, the orange in memoriam, and then to the little tombstone marking my twin brother's grave and I quietly promised them I'd come again soon. Grandpa used to say I was very perceptive, but this death business put me in a mental jumble. I felt some relief and comfort in Mother's repeated declaration, "*I'll just never understand it.*"

Dad was whistling some nameless tune while Mother began another diatribe on furniture in storage getting bugs and the carpeting most likely being eaten by moths and the books getting silverfish. I could feel creepy things crawling all over me.

"Toot, will you settle down? There's not enough room for you to squirm around like that. Now just sit still. We'll soon be to your Auntie Katie's, although heaven knows I really don't like it one bit. I don't feel like we're going for a visit since we sold the house. It's like we don't have a home and are just imposing on them, and I know she said we were welcome to come and any other time I'd be glad to but I don't like all those women thinking we're just poor relations. You know, Papa said you could find work down there. He said he just couldn't understand why you would go down in those coal mines surveying when there's all kinds of work above ground and I told him that you say you like it and its good money and someone's got to do it and Papa said, you ought to care more about me and the children than to just lose your home out from under you like that. I said, 'Now, Papa, we can't help that. You know we lost a bundle when the banks closed and then Father and Mother Mason lost nearly everything and then gave practically everything else to Katie and Ralph and what with all of the expenses we can't do much more than keep body and soul together' and then Mama said, 'Why don't you make Riley sell some of those guns? Seems to me like he cares for them more than he does you and the children' and I said, 'Mama, Riley says some of those guns have been in his family for two hundred years and nobody else appreciates them like he does and he says too that they're better than money in the bank and they're our future security' and Mama said, 'It doesn't look to me like they're doing you or anybody else any good and now you don't even have a home to keep them in' and Papa said, 'Peggy', you know how he always calls me that, he said, 'Peggy, I don't like seeing you so unsettled! Here you are in that delicate condition again and no home and nothing coming in, but, you know you've always got a home here with me and your Mama and . . .'"

Dad's mouth had become a tight line and his eyes narrowed. He took off his hat and put it down on my lap and wiped the perspiration from his brow. The bright afternoon sunlight breaking through the trees lining the road had a dizzying effect on me and I closed my eyes tight as my stomach started churning. Dad patted me on the arm and said, "We'll soon be there, Toot. Just a few more minutes."

Mother was mumbling something about losing such a nice home. Dad reached down and got his hat and put it back on and said,

"Martha, your folks are good people and I understand their concern for your welfare. I know the last few years have been more hell than you'd bargained for but it's been more hell than fun for all of us. We haven't had it as bad as a lot of people. Matter of fact, you well know, I've been in an enviable position. Many a man would have given his eye teeth for such a job but we knew all along that it couldn't last. I could have drawn that work out for myself for a few more weeks or months but that would have made it difficult for some of the other men and they have families too, as well as there's an honor in doing the best job you can as quickly and efficiently as possible, especially when it's in the publics' interest. And about that house—I wish you'd quit harping on it. Can't you get it through your head that we sold it? We did not lose it! We sold it for a good price—more than it's worth on the market today. And I promise you within a week's time we'll have another one. I've got the name of a fella to see tomorrow about a job surveying with the mines and I'll be hearing from Thompson tomorrow or the next day about that opening with the Highway Department in Nilesville. I know you prefer living there and if I get that position then I'd thought we might get the old Jackson place out on the west hardroad. It's available."

It was hard to keep my eyes open traveling into the setting sun. Dad started whistling again and Mother mumbled quietly as she stared out the window. I hoped fervently that no wild animals got that orange. I knew Grandpa knew it was there.

Dad maneuvered a hair-pin curve that caused me to lean toward him. Suddenly, the blinding bright western sun seemed to be hanging directly over the long ribbon of a road that stretched and swirled seemingly endlessly through the freshly turned and plowed fields and the encroaching woods.

It seemed everyone was dozing except for Dad and me. He was whispering whistling a happy sounding tune. I looked up at him and laughed. He winked and quietly trilled a high note.

"You sound like a bird, Dad. Dad, do you think . . . God cares about, . . . well, about sparrows?"

He chuckled, "Of course He does."

"You're sure?"

"Damn sure! That's why He made worms—to feed the sparrows."

"Oh Daddy, I'm serious."

"Well, now, I know you are, Toot, and I'm serious, too. There's a beautiful song, a hymn, that your Grandma sings and plays on the piano that tells us, 'His eye is on the sparrow and I know He watches me.' Haven't you heard her singing that?"

I nodded "Yeah, it's so pretty. I was just wonderin'. Guess that's why I asked you."

"Well, you know what? I asked your Grandma about that one time and she said that the Bible says God cares for and values the tiny sparrows, so how much more He must care for you. So guess what? I looked it up in the Bible, and sure enuff. It was right there. In three different places, both the Old Testament and the New Testament; Psalms, Matthew and Luke. God watches over the sparrow and He watches over you, too."

Dad smiled down at me and putting his arm around me, pulled me close to him.

"Yes-sirree, Toot. Why I'd bet my bottom dollar on it."

I snuggled against him and went to sleep with the sounds of his soft whistling in my ears.

2

YOU CAN'T EAT GUNS

Uncle Ralph had met Grandma at the train station and had put the long heavy gun boxes in the barn. Dad didn't like it but there was no place for them in the house.

Aunt Katie was a lovely lady, quiet and nice to be near. Uncle Ralph was a big man with wavy iron-gray hair and laughing eyes. He teased me about my black eyes and called me 'Black Eyed Suzie'. Their son, Kenneth, was older than Alf, and did a lot of work with the men on the farm. Lizzie and Sharon, who I knew well from their week-end stays in our home, were contemporaries of Marj and Loralee, but they usually tolerated my tagging along.

I awoke, that first morning on the farm, to strange noises. A rooster was crowing, men's voices were calling and bantering, and cows were mooing. I stood at the upstairs window watching the activity out around the barn. I saw Dad and Uncle Ralph walk out to our car and stand talking for awhile before Dad got in and drove off.

Grandma and Mother helped Aunt Katie and several other women prepare the noonday meal for all of the hired men. They ate at a long table set up on the side porch. I had the big important job of shooing the flies away with the biggest fan I'd ever seen. The men laughed and joked all through dinner. One kept saying, "Pass the honey, Honey."

Another kept insisting they should take a nap after dinner like they do down south. One asked me if that boy out there in the barn was my brother and they all laughed when I said, "I don't know. I'll have to go see."

Another asked Uncle Ralph what was in those big wooden boxes out in the barn and he replied, "Oh, just some of Black Eyed Suzie's toys and some of her Daddy's gear. He's a Civil Engineer and Surveyor. Gone to see about a job today."

One of the older men said, "You ought to take him on here, Boss. You could use another hand."

Uncle Ralph laughed, "Aww, come on, Joe. Hell needs a fire, too. Besides, he'd be the first to tell you, he wouldn't know which end of a horse to hitch a plow to."

The men roared with laughter and wisecracks. I gave my fan to Sharon, who, seemingly oblivious to all around her, kept singing, 'Shoo Fly Pie' and swinging the fans to the exaggerated beat. I walked out to the fence around the barnyard. I was terrified of all the chickens clucking and walking about and the cows that looked at me so suspiciously. I called, "Alf-ie! Alf-ie! Are you out there?"

He looked down at me from the hayloft. "What do you want, Toot?"

"What are you doing out there?"

"Dad told me to hang around here and watch the gu–, uh, boxes. Go tell Loralee to bring me something to eat."

"Alf? Are those wild animals?"

"No, dummy, they won't hurt you. Just ignore them. But don't wear that red dress out in the pasture where the bull is or you'll make him mad and he'll tear you to pieces."

I ran for the house, scattering frightened chickens, startling contented cud-chewing cows, exciting the curious skittish cats, and causing the sleeping dogs to jump up barking. All of which prompted concerned glances and aside comments on the city girl's peculiar behavior.

Loralee was in the kitchen preparing a tray of food for Alf. She poured ice cold milk and covered it all with a tea towel. We made our way back to the fence gate where she called in country fashion for Alf to come fetch his dinner. He teased us about being afraid of the barnyard and called us big sissies and citified dummies and to show us how brave he was he ran at a cow and said "Boo!"

The startled creature veered away and Loralee shamed him for scaring it. He said Uncle Ralph had done that this morning to show him that the animals are really afraid of us.

"He said that's why they keep watching us. If they get in the way, all you have to do is yell 'Boo' and they'll go off."

He bragged about seeing something that would make us puke. Loralee ignored him but I begged him to tell me what it was. He considered it while trying to spit through his teeth like he'd seen some of the men do and then he told about seeing two of them wring the chickens' necks early that morning. He went through the motions and described how the headless bodies had flopped all around all over the yard. He pointed to where one could still see feathers about and described how they had dunked them in tubs of boiling water before plucking the feathers out and he wrinkled his nose when telling of how the feathers stank. I felt scared and sick. He lifted the tea towel and said, "See, Toot? That's where that fried chicken came from."

I looked from the golden crusted chicken pieces on the plate to the chickens walking around clucking, picking at insects, turning their heads about and pecking at their wings, and felt a rush of sympathy. Loralee said, "That's alright, Toot. I know it sounds gory, but chickens are intended to be food for people."

"Eggs", Alf said, "Don't forget the eggs. That's where eggs come from, too."

I shuddered involuntarily. "You mean chickens eating bugs and worms make eggs?"

Alf succeeded in spitting through his teeth and grinned, "Yep! Best eggs you can buy."

We watched the chickens scuttling about and laughed at the rooster holding one foot in the air before setting it down to take a cautious step. Alf ate the chicken with relish and teased me to take a bite. I had never thought about where fried chicken or eggs came from and the knowledge was unsettling to my stomach.

We could hear the men coming out the back in our direction. I pointed to the one who had been so inquisitive. "Alf, that man with the whiskers was asking about the boxes." He watched him a minute. "Yeah—He's the one that was asking me about them, too. Go tell Uncle Ralph."

"He knows."

"Well, then, it'll be alright. You all come out here to play in the hay when you get through in there."

Loralee pointed to a cow that was chewing its cud and talked about its big soft brown eyes. We gingerly made our way up to it and stroked it on the neck. It would ripple its skin and swish its tail and it didn't seem like anything to be afraid of. There was a nanny goat that was big with kid and there were cats and kittens of all shapes, sizes and descriptions. Two Shetland ponies grazed in the pasture, shooing flies away with their long fluffy tails. There were lots of dogs; bird dogs, hounds, a black Labrador that would fetch corn cobs or sticks as long as anyone would throw them and a big brown and white collie that would round up the cows each morning and evening at milking time. There was an old brown spotted hound dog that Sharon claimed was more than a hundred years old. It just ate and slept, moving from the sun to the shade and back again.

The barnyard was a fascinating place; fun and busy, clean and earthy. We giggled at having to be careful where we stepped and when a cow raised its tail to nature's call we stopped and stared, and then, blushingly, turned away and giggled.

The cool shady interior of the barn smelled of sweet hay feed and animal's droppings. Strange tools, harnesses and tack of all descriptions lined the walls. Old saddles were stacked on sawhorses and the ladder to the hay loft was perpendicular, which made it particularly daring and exciting to climb. There was a huge mound of hay on the lower level and Alfie dared us to jump in. Loralee went first, and, I, with much coaxing, followed. After surmounting the initial awesomeness of jumping from such heights we were delirious with the rapturous delight of bounding off into space.

Joe and Charley, who were both regular helpers, made several trips in and out of the barn for supplies that they were loading into the truck. They would look askance at us playing in the hay and diving through the air and cautioned us several times to be sure and land where it's piled up or "you'll break a neck or a leg".

When they were leaving with the last load they stopped at one of the stalls, snickering and guffawing. Then, Charley walked back toward the hay mound as though he was looking for something he had dropped. He took a big red bandanna out of his back pocket and wiped his brow and spoke confidentially, "I don't want to alarm you kids, but, maybe you ought to know, in case you haven't seen any yet—uh."

He hesitated, looked about and moved some of the hay with his foot as he continued, "We've got some milk snakes around here."

I screamed and ran to Alf. He shook me off and looking around, asked, "What's a milk snake?"

Loralee was cautiously backing down the ladder. Charley held his hands out at arms' length and considering them, said, "Well, I reckon they're about that long. Just about as long as Suzie is tall."

I gasped. Loralee seemed glued to the bottom rung of the ladder. Charley wiped his face again with the limp bandanna. He shuffled about, poking the toe of his boot about the straw-strewn hard-dirt area. He continued, "They're kinda hard to see, 'cause they're gray with blotches, uh, kinda big black and brown blotches, all over the back and sides. They're real hard to see 'cause they're camouflaged, you see, the way they're colored. They generally stay all curled up so you're not apt to notice 'em, unless they're hungry or you step on one."

Joe had been listening from across the barn. He moved nearer, scooting the many clumps of hay and called, "Charley! How many do you think we have of those mean ole milk snakes?"

Charley nodded his head, put his big callused hands on his hips, and studied the milieu. "Reckon I can't say how many there is. But, they're always 'round barns and cows. They like milk. They drink the milk right from the cows. Why, some mornings we have to fight them off the cows before we can milk them."

I was petrified with fear and thought I'd never drink milk again. My voice was as weak as my knees when I asked, "Where are they now?"

Charley drawled, "Well, they usually stay all curled up in the hay!"

Joe turned quickly to leave. Charley looked after him and had a fit of coughing. He took his hat off and scratched his head and said cheerily, "Well, you kids have a good time! Just be careful."

We watched him as he strode briskly toward the exit. He kinda slowed down, then stopped, turning back and called, "Actually, I don't think those snakes will hurt you. They do a lot of good around the barn here— eating rats and the mice. Well, have fun!"

He waved and disappeared out the door. I pulled at Loralee and begged to go to the house, terrified of taking a single step by myself. Loralee kept looking all about. Alfie shook his head in bewilderment. "I've been out here all day and I haven't seen any snakes and I'm sure Uncle Ralph would have said something about them."

Loralee asked, "Did you see any rats or mice?"

Alf shrugged, "No. I didn't. I wasn't looking for them. But, I wouldn't think there would be any with all of those cats around here."

I offered, "He said the snakes are curled up in the hay."

Alf bravely poked his foot in some hay exploring. Loralee poked him in the ribs: he jumped and shrieked as though he had been bitten. Loralee screamed with laughter and the two of us ran for the house, laughing hysterically, scattering the chickens, frightening the cows, exciting the cats, waking the dogs, and causing the grown-ups to stare and smile and wonder.

Kettles of water were steaming on the stove. The women washed the dishes in sudsy water and then poured the boiling water over them to sterilize them and make them easier to dry and most importantly to kill any germs because, "you never know what some of those men might be carrying."

I sat at the kitchen table and studied the women and absorbed their talk as they tidied things up. They were catering to Mother and sympathizing with her. Joe's wife was obviously in charge of the supervision of the kitchen and would have been even if Joe were not the foreman. Everyone called her 'Aunt Ruth'. She was roundish all over and her ankles actually hung down over her plain brown oxfords. She had grunted a short-breathed greeting to me in the early morning as she had come plodding up the long steep driveway carrying a fresh supply of tea towels made from flour sacks. She was kind and laughed a lot and it seemed all of the women sought her opinion or her approval on whatever task was at hand. She had a way of clucking her tongue that could express either approval or disapproval. A higher sound was favorable: the lower register was disapproving. She was the biggest woman I had ever seen, but as she stirred about the huge farm house kitchen, I marveled at her swift, sprightly, graceful strides.

Mother was basking in the limelight of attention as they asked her about her expectations and experiences. One sympathized, "You poor thing! In your condition and having to move."

Mother sighed and put her hand to her head as though she were about to faint. They urged her to sit down and Aunt Katie got her a cold wet towel, and winked at me and said, "Martha, do you think you're going to have twins again?"

Mother laughed and asked if they all knew that I was a twin. I flushed with self-consciousness as they all looked at me and laughed and commented on the "double blessing" and "double trouble".

"Did you know before hand?"

Mother was completely revived and titillated. "Why, I had no inkling a 'tall! Absolutely no idea. Of course, I knew something was different but there had never been twins on either side of our families, so, it would never have occurred to me that I would have twins! And they were born early wouldn't you know, at least two weeks early. It was on the day before Thanksgiving and we were having all of the family come to our house the next day for dinner."

"Twins! Imagine."

"Martha—was it twice as bad?"

Mother daintily pressed the cold towel to her forehead and grimaced as though the memory were too much for her. "Oh, I'll tell you, I didn't think it would ever end! I'm sure I'd never have lived through it if it hadn't been for Dr. Matthews."

"Were you in labor long?"

"Well, looking back on it, I'm sure I must have been, but I just had so much to do I couldn't take time to pamper myself. Why, I was baking pumpkin pies and I'd just taken them out of the oven when I was bent double with pain."

"You shouldn't have been doing all that work that near your time."

"Oh, I've worked hard all my life, but, when the doctor ushered Billy into the world and then said, 'Why, Martha, you're going to have twins', I sure had some second thoughts!"

Alberta, the tall thin woman with the pinched face, said, "I'd have died right then!"

Everyone laughed in agreement but comments ceased as Mother continued, "Well, I'll tell you the truth—I would have changed my mind about the whole thing right then if I could have."

Josie set seven glasses on the table and looked to Aunt Ruth for approval before pouring iced tea for each of the ladies. Aunt Katie gave me a glass of cold milk. Josie said, "I never wanted to go through that once but ended up having to do it four times. Never again though, thank God! I'm too old for that kind of foolishness. I just set the law down and told Charley if he wanted to romp he'd have to be mighty careful."

Elvina, a pretty lady who was Aunt Katie's best friend, giggled, and confided with naiveté, "We had three babies before we found out where they were coming from."

Spasms of laughter seized each of the ladies. I was fascinated with Alberta's high-pitched, "Tee hee hee hee". Mother waited for quiet. "Well, I still don't know where the twins came from. Why, when Dr. Matthews told me I was having twins I was just flabbergasted! It was the first time he had ever attended the birthing of twins and he stayed all day and all night. Said he wanted to watch those babies. Folks started coming and everyone was so surprised."

Aunt Katie mocked consternation: hands on hips, eyes wide, head tilted to one side, she said, "Sur-prised? Why, Martha, that's hardly the word for it! And that trick Riley pulled on me—why, I don't think he'll ever grow up."

They urged her to tell about the trick as they refilled their tea glasses, enjoying the cooling off before leaving for the day. Mother sipped her tea and looked fondly at her sister-in-law. Aunt Katie was sitting beside me and slipped her arm about me and said, "Honey, did you ever hear what your Daddy did to me the day you and Billy were born?"

I shook my head and murmured, "No, mam."

"Well, you've got to know that your Daddy and I were the only children in our family. He was the oldest, the biggest, and the most mischievous big brother anyone ever had. He was always pulling tricks on me and most of them were funny but I got so tired of them and Mama and Papa would just laugh at him."

Grandma walked into the kitchen and accepted a chair and a glass of tea from Alberta. Aunt Kate looked to her for verification. "Now, Mama, you know, you and Papa just laughed at his tricks."

Grandma smiled and nodded in agreement, but then she raised her hand and said, "There was one time when your Papa spanked him, the time he sat you down on the cactus. I liked to never got all of those needles out of your bottom."

Aunt Katie frowned and squirmed with the memory, and then leaned toward me.

"Well, anyway, your Daddy always thought boys were better than girls, and it just galled him when I had a son before he did. When your big brother, Alfred, was born, your Daddy was walking ten feet off the ground. You see, then, we each had a son and two daughters, so, when we found out that your Mama was going to have another baby, your Daddy bet us that it would be a boy. Now, the day you were born, we were about the last of the folks to arrive. Dr. Matthews was drunk and asleep in the library. Your Daddy had put everyone up to acting like your Mama only had one baby, but you know none of your people will lie, so they just weren't talking and I thought it was awfully strange for them to be so quiet when we arrived, but then, Riley came running downstairs looking for us and he was all excited about having a bouncing baby boy and insisted we hurry right upstairs to see it. And, I'll tell you, when I walked into that room and saw your Mama lying there grinning with a baby on each arm, I said, 'What? Twins?', and your Daddy said, 'Oh, I forgot to tell you—we have a girl, too.'"

Mother took up the story. With a sweep of her hands that took in the entire gathering she said, "And Katie fainted! Fell—just crumpled forward on the floor. And they couldn't wake up Dr. Matthews to tend to her. Riley laughed for days about putting that over on you, Katie."

The women repeated parts of the story and reminisced about their own experiences. Aunt Ruth asked, "Martha, if you don't mind my asking, whatever happened to the twin boy?"

Mother clasped her hands in her lap and looked toward the ceiling as though searching for an answer. Grandma spoke up in her gentle, firm, matter-of-fact way.

"Billy died when he was sixteen months old. The doctor said he died of bronchial pneumonia."

Things got a bit quiet then. Mother said she would never understand it and others told of babies they had known of who had been lost to illness or accident.

We had a cold supper of leftovers, picnic style and afterwards we children played hide-and-seek in the huge front yard. My initial fear of the chickens and animals turned to fascination as I watched them and learned more about them. Even the rooster looked quite harmless roosting down. I loved the ponies and riding them was sheer delight.

Dad arrived at dark with the good news that he had gotten the job in Nilesville and we would be moving into a new home in four or five days. Loralee and Marj were happy that they would not have to change schools and Alf, though quiet, seemed to be relieved. Mother asked lots of questions about Dad's new job and our new home. Long after we children were bedded down upstairs we could hear the grown-ups talking in the kitchen.

The windows were up and the curtains tied back so that what breeze there was would not be hampered coming in. It was fascinating to see how bright it was outside from the full moon. We could hear a mockingbird and frogs and katydids and the soft 'who who' of an owl in the distant woods. I liked the cozy surroundings and being in the same room with four big grown-up girls. Lizzie and Sharon each had a double bed, dressing table and chiffonier. Loralee was sleeping with Liz, and Marj with Sharon. I had a big thick pallet on the floor at the far side of the room nearest the windows. Alf was sharing Kenneth's room, but had been in our room teasing us girls at bedtime. Kenneth was out on a date so Alf claimed he was 'lonely.' Marj yelled at him to go to his own room before she called Mother. He offered to trade places with her and Sharon shrieked with giggles and dared him to, "just try and get in my bed and see what happens to you, Mr. Smarty-Pants!"

Alf ignored her and the teasing taunts died down to whispers of confidantes. I lay on my pallet listening to the congenial voices below, and the fascinating cacophony of new sounds without.

Sometime later I was awakened by the telephone ringing downstairs. I heard Aunt Katie answer it and call, "Ralph! Riley! Come here quick!"

There was a bit of commotion and then Uncle Ralph's voice cut through the air.

"That bastard! No, you don't need to come. Riley's here. Call the sheriff though, and tell him to get out here on the double!"

I could hear Aunt Katie and Mother urging caution and then for the longest time there seemed to be no sounds at all. I got up to look out the window; it looked over the back yard and I could see the end of the driveway where our car sat next to Uncle Ralph's truck. I could see the shadowy forms of the cattle in the barnyard and out in the pasture and then, I saw a man carrying something out of the barn. The girls were asleep. I padded into Alf's room and shook him awake. We hurried back to the window and quietly woke the girls. We could clearly see that there were two men removing the gun boxes from the barn and loading them into Uncle Ralph's truck. We could not see Dad or Uncle Ralph anyplace, until, hoods were lifted from two lanterns and there was a shotgun blast and a voice piercing the night.

"You Goddamned son-of-a-bitch! Stop right there or I'll shoot you on the spot!"

That was Uncle Ralph's voice. Dad yelled, "You in the barn! Get your Goddamned ass out here or I'm comin' in shootin' to kill!"

We were all crowding about the window straining to see. Marj said,"Ummmm—did you hear that?"

We were all speculating as to what was going on and shushing each other so we could hear more from outside. Alf said, "There he is! He's comin' out!"

The dogs were barking up a storm and the angry voices continued to shatter the night air, as we whispered about what we had seen.

Loralee and Alf agreed that it was probably that whiskered man who had asked questions about the boxes. Liz said he was a drifter and that her mom didn't like for her Dad to hire such people but they had never had any trouble before, other than, they were not dependable. They were trying to determine who the other one could be. Alf re-enacted the apprehensions and kept repeating the cussings until Marj, tired of laughing, threatened to call Mother.

We heard the sirens in the distance and watched the red revolving lights turn up into the steep driveway. Several men jumped out of the sheriff's car and minutes later hauled the thieves off.

Dad and Uncle Ralph carried the boxes of guns into the house and stacked them in the front room. We children had all gone downstairs but after a few minutes were told to go back to bed.

"Go on and go to sleep now. Everything's fine. Don't forget to say your prayers."

Liz and Sharon scrambled for the hot air register between their beds. They finagled with it until they got it to slide open. The dining room was directly below and the grown-ups were in the kitchen. We couldn't see them but we could hear their voices distinctly as they talked about the 'trouble'. Uncle Ralph said, "I'd kept a close watch on that bastard all day, for he was so Goddamned nosey about those boxes. He'd had no business even being near that barn—just lookin' for somethin' to steal! Don't know who the other one was—never saw the bastard before. So many lead-assed bums and Goddamned hobos roamin' the countryside— lookin' for a handout—you can't trust a one of 'em!"

Dad's voice cut in. "For the love of Christ, Ralph! You shouldn't hire just any poor bastard that shows up! I know you're a soft touch but you've always been a good judge of men as well as horse-flesh, but, Gawd Almighty—that thievin' son-of-a-bitch had some—heh eh,—that brazen idiot had his gall—loadin' 'em into your truck!"

Dad was chuckling and Uncle Ralph was laughing and cussing about how he had hired him, given him a place to stay and fed him and although he had never really trusted him, he wouldn't have thought about him trying to steal his truck. Dad said, "Well, we got 'em. Caught 'em red handed. Thanks to Joe warnin' us. How come those dogs didn't bark?"

"Oh, those Goddamned dogs aren't worth shit. They won't even fight their Goddamned fleas."

Grandma's voice came up to our singed eardrums. "Now, you boys hush that talk. There are ladies present in case you hadn't noticed and I suspect the walls have ears, too."

We could almost feel her looking up at the ceiling thinking about us listening. Aunt Katie said, "I don't know why you're laughing about it . . ."

Both men began laughing harder with guffaws and chortles. Their laughter was infectious and we were convulsed with giggles while still straining to hear. Dad was trying to explain. "To put it delicately, ladies—heh, heh, heh—the fella in the barn. . ."

Dad was chuckling and Uncle Ralph whooped and laughed, "I thought he'd stepped in something!"

Dad continued, ". . . lost control of his bowels."

We had our hands over our mouths trying to stifle our own laughter in order to hear what they were saying. Aunt Katie said, "I don't know what we would have done if they had stolen that truck. Why, we spent our last red cent on that and we use it for everything."

Dad said, "Well, Katie, they didn't steal it, did they? We stopped the Goddamned thieves and I hope to hell they rot in jail."

Mother's reproachful voice wafted up, "Riley! You ought to be thankful—"

"Thankful?" Dad chuckled, "Why, I am thankful! You can bet your bottom dollar I'm thankful. I'm thankful we caught the Goddamned thievin' bastards!"

We were all whispering these exciting, seldom heard, prohibited, cuss words. We would try to intone them just as we had heard them until someone would mimic Grandma and we would collapse in shushed giggles. It was more fun than ghost stories; scarier, too, for it was real.

The following morning I was the last one to get up. The chamber pot, or the slop jar, as it was usually referred to derisively, was nearly full and I was afraid to sit on it. We had always had a proper bathroom and while I was unsure of the chamber pot, I was absolutely terrified of the two-holer out in back. I was not really afraid of falling in, but I was sure something would leap up and bite me if I sat down on it. I was poppin' to go and I did not know where I could go. I was doing a bit of a jig and trying to get my anklets and shoes on when Alf came whistling up the stairs.

"Hey, Toot! Did you wake up?"

"Yes, I'm awake!"

"Well, you don't have to snap my head off."

"I've got to go to the bathrooomm . . ."

"They don't have a bathroom."

"I knooooww."

"Why don't you use the slop jar?"

"Because it's fuuulll!!"

I had sat down on the side of Sharon's bed and was bouncing furiously. Alf looked from me to the brimming pot. He grimaced and said, "I guess I can empty it for you."

"But, I can't waaitt."

He picked it up; said "Yech!" and made a vomit sound. I crossed my legs tight as I began to laugh. He carried it carefully to the back window and resting it on the window sill, he unhooked the tiny latch to the screen, and with a "Whew!" gave the contents of the slop jar a wide toss. We heard the old hound dog yelp and go whining off. Alf said,

"Well, if I didn't hit the Goddamned dog!"

I collapsed on the bed in convulsive laughter. All of the excitements, the strangeness, and my bladder just gave way. As I realized what I was doing, I could only laugh harder.

Alf was still looking out the window calling to the poor old dog that had gone under the porch and would not come out. When he saw what I had done he looked incredulous, and then frowned and moaned, "Oh, Jesus Christ, Toot. I told you I'd empty it for you! Why didn't you wait? Boy, you're gonna get it."

I wailed in humiliation, "It's your fault, Alfie. I just couldn't wait any longer and it was so funny when you threw it on the dog."

"My fault? I was trying to help you. Yuch!—I didn't even see that poor old dog down there."

He shuddered and began imitating the yelping dog, embellishing it as he went, getting on his hands and knees and looking ceilingward, exclaiming between very realistic doggie yelps, "Good Gawd! It's raining slop jars of pee."

Eventually, weak with laughter, we surveyed the situation. The beds had been neatly made, but now, Sharon's bed was soaked. Alf grinned mischievously, "That's where Sharon and Marj slept, isn't it? - Tell you what, Toot. You hurry and change clothes. I'll sneak those out to the wash house for you. Don't tell anyone about this, OK? They're so smart, we'll just let them figure it out."

The implication escaped me but I hurriedly changed clothes and followed him downstairs.

"By the way, Toot," he cautioned, "don't say any bad words. Mom's mad. She said if she heard anyone say a bad word she'd wash all our mouths out with soap."

The door to the front room was closed. Aunt Katie and Aunt Ruth were supervising the women in the steamy kitchen as they prepared two-crusted pies and shaped loaves of bread. The talk was of the night before. Aunt Ruth was telling of how Joe had overheard the two men talking at the tavern, and making plans to steal Mr. Mason's guns. Aunt Katie said, "Well, we just can't thank you enough. They were going to steal our truck, too, and I just don't know how we could get along without it."

They saw me a bit shy walking into the biggest and busiest kitchen I'd ever seen. I couldn't help but giggle amidst the cheery greetings of, "Well, look what the cat's drug in."

"You missed your breakfast, Honey, but, we'll find somethin' better."

"Did sleepy-head decide to get up?"

I noticed Mother sniff suspiciously and look at me closely, but she only said, "Honey, you go out to the pump house and wash rea-ul good. Your breakfast will be ready when you get back."

The old hound dog was once again lying in the sunshine, and raised his eyes to me accusingly. I said, as I ran on to the pump house, "I'm really sorry, doggie."

The water was deliciously cold as it gushed from the squeaky pump and the strong smelling yellow soap made me feel tingling clean. I toweled myself off and ran back to the kitchen.

A bowl of strawberries and cream, a plate of hot buttered biscuits and a Hop-a-Long Cassidy cup of hot milk and coffee were ready for me. But what I was really hungry for was their talk. And, as I sat there slowly savoring each mouthful, or, as Mother called it, dabbling in my food, I absorbed their conversations and was enthralled with their cadence of speech, their accentual diction and their inflections. I feasted my eyes on their various shapes and postures that were as different as the print dresses they wore and yet as similar as the aprons that protected them. I marveled at their graceful restrained moves from stove to table to wash stand, as they stirred, tasted, peeled, rinsed, snapped, chopped, seasoned and all the time they were talking, exclaiming, bantering, chattering, expressing their own honest opinions punctuated with, "if you want to know" or "for what it's worth" or "I'll tell you".

I gathered that everyone knew about Grandpa's guns. He had made some mighty fine gun stocks himself and there were those, collectors, who would pay good money just for one of those. Alberta seemed to know a lot about collectors and she exclaimed with feeling, "Why, imagine! They'd pay more for one gun to put up on the shelf than we make in a year of good crops!"

Elvina, who had been frightened of the close call Katie had had the night before, said, "I just cain't understand why Mr. Mason won't sell them guns, Martha—what with him bein' out of work and a family to see to."

Mother looked woebegone, and began her lament. "My Mama says Riley cares more for those guns than he does for me or the children."

I felt an unexplainable flush of shame, outrage and loyalty to my father. I wanted to scream bad words at my Mother who continued to tell how she had, ". . .pleaded with him to sell just enough so we could keep our house, but, no, he just wouldn't listen to reason and what's more, he's never satisfied with what he has! He's gotten so he spends every dollar he gets a hold of on more guns. A lot of people are selling them cheap now a days, but they're a lot smarter than we are. You can't eat guns! I keep telling him when you've got a family to care for you've got to keep food on the table and the way prices are sky-rocketing it's getting harder and harder to make ends meet. Why, last night wasn't the first time thieves have tried to steal those guns and it probably won't be the last time and then where will we be?"

I saw Grandma standing in the doorway. Her countenance was calm, serene, but stern. Her blue eyes were fixed on Mother. As others became aware of her presence, they anxiously busied themselves in self-conscious activities. Mother was the last to see her. Grandma's glance took in the whole room and returned to rest on Mother. Her words seemed to hang in the air as she spoke patiently but with authority.

"Martha, can't you understand that those guns are all we have left? They are a part of this family's history; a part of this country's history. They represent the very birth pains of our country as well as the lives of the men who made them. The Mason's were all gunsmiths. They came here from Germany nearly a hundred and eighty years ago. They were good, honest, hard-working men and the fancy, modern, machine made guns of today would never have been possible without their inventions and trial and error discoveries and constant improvements. Oh, they didn't get rich on gunsmithing, but the guns the Mason's made were dependable and men knew it and respected them for it. They stopped many a Red coat and they put food on the table and clothes on their backs and women and children were safe from thieving savages because of them. The gunsmiths are our unsung heroes! None of them were President and none of them signed the Declaration of Independence. They're not even mentioned in the history books, but I'm telling you the very freedom of this country was shaped and forged in the hot fires and on the anvils of the Mason's Forges. Riley is our only son and he was named after his great grandfather who was a highly respected gunsmith. These few guns we have belong to this family and as long as I have breath not one of them will be sold for any purpose."

Grandma's cool glance swept the room, resting briefly on me. All activity had ceased as the women listened and watched in rapt attention. Steam was hissing from a tea kettle. The lid of a huge stainless steel pot was jiggling from side to side in response to the escaping steam. Elvina stood, poised with knife in hand over the chopping block that was laden with heads of cabbage, carrots and mangoes. Alberta's face looked longer than usual as she gazed, round eyed and open mouthed, forgetting momentarily, the half peeled potato in her hand. Aunt Ruth, who had been kneading a huge, smooth, elastic, well-floured, shapeless mass of dough, seemed unaware of the flour on her face, bosom and arms. Aunt Katie had been skimming the morning's milking and leaned thoughtfully against the new Frigidaire. Mother was sitting at the table shelling new peas into a dish pan. I thought I detected a slight twinkle in Grandma's eyes as she turned to leave and I felt safe and strong and proud.

Alberta's voice had a note of awe when she spoke. "I wish I could talk like that."

I did not know why it was funny but everyone laughed. Aunt Katie said, "Mama doesn't talk much, but when she does it's worth listening to."

Mother sat with wrinkled brow, chewing on her lips. She tossed her head from side to side and said with mock sincerity, "Oh, I do hope and pray I have a son, even twin sons! And I hope they're born with guns in their hands!"

The kitchen exploded in boisterous laughter and, Mother, once again the center of attention, told me to run out and play.

3

🦃 FOR A DURIS EGG FLINTLOCK

The work on a farm is demanding, never-ending and fascinating. Everyone was busy with work or chores or talk. Alf had gone with Kenneth and the men he was working with out to a far field. I walked about the yard throwing a stick for the black lab to fetch and wished I could go pony riding.

Uncle Ralph came hurrying out from the side porch carrying a long white envelope.

"Hey there, little Black Eyed Suzie! Have you seen Sharon around?"

"No, Uncle Ralph. Lizzie said she went down to the main road to meet the mailman."

"She did? Huh! She's going down there an awful lot lately. Must be expectin'—somethin'."

He looked off down the lane toward the dirt road that led to the crossroads where several boxes were located.

"So, she's already gone, huh? Well, gosh darn it to smithereens! I wanted to get this in the mail today."

"I'll take it down there for you, Uncle Ralph."

He hesitated, rubbed his chin, looked at me and smiled. His eyes were all crinkly and his teeth broad and white. His face was deeply tanned except in the white creases of his forehead and around his eyes where he squinted against the sun. His dark gray hair was turning white above his ears and had a gentle waviness that always appeared a bit wind-tousled.

"How old are you, now, Suzie?"

"Six. I'll be six my birthday."

"And that's next November?"

"Yes, sir."

"My, my—if you're not something else! Just as sharp as a tack and a durn sight prettier."

I grinned at him because I thought he was 'something else' too. He seemed to weigh the envelope in his hand, and then looking quite serious, said, "Now, listen, Suzie. This is very important. I would like to get it in the mail today, but, I can't spare the time to run down there—I've got men waitin' out in the far field for the truck."

I repeated, "I'd like to take it down there for you, Uncle Ralph."

"It's a long ways, Suzie. Nearly half a mile to the mail box." He put his hand on my shoulder as we walked to the top of the lane. "It's just straight down that road there, over the hill and around the bend. There's just woods on both sides of the road, but there's nothing that'll hurt you and you can't get lost. What I want to know though, is—would you be scared or afraid? Or is it too far for those little feet and fancy shoes?"

I was not too sure about walking through a woods but I trusted him and he said there was nothing that would hurt me and I did want to be helpful so I assured him I was not afraid at all.

He took out his pocket watch and contemplated the time and distance. He said, "You may catch up with Sharon. I don't know how long she's been gone. Leastways, you can walk back with her. Nick usually comes around ten. You've got plenty of time, but don't dally goin', alright?"

"No, sir."

I started off in a run. He told me to hold up for a minute and whistled for Old Sam, the collie, and told him to stay with me.

The dirt road had ruts and it was hard to find a smooth place to walk, but I felt adventuresome and helpful and it was fun having the dog along. The road was narrow with green grass growing between the tire ruts and grass-grown ditches on either side. I could hear the grass rustle from time to time and Old Sam would pick up his ears and look longingly towards the sound, but he never left my side.

We had crested the hill and I was feeling breathless and sweating after running down the hill, in spite of the cool musty breeze, when a car came around the bend, stirring up the dust. I stepped to one side of the road for it to pass and saw that Sharon seemed to be driving it. She was sitting on a man's lap, laughing wildly and bouncing about. Her hands were on the steering wheel, but as they passed along side of me I could see her dress was all bunched up around her neck. Sam heard Sharon's voice and started to run toward the car, but, then he stopped and turned and looked at me. I was sure that Sharon had seen me, but, she pretended she hadn't , and they kept on driving slowly down the road until they began to climb the hill on the other side of the cluster of mailboxes. I told Old Sam to stay. He was kinda excited about running to the car. He would run forward a few feet and then look back to me. I didn't like the looks of the man and I didn't like the way Sharon was acting. For some reason I just wanted to run back to the house, but, I had told Uncle Ralph I would mail the letter so I kept on walking, slowly, toward the mailboxes and watching the car. When we got to the mailboxes, I could not figure out which one was Uncle Ralph's. They all looked alike and I looked toward the car for Sharon, but she wasn't in it. I looked all around but, she seemed to have disappeared. Old Sam had his head cocked at the kinda strange, kinda muffled half-yelling sounds in the air.

For some reason it all seemed scary and I really wanted to go back to the house. But, I had told Uncle Ralph I would mail his letter, so, I guessed I had to wait for Sharon or the mailman. I heard the car start up and go through the grinding motions of turning around on the narrow road. I didn't know what to do when they pulled along side of me, but Sharon jumped out from the passenger side and said, "Hi, Toot. Have you got a letter to mail?"

"Uncle Ralph wants this mailed. I'm 'spose to give it to Nick."

Sharon took the letter, handed it to the man and said, very matter-of-factly, "This is Nick. He's the mailman."

He ignored me as he busily distributed mail and newspapers into the weather-worn mailboxes. Then he swung back in his car and shifted into gear.

Sharon said, "Thanks for letting me drive."

He said, "You just be here anytime you want to do it again."

She traced her fingers around the fancy side-view mirror.

"Do you 'spose, maybe, next time, you could let me drive it all by myself?"

Nick plopped a piece of gum into his mouth, without offering us any, and inched the car forward, "We'll see. But I think you probably need more practice steering first. Maybe we'll go a little longer next time. And, who knows, maybe we'll go for a real long ride!"

He raised his eyebrows and grinned at her. She looked down at the road and he sped off, whirling the dust all about us.

Old Sam was having fits to start home. I felt strangely awkward with Sharon and we walked most of the way in silence. It was embarrassing the way she kept stopping to hoick and spit. She stopped from time to time to pick up a stick or to pluck a wild flower growing alongside the road. As we neared the lane leading up to the house she said, "Toot, promise me you won't tell anyone about me and Nick."

I looked down at my dusty shoes and once-white anklets that were streaked with brown dirt. I asked, "What were you doing, anyway?"

She looked toward the house and then frowned at me. "You wouldn't understand."

She started on toward the house and then stopped.

"Nick said he'd teach me to drive! But we have to do it his way."

I said, "I don't like him at all."

Sharon narrowed her eyes and spoke with vehemence, "I hate him! He's so nasty!"

She spat again and wiped her mouth, smoothed her dress and stood between me and the house as though blocking my way. "You've got to promise me you won't tell!"

"Won't tell what, Sharon?"

"Oh, Goddamnit! You're such a stupid little brat! Everybody thinks you're so smart. You don't know nothing! But, you'd better not tell anyone, anything! Do you hear me?"

"Alright, Sharon. I won't tell. But, if you hate him, why do you let him tickle you like that?"

Sharon's face crumpled and she looked like she was going to cry. " I don't know. He said he would teach me how to drive." Tears streamed down her face as she whirled about and hurried toward the house.

Loralee and Lizzie were in the living room with a big roll of material spread out on the floor. It was pinned with patterns for a dress and a skirt. Loralee sat on her heels clutching a huge pair of stainless steel shears; afraid to start cutting. Lizzie checked the pinning's to be sure they were on the straight of the material and urged her, "Go ahead now and cut it out. It'll be fine. You'll see."

I sat down at the sewing machine and peddled it, fascinated with the way the needle went up and down. I was earnestly trying to see how fast it would go when Liz yelled at me.

"Stop that, Toot! That's not a toy—go peddle your papers someplace else."

I looked to Loralee but she was preoccupied with the material and didn't seem to notice me.

The hallway was cool and deserted. I opened the door into the parlor, still piled high with the long heavy gun boxes. I sat on the Victorian sofa and traced my finger around the subdued flowered patterns in the brocade. The intricately carved mahogany frame had a reddish hue that gleaned with the patina of many years loving care. I had heard Mother talking about how Grandma had given all of her fine old furniture to Aunt Katie as though the farm and all that land wasn't enough. This sofa looked like Grandma. It wasn't anything like our big overstuffed one. This one was so elegant and there was a slight tobacco-e smell that reminded me of Grandpa. I curled up comfortably. Marj was leafing through a stack of sheet music, picking out the melodies. I climbed over the boxes to sit beside her on the piano bench. She elbowed me sharply in the ribs and yelled, "Go away! You're not 'spose to be in here. Go on out to play."

I sulked out, hating this place and wishing I could go home.

The sun was high and the threatening sweat bees and flies kept my arms flaying and my feet stomping as I wandered about the huge green yard in search of something to do.

Voices wafted from the kitchen and the back porch, punctuated with sweet-tempered laughter that only increased my dejection and stung my eyes with tears. My feet were sweating and burning and I could feel a squishiness between my toes. I sat down under the shady mantle of the old oak trees and took off my shoes and socks. The grass was cool and soft and inviting. I lay down and watched the leaves on the branches high above me, hanging motionless in the heavy noonday heat. From the distance drifted sounds now familiar of the chickens constant clucking, the cows mooing, the horses neighing, the men's voices calling and bantering, and closer, a fly buzzing. I dozed. The tickling, buzzing, tickling around my face was annoying. The fly called one of his mates and together they began to boldly explore and make sport with this unresisting terrain. I became conscious of something very lightly tickling the sides and tip of my nose and crawling about my mouth. I heard a buzzing and again felt something lightly tickling my mouth. In my mind's eye I envisioned the nasty green flies I had seen on the manure piles and in the horse biscuits and my mind screamed "They're on me!"

I jumped and ran screaming and crying toward the house. Aunt Katie and others came running out to me. She grabbed me and held me and as others gathered about demanded to know what was wrong. I saw Sharon in the doorway, watching and listening with narrowed eyes. I gasped, "A nasty . . . my mouth . . . a nasty ole fly . . . was on me . . . on my mouth. . ."

Aunt Katie looked and acted both relieved and annoyed, as others made laughing comments. Alberta washed my face with a washrag and made soothing sounds about how she, ". . .wouldn't want those nasty ole flies on me either."

Mother noticed my bare feet and began a harangue on the dangers and evils of going barefoot. Aunt Ruth shook her head and mumbled, "City folk—umph ummmm!"

Sharon offered to let me ring the dinner bell and even let me have first choice on the daily betting game of guessing who would be the first man to the table.

Bedtime always came early on the farm. After being up so late the night before no one seemed to mind going to bed with the chickens.

Sharon and Marj were puzzled about their bed being dampish. Alfie and I had the giggles, reinforced by him yelping like a frightened dog. The others would laugh and ask for explanations but we would just giggle all the harder with our secret.

It rained during the night and the bright early morning sun hung heavily in the cloud-strewn eastern sky making a promise of oppressive heat and humidity for the day.

Dad and Uncle Ralph were at the breakfast table talking about the proven, unbeatable merits of the new tractors and farm implements over the ancient models he had in use and the tremendous advantages to be gained by installing a milking machine. Uncle Ralph claimed he had no argument with modernity and progress other than he could not afford it and was not about to go in to debt for it. Dad was fascinated with the mechanical aspects of motors and motor driven devices. He was good at figures and always had an indelible pencil with a sharp point at hand. He showed Uncle Ralph how he could increase production, both grain and dairy, expand his orchards, lessen man hours and earn considerable more profit just by using the new machinery and installing a milking machine. Uncle Ralph listened thoughtfully, nodding assent. Aunt Katie never seemed to tire of carrying the heavy blue and gray spotted, enameled percolator from stove to table to refill the thick white mugs with steaming black coffee as she looked over their shoulders at the purple figures scrawled in front of them. Uncle Ralph had taken the pencil and slowly made some columns. He put the pencil down, slid his chair back, stretched and then leaning wearily on his elbows, said, "Well, there's just no way in God's blue heaven that I can do any of this!"

Aunt Katie sat down and sugared her coffee and sat musing, stirring, staring, as though the answer lay in the swirling liquid. Mother reached over and patted her on the arm and said, "It seems such a shame for Riley to talk like this and get your hopes all up. But you know Riley. He's always planning and figuring on something. But it's kind of a dirty trick to get your hopes up if there's no way of doing it."

Dad sounded exasperated as he insisted, "But it can be done! That's what I'm trying to tell you."

Uncle Ralph cut in, "I don't doubt your figuring, Riley. According to my calculations I'd say you've been conservative, in estimating the profits. But! based on the going prices and allowing for no emergencies—it'll be at lease three years before I can get enough cash on hand to. . ."

Dad put up his hand to stop him. "Tell you what I'm goin' to do. I was talking with the manager of the Farm Implement Company. Mama still owns about forty shares and that entitles us, among other things, to buy on time, no interest. I've got about a thousand dollars here we can use for a down payment and in three years time you'll be rollin' in dough and you can pay me back, or, what the hell, as long as it's in the family!"

Aunt Katie was stammering, "Why, Riley, you can't do that! You've got to buy a house and with the baby coming? No, now, you're liable to be needing that."

Dad put his arm around Aunt Katie's shoulders.

"Now listen here, Sis. I know what I'm talking about and I know what I'm doing. Your Mama and I have given this a lot of thought and I don't see why you should object. You were dragging around here last night, bitchin', 'scuse me, griping, about the hard work and the heat and all. Well, I can't do anything about the heat but we can make the work easier for you. And, I promise you, no tricks."

Dad squeezed her and untied her apron as he moved away.

Uncle Ralph added pure cream to his fresh cup of coffee and stirred thoughtfully.

"You say you've gotten the old Jackson place?"

"Yep! And it's a good deal, too—Better than I could have hoped for."

Mother stirred from her preoccupation with the purple figures and asked, "How many bedrooms are there in that place?"

Dad chuckled, "More than we'll ever need unless you keep having twins."

Mother acted a bit riled and petulant and quipped, "Riley, really! I'm not having them by myself you know!" Dad laughed and said with emphasis "I know you're not!"

Uncle Ralph grinned broadly and Aunt Katie sighed "Oh, you men, honestly."

Mother got Dad's attention and nailed him with a 'I mean business' look and railed, "It does look like you could tell me something about this house, Riley. I mean, I'm the one who's going to be living there day in and day out for no telling how long and it's only to be assumed that I'd be curious as to what it's like, but then, that'd never occur to you, would it?"

Aunt Katie patted Mother on the shoulder and said, "Now, Martha, you know these men can't think of everything, and, you know, just from passing it on the road, it's a beautiful home."

Mother wheedled, "Well, it does look like a body's entitled to being informed, especially when it pertains to their own welfare."

Dad shook his head and sighed heavily and explained in soft, measured tones, "Martha, I was hoping to surprise you with how nice it is. There are seven bedrooms, three bathrooms, a modern kitchen with all of the latest conveniences, a full basement with a nice separate washroom and a half-bath. There's a big attic for storage and for a playroom. It has a good furnace and a good deep well and the cistern is in good order. The paper's good throughout the house and they're leaving the blinds and most of the curtains and draperies."

Mother said, "Well, I guess beggars can't be choosers. Heaven knows, anything's better than nothing and at least it'll be a roof over our heads."

A dark frown passed over Dad's face and I saw Uncle Ralph's mouth drop in disbelief. Aunt Katie looked perplexed and began talking in a forced, cheerful, coaxing voice. "Why, Martha! That sounds like a near mansion! And, my gosh, girl, three bathrooms! Imagine! Oh, someday we're going to get a bigger cistern and run water in here for a bathroom. Oh, Riley, you did out do yourself. It sounds wonderful!"

Aunt Katie kissed him on the cheek and as she moved away, Dad slyly mischievously, untied her apron again, without her knowing it until it started to slide off. To Mother he said, "You'll like it, Martha. It's soundly built and it's nice. 'Pert near as big as your folks place. Lots of shade trees and some fruit trees. New screens and new shutters all around the house. Nice big yard with that blue-grass all over it. Why, I'd have been a fool to pass it up."

Mother eyed him suspiciously, "Well, then, if it is so good, like you say it is, why are they selling it?"

The chair scraped back on the linoleum as Dad stood up and moved away from the table. He had a worried, pained expression that seemed to melt away as he rubbed the back of his neck and turned his head from side to side. He glanced over at me and Grandma, clinched his mouth and turning to Mother, explained, with long-suffering patience, "They sold it because Mr. Jackson's been dead and gone for three years now and the two boys have settled with good jobs up North and Miz Jackson's going to go join them and their families up there now. She's not able to do for herself anymore, so, they decided to sell it and be done with it. The older boy, Jeff, is a Mason and somewhat of a gun collector, in a small way."

Dad rolled his eyes and grinned in a derisive manner which implied his contempt for the unlearned, mercenary, run-of-the-mill gun collectors. Mother sat up straight and a look of consternation mingled with disbelief and near delight played across her face.

"Why, Riley! You don't mean—you've sold the guns? Did you?"

Dad exploded "Hell, no!"

Grandma didn't register a lot of expression on her face. She usually had a smooth, almost porcelain like countenance that suggested tranquility, a peace, a strength, that was always comforting. Yet, her blue eyes spoke volumes and the little folds of skin about her eyes seemed to undulate with her innermost thoughts. Her forehead was high with rather prominent 'intelligence bumps' over the brow line, but the worry lines were negligible. The little folds about her mouth were usually relaxed in self-confident assuredness, as though she viewed 'the children' in the greater perspective of her own life time of experiences, and consequently, with the wisdom of her years. She asked Dad, "Did you meet this Jeff Jackson, uh, Mason, and, uh, gun collector?"

Dad nodded. "I surely did. I stopped by there the other day after I learned I'd gotten the job with the County, and talked with Miz Jackson. She told me Jeff was coming down to take care of the sale of the house and the moving. We talked for awhile and then we called him and I told him I was interested and he said a couple of others were too and he was just getting ready to drive down for a couple of days. So, the next day, I went by and talked with him and found out he's a Mason and interested in guns. I told him I had a few and asked if there was anything in particular he'd like. He said he'd been looking all over the country for a Duris Egg Flintlock shotgun and that he'd give his eye teeth to get a hold of a really good one. I said, 'Well, Sir, I've got a good one and it's a dandy, but, I don't need your eye teeth. How about giving me a good deal on that house?' and he said, 'Mr. Mason, if that gun's as good as you say and if you can deal in cash, that house is yours.' So, I bought it for nearly two thousand less what we sold the old home for, but, I'm telling you, it's a good sight better'n the one we had. Did I mention there's about twenty acres of good pasture with it? The people to the east are wanting to use it for a good price."

Mother sat with her elbows resting on the table, hands wrapped around her coffee cup and looking up at Dad, asked hesitantly "How much was that gun worth?"

Dad shrugged his shoulders and gestured with both hands spread out.

"It depends. I didn't pay money for it. I took it back in 'thirty-one in payment for a surveyin' job that an old man had to have done before he could sell his farm. He'd told me he didn't have any money but that he had some fine old pieces and when I saw them I told him I'd be proud to do the job for any one of them. He gave me two and a high recommendation to his old cronies. I still get calls from them."

Aunt Katie was beaming with pride at Dad and Uncle Ralph shook his head in admiration and teased Mother, who was shifting her extra weight about conspicuously.

"Well, Martha, it sounds like you're going to have a really beautiful home to have those babies in, after all. Here you've been so worried—all for nothing."

Dad said, apologetically, to Mother, "I kept telling you not to worry about it. I couldn't take you to see it, because Miz Jackson didn't want it being seen until after she'd moved out. I really was hoping to just pull up in front of that big beautiful house and just surprise you with it. But, now you know the ins and outs of it."

Mother acted hurt and offended and protested in child-like innocence, "Well, you don't have to get huffy. I just asked a simple question that does pertain to my circumstances. I wasn't accusin' you of neglect or not carin' or anything and I wasn't questionin' your judgement, but heaven knows, you can't get somethin' for nothin' in this day and age and it was a shame to lose that house we had, although this one does sound almost too good to be true. I just don't like to get my hopes all up and then have 'em bashed against the rocks again, but then, if I'd had any idea you were fixing to surprise me—why, I wouldn't have said a word."

Dad's cheeks were flushed. He cupped his hand over his right ear as though he were suctioning something out and shook his head as though to clear it. He looked at Mother and turning away, said, "That'll be the day!"

Uncle Ralph seemed to sympathize with Dad's discomfiture. He clapped him on the shoulder and mischievously baited Mother.

"Martha, I don't think you'd be satisfied if he gave you the moon on a string. No, Sir, —she'd want it on a gold chain!"

Mother sat her cup down with a clink and looked at Uncle Ralph, coyly, "Why—Ralph? Whatever are you talking about? Why, Heaven knows, I'm not hard to please. I've never asked for much and I don't complain when I don't get it. I know, very well, a person just has to do the best he can with what he has and then make do with that."

Dad took his wallet out and riffled through the thick bulk of bills.

"Come on, Ralph! Let's run into town, before we lose all morning. You can drive the new tractor home and I'll bet we can get a milking machine installed tomorrow."

Uncle Ralph walked over to the bay windows where Grandpa's old roll-top desk sat to one side. He opened a secret drawer and took out a well-worn fat envelope. He looked at Aunt Katie and she smiled and nodded back at him. He said, "Your brother may not be much of a farmer, but he's got a mighty good head for business on his shoulders and I think it's high time I listened to him on some of these matters."

Aunt Katie smiled approvingly and waved them on "You boys shoo. It's almost eight o'clock, and you know the early bird gets the worm."

Arrangements were made for us to move into our new home on Sunday morning. Grandma decided to ride back to Nilesville in the car with us, since there was no train until late afternoon. Uncle Ralph and Kenneth were going to drive the truck to carry the gun boxes and the luggage.

I sat in the back seat with Alf, Loralee and Marj. Grandma and Mother sat in the front seat with Dad.

We were excited about the drive and seeing our new home in spite of Mother's protesting that Sunday was meant to be a day of rest, not work, and we really should be going to church to worship and pray. Dad chuckled, "Why, Martha, those moving men were praying for some extra work and they thought it was an answer to prayer when I asked them to move us today. And here you are wanting us to go pray and put them out of work."

Mother shook her head and chewed on her lip and tried to justify her position by recounting, "The Lord gave us six days to work and one day to rest. Now, He knows better than we do that all work and no play makes Jack a dull boy, and Papa always said, 'If you give the Lord one day a week, you'll accomplish more in the remaining six then you could working all seven' and Dr. Burns used to say, 'If a man works seven days a week he'll burn out before he's fifty' and, you know, when a man has children it's important for him to set an example of going to worship on Sunday."

Grandma had been gazing out the window. She asked if the breeze was to much for us in the back seat and smiled knowingly when Alf answered, "Indubitably!—but please don't roll up the window. The fresh air feels good."

Grandma ignored the double-entendre, and said to Mother, "I respect your views on Sunday worship, Martha. I suspect God had a hand in Riley's buying this home which is in itself an answer to prayer. I'm sure He won't mind us doing what needs to be done."

Mother mumbled acquiesces and then, brightly, half-turning in her seat, announced, "I know! Let's sing Sunday School songs!"

Loralee moaned and Marj muttered under her breath as Mother began happily singing, "*Jesus loves me, this I know.*"

Alf began sputtering with laughter. He covered his face with his hands and bent over double when Mother looked over her shoulder and ordered, "Sing!"

"*For the Bible tells me so.* (Sing!)
Little ones to Him belong, (Come on, sing.)
They are weak but He is strong."

Mother never missed a beat and seemed oblivious to the bedeviling in the back seat. Alf had a paroxysm of laughter and was alternating between doubling over and sprawling all over the three of us girls. Every time Mother would demand us to sing he'd whoop and jerk spasmodically. Marj's mutterings had turned to giggles and she began shrieking each time Mother said "Sing." Loralee was convulsed with laughter and I never felt such explosive belly laughing in all my life. Mother continued without missing a beat, and urging in a one-note chant,

"Now, I know you know this—sing!
Yes, Jesus loves me, Yes, Jesus loves me.
Yes, Jesus loves me, The Bible tells me so."

We clapped and cheered to make up for not joining in. Mother pouted, "I didn't know I was going to have to sing a solo."

The camaraderie continued as we traveled through the nearly deserted countryside on that early Sunday morning; piercing the quiet peacefulness with the steady droning of the motor, the flip, flip, flip of the wheels on the pavement, and the whishing of the wind we stirred as we sped up the long hills that seemed to climb to the sky, only to diminish in size as we neared them. The narrow two-lane hard-road had bends to the left and bends to the right and we would lean in the direction of the curve nearly mashing each other.

Dad had been reminded by Mother's rendition of his own repertoire of paraphrased church hymns that were only mildly sacrilegious. We children thought they were hilarious. Mother would look disapproving and laughingly admonish him, but Grandma would actually laugh out loud at them.

We had arrived at the outskirts of town and could hear the church bells peeling out an old familiar tune. Dad snapped his fingers and chuckled, "By God! There's one I forgot."

He began singing, with the bells for accompaniment, in a loud, clear, baritone, using a falsetto for an echo.

"At the bar, at the bar,
Where I smoked my first cigar,
And the money in my pockets rolled away. (Rolled away)
It was there, by chance,
That I lost my Sunday pants,
Cause the hootchie girls were workin' night and day (Night and day)."

We pestered him to sing it again, while Mother doubted the wisdom of teaching the children such as that, ". . .for heaven knows they'll learn it soon enough as it is."

Grandma's bright blue eyes twinkled with amusement and she wondered aloud if that organist had any idea we would have such fun with that old hymn.

Dad said, "Mama, do you remember the time when. . ."

Grandma was nodding her head and laughingly interrupted, "I'll never forget that. Your Papa was laughing so hard he shook the pew. Katie was so embarrassed she tried to hide under the seat and the preacher was so mad he was hopping about like a flea on a hot skillet. That really was naughty of you boys!"

Alf was sitting up on the edge of the seat asking, "What'd you do, Dad? Huh? What happened?"

Dad conceded, "Your Grandma can tell you better than I."

She began, "Your Dad was about your age, Loralee, and he was feeling his oats from time to time. A good boy, mind you, but never-the-less, boys will be boys. This happened on an early spring Sunday night. Our little church was having a revival service and people had come from miles around. Your Dad and three of his friends were sitting on the back row, where mischief usually begins. I'm sure they'd have rather been somewhere else, and in all fairness, I must admit the service wasn't very interesting. The preacher kept announcing song after song and I think everyone was tired of it. Then, he announced he wanted us all to turn to page thirty-seven and really sing out on it. And did those boys sing out! —in harmony—just like a quartet—and loud—drowning everyone else out. Of course, the whole congregation stopped singing and started listening when they realized the words were—uh—different!"

We all begged Dad to sing it again and he clownishly obliged us, leering at Mother and winking at Grandma when he sang about the hootchie girls. Mother asked her, "What did the preacher do?"

Grandma thought for a minute and then replied, "Well, it was what John, your Grandpa, did that mattered. When he finally quit laughing, he made all four of them apologize for disturbing the service and then he told the preacher he had a good quartet for special music every night that week."

Mother looked at Dad in surprise. "Why, Riley! You never told me you'd sung in a quartet."

Dad grimaced, and replied sheepishly, "It was just for one week."

The car slowed and Dad extended his arm, signaling for a left-hand turn. We all stared at the big white house up on the rise that seemed to grow larger as we drove slowly up the lane.

"It's beautiful!"

"Gee—it's huge."

"So well kept."

"It's going to be a job cleaning it!"

We were all excited and happy about our new house and as the old familiar furnishings and the accumulations of many years were situated about the rooms it began to look and feel like home. Mother was obviously pleased with the house although the most she would say to our rapturous exclamation of pride and delight was, "Well, yes, I suppose it'll do. Any shelter in a storm."

We each had our jobs to do and in spite of the heat and confusion there was a happy, party-like atmosphere. Word had spread quickly that we were moving in and old friends and former neighbors, as well as new neighbors, came to call and to bring covered dishes and cakes and pies for supper. Some stayed to help unpack and arrange the furniture since, "Poor Martha is in no condition to be doing this heavy work. Why, a woman as far along as she is shouldn't be lifting her hands over her head or going up and down those stairs or lifting anything heavier than an iron."

Mother would smile wanly and say in a woebegone voice, "Oh, I'll be alright. Why, I wouldn't know how to act if I didn't have more work than I could shake a stick at."

Grandma sighed wearily and said to no one in particular, "Some just don't know when they are well off."

The movers unrolled the pads and rugs and placed them according to precise directions. The movers repeatedly confused the front room, the living room and the study, so it was necessary to move the same pieces of furniture from room to room before it was eventually placed. The three pianos gave them fits and they waited until Mother was sure of where she wanted them before carrying them in. She had decided to put the old practice piano in the living room and the baby grande in the front room, which, as one of the movers pointed out, would have been called a 'parlour' in olden times. The player piano, my favorite, was relegated to the basement to the chagrin of the men who had carried it to the study.

There were pictures, paintings and mirrors to be hung and everyone seemed to have an opinion to express about what would look good where, but things, actually, seemed to find their own place and it was astonishing how quickly a big strange house could become one's cozy well known home.

Uncle Ralph and Kenneth arrived with the boxes of guns. Dad and Alf helped them carry them to the basement and stacked them off to one side out of the way.

Uncle Ralph joked about Dad getting the house in trade for a fancy shotgun and the fiction was told for fact before the day was over.

We children had been told we could each have our choice of the bedrooms, and, as could be expected Marj belatedly decided she had to have the one Loralee had chosen. Dad pointed out the two rooms were the same size, each had two windows, a big closet, a classy brass ceiling fan, and a bathroom was in between them. Marj usually favored anything blue, but pouted that the blue paper in her room was ugly and the rug had a bare spot in front of the window and Loralee always got the prettiest and the nicest just because she was the oldest.

Mother told her, "You ought to be thankful to have a room to yourself. Not everyone is so fortunate. Of course, I prefer the yellow roses for they are so cheerful, but, again, that blue paper is really good quality and could make a really beautiful room with that brass bed and blue comforter. You could put a throw rug in front of the window with a little reading chair."

Marj continued to pout and be quarrelsome until Loralee gave up her claim on the yellow room, and told her saucily, "Since it's so very important to you, you may have it! I really wanted the blue one all along, so, there, Miss Stingy."

Marj's bittersweet victory seemed to sour her even more and the ensuing inflammatory wise-cracks held no humor and threatened to spread beyond the second floor. The moving men, unwittingly seemed to cater to Loralee, who would politely and decidedly tell them where to place things. Marj would ignore them with their heavy loads and when they would inquire where to put something she would tell them haughtily to "just put it down".

Alf refused to help her move the furniture, infuriating her even more by calling her a "stubborn German".

Marj could not close the door to her room since the furniture was placed so haphazardly. I could hear her heaving and grunting and occasionally swearing, as she struggled to move things about. I went to her door and waited until she noticed me. Her eyes looked red and watery. I said, "Marj? I'll help you."

"What do you think you can do, you little squirt? You think you can move something I can't?"

"I'll ask Dad to help."

"No you won't! I don't want his help. I don't want anyone's help. Now get out of my room and leave me alone!"

I stuck my tongue out as far as it would go and blew as rude a noise as I could muster. I turned to run and bumped into Grandma. She looked surprised, "My, my. That didn't sound very polite."

I looked down at my shoes for an explanation but Grandma patted me on the head and looking into Marj's room observed, "Moving can be awfully hard on one's disposition. Toot, go tell Riley I want one of those movers up here right now."

I ran down with the message. Dad asked the one with the reddish face if he would see to it. He groaned good-naturedly and told me to lead the way.

Grandma thanked him for ". . .being so kind as to help with these heavy pieces. I'd move them myself if I could."

He said, "Oh no, mam, don't you even consider trying to move this stuff. You just tell me where you want it."

Grandma said she was much obliged and suggested he move the dresser to the far end of the long wall, the chiffonier to the short wall by the closet, the head of the bed to the inside wall with the cedar chest at the foot of the bed, and the table and chair in front of the windows. It was all done very quickly.

Grandma thanked him graciously and said to Marj, "Now that it is within reason, you finish it. And remember, whether it is in your room or in your attitude, you have to lie in the bed that you make."

My own room had a multi-colored paper with pastel Nosegays and roses with various shades of green leaves and vines. The dominating colors were green and yellow and the pleasing leaf green was repeated in the rug and draperies. The big double window looked out over the backyard and I could see our nearest neighbors barn and tree-enshrouded home across the pasture to the east. Fields of wheat and corn stretched out as far as the eye could see directly behind our home and to the west stood a dense woods. Our lane curved from the front around one side of the house and forked in the back so that one could turn in near the back porch or continue on down toward the woods. There was a neglected vegetable garden in the far back that was partially concealed by a grape arbor and flowering shrubs. Flower borders showed loving care and little green pears were growing on a huge old pear tree.

A giant oak spread its massive branches to the sky offering shade from the sun and homes to numerous birds and squirrels. Grandma said its roots grew as deep and spread as far below the soil as its trunk and branches extended above the ground.

My favorite room was the study. It had a fireplace that was almost big enough for me to stand in. The mantle was of blue and gray motteled marble and even on the hottest days it felt as cold as ice. The colorful wool Alexander Smith rug had a strong smell that permeated the whole room but the movers said it would soon go away; it was from Mother packing it so liberally with moth balls. One could detect that odor throughout the house for days, even though the windows were open and the fans were working to dissipate it.

Oak bookcases lined one wall from floor to ceiling. Each section had a glass door that lifted up and slid back in place. Cardboard boxes of books were stacked on one side waiting for someone to get to them. Big brown leather chairs were placed to the sides of the fireplace and the long oak library table was set in the middle of the room with the straight-backed chairs at both ends. Dad's big desk and his drafting board were on the far side of the room. A seven foot wide painting of Gethsemane hung over the mantle and seemed to create a meditative atmosphere.

The kitchen was bright and crowded with people sitting and standing and coming and going with snacks and coffee and tea. The movers ate before leaving and as Dad was settling with the foreman, the one with the reddish face asked Mother, "Is it true that Mr. Mason traded a fancy shotgun for this house?"

Mother took a deep breath and smiled and fluttered her eyelashes and clasped her hand to her breast and prattled, "I was simply shocked out of my wits! I just couldn't believe my ears when Riley told me how he got this house. But, then, you men never cease to amaze me!"

Mother moved on and the man shook his head as though he couldn't believe his ears. He walked off muttering about how that must have been "some gun!"

4

🐦 HANG THEM IN THE ATTIC

Dad left early the next morning for his first day on the new job. Mother was anxious to get the house in apple pie order—a place for everything and everything in its place—before the baby came. She anticipated being in bed for two to three weeks after giving birth, so from dawn to dusk she was scrubbing, polishing, waxing, shining, arranging and rearranging, or as she called it "setting things in order".

The back stairs led from the kitchen all the way to the attic. Alf was the first to explore the attic and eagerly called us girls to come and see. We ran up the stairs expectantly. The movers had put a few things up there for storage, but there remained a large area open for play. The rafters were high in the middle sloping down on the sides. A piece of knotted, frayed rope hung from a hook in the peak of the highest rafter. There were tiny little windows and the sun streaming through them emphasized the dust in the air. Marj gasped, "Oh, how creepy!"

Loralee said, "It isn't creepy—just dirty."

Alf pulled a cobweb down and slung it on Marj, who shrieked and jumped and yelled, "That's creepy!"

There was no debris but a thick layer of dry dust covered the wood oak floor boards and the few items the Jacksons had left there. Loralee wrapped a rag around a broom and she and Alf knocked the cobwebs down. There were giant dust balls and stretchy strands of lint milling about. We gingerly brushed the lint from the shriveled up crab apples and rolled them next to the wall for everyone knew they kept the bugs away. It was frustrating trying to get rid of the years' accumulation of dust, and in a short time we were all sneezing and coughing in the fog we created in our enthusiasm to clean it.

There were trunks of old clothes; fashions of long-gone eras, baby dresses and tiny worn shoes. Quilt tops, begging to be quilted, were piled by a long deserted quilting frame that was frightening with all of its needle-like nails marching around the sides of it. A dress frame that had been extended to its full capacity for some hefty lady's well endowed figure became our 'Aunt Jemimah' as Loralee practiced her newly acquired sewing expertise by fitting out the frame and topping it with a head complete with a black smiling face and a red bandanna. Her gloved hands were clasped in front of her over her massive apron covered front. I talked to her and there were times when she seemed to respond.

There were only bare light bulbs hanging from the rafters and they were never very bright, so on cloudy days it was dreary and a bit spooky. Marj was an excellent teller of ghost stories. We would hang on her every word or groan she would utter and it seemed even the house and wind would oblige her tales by creaking and brushing branches against tiny windows at just the right moment to heighten our giggly anticipated shivers of fright and delight.

On the farthest side of the attic stood the big double crib that Dad had built for Billy and me when we were babies. It was large enough for two toddlers, divided in the middle with white hard rubber padded bars; each half with its own mattress. Foot pedals were situated on one side to operate the guard rail so that half of it would slide down independent of the other side. The head and foot boards were identical except one had blue teddy bears in a field of blue flowers and the other had pink teddy bears in a field of pink flowers. It made the fact of my babyhood, and Billy, very real to me.

I heard Grandma calling me. "Toot? Toot! —Come meet a neighbor! This is Dean Swanson. His people own the horses out there in the pasture. His mother sent these lovely tomatoes over for us."

"Hi."

"Hi yourself. Da ya have any brothers?"

"Yes, one. But he's big."

"None my age?"

"No. Do you have any sisters?"

"Nope! No girls at our house, 'cept Mom."

"You don't like girls, do you?"

"Nope—They're dumb."

"I'm not dumb."

"Well—you're little."

"How old are you?"

"Nine."

"Are those your horses?"

"Yep! Know how to ride?"

"Yep! Well, ponies."

"Same thing."

"Really?"

"Sure. I'll show you sometime."

"You leaving?"

"Yep. Got things to do."

"Bye, Dean."

"Is your name really Toot?"

"Yep."

"Funny name. Bye, Toot."

"Dean? I have another name, too."

"What's it?"

"Olivia."

"I like Toot better. See ya, Toot."

Grandma hired a Mr. Aiken, a perpetual grumbler, to care for the yard and help with the gardening and flowers. Mother said she wasn't questioning her judgment but she didn't see how she could tolerate his grumbling. Grandma said, "He is a chronic complainer, alright. But Mr. Aiken is a good worker, and I believe he is as honest as the day is long. He does everything I ask him to, and more." Mother laughed, "Well, that's not surprising. You could make a lion purr."

Grandma shook her head disclaiming, "No. He's a proud man. I suspect he's known better. It is strange the way he showed up when I was really needing help. Makes me wonder if he's an angel unaware."

Alf helped the old gentleman with the spading and weeding and trimming and pruning. His mimes and imitations of the quarrelsome old man would regale us. Mr. Aiken didn't talk much but when he did his speech ranged from the crude illiterate to the folksy, to the refined country. The first time I 'pestered' him he took out his pocketknife and said he was going to cut my nose off. I had run to the house scared silly and tried to keep my distance after that, but he was everywhere from dawn to dusk: weeding, hoeing, fertilizing, watering, repairing fences, whitewashing, gathering vegetables, cutting flowers, sharpening scythes. I was afraid of him. Every time I would go outside he would appear within a few feet and say something. "Hey! C'mere 'n let me cut your nose off!"

One morning I was sitting in the swing on the front porch when he came around the corner of the house and walked up to the steps and grinned and put his hand in the pocket of the overalls that he always wore on top of his other clothes, and asked, "Ya want me to cut that there pigtail off?"

One afternoon I had not noticed him walking up behind me until he said, "Somethin' wrong with your ears? Ya want me to cut 'em off?"

I had run to find Mother and gasped out my fears. She had scoffed "Oh, pshaw! He's just trying to be friendly."

That night at supper, after grace, Dad said, "I had quite a talk with Mr. Aiken, today."

He filled his plate and urged the rest of us to do the same. Marj said, "He's cantankerous."

Alf said, "He told me he was a mendicant from Missouri."

Loralee asked, "What's a mendicant?"

Dad chuckled, "That's a fancy word for a beggar. I don't doubt he's from Missouri. He's a democrat."

Alf bellowed, "Hee Haw! Hee Haw!" Mother shushed with, "Alf! Not at the table."

Grandma looked concerned and spoke quietly, "He does a fine job, Riley. I'd hate to have to let him go."

Dad raised his hand for quiet, glanced warningly around the table at us children who were still snickering and hastened to reassure Grandma. "Oh no, Mama. I didn't mean to imply that at all. Why, he's a fine worker. Just needed a chance and someone to prod him." He started chuckling again, and continued, "You've made a believer out of him. Like I said, I don't doubt he's from Missouri or has rheumatism or has been down on his luck, but, I'm telling you, Mama, he thinks you are the salt of the earth and if you told him to move a mountain he'd probably start shoveling."

Alf scooted his chair back and began imitating a shoveling motion and spoke in a thick accent,

"Wull, if'n muh back don't break or muh armn don't fall off, I might manage to get this 'ere mountain moved 'fore dark but I'm ahurtin' so bad, I doubt if'n I'll live to see the light of a 'nurther day a dawnin'."

Mother admonished him for his mimicry and the rest of us for laughing at him and repeated one of her favorite platitudes.

"As the wise old Indian said, 'Never judge a man until you have walked for two weeks in his moccasins'." Dad joined in the stock reply that we all chorused, with raised right hands. "How!"

Mother relentlessly began a homily: "Now, alright, make fun if you will. I've no quarrel with a bit of humor. The proverbs tell us that a merry heart is the best medicine. But you children have got to learn the difference between laughing at people and laughing at situations. Everyone does comical things from time to time, often without meaning to and it's good to laugh at one's self, but I won't have you making fun of people or depriving them of their respect simply because they're different from us. God, in His infinite wisdom, devised that no two people should be exactly alike."

Dad raised his eyes toward the ceiling and muttered, "Thank you, Lord." Grandma discreetly covered her mouth with her napkin but I could see her eyes twinkling as the rest of us struggled to control our tittering. Loralee looked to Mother who had busied herself with eating.

"Mother, in the movies they make fun of people all the time. I mean, even cruelty is made to be funny. Charlie Chaplin is famous for it and of course, Laurel and Hardy are hilarious. But it's just acting and that's the way I see it when Alfie imitates Mr. Aiken or the savages or the coloreds or the Indians or the Pilgrims. I mean, it's just acting. There's nothing wrong with that, is there?"

Mother hesitated, contemplating, "In the movies everything is exaggerated and I must say Alf's good enough to be in the movies himself. I just don't want any of you to be cynical, or sarcastic, or conceited. You must not think that anyone different from us is funny just because they're, uh—different."

Grandma spoke quietly, "Your Mother's right. Look at the food on the table. The roast is brown, the potatoes are white, the tomatoes are red and the corn is yellow. That chocolate cake is very rich, but the pitcher of water, although life-giving, would be very poor food by itself. Each dish of food is perfect in it's own way, but it takes all of it together to make a complete meal. There are many races and cultures amongst the people of the world. It is important to honor all with respect and to value each for their individual worth."

Mother said, "Exactly. That's just what I was saying; one cannot generalize or categorize people just by their color. Now, see, those potatoes were mashed; but they could have been prepared in a dozen different ways that would have altered them or improved them from their original state."

Marj sniggered and pointed to Alf's plate. "Look what Alfie did to his! He's the only one I know of who likes mustard on his mashed potatoes!"

Alf grinned self-consciously, as he marbled the mustard into the mound of mashed potatoes on his plate. Dad said, "Well, now, that's alright. That's his privilege. 'Course, we may laugh about it, but, we're not laughing at him, are we? It's just a bit amusing to see mustard on potatoes."

Marj shuddered and said, "I think it's sickening."

Grandma continued in a firm voice, "I'd like to make two points. The first is: people look, speak, act, think and even live and eat in many different ways, depending on their race, education and culture. But, basically, we are all the same inside and we all have the same needs. The big difference is that we each react to and reflect our lot according to the light that we have. Our family has suffered much sorrow and ill-fate, but we are still more fortunate than many, because we are strong and resilient; however, we must not criticize or make fun of those who are down and out. Your Grandpa used to say, 'There, but for the grace of God, go I!' You see, one person can never know the private hell of another. That's what that ole Indian meant when he said not to judge someone until you have lived his life. Now, my second point is just to ponder: Have you ever noticed how similar laughing is to crying?"

Alf said, "But, they are opposites." Loralee leaned toward Alf and said, "I've laughed until I cried before, lots of times, at you!" Marj asked, "Were you laughing at him or with him?" Dad added, "Or at what he did to those potatoes?"

Mother said, "Well, if I can have my druthers, I'd rather you be laughing than crying any day of the week. Heaven knows there's too much to cry about in this life, but crying can't change things and laughing does make them easier, somehow." Dad said, "A good belly laugh never hurt anybody. Now, if someone would be so kind as to pass that good brown roast and those juicy red tomatoes, I'd be much obliged, although, after that analogy, Mama, I feel a bit cannibalistic."

Marj wrinkled her nose and groaned. I said, "What's that mean, Dad?" He motioned to Mother and whispered, "Ask your Mother—later." Grandma said, "Son, were you satisfied with Mr. Aiken?"

Dad said, "Yes, mam! Matter of fact, before I got sidetracked, I was going to tell you all about our conversation this morning." We were all curious about this crusty oddity who ruled our yard and garden with an iron hand and a green thumb.

"He's had quite a life of it. Said he used to be a gin runner during prohibition. He was in France during the Great War but couldn't find work when he got out of the army, so he odd-jobbed it until he got into gin running and then was making money hand over fist until the big racketeers took over his territory and he started drinking. When the banks failed he lost everything, his wife died, his children disowned him and he'd been wanderin' around the country in a stupor for years. He doesn't even know when or how he got down here in this part of the country. He woke up in jail with the tremors and after the sheriff released him he started walking down the road. He said, 'I's so weak and thursty I thought I'd die. Then I seed that beautiful lady a-waterin' that border of flowers. I walked up to her and asked fur a drink and she says, "this isn't clean—come to the kitchen door" and then she brought me out a tray with meat 'n cheese 'n pie 'n tea, and I've seed a lot of hand-outs, but never nothin' like that, and after I et she asked, 'ave you a place to stay?' 'n I says, 'No, Mam,' and she says, 'If you can work a coupla of hours I'll give you your dinner and a week's pay in advance, so you can find a room.' 'Magine! Jest like that. She gave me a new lease on life!"

Dad paused for a drink. Mother reached over to pat Grandma on the arm affectionately, saying, teasingly, "I don't doubt your judgment, Mother, but he surely doesn't sound like an angel unawares to me." Grandma smiled and glanced around the table. "One never knows, does one?"

Dad chuckled, reached for another piece of cake and said, "If he's an angel it's because you laid the law down, Mama. He told me he felt better than he had in years, that he was getting some of his strength back and that he would never take another drink as long as he lived. What'd you tell him anyway?"

Grandma replied softly, "God helps those who help themselves."

One cool day in August, about a month after our baby brother was born; I was dawdling away the morning hours in the attic. I seldom spent time with dolls but on this occasion I was undressing and redressing them; my idea of playing with them. Marj was riffling through a stack of magazines and suggested I put the dolls down to sleep in the crib.

"I'd never put anything in there!"

"Why ever not?"

She looked at me with interest. I told her I hated those ugly gray striped mattresses. She looked at me curiously and said, "Well, you can put sheets on them, Silly. And there's a bunch of blankets and a couple of bedspreads with bears on them."

"Really?"

I jumped to my feet and gathering up the dolls and paraphernalia, urged her, "Help me, Marj! Please get them for me and help me fix them, please!"

"Well, for Pete's sake, Toot! I don't know where that stuff is."

She let herself be caught up in my enthusiasm and began searching diligently, almost feverishly, through trunks, chests and cardboard boxes. At last, she found them where they had been packed away; clean, ironed, folded and sprinkled liberally with mothballs. Marj smoothed the sheets over the mattresses, tucked the blankets tight and arranged the bedspreads neatly, corresponding the blue and pink bears with their right mates on the head boards. The bed was beautiful. I wondered aloud if Billy would mind having dolls on his side. Marj said he had been such a little doll himself she was sure he would not mind. She asked, "Has Mother let you hold Joshua yet?"

"No."

"Well, be patient. Did she tell you to practice holding the dolls?"

"Yes."

Marj laughed and poked me on the belly. "Toot, she was the same way when you and Billy were babies. She made us all practice holding dolls and washing dolls and dressing dolls before we could even touch you."

"Did she feed us like that, too?"

"Of course, Silly. That's the way babies are 'spose to eat. God planned it that way. They're 'spose to nurse at their mother's breast until they get their baby teeth and learn to drink from a cup."

"All babies eat like that?"

"Of course, dummy! I just told you. God planned it that way. Even animals get milk from their mothers—dogs and cats and cows and horses."

"I didn't know horses had milk, and dogs, and cats. Yuk."

"Well, they do when they need it."

Marj sat on a trunk and pulled her knees up under her chin. She glanced over at the dolls in the double crib and ran her hand through her ash blonde, shoulder length hair.

She smiled and said, "We were hoping Mother would have twins again. You and Billy were really a lot of fun. You know how Mother talks a mile a minute and puts in every little detail and never stops for breath?"

Marj gasped several times as I laughed guiltily at her apt description of Mother's monologues.

"She used to talk about you and Billy nursing and would tell every little thing; how long each took, how you'd burpeeboo, how she couldn't eat cabbage 'cause it'd give you gas. We used to roll on the floor laughing at the things she'd tell. And, then, when the two of you got older you were so cute and so funny, we watched you all the time just to see what you'd do next. It won't be long until Joshua will be sitting up and then you can play with him, or push him in the buggy. That's the same buggy that we used to push you and Billy in. Of course, we lived in town then, and everybody wanted to see you for twins are so unusual."

"I wish he hadn't died."

"Well, I do too. But, people always die when they get pneumonia."

"Did you ever change our diapers?"

"Sure. Lots of times."

I looked at the three lines of rope Dad had strung up on one side of the attic to dry diapers on rainy days. I said, "It takes a lot of them, doesn't it?" "But of course! One has to keep the baby dry."

"Marj, which one of us did you like the best?"

"That's not a fair question. In a family, you like everyone the same. We've all got the same blood and blood's thicker than anything. Why do you ask such a dumb question?"

I looked around for an answer. Aunt Jemimah's black flat face grinned a perpetual fetching red rickrack smile. The baby dolls looked happy and content in the newly made up crib. Dirt daubers were buzzing around the window on one side and from the far off distance came the distinctive, hauntingly lonesome sounding, pleading toot-tooot- toooting of a freight train. I said, "Oh, I don't know—just something Mother said."

Marg sat down on the floor next to me and cupped her hand under my chin. She pushed my hair back, made a silly grin and poked the dimple in my chin. She spoke kinda whispery, "Toot, I'm gonna tell you a secret. I don't think she means everything she says. She's very happy that he's a boy. I am, too. Aren't you? See, we already have three girls in the family and now we have two boys. You see, the boys carry the family name on."

"I don't like the name, Joshua."

"Why ever not?"

"It doesn't sound like a baby's name."

"Well, he'll grow up. It's a good name: it's a family name. There's a Joshua in the Old Testament, too. I'll read you the story about him sometime, OK? But, now, I wanna read this."

Marj had opened her book and was instantly totally engrossed in it. I felt a familiar pang of rejection and an inexplicable loneliness. I opened the door that led out to the stairs. Marj didn't notice. I reached up to flip the light switch the way Alf always did, but I hesitated, for I knew she'd yell. Sometimes, teasing her was fun, but then again—

"Toot?"

I looked around expectantly, "Yeah?"

"Don't you bother that light! And quit saying 'yeah'. That's not nice."

I ran down the stairs to the kitchen where the familiar strains of the noontime soap opera filled the air as the announcer's voice queried whether a coalminer's daughter could find happiness as the wife of a nobleman. The fresh smell of cucumbers and onions permeated the kitchen. Grandma was making little sandwiches and told me to have a little snack before changing for the new preacher's wife was coming to visit. She peeled a cucumber for me, sprinkled it with salt and laid it on a plate with two cold biscuits that had been split, spread with a thick creamy salad dressing and graced with sweet white onion slices. She added thick slabs of sharp cheese and poured me a glass of iced tea.

Mother was nursing the baby while listening to the radio. The curtains were blowing in the breeze and the baby seemed more interested in watching them then in nursing. Grandma arranged the dainty little open faced sandwiches on a silver tray.

Mr. Aiken called from the back door. "Will these be enough, Mrs. Mason?"

Grandma answered, "Please bring them in here."

Mr. Aiken walked in carrying a bucket full of flowers. He beamed with pride when Grandma exclaimed, "My gracious! Yes, that's just right. They're lovely, thank you very much."

He put them down by the kitchen sink and shook his head in bewilderment as he eyed the tray of dainty sandwiches. "Well, I'll be danged! If they don't beat all! I've heered tell of such but I neer dreamed I'd ever see 'em."

Grandma laughed and offered him one. He declined saying it looked like food for fine ladies, not an old oddjobber. Grandma handed him one and told him it would whet his appetite for the cold roast beef plate she had ready for him. He grinned his thanks and the incongruity of that dainty sandwich in his huge work hardened hands gave me the giggles. He teased me that the cucumber would give me a bellyache. I showed him my biscuit and onion sandwich and he exclaimed, "My Gawd! You sure do eat funny."

Mother adjusted the hanky over her breast and Mr. Aiken flushed with embarrassment as he realized the baby was nursing. He turned away quickly excusing himself and made a quick exit after Grandma gave him his lunch and thanked him again for cutting the flowers for her.

I watched Grandma as she quickly arranged the glads and Sweet Williams with the smallest or tightest buds in the lightest colors at the top graduating down to the deepest, most vivid colors of the large round zinnias tucked in amidst the fully opened blossoms of the dominant varieties. Grandma was only about five feet, two inches tall and the tall cut glass vase was sitting on the counter top. The tall stems of the multi-colored flowers towered above her giving the impression that she was working in a cloud of flowers.

Mother admired the beauty of the arrangement as Grandma carried them into the front room. Grandma laughed and said she thought she had enough flowers for every room in the house. She made a small arrangement of anemones for the dining room table and combined several stalks of glads in an urn for the study. She wrapped the stems of the remaining flowers in a newspaper and stood them down in the bucket of water remarking that the Preacher's wife would probably enjoy having some to take home with her.

We girls were expected to be present when company came, especially if they had called and had an appointed time. It was a matter of sitting quietly, listening politely and speaking only if spoken to. Loralee had pointed out how to gauge the importance of the company by which tea pot Grandma or Mother used. The red clay pot was for everyday use; sometimes neighbors or close friends, who just dropped in, and shared tea from it. The silver tea pot was for parties or special days. There were two bone china tea pots. The plainer one was used for "just acquaintances". The other bone china tea pot was decorated elaborately with gold trim: it was used for semi-important social occasions. The gold trimmed tea pot set on the ready for brew time. A needle point tea cozy lay near by.

Loralee had put two coats of white shoe polish on my scandals and cautioned me not to scuff them or get polish on my ankle bones. Marj had braided my hair too tightly and my scalp itched and burned. The starched pinafore rubbed my shoulders as I stood waiting for Loralee to be satisfied with the bow she was tying. I scratched my tight scalp and self-consciously kept my feet inches apart and pouted that I was going to stay in my room. Loralee said, "You can't do that, Toot. You have to learn how to entertain so when you grow up and have company you'll know what to do." Marj mocked, "Oh, won't you have some tea, muh deah? It only has a touch of arsenic in it!"

They speculated about what the visitor would look like and how she would talk. Marj predicted, "She'll be fat and dressed in black with her hair pulled tightly back. She won't have any make-up on and no jewelry cause that's too worldly and she'll probably talk about fun things being sinful and that the young people are going to the dogs." Loralee laughed and said, "No. That sounds more like a Nazarene! She won't be that bad—or good! She's a Methodist. She'll be nice—I mean, my gosh— she's a preacher's wife."

Mother's voice called to us, "Come on now, girls!" Loralee coaxed me, "Come on, Toot, it'll be nice! Grandma's made some party sandwiches and cookies. Listen—she's already playing the piano."

I reluctantly trailed them down the stairs and slowly made my way to the front room. Grandma sat at the piano playing melancholy ballads of the misty isles. Mother picked up her violin and the rich, sweet melody of *The Londonderry Air* wafted out into the afternoon's stillness. I saw Mr. Aiken, working out in the flower bed, straighten up, and stand looking toward the house as though awe-struck. Mother played with such clarity and expression one could almost hear the words of the beautiful old song: the plaintive pleading of a father's heart to his son and homeland. The piano accompaniment continued and without any verbal exchange, the lilting strains of *Loch Lomond* made our feet meet the beat. I loved the legend that Grandma had so oft repeated as she played the melody. I sat back in the chair, crushing the bow and crossed my feet, scuffing the shoes, and remembered Grandma's words.

"Long before the Pilgrims sailed for this land of Liberty, two highlanders were involved in what was called *The Gunpowder Plot*; just one of the Scotsmen's many fights for freedom. They were captured and imprisoned in the terrible Tower of London. One was released and sent home to Scotland with the message to his clan that they must no longer resist the laws of the English Parliament. The other man was sentenced to die. All Scotsmen believed their souls would return to their homeland, and the doomed man penned the poignant lyrics of how his friend would take the high road, but he would travel the low road and be there before him, although unable to meet his true love, who was waiting for him on the beautiful misty banks of Loch Lomond. The message from Parliament was scorned; but the lyrics in the letter had been sung to the tune of an old Scottish folk melody and served as a rallying cry for the clansmen."

The hallway clock struck two o'clock. We were all aware of the car pulling up the drive, but neither Grandma nor Mother seemed to notice as they began the stately euphony of *Nearer My God To Thee*.

The pretty portly middle-aged lady in the print dress with pink beads and black walking shoes extended her white gloved hand which Mother took after only a second's hesitation. She matched Mother's effervescence as they exchanged pleasantries. Mother ushered her into the front room and introduced Grandma, who kept her hands folded in her lap, but nodded a bow with her greeting of, "How do you do?"

Loralee, Marj and I each stood as we were introduced and Mrs. Ross insisted on giving our hands a hearty shake. It was hard to keep from giggling for we knew Mother's disdain for such and her frequent quote, "A lady never shakes hands."

The three ladies were very shortly engrossed in a lively, animated conversation on the advantages and disadvantages of moving and the unpredictability of: the weather, the congregation and children.

Mrs. Ross was fun to watch. She was a gracious, accomplished conversationalist with a charming, fascinating way of putting pauses both before and after her words, creating the illusion of a painting being framed. She did not talk 'religious' as Marj had bet she would. She laughed easily, expressed herself openly and sincerely and communicated a warmth and friendliness that could not be denied or ignored. It was readily apparent that her sense of humor bordered on the mischievous and was at high tide as she confided the complexities of their decision to accept the appointment to First Church in Nilesville.

Mother regretted our inactivity in the church in recent months and explained that she had been busy, as well as the Reverend Smith's obesity was abominable and she had thought him opinionated, dogmatic and pedantic and resented the way he had used the pulpit to strut his stuff.

Mrs. Ross looked a bit uneasy and Grandma said she did not hold with criticizing any man, especially a man of the cloth. "But, when one gets so pious they think they can walk on water, it's high time they had a good ducking."

We all laughed at the imagery. She continued, "He'll learn. He's a good scholar and a good-hearted man. He just needs a little more experience in dealing with people."

Grandma excused herself to get the tea and refreshments. Mother took Mrs. Ross to see the "little bundle from heaven".

Loralee commented on how nice Mrs. Ross was and Marj agreed, but giggled about having to shake hands.

Mrs. Ross was remarking on how lovely the house and flowers were when they rejoined us. Grandma poured tea and let me pass the tray of dainties around as the conversation stemmed about the niceties of the summer wedding parties and the church socials.

Mrs. Ross told of a faux pax she had made at a recent tea that had prompted some to tease her about being careful not to get a reputation for putting her foot in her mouth like Anna Smith, the last preacher's wife. Mother said, "I wouldn't be a preacher's wife for love nor money. Having to deal with so many different kinds of people from so many different walks of life would be just like skating on thin ice!"

Mrs. Ross accepted more tea and another cucumber sandwich. She explained that she refused to be bothered by parishioners' preconceived notions of how the preacher's wife should act, but admitted to altering her activities considerably in order to not offend anyone unnecessarily. She said her biggest problem was with getting tickled at the wrong time and laughing at the wrong thing. Mother looked surprised and quipped, "That's a funny problem."

Grandma observed, "There would be fewer problems if people would keep a sense of humor. 'A merry heart doeth good like a medicine'." Mrs. Ross smiled and nodded, "Proverbs: Seventeen, Twenty-two. One of my favorites!" She paused and seemed to be contemplating something.

Mother refilled the tea cups and Mrs. Ross said, "If you'll promise not to think me a gossip, I'd love to tell you a funny story about Anna." Grandma looked down at the cup of tea she was holding in both hands on her lap. Mother looked apprehensive as she glanced at us children. Mrs. Ross hastened to add, "It has to do with the Jackson's."

Mother said, "Oh?" and sipped her tea. Mrs. Ross began, "Mr. Jackson just couldn't reconcile himself to his losses when the banks failed. He lost the railroad and he nearly lost the shirt off his back. He withdrew into himself and became a recluse the last few years of his life. One morning Mrs. Jackson couldn't find him anyplace but she figured he'd gone down to the woods. Late in the afternoon, she had a peculiar feeling, and went up to the attic. She found him there, hanging from the rafters."

Marj rolled her eyes at Loralee. I gasped audibly and we listened closely in fascination. Mother exclaimed, "How dreadful! I had no idea." Mrs. Ross continued, "It was a terribly traumatic experience for Mrs. Jackson, but Reverend Smith excelled at counseling. He was conscientious, sincere and well-trained and he gave a lot of time to helping her. Anna had a good heart but she was a trifle scatter-brained and he was leery of letting her pay her respects but he finally relented on the condition that she only stay five minutes and only talk about the weather. Anna eagerly agreed and promised that she would not say anything that would set Mrs. Jackson off or remind her of the tragedy. So, Anna called on Mrs. Jackson and asked her how she was. She said, 'Oh, I'm doing pretty fine, now, but I've put the wash off for so long and what with all of the rain, I don't know how I'm going to get the bed linens dry.' Anna piped up with, 'Why, that shouldn't be any problem. You can always hang them in the attic!'."

Grandma's cup was clinking in the saucer and Mother was having trouble setting hers down on the table. Mrs. Ross had her chin on her chest and was doubling over. Each lady seemed to be caught in the throes of some compelling force, bridged between hilarity and pain. There was an audible intake of breaths and each collapsed in laughter that was highly infectious. Mother regained her composure enough to murmur, "Hang them in the attic."

A renewed surge of laughter swept through the room binding us all in pangs of delight. Out in the far side yard Mr. Aiken and Alf looked toward the house inquisitively, talked awhile, laughed and resumed their work. Mrs. Ross said she really must go and confided she couldn't remember ever enjoying a visit so much as she had this one. Grandma gave her the flowers and as soon as she left we girls hurried to the attic.

Loralee opened the door and reached in to switch on the light. The heat was oppressive and the interior darker and more forbidding than I remembered it. Marj was saying, "I told you it was creepy and spooky. I'll bet his ghost is still here!" Loralee elbowed her, "Don't be dumb! There's no such thing as ghosts."

I looked around at Aunt Jemimah with her red rickrack grin, the dolls nestled in the crib, the stacks of magazines, the trunks and chairs and quilting and curtain frames. I whispered, "It's just the same."

Marj whispered back," No, it's not. It'll never be the same again. His ghost is here. See that hook up there? I'll bet that's the one where he hung himself. That's a piece of the rope still on it!"

Loralee laughed weakly "Marj—don't scare Toot." I moved closer to Loralee and said, "I'm not sca-scared." Marj's eyes were as big as saucers and her tone ominous, "It's a proven fact that when a man commits suicide his ghost stays right there where he did it until his predestined time of death."

Loralee put her hands on her hips and defiantly faced Marj. "Hogwash! That's just out of one of your stupid Halloween stories. No intelligent person believes in predestination or ghosts!"

Loralee's voice was loud with just the slightest quiver. She put her arm about my shoulder and said firmly, "Now, Toot, don't you take her seriously. She's just joking."

Marj yelled, "I am not! It's the gospel truth."

I asked, "What's predes. . . ?"

Marj hissed, "You wouldn't understand!" She leaned near and whispered ghoulishly, "But you know what a ghost is, don't you?"

Loralee's eyes were looking up to the hook with the fragment of rope dangling loosely between the beams. Marj was looking up at it, too. My glance caught the clothesline rope that Mr. Aiken had strung up for drying diapers. I started laughing and said, "Look!" Loralee and Marj were looking curiously, furtively about. I pointed to the triple rows of rope with diapers drying on them and blurted out between gasps,

"Hang them—in the—attic." Marj shrieked with giggles and Loralee laughed until the tears streamed down her cheeks. Grandma walked in fanning herself against the heat. "I'm so glad you girls are not entertaining any foolishness about being shy of the attic. It's such a nice place for you to play and . . ." She leaned closer and whispered, "Girls should always have a quiet, secret place." We all giggled and Loralee teased, "Yes, it is a good hang-out." Grandma beamed approval. She turned to leave and laughed, "I can hardly wait for Riley to get home. That's the funniest story I've heard in years. I know it'll just put him in stitches."

5

🐦 WELL FED ON CONTRADICTIONS

I started to school in the fall and Miss Lamb put me with the second graders. I liked the conformities and the challenges of the classroom and it quickly became the center of my world. Each afternoon I would rush home and tell about the lessons of the day and eagerly read or memorize the assigned work. Mother and Grandma would listen attentively and coach me diligently; tirelessly elaborating on the lessons. If I were baffled over a new spelling word or problem or situation, they would use it repeatedly, good-naturedly surprising me with its common usage until it would become a part of my vocabulary or understanding. Both of them would tell stories of how it was when they were going to school.

One day Mother got a china doll out of her keepsake trunk in the attic and told of how she had had trouble with her multiplication tables, especially, six times nine equals fifty-four, so her Papa bought her the dolly and told her its name was 'Six Times Nine Equals Fifty-Four'. She cuddled it to her lovingly and laughed, "I never forgot that one again and it made all of the others easier too."

Miss Lamb was a tiger for perfection. Anything less than one's best was not acceptable. Slouching or sloppiness in any form was simply not tolerated. I thought her queenly: Her impeccable manner and bearing were an inspiration. She ruled the classroom serenely, though sternly. We students all worshiped her and learned to take pride and pleasure in hard work, extra work, doing more than was assigned and doing it to the best of our ability. Excuses, fawning or brown-nosing as it was called on the playground, were "not proper". Responses of, "Yes, Mam" and "No, Mam" were proper but an obsequious or servile attitude denoted a problem or a weakness in character and Miss Lamb left no stone unturned in search of the rot and worms that were defying a strong durable base of support for her students growth and self-confidence. I loved her. I thought she was perfect.

Late one afternoon in early October after I had discoursed on my day at school, Mother commented, "Miss Lamb—such a nice name. I'm sure if she's half as nice as her name, you'll just love her, and it's so important to like your teacher—Gets you off to a good start for all your school years. I do hope she's well qualified. So many of the older women didn't even go to a teacher's college and it just makes me wonder how effective they can be at teaching."

Grandma looked up from her tatting. "Maybe you should consider teaching, Martha. You've got your certificate and from what I see in the papers they're begging for teachers this year."

Mother squirmed uneasily. "Why, Mother Mason. Here I am with a baby and him still nursing and so much work to do I don't even know where to start. My goodness! I haven't been in a classroom for years and I never did have a yen for it. Papa just assumed I'd go to Normal and be a teacher. He never once asked me what I thought about it and it never occurred to me to tell him. Truth of the matter is, I didn't know. But, children make me nervous! I don't mean my own. I always wanted a big family. But, other peoples' kids get on my nerves!"

Grandma nodded, sighed, and held up her tatting for scrutiny. She adjusted her glasses and smiling lightly at Mother, said, "You do a good job with your children, Martha. I've heard you helping then with their studies and you worry them 'till they're done."

Mother smiled quizzically, as Grandma continued, "I've known some good teachers whose only qualifications were their love for teaching. But, times are changing. Life's getting more complicated—Seems there's more to learn now."

Mother made a production of rethreading her needle, stabbing the air with the thread, weaving from side to side with the needle held toward the window at arms length and mildly protesting. "They're making the needle eyes smaller than they use to."

Grandma frowned, "You'd better have your eyes checked. I'll fix some carrot sticks. They'll keep nicely in a jar in the fridge. That way, you can just help yourself when you take a notion for one."

Mother stifled a yawn and began darning another sock. She said, "Oh, don't get up, Mother. Carrots are a good idea but they can wait until later. I agree with you that it's important for a teacher to have a love of teaching. But, ideally, they should have a degree as well."

Grandma reminisced, "I always just left Riley and Katie be. Of course, he took to books like a duck takes to water, but Katie just poked along doing no more than she had to. She'd rather cook or sew than read a book. I read the classics to her, but she didn't listen half the time. I don't mean that to be critical, though. Katie's the best seamstress this side of Sant Louis, and she runs her kitchen and house as well as Riley runs his office."

It was cozy and comfortable sitting at the kitchen table doing my homework. I heard, without listening, the conversational nuances, the affable exchanges, the agreeable good-natured humor and sound reasoning. It was not distracting. The atmosphere was conducive to study. It was easy to concentrate here in the peaceful, quiet late afternoon rest hour that precluded the hustle-bustle activities of supper preparation. But, suddenly, a word stood out, struck a chord and I blurted out, "Grandma, Miss Lamb said we shouldn't say 'Sant'. She said that's wrong. We're 'spose to say, 'Saint' Louis."

Grandma looked pensive. The thread relaxed, the slim silver hooks were stayed as though caught in an unexpected tangle.

Mother scoffed indignantly. "Oh, Bull! Who does she think she is? Where's she from anyway? You can bet she isn't from around here! If there's one thing I can't stand it's some teacher trying to pour each student into a little mold. Grammar is one thing with hard fast rules of usage. But dialect is flexible and as free as a flag in a breeze, and any teacher, who's worth her salt knows that! Why, everybody in Southern Illinois says 'Sant" whether they're talking about Sant Louis or Sant Peter at the pearly gates. Now, don't you get me wrong, young Lady, I'm not going to have you talking crude, saying things like cain't or ain't, but when it comes to the pronunciation of certain words, it depends on what part of the country one's from as to what's right or wrong. And here, it is right and proper to say 'Sant'. Just remember to spell it with an 'i' sandwiched in the middle."

I felt rebuffed, strangely embarrassed and just a little confused. Grandma wound the loosed thread on the little fat spool and enfolded the spool, thimble and hooks in the hankie. She removed the reading glasses that she also wore for close work, sighed heavily and said to me,

"We've all got a lot to learn, Honey. That's something we never get through with, because we can never learn everything we're meant to know. Don't be embarrassed to talk about new ideas or to ask questions. You're going to be learning about a lot of things I've never even heard of."

Grandma patted me on the shoulder and I smiled my thanks. Mother was hastily gathering her mending and sewing paraphernalia. She said,

"If I don't get supper started I'm liable to have a hungry crew in here threatening to fire the chief cook and bottle washer. You listen to your Grandma, Toot. They say curiosity killed the cat, but, God meant for us to be curious and inquisitive. That's how new discoveries are made in science and medicine and technology. Somebody saying, 'Why? Why?' and building on to what others have learned and taught and shared. But learning new ways and new things does not necessarily mean that the old ways are wrong! And you must remember that there are many roads that lead to New York—or Sant Louis."

I picked up my books, papers and pencils and went into the study. The oversized oak roll-top desk was laden with papers, rolls of maps and charts and correspondence. An assortment of ink pens and a copper ink stand reminded me of a penmanship assignment, so I sat at the cluttered desk making oval O's and elongated L's, sweeping S's and curvy C's. Line after line of A's, F's and Z's. *Dip the pen, rest the wrist, keep your back straight and your head up, point the tip of the pen toward your right shoulder, now write, write, blot. Begin again. It is wrong to say 'Sant'! Mother said, "Bull!" Miss Lamb is wrong. It is easy to make a lamb out of an O or U. S's become snakes and pretty graceful swans and huge awkward dinosaurs. O's become faces: smiling, frowning, and then individuals countenances take shape. L's make graceful ballerinas all in a row standing on their toes. Why don't they fall? U's become a mixture of sheep and tulips. The black ink is no good for shading, but the purple indelible pencil, touched to the tip of the tongue, makes a rich purpley color that lightens as it dries.*

"What are you doing at Dad's desk?" I had not noticed Marj come in. She towered above me like a threatening storm cloud. I answered defiantly, "I'm doing my homework!"

She peered over my shoulder and smirked, "That doesn't look like any homework to me. If it was, you've ruined it! And I'll bet you've ruined Dad's pen, too. Boy! Is he gonna be mad!"

She flipped on the reading light and flopped down in a chair. "Why don't you go someplace else, Squirt? I've got to read this."

I wiped the pen on a soft rag and replaced it in its holder. I gathered my things and started to leave. Marj was totally engrossed in her studying. I said, "Marj?" She did not answer me. I walked nearer her and said, louder, "Marj!"

She plopped the book down in her lap and scowled at me, "What?"

"What's the name of that big city that has the bridge over the river?"

She sneered at me. "You mean Sant Louis?"

I said, "Oh, yeah", and ran snickering from the room.

The evening meal was usually called supper or supper-time, and the entire family took their places about the long rectangular oak table in the dining room. It was set with good china that varied with the seasons of the year, and one of three patterns of silver flatware, depending on which of us girls set the table. We each had our "favorite" and were told that "someday" it would be ours to place upon some table in our far distant future.

A huge mirror with three sections and an elaborate gilded gold-leaf frame covered the wall above the buffet and reflected the gleaming crystal chandelier that hung over the center of the room.

To one side stood a large heavy ornately carved whiskey-cabinet, which was used for storing linens and "good" candies. Whiskey was taboo, but, wine or sherry was okay for grown-ups, although Mother sometimes seemed to worry about some abstinence card she had signed one Sunday morning in church, when some visiting preacher had insisted everyone had to sign a card and he refused to dismiss the service until they did. Dad had asked her, "Why didn't you just leave?"

Mother had fluttered her eyes and put her hand on her chest, "Why, I couldn't do that. There must have been nearly a hundred people there. I didn't see anyone leave. You know how they talk about the least little thing. I'm certainly not going to make a spectacle of myself or give them any fodder for gossip."

An oak china closet with a curved glass door and curved glass petitions on either side stood on the wall nearest the kitchen. The mirror in the back of it was nearly obscured by the piles and stacks of china plates, bowls, cups and saucers. Crystal glasses with gold rims stood on the ready for company. We used plain ones for family.

I had been taught the proper way to set the table, lay the silver and fold the napkins, before I was tall enough to reach the kitchen faucets. Grandma liked a pretty table, and frequently commented, "If it looks good, it's bound to taste better."

Grace was usually said by Dad or Mother or Grandma. Sometimes one of us children would recite a Sunday School prayer or intone some Scripture verse. Dad would usually get a chuckle with his very brief table blessings. Grandma spoke in thee's and thou's. Mother went over-long, tending to verbalize her thanks to God for each one of us and for the very air that we breath and the ground that we walked on and seeking His guardian angels to protect us each step of the way and always the closing line, ". . .*now bless this food to the nourishment of our bodies and feed our souls upon the everlasting bread of life that we may be worthy and fit vessels for Thy Heavenly Kingdom, In the name of our gracious Lord and Savior, Jesus Christ, Amen.*"

Dad had been known to murmur a soft "Whew!" at the conclusion. I do not believe it was meant disrespectfully. Mother seemed to take it as a compliment and Grandma always smiled. Somehow, it seemed appropriate.

Food was dished out as generously as home-spun philosophy. There were lessons to be chewed over, sermons to be absorbed, and tantalizing moralizing for food for thought.

Opinions and witticisms were dispensed as freely as the salt and pepper, but within the confines of good taste and propriety. Too much seasoning will spoil the broth and hurt the stomach and not all topics are appropriate for table talk. So, within the fine lines, that were as well established and adhered to as stringently as the Old Testament food laws about what shall and what shall not be eaten, there was an even flow of conversation, centering around the day's events, sprinkled liberally with good humor and laced with love, affection and respect amongst the three generations at the table.

We seldom used the word "kosher", but the Food Laws were considered to be on the same plane as the Ten Commandments. We did not have separate courses, but rather ate family style with meat and vegetables on the same plate and salads were eaten along with the meals. It was not considered healthy to drink milk at suppertime. Milk was a part of breakfast and encouraged for snacks and lunch, unless we were having salmon patties. *"Heaven forbid you drink milk and eat fish together! It'll kill you, if not sooner than later."*

Mother catered to the individual likes and dislikes of her family's palates and respected our individual tastes and preferences. She never insisted we eat something we did not like, but would query, *"How can you know if you like it or not if you don't try at least one tiny little bite? God knows I wouldn't have fixed it if it were going to hurt you."*

She insisted we eat sensibly for one must feed the mind and spirit as well as the whole body. I was amazed to learn in school that all foods go to the stomach. I thought they had specific destinations, based on Mother's admonitions.

"Eat your eggs. They'll make your hair grow and shine."

"Meat and cheese are good for the bones and teeth, but you mustn't eat them together or they'll make you sluggish."

"You must not drink coffee until you are through growing, but tea is fine; iced, hot or lukewarm; with honey and lemon it's medicinal and a proper tonic any time of the day or night for any ill, either real or imagined."

"Milk gravy is fine for breakfast with eggs, even with eggs and cheese, but only broth gravy should be eaten with meat."

"Crunchy raw vegetables will make you as fleet as a deer, and they're good for the eyes, too. You never saw a deer wearing glasses, did you?"

Vegetables had to be thoroughly washed and rinsed. It was unthinkable to overcook them or to overload them with heavy sauces and downright sinful to season them with meat.

"What's the world coming to? Why would supposedly intelligent people doubt but what God knows best? If He'd meant for us to have greasy vegetables He'd have made them that way."

"Seafood and shellfish are an abomination. God made them to keep the water clean. They're scavengers! They should be left alone to do what they were made to do. Imagine eating such! It's no surprise for me that some people have such horrible diseases. You are what you eat!"

Eggs were thoroughly cooked. No drinks or sauces or new desserts that called for raw eggs would even be considered. Meats were thoroughly cooked, and the seasons were reflected in the meals. Cold weather meant heavier meals for, *"Everyone knows, you burn more fuel in the winter just like the furnace."*

In the fall there would be quail, pheasant and venison to augment the beef, mutton and chicken. Special occasions usually called for turkey. Spring time saw an abundance of trout, bass, lamb and veal.

There were always a choice of salads; two, if not three vegetables, and potatoes; usually mashed, sometimes, baked, French roasted, fried, braised, or par-broiled.

The proper drink for supper was water if one must drink during the meal, but iced tea was permissible. *"If you really feel you need it and will be careful not to overload your stomach."*

Desserts were the crowning event to every evening meal: fruit pies in season, creamed pies; chocolate, lemon, coconut and butterscotch were the favorites; angel food cake, applesauce cake, devil's food cake and the joshing that went with it as surely as the thick fudgy icing and a Hickory Nut Cake with a boiled sugar icing that was Dad's favorite cake. It was an old recipe from Mary Todd Lincoln. She had written that it was Abraham Lincoln's favorite cake too, so the talk always centered around Abraham Lincoln when we had that cake.

After school snacks would be any combination of left-overs for sandwiches or any of a variety of puddings, and sometimes fruit and nut breads and cookies; molasses cookies, oatmeal cookies, chocolate cookies, peanut-butter cookies and, my favorite, cheese cookies. All served with the warning, *"I do like to see you enjoy your eating, but too much of a good thing will do you more harm than good."*

I had nearly finished redoing my penmanship exercise when Dad knocked on the door to my room. "Toot? Didn't you hear the bell? Supper's ready."

I was still mulling over the earlier elucidation on dialect and the subsequent painful conflict between my Mother and my teacher. I could not resolve it, neither could I understand it. Mother was convincing, but Miss Lamb was my teacher.

Dad, unaware of what had gone on before, innocently asked, "Pass the tomatoes, please, and help yourselves. There won't be many more this year. Better enjoy them while you can."

Mother picked up the decorative platter of bright red, juicy, round, generous slices of tomatoes and said a bit saucily, "You mean, tuh-MAH-toes?"

Dad looked quizzical and shrugged, "Tuh-MAY-toes, tuh-MAH-toes, love apples—a rose by any other name is still a rose."

Mother laughed, "Ah, yes! But, we're talking about tuh-MAH-toes. Most important to WAR-sh, or should I say, WAH-sh, them before slicing."

Dad grumbled, "I trust your judgment in war-shing the tuh-may-toes. Now, if you'll pass them instead of just admiring them, I'll show you how to really enjoy them."

Alf speared a helping with his fork as he passed the dish on and Mother's quick eye saw and she rebuked him with,

"Alf! I haven't reared you to be rude at the table."

Alf grinned mischievously, leaned toward her and gave a good husky voiced imitation of W.C. Fields, "Yas, mam, I mean, no, mam. You raised me to be neat an tidy and above all things, un-rude at the table. Umm, yas, un-rude I say."

Josh, from his high-chair, murmured something that sounded like, "Yas, yas."

Laughter and confusion reigned momentarily as several of us tried to imitate somebody else or get Josh to repeat some foolishness.

Grandma addressed Alf as she said, "One may raise corn or chickens, but parents rear their children."

Marj asked, "Is that like a horse rears?"

Dad plopped some mashed potatoes on his plate and in mocked exasperation threatened, "I'm gonna raise a little cane and maybe do some rearin' around here myself if someone doesn't tell me about what's a-goin' on."

I felt a tinge of embarrassment and guiltily toyed with my food. Mother gaily chirped, "Toot's teacher, Miss Lamb, told the class today that we should say 'Saint' instead of 'Sant'."

Dad looked around the table and winked at me. "Well, what's wrong with that? Most people would agree with her. That's probably the way they say it everyplace else."

Mother bridled, "But that's the whole point. It depends on the locale and the dialect as to what is right or wrong. Common usage constitutes what's right. You know that! It just makes my blood boil to have some outsider come in here and tell our children we aren't pronouncing words correctly."

Dad put his hand up like a stop sign and said, "Whoa now. We're paying these teachers a good salary to teach and I don't think we ought to be undermining their efforts here at home."

Mother, taken aback by the gentle chiding, feigned hurt. With one hand held delicately against her chest, she tossed her head from side to side as she glanced around the table and defensively demanded,

"Have I ever once discouraged any of you children in your learning? Why, I'd bite my tongue before I'd do or say anything that would keep you from your studies and I'd certainly never rob any teacher of their due respect. But, teachers are only human and they're still learning just like the rest of us and Miss Lamb is way off base when it comes to dialect. I'm not saying she isn't a good teacher. And nobody can accuse me of not wanting you to talk as well as act, proper, but I'm not going to have you putting on airs or correcting your elders and you can just remember to 'when in Rome do as the Roman's do'."

Dad teased her. "Why, Martha, I wouldn't have thought you, of all people would be a party to that philosophy." Mother feigned hurt and said, "Make fun if you will, but you know I speak the truth."

Alf said, "I thought this was Little Egypt."

Marj said, "For your information, this is SOUTHERN ILLINOIS, soon to become the FORTY-NINTH STATE in the great UNITED STATES OF AMERICA"

Dad chuckled, shook his head, winked at Grandma and buttered another helping of potatoes.

"Like the way you think, Miss Marjie, but, don't hold your breath. There's one thing for sure that no-one in their right mind would argue about Southern Illinois. We certainly have a fair share of idioms and a good sprinkling of dialect you can't find any place else. There's a poor fella in jail down in Eldorado that could attest to it."

We all looked to Dad. The gold watch fob was dancing on it's chain from his stomach heaving with contained laughter as he buttered another big slab of cornbread, obviously savoring the telling of the tale as much as the taste of the rich textured, golden-crusted cornbread, and debating which to start first. We did not give him a choice for we were all curious about who the poor fella was and what would he attest to and why was he in jail.

Dad reluctantly placed the bread on the edge of his plate and wiped his mouth with his napkin as we all sat in suspense. Mother seemed to be as curious as we children while Grandma looked on as though viewing her favorite pastime. Dad complied with, "Well, there was an article in the newspaper the other day about a well-dressed man who went into the bank down in Eldorado and wanted to cash a good-sized check. The lady-teller looked at him the way they have of looking at someone they don't know, and she asked, 'What is your home address?' He gave her an address on Oak Street and she said, 'What town?" and he said, 'Why, right here in El-do-rah-do.' She knew right off he was lying, but she asked, 'Do you live here?' He said, 'Yes, I was born and raised right here in El-do- rah-do.' So, she excused herself on some pretence and went back to the bank president's office and told him to call the Sheriff and the stranger was arrested and what's more, he was wanted in several states on bad check charges."

Loralee said, "I don't get it."

Alf asked, "How'd she know he was lying?"

Mother was beaming with interest and delight in the story as Dad continued. "Well, that stranger didn't understand it either at first. However, if he had known your Mother and her thinking on dialect he'd never have made such a serious mistake."

Mother sounded please as she said, "Oh, Riley, you do go on!"

Dad elaborated, "You see, it was his ignorance of dialect, or common usage, that tripped him up. The lady-teller knew that no one from around there would say, Oak Street. All of the residential streets are called Avenues. No-one from Southern Illinois would say 'El-do-RAH-do'. It's El-do-RAY- do. Now, out in the West there's several towns called El-do-RAH-do, spelled the same, but, pronounced differently. And, now, for the coup de grace, that is, the clincher; folks from here abouts, would say they'd been reared, not raised. So, you see, the fella got what was coming to him, because that lady-teller knew her dialect as well as your Mother does."

Mother basked in the favorable comments that followed. I asked Dad if I could tell that story to Miss Lamb. He replied, "Let's see if we still have that paper about."

He smiled and gave a devilish look to Mother and added pointedly, "It was in the Sant Louis Trib."

Mother beamed, "I'm sure Miss Lamb would find it interesting and enlightening."

After supper Dad and I found the article. He watched as I carefully cut it out with a big pair of scissors. I said a bit grimly, "Now, Miss Lamb will know that she's wrong."

Dad rubbed his chin and eyed me closely. I blurted out, "I didn't think teachers were 'spose to be wrong!'"

Dad half-whispered in a confidential tone, "Well, now, I'm not sure she's wrong at all."

"But, Dad! She said it's wrong to say 'Sant'."

"Well, I believe she is right to teach you the proper pronunciation of words. It is very important for a young lady to know that. No, I wouldn't say she was wrong at all."

I stared at him. My mouth opened and I inhaled audibly. Dad laughed. I protested, "But, Mother said—You said—" Dad interrupted my stammering.

"Now, listen. You go to school to learn. Learning can be fun, but it can be hard work, too, and sometimes, it can be a bit painful. You are going to have a lot of teachers over the years. Many of them will have ideas, opinions or ways that are different than our own here at home. That is not to say that they are wrong or that we are wrong. You must keep your mind open to their teachings and remember that things do not have to be labeled right or wrong just because they are different. I'm glad Miss Lamb is teaching you the correct pronunciation of words. But, learning is a two-way street, and I feel sure she will be interested in learning our dialect here. You see, dialect is fun, but it isn't nearly as important as being correct. Besides, you want to know a secret? It makes spelling a lot easier if you pronounce the words correctly and enunciate them clearly."

I did not realize I was frowning until Dad said, "If your face freezes in that dark frown, you'll scare the goblins on Halloween." I tried to keep from smiling.

He said, "What's bothering you?"

"What do you mean about a two-way street?"

Dad said, "Oh, well, you know cars go both ways on a two-way street. With learning, that means the teacher learns from the students while the students are learning from the teacher."

I grinned broadly, pleased with the aspect of a teacher learning from her students. "Really?"

"Sure!" he said, and poked the dimple in my chin. "Of course, the students never let on that they know that. It's one of those things that is best left unsaid. Understand?" And he winked at me real silly. He told me to go put the article with my homework and then to meet him in the study.

Dad and Grandma were laughing quietly over some secret whisperings when I ran into the study moments later. Grandma opened her arms to me and I hurried to them and stood between her and Dad, encircled in her cocoon of care, enveloped in her loving concern, and fortified by her quiet strength. Dad was rubbing an oily cloth over a long gun. The pungent smell of the oil tickled my nostrils. Dad held the piece aloft, admiring it and said to me,

"Looky here, Toot! See that fine scroll work on the stock? And just look at the elaborate tooling on the barrel. It's a work of art! But, you want to know a fact? This gun can't shoot worth a hoot. It was the one of the first long-guns made and they hadn't figured out yet about the number of spirals necessary on the inside of the barrel to project a ball, so, although this piece is a thing of beauty, it just couldn't cut the mustard."

Dad chuckled and sighted it. He continued, "Yes, sirree, one of the first long-guns ever made! And, it was your great, great, great granddaddy that made it. See his sign there? But, when they'd pour the powder in and tamp it down, and then drop the ball in and fire it, there'd be a flash and a blue tail of smoke and the ball would just fall out at the end of the barrel, easy like, ker-plunk. So, they scratched their heads and thought on it, and then more than likely, some outsider come along with a new idea and says it's wrong to have such a long barrel without a corresponding number of spirals to give the ball the speed it needs to project it. So, the gunsmith thought just maybe, there was something to what he said, even if he was an outsider. So, he made another one, with the additional spirals cut into the innards of the barrel, and sure enough, it worked. The thing is, they kept learning and trying new ideas and working at it and sharing their knowledge with others until they finally perfected it and had something they could be proud of and a long-gun that could be depended upon."

Grandma's hands rested gently on my shoulders. She said, "It's still like that with learning, Honey. Sometimes, you have to look deep inside things to understand what makes them work. Why, some folks say there's nothing new under the sun, but, everyday there are new ideas and new discoveries that affect all of us. Do you know that when I was your age we didn't have electricity or automobiles or telephones?"

We all laughed. Dad said, "How'd you ever survive, Mama?"

Grandma continued, and shook her head in wonderment, "My gracious. I have seen a lot of wonderful things become commonplace. I'm sure there will be even greater advancements in your time, Toot. I want you to be receptive to new ideas and new teachings, and, please, tell me about them, too . We can never learn everything we're meant to know."

Mother came bounding in. "So! This is where you all are. I might have known. Toot, you'd better run up to bed. It's after eight o'clock and tomorrow is another day. Did you find that article? Well, good! That'll give Miss Lamb some food for thought. It just makes my blood boil to have some outsider like that. . ."

6

🐦 CLIMBING THROUGH FENCES

The telephone jangled in the kitchen and Mother fussed, "It never fails. Just let us sit down to eat and the telephone has to ring. We can't seem to have a decent meal without the phone interrupting!"

Alf and Marj both jumped to answer it. He won out, as usual, in their scramble for it, blocking her with an exaggerated posture as he answered in a mellifluous voice, "Hel-loo?"

Dad chuckled and Mother sighed adoringly, commenting, as though in surrender.

"Ummm, that boy! I don't know what we're going to do with him. Such a cut-up!"

We all listened to see who was calling. Alf's tone changed quickly as he answered, "Oh, hi, Uncle Ralph—No, we're just eating—Sure, he's right here—Dad! It's Uncle Ralph."

Mother wondered aloud what he was calling about. Dad hurried to the phone. We were all curious but from what Dad said it sounded like they were talking about acreage and harvesting and machinery. Loralee asked about going shopping for a new dress for the school dance and talk turned to the family of the boy she was seeing. Grandma said she would like to go shopping on Saturday, "Seeing as how someone's going to be having a birthday one of these days."

All eyes focused on me as Mother asked teasingly, "Well, now, I wonder who that could be?" We had finished with dessert and were idling about the table when Dad rejoined us and in answer to our queries told us, "Everybody says, 'Hi.' Your Uncle Ralph says he wished he'd gotten that new tractor years ago and now that he's gotten that milking machine he's going to increase his herd of Jerseys."

Dad pushed aside his unfinished plate of cold food. Mother poured him coffee and offered him a choice of pies, bemoaning the fact that we children just didn't like pecan pie if there were chocolate or butterscotch about. Dad said we didn't know what was good and then asked, "Was there any mail this morning?"

Grandma said, "Just the St. Louis Trib."

Dad bragged on how good the pie was. Mother regretted it was a bit chewy around the edges and hoped her indulgence would not give the baby gas. Waves of self-conscious tittering grew into billows of laughter amongst us children as an anonymous individual gave a punctuation mark to Mother's worry about the baby's indigestion. Grandma kept her glance discreetly down and held her napkin over her mouth for some time. But I noticed her shoulders were shaking with silent mirth. Dad attempted to restore a degree of decorum by ignoring the tomfoolery and asked, "What time does the mailman come by here? Have any of you met him?"

We each volunteered some tidbit of information and Mother told of how nice and friendly he was. She said, "I was walking Josh up and down the lane this morning when he pulled up. He admired him and said they're expecting their first grandchild any day now. There were some geese flying over and he said they were probably going down to Horseshoe Lake and that he had seen some black wooly worms, too. We'll probably have an exceptionally cold winter."

Dad said he would sure hate to have to have a mailbox half-a-mile down the road like Ralph and Katie. Mother philosophized, "Well, when one's accustomed to something like that, they don't see it as an inconvenience. They just take it as a matter of course." Dad nodded agreement and looking around at us children, asked, "Did any of you see their mailman when we were out there last summer?"

Loralee shook her head no. Marj said she had offered to walk down with Sharon, but she never wanted her to. Alf said he was always too busy and had not even thought about them getting mail way out there. Dad looked at me questioningly. I said I had taken a letter down for Uncle Ralph one time. Dad contemplated a forkful of pie, put it down and drank some coffee. He looked at me searchingly, "Did you see the mailman, Toot?"

I squirmed in my chair, remembering. I studied the centerpiece of bronze and yellow mums and looked at Dad's intent blue eyes.

"Yes Sir. I saw him."

Something clouded his eyes: worry, fear, concern, anger? I did not know what, but it was a relief when he folded his napkin and said cheerily,

"Which one of you pretty ladies baked that pie? I swear it's the best I've ever had and if I don't leave this table I'll be tempted to have more than I should."

Grandma said Mother had made it. Mother said Grandma had made the pastry and that was what made it so good.

The grandfather clock struck seven o'clock and Alf and Marj ran for the radio. Loralee was helping clear the table. Dad touched me on the shoulder and nodded toward the study. I reluctantly, but curiously, followed him. He closed the door, walked over to the fireplace and poked the logs, making sparks fly and flames flare up high.

"Toot? I'm curious about a thing or two. You can help me by answering some questions, OK?"

I sat down in the rocking chair but did not trust myself to rock it. Apprehension, an unexplainable guilt and a dread of embarrassment engulfed me, but I could not understand why. I knew he was going to ask me about that nasty mailman and I was not sure what I had promised Sharon I would not tell. Dad sat down in the wing chair facing me.

"I've just got a minute or two, because I've got to leave shortly. Did you want to hear that program?"

I shrugged, "I don't care."

"The day you took that letter to the mailman for your Uncle Ralph—the time you saw the mailman—did you talk to him?"

"No. I gave the letter to Sharon. She handed it to him. Did it get lost?"

Dad looked surprised and a little amused. He patted me on the arm and said, "Oh no. The letter, uh—that was fine. Then, Sharon was with you?"

"Well, yes. I walked down there with Old Sam, but Sharon was there with Nick, that's the mailman's name."

"Were you in the car with him?"

"Oh, no. I was just on the road waiting for them."

"Sharon was in the car with him?"

I looked down at my lap. Dad waited. There were worry lines in his forehead and his mouth was in a tight line as he took out his watch and sighed heavily. I squirmed in my chair and my hands kept clutching the hem of my dress, twisting it into tight wrinkles.

"Dad? I promised Sharon I wouldn't tell."

He exhaled through his nose and ran his hand through his hair.

"Toot, did he say anything to you, or touch you or give you anything?"

"No. He had some gum but he didn't offer us any."

"Did he ask you if you wanted to ride in his car?"

"No. He just talked to Sharon. He didn't talk to me at all."

Dad sighed again and rubbed his forehead.

"Did you see Sharon in the car with him?"

I looked down, remembering my promise not to tell, about what— Her learning to drive—Or him tickling her—Or both? Dad spoke sharply, "Well, did you?"

"Yes—but she made me promise I wouldn't tell."

Dad frowned darkly, closed his eyes for a moment, then, got up, stoked the fire, put another log on and brushed his hands off on his trousers.

"I see. Well, Honey, I don't want to make you break a promise."

Dad walked over to in front of my chair, took my hand and pulled me to my feet. He knelt down on one knee so that we were eye level. He brushed my bangs back from my forehead and cupped my chin in his big hand.

"Toot? You're sure he didn't touch you at all?" I shook my head no.

"He didn't touch me, Dad." I thought for a minute and then added. "I didn't like him. Neither did Sharon. She said he was nasty."

Dad rose slowly with great effort, as though he were very tired, and turned toward the fireplace.

"Please go tell your Grandma I would like to see her for a moment— and, Toot—Don't say anything about this to anyone else. Okay?"

Grandma was drying dishes and joshed to Mother and Loralee about not finishing until she got back. I got a wrap and slipped out into the heavy, chilling darkness onto the front porch that bordered the study. There was a window with lace curtains and I could hear without being seen. I knew I would be in real trouble if I were caught. I was trembling from both the November chill and the guilt of spying, but I sensed something was brewing and the curiosity stayed me. Their voices were low, but carried distinctly.

"Mama, that was Ralph alright, but he was calling about—something else. Martha doesn't need to know any of this. She'd just likely get worried and all upset."

Dad took a shotgun from out of a side cabinet and wrapped it in a sheet of drafting paper. Grandma asked quietly, "What is it, Riley?"

"My God, Mama—I hate to tell you such ugliness! But, Ralph and Katie are so broken up over it. I told him not to do anything until I get there. God—It's a mess!"

Dad paced back and forth. He unlocked another gun cabinet and took out a hand gun and shoulder holster.

Grandma stood quietly by the library table. Dad ran his fingers through his dark wavy hair, walked over to the fireplace and turned to face Grandma.

"I'm sure everything will work out fine, but, I felt I should tell you— just in case."

His voice trailed off. Grandma walked over to the wing chair and sat down.

"It's sodomy, Mama—and indecent acts against nature—wrongful carnal knowledge of children—God! I don't know what all. We don't even know for sure how many children are involved. That—mailman, Nick Tucker, was bribing some of the young-uns. Teaching them to drive his car in exchange for them pleasurin' him. Sharon's been with him—wouldn't admit it at first, but she finally broke down and told them everything. There's two other girls and two boys that they know of. All on the same mail route."

Grandma had been staring at Dad intently. She asked, "Is Katie—taking it alright?"

"She's sick over it. Blames herself, somehow, and worried over how it might affect Sharon in the long haul. She doesn't want any publicity and neither do any of the others. It's bad enough for the kids without everybody knowing about it and shaming them more."

Grandma's voice was as cold and sharp as icicles as she said, "He can't just get by with it!"

Dad sighed audibly. "He's not going to get by with it, Mama. But, if it is reported to the authorities and he's arrested for it, there'll be a trial and an awful lot of unpleasant talk. There's no doubt about the bastard being guilty."

"I hope they're not thinking of the Klan."

"Not at all! We don't need any hotheads running around causing more grief. Ralph said Nick's parents are good people and they're up in years. It'd break their hearts to know what he's done. He's got two or three brothers and sisters with families: all good people. Funny thing—Nick's the only bad one in the bunch!"

"How'd Ralph learn of it?"

"One of the little girls got sick; kept vomiting and crying and carrying on—finally told her Mother about it. She called another family with a young girl and they questioned her and sure enough, he'd gotten to her, too. One thing led to another until they had five children for sure. You see, Nick had told them about each other, egging them on. Goddamned bastard!"

Dad riffled through some papers in the desk drawers; glanced over a chart and map on the drawing board and said, "This'll have to wait. My personal papers are in order. I'll tell Martha I've got to go out on business."

Grandma walked over to Dad. "Should I ask you what you're going to do?"

"No, Mama—I'm going to meet Ralph and the fathers of the others. They're too involved to think rationally. But, no one else is to know. If we can keep it quiet, maybe it'll just die down without hurting these poor kids anymore than they've already been hurt!"

"Riley—be careful, Son. I know you have good judgment."

Grandma kissed Dad. He embraced her and then left hurriedly.

The late November sun was streaming into the east windows melting the hoarfrost into tiny riverlets that provided a moment's fascination as it yielded to the pull of gravity. I was feeling pouty over the long underwear that Mother insisted I must wear since it was cold outside and I seemed to have a bit of the sniffles. It was impossible to pull the long brown stockings up smoothly over the thick underwear. The bulkiness was both irritating and frustrating, but what really singed my feathers was that Loralee and Marj didn't have to wear them. Alf understood my discomfort and sympathized in his big brother manner. He announced to one and all that having to wear underwear was not so bad. It was having to put it on that constituted one of the greatest cruelties of childhood, unless you took into consideration that, most probably, sometime during the day, one must answer nature's call, and it was practically impossible with long underwear on, especially if it had the up and down slit. He reckoned the button type would be easier but doubted anyone, other than a contortionist, could button them back up. The visual image he conjured up made us all laugh. Loralee told of how she had struggled with them in years past, getting then all tangled up trying to put then on and would inevitably put her foot through the arm.

Mother was laughing but she chided us with, "Now, you children shouldn't be indelicate at the table. Hurry up and finish your breakfast."

Dad was still home. Ordinarily, he would be gone for work before we came down of the morning. Grandma dished up oatmeal and scrambled eggs. Mother was bustling about making salmon patties for our lunches. The radio was on and Mother was talking about how every year it seems there's more and more hunting accidents. Some farmer had just found the body of some man that'd been out duck hunting.

"You just mark my word. One of these days, they're going to wise up and require a man to take a test and prove his expertise before allowing him to go out hunting, and well they should, for heaven knows, with some of these idiots, now a days, I wouldn't want to go out hunting for love or money. Why, they're just as likely to shoot at you as not, if they don't shoot themselves first. Why, even I know enough to not go climbing through a fence with a loaded gun."

Mother's monologue seemed to have no effect on Grandma as she sugared my oats and told me to say "when" as she poured on the cream and then stirred them noiselessly, but thoroughly.

Alf asked Dad if he'd like to go hunting on Saturday. He said, "We'll see. The dogs do need a good workout and I've heard there's several braces of pheasant about. You want to go colonial?"

Alf's eagerness overshadowed the silent envy of us girls, as he enthused, "Yeah! Let's take the muskets and the powder horns. Boy, I don't know anyone else that goes hunting with muskets."

Grandma said, "That used to be all they had, other than bow and arrow or traps. Of course, they weren't hunting for sport so much as food for the table."

Mother fastened the clasp on the last lunch pail and poured Dad another cup of coffee. She seemed worried and preoccupied as she poured herself a cup of the hot, steaming black liquid and hot milk, and addressed her remarks to Dad.

"It just makes me so uneasy to think about you going out hunting. I mean, it isn't as though you had to, and accidents do happen, just like that one this morning. That poor man. Of course you won't be climbing through any fences."

Dad seemed to be forcing composure, but he smiled and said teasingly, "Would you like to come with us, Martha? You haven't been out hunting in a long time. It'd do you good to get out for a change."

Mother looked indignant and a trifle flustered. She filled her plate and smiled coyly at Dad, "Why, Riley, you know I couldn't hit the side of a barn if my life depended on it. I told you the one and only time I ever went out hunting with you that I'd never do it again. Why, my shoulder was sore for a week."

Mother rubbed her shoulder with the memory and even I was familiar with the kickback. Dad laughed and said he and Alf would be glad to get the pheasants if she wouldn't mind cooking them. Mother persisted, "Now, I'm serious! You just can't be too careful out like that. That announcer said that man probably got his gun caught in the barbed wire fence and it blew his head right off!"

She shuddered, and continued, "How tragic! He said he was a rural carrier up around Oakville. You don't 'spose Katie or Ralph would have known him?"

Dad said, "Well, it's tragic, alright! Are there any more biscuits?"

Mother buttered and jellied some biscuits that were being kept hot under the cozy and teased Dad, "My, my. Such an appetite this morning. My gracious, you're going to get a bay window for sure, and if you don't quit staying out so late, you'll get purple bags under those sleepy blue eyes. I didn't know this job was going to require you staying out all hours of the night."

Dad got up for more coffee. He kissed Mother on top of the head and said, "Don't you worry about it. It won't happen again, I'm sure. Joshua's mighty quiet this morning. Did he go back to sleep?"

Mother bragged on how he had slept from his ten o'clock nursing until six o'clock and she had slept, too. She said she had not even heard Dad come in or noticed him getting up, but someone had left a light on in the study all night and whoever it was ought to be told a thing or two about burning a candle at both ends.

Dad offered to give us a ride to school if we were ready, so we hustled for our wraps and books. Dad yawned, 'scused himself, stretched and yawned again. Mother said, "Serves you right."

Grandma acted concerned, "I'm afraid you're going to have a long day."

She handed him a big thermos and said meaningfully, "Strong, black, coffee."

He grinned appreciatively. "Thank you, Mama—I'm afraid you didn't get much sleep last night, either—Try to rest today; everything's fine."

Mother looked from one to the other inquiringly. Grandma's eyes were shining and wet but she smiled, "Yes, Son. I'll rest well, today."

7

THE FOUR-LEAF CLOVER

A large, fading, red white and blue, "Wilkie for President" sign had been removed from the front yard, but was propped against the back porch and was visible from the lane. Mother worried about it because some of the relatives coming for dinner were staunch supporters of Roosevelt, who had already been elected in spite of Dad protesting that it was dangerous for the democratic process for him to be elected for a third term. He was adamantly opposed to the nuts and bolts of the New Deal and, although he approved of Roosevelt's foreign policy, he believed Wilkie had a larger view of the world situation and would use a firmer hand at the controls. So, the sign, weeks after the national election, stood fading, a reminder of the gallant efforts by the local Wilkie Club to elect a man they believed more capable and far superior to the aristocrat who only narrowly carried the popular vote.

Christmas Day, 1940, brought snow and relatives. Snowflakes drifted down with an easy steadiness as the overcast skies unburdened themselves in some divine plan to lavish an awe-inspiring, mystical quality to the countryside. The snow flakes seemed to float and drift lazily about as I watched from the living room window by the Christmas tree, but the fence posts and trees seemed to shrink in height as the morning advanced and the potentially perilous accumulation grew higher and higher.

We had been up early to open our presents and to get organized before our company arrived. The smell of turkey baking permeated the whole house and breakfast was forgotten as we stuffed ourselves with chocolate covered cherries and chocolate creams and hard Christmas candies.

It was custom for us children to hang up our longest stockings for Santa. He never failed to delight us with the imaginative gifts he stuffed them with. There would be something very nice, something fun, and suited to our individual tastes and ages, and always an orange. Loralee was thrilled and we were all amused with her stocking full of a dozen pair of silk hosiery. She had a penchant for them and wore them daily in spite of being beleaguered by 'runs'.

Our gifts for each other were carefully guarded secrets, whispered confidentially to all but the recipient. All of us children knew that Dad had gone to a fur auction in St. Louis to buy Mother a new coat and we were eager for her to open the big, beautifully wrapped box with the little card that read, "To Martha, Wife and Mother, Merry Christmas with love."

Mother unwrapped the box, cautiously, frowning and muttering about Christmas being for children. She slowly lifted the lid of the box and sighed. We were all very quiet, containing our own excitement, awaiting her reaction, watching closely for that moment of realization when she would be delighted and pleased. Warily, she folded back the tissue paper and revealed the most luxurious sight I had ever seen. "Ohh's" and "Ahh's" escaped from our throats as we eagerly awaited her cries of delight. Mother murmured, "My, my. What have we here?" She seemed reluctant to lift it from the box even though we were all urging her to.

Grandma sat quietly gazing at the Christmas tree, as though enwrapped in memories of other Christmases. Her long, tapering fingers sought the brooch pinned in the folds of soft beige lace at her throat. The diamonds shone in brilliance in their yellow gold setting and Grandma's eyes were tearing as she smiled to herself. She sighed and turning to the activity in the room centered about Mother, she said,

"What a beautiful fur, Martha."

Mother sat on the sofa with the opened box beside her. She wore a worried expression and nervously chewed on her lip as she looked at the fur and murmured, "Umm umph!" Dad insisted she try it on. She relented, saying, "Well, I can see I'm not going to get any peace around here until you all have your way."

Dad held it for her as she slipped her arms into the sleeves and self-consciously enfolded herself in the luxuriant, perfectly matched pelts. The coat was a rich looking dark brown with brighter hues highlighting the soft thickness of the fur. It hung beautifully and the softly rolled collar gracefully accented the neckline. Other gifts lay forgotten as we all admired it, carefully stroked it and lavished praise on its beauty. Dad kept asking Mother if she liked it. She would hum and haw and twist and turn about and finally, with wrinkled brow, commented, "Well, now, truth be known, I don't need anything like this. Why, I never go anyplace to speak of, and, you know, I always say, Christmas is for children! You shouldn't have done this. It isn't mink, is it?"

Dad said, "That's stone marten, Martha. It's a good sight better than mink."

Mother said, "I don't know what ever possessed you to make you buy something like this. I like my beaver coat just fine and it's still perfectly good."

Dad looked a bit perplexed. He said "Well, if you'd rather have mink, we can exchange it. I want you to have what you want."

Mother said, "Oh, it's alright. This'll do fine." She slipped it off and held it up to look at it, while frowning and clinching her mouth and shaking her head. She sighed and laughed and laid it on the sofa, saying, "It surely is warm. Why, that'll keep me just as snug as a bug in a rug."

Grandma said, "It surely is beautiful, Martha, and it looks lovely on you. Riley, you do have good taste."

Dad clinched his mouth in a tight smile and then turning back to the tree to finish distributing the gifts, said cheerily, "Well, now, let's see what else we have here!"

Relatives began arriving in mid-morning and the much-sung Christmas theme of peace on earth was cast aside with the crushed, crumpled and torn colorful wrappings and lovely ribbons amidst Mother's protesting, "We should save that pretty paper. We could use those ribbons again. Let's not have any talk about politics!"

Dad wore an ivory elephant in his tie. Uncle David, Mother's brother, had a big donkey with a monocle and huge teeth clamping a cigar pinned on his lapel. Aunt Venita was swathed in mink and daintily stomped the snow from her fur-topped boots as she called, "Riley, you darling you! What in the hell is that hideous sign doing out there?"

Dad pecked her dutifully on her proffered rouged cheek and said, "Why, Vennie, that's the latest thing in lawn decorations. I'd be glad to get you one, if you'd like it."

Uncle David laughed, "Like hell you will!"

Mother's parents arrived with armloads of presents and fruitcakes and cookies. Cousins invaded even the privacy of our bedrooms. Aunts and uncles hugged and kissed and exchanged news of family and friends and everyone hoped the snow would soon stop.

Pandemonium reigned as cousins ran through the house exploring from basement to attic. We bragged about our ghost and pointed out the frayed rope. One claimed to see the ghost hovering in the dark recesses of the attic and scared everyone else out of their hides. The ensuing stampede down the back stairs into the kitchen full of busy, visiting ladies, prompted Mother to insist we all go outside to play in the snow.

Later, Marj and Sharon were caught smoking out in back by Aunt Venita and Aunt Dorothy, who had sneaked out for a smoke themselves.

The older group of boys built a huge snowman, the biggest and best I had ever seen. It was destroyed in a snowball fight that became a free-for-all. Someone broke my new sled and no one seemed to care. They were all older, bigger and better at everything than I. They played hard and rough. It was fun watching them but the snow was so cold it burned when Willy washed my face in it because I had laughed at Alf getting the best of him. I waded through the knee-deep heavy white stuff, holding my face skyward to feel the fresh flakes that were slowly drifting down.

Grandma had said that each snowflake is different: no two are alike and each one is beautiful, like a bit of lace, but more intricate, more delicate. I made my way to the far backside of the yard where the snow was pure and spotless, undisturbed, and perfect for angels-in-the-snow. I lay down, spread-eagled, and worked my legs and arms back and forth. The trick was in getting up, carefully, so as not to disturb the image. I made a choir of angels-in-the-snow, and in my mind's ear I could hear them singing, *Joy to the World*, just as the church choir had sung on Sunday.

I was shivering with the cold and the wetness but felt strangely warmed as I looked up at the cold gray sky wondering if Grandpa could see my angels-in-the-snow. Do they have Christmas in heaven? Maybe Grandpa and Billy were both watching me. I smiled and waved toward the sky and called loudly,

"Merry Christmas, Grandpa! Merry Christmas, Billy!"

I heard a horse neighing and looked out across the pasture. Dean, his two older brothers and Mr. Swanson were out riding in the snow. They waved and called greetings and I watched as they cut new paths through the blanket of snow. Dean cut away from the others and came galloping toward me.

"Hi, Toot."

"Hi, Dean."

"Ya got a houseful?"

"Yeah."

"Ya wanna ride?"

"Yeah."

"Gimme your hand."

He pulled me up in front of him and reined the horse about and we galloped off to rejoin the others. Mr. Swanson called, "Let's go through the woods!"

He and Frank led the way as Bob rode by Dean and me. Bob asked, "Toot, did you ever see the woods in the snow?"

I said, "No, not yet."

He laughed, "Its mighty pretty!"

We galloped along the edge of the cornfield, cut over into the lane on higher ground and walked the horses into the snow-covered path that led through the woods. The creek was frozen and looked like a long narrow crooked bed of thick snow. The branches hung low with the weight of the wet snow and the bushes and brambles were heavily draped in the white fluff. Dean's breath was warm and smelled like peppermint. I asked, "Did you get what you wanted for Christmas?"

He grinned and said, "Yep."

"What?"

"You're ridin' on her."

"Oh, Dean, I didn't know this was a new horse."

"Yep! They just brought her out this morning. Surprised me."

"I'm glad."

"Me, too."

Mr. Swanson reigned up and pointed to his left. We looked and saw a bright red cardinal with a crest of feathers on its head that looked like a peaked cap. The black marking around its red bill looked like a tiny beard. He and his mate, a dull-colored, buff and olive-gray cardinal with a bright orange bill, were flying around the blackberry bramble. Bob pulled a sack out of his pocket and took out a big slab of beef suet that was tied in a string net. He stood in his stirrups and tied it to a branch. We moved on through the winter wonderland and rode out of the woods into the far field that belonged to the Andrews. We could see their home across the way and smell the smoke from their chimney.

We stood four abreast and the horses excitedly sensed what was to come. Laughingly they held them in reign as Mr. Swanson ordered, "Now, watch that stubble and no jumpin' fences! Last one back's gotta carve the turkey!"

He took the lead but was quickly overtaken by Frank and Bob, who whooped and yelled as they split for home. We saw them sail over the fence to the pasture as they pressed homeward. Mr. Swanson was laughing and as Dean cut off toward our house he called, "Tell your folks Merry Christmas, Toot! You hurry home, Son."

My face was cold in the wind and the snow, but it felt so good to be out riding with Dean. I chattered about the thrill of the ride, the beauty of the woods and feeding the birds. Dean said, "We always ride in the snow at Christmas! When you get big enough, you can too, if you want to."

"Oh, I do, Dean."

"We're gonna breed Jessie. Frank wants the first foal, but you can have the second one."

"For my own?"

"Yep."

"Ohhh. Thank you, Dean."

We trotted up our lane. A shrill whistle pierced the quiet air. We looked toward the house and saw Alf and Willy and James gesturing, waving me in. "Hey Toot! Come on! It's turkey time!"

Dean held my hand as I slid down. Jessie whinnied and I stroked her on the neck. As Dean turned her about, I said, "She's so pretty. Thanks, Dean, for everything."

"Merry Christmas, Toot. See ya."

The grown-ups were gathered around the dining room table. We children sat wherever we could find a seat, mostly in the kitchen and breakfast nook. There was a general shushing for quiet so Grandpa Bentley could say grace. I loved that part. He prayed in Old English with thee's and thou's in a deep rumbling bass voice and it seemed as though surely God Himself must listen when Grandpa Bentley prayed, because it was for sure everybody else did. I really liked him a lot and I loved his sense of humor and his wonderful laugh and his deep bass voice that seemed so clear and majestic. He called me "Peggy". And he called Loralee and Marg and all of our girl cousins "Peggy". He even called Mother and my aunts "Peggy". When I asked him why he called all of us Peggy he said he just loved the name Peggy and loved to sing "Peg Of My Heart", but none of the Mamas would name their baby girls Peggy so he just called us all Peggy so he could sing us one of his favorite songs, and then, he would sing a few lines of, "Peg of My Heart" and everyone would stop to listen. It made me feel so special—kinda embarrassed, but, I really liked it. Seemed like there was a song for every occasion, and he knew them all.

Aunt Venita said, "I wish my name really was Peggy." Mother said, "I wish my name WERE Peggy." Aunt Venita gave her a quizzical look and said," Well, that's what I just said. But, I guess we can both wish we'd been named Peggy."

Everyone laughed and Dad began, ceremoniously, carving the turkey. Uncle David said, "Might know a Wilkie man would serve turkey! I'd rather have a ham any day of the week."

Dad chuckled and replied, "Only a jackass would prefer ham to turkey."

There was a chorus of comments but above them all we could hear Mother, "Why, Davie, you can't be serious! Have you really started eating ham? You used to love turkey. Oh, you boys! Now, this is Christmas and I don't want any more talk about Wilkie or jack, uh, donkeys! Let's just talk about neutral subjects. Uh, are you really thinking about running for Governor, Davie?"

Everyone laughed at the incongruity of Mother's comments and began eating and talking pleasantly.

Grandpa Bentley continued, "So, who likes history?" Aunt Venita and a few others moaned but the majority clamored for more. Grandpa laughed and asked, "Who knows what symbol the Republican Party had when it reformed from being the Whig Party?"

Dad and a coupla of the Uncles laughed. Mother said, "Raccoons are so pretty. Their faces are kinda like the panda bears with their black eyes and they are so clever and quick. I could never understand how people could hurt them, let alone eat them. Why, they don't do any harm." Dad said, "Actually, Martha, I'm afraid our farmers wouldn't agree with you.

Uncle Ralph said, "Raccoons eat anything, everything. They are known to raid hen houses, ruin corn crops and fields of vegetables. They're excellent climbers and they raid any and all of the birds' nests for their eggs and they devastate the pecan and walnut and hickory crops."

Dad said, "They have almost obliterated the Hickory Nut Trees –and you know, I take that personally . . ."

We all laughed and everyone was talking about the Hickory Nut Cake with Boiled Icing. We had all smashed our fingers and thumbs trying to crack the hard shells and working so hard on the difficult task of picking out the unusual and most delicious nut meats. Aunt Venita asked Grandma Bentley, "Mama, I've lost that recipe that you gave me that was Mary Todd's. You know the one that was Abraham Lincoln's favorite cake."

Several chimed in with how good that cake is and they can hardly wait for all of their favorite desserts.

Dad said, "Ya know, our conversations are always fun and kinda crazy but we sometimes lose our train of thought."

Everyone started talking and laughing in utter confusion. Aunt Katie said, "Now, don't leave me up in the tree here. We were talking about, . . . what?"

"Oh yeah."

"'Bout symbols. When did we have Whigs?"

"Were the Whigs like Republicans or Democrats?"

"Oh, what fun! I love it when a thinker throws down the gauntlet."

Grandpa Bentley's eyes were twinkling as he continued, "The Whig Party was very popular about a hundred years ago. In the 1830's the Whig Party had the Raccoon for its emblem."

Alf said, "I knew it. That's why Mom was talking about the raccoons."

Grandpa Bentley laughed, "Members were called 'coons'. They always had coonskins hanging on their log cabins or on a gate or fence, and, of course, coon skin hats were long popular and still treasured in some parts."

Several of the cousins were talking about having coonskin hats, and giggling about calling each other "coons." One asked, "Did they really call people "coons"?

Grandpa Bentley nodded, "Yes, of course. It was just a nick name for the members of the Whig Party. Daniel Webster and Harrison and Tyler and all of the philosophical thinkers debated over the question of slavery. By the 1840's, most of the Southern Whigs went with the Democratic Party. The Northern Whigs had joined the newly formed Republican Party, and what is their emblem?"

We children and some adults chorused, ". . . the Elephant!"

"And the Democrats use—?"

"A donkey!"

"Hee Haw, Hee Haw, Hee—"

"Josh! Not at the table."

In the early afternoon the snowflakes seemed to lose their individuality as the gray heavy-laden skies spit a hard icy substance with a vehemence that coated our little world with a bright crustiness that seemed to be studded with diamonds. The older folks became anxious about driving conditions and most began leaving right after dinner, amidst a festive melee of apologies and felicitations.

Uncle David, Grandpa Bentley, Uncle Ralph and Dad were talking guns in the study. Alf, James and Willy had come in and the two cousins were aggressively intruding. I saw Dad clamp his mouth in the familiar tight line that meant he was holding his peace when Uncle David swung the piece he was sighting around and banged it against the door sill. His sons, strangers to guns, were fingering everything. One picked up a handgun and pointed it at his brother, clicking it and saying, "Bang! Bang!"

In one fleet motion Dad grabbed the revolver from him and gave him a swift sidekick in the seat of his pants. Uncle David cleared his throat as a very red-faced James whined, "I didn't mean any harm. Just funnin'."

Dad said, "And how did you know that gun wasn't loaded? What if you'd killed your brother? Then would it have mattered that you were 'just funnin'?"

I had never seen Dad so angry or heard his voice bristle with such acrimony. He placed the gun on the table and then faced James. He put his left hand on James shoulder and waited for James to raise his head. He punctuated his words with the index finger of his right hand as he emphasized the cardinal rule that I had assumed everyone was born knowing.

"Don't you ever point a gun at anyone like that again. These are weapons! They are not toys. They'll kill! Do you understand me?"

James murmured, "Yes sir."

Dad turned loose of his shoulder and continued, including both of the brothers in his talk. "You need to know how to use a gun, how to care for it, and I'll teach you if you want me to, but don't ever handle them foolishly again. It's kinda like driving a car.

There's a lot more to it than just steering the wheel, and there's a lot more to using a gun than just clicking the trigger."

Grandpa Bentley said they had had a valuable lesson and Uncle David said they had better be going since it looked like the snow was turning to ice. Uncle Ralph teased him about not getting his money's worth on that new car since it did not have any running boards to speak of. They started discussing the technicalities of coiled springs and sealed beam headlights, so, I moseyed over to the mantle where Dad and Grandpa Bentley were talking confidentially. I was hoping they would not notice me, but they did and I was told to go on and play with my cousins.

In the kitchen, the remaining womenfolk were still tidying up. Aunt Katie had brought a big box of homemade fudge and peanut brittle. They were commenting on it and exchanging recipes, when James and Willy came sulking in and whined to Aunt Venita, "We want to go home."

Aunt Venita looked at James quizzically, "Why, whatever's the matter with you?"

He looked like he was going to cry and wailed, "He kicked me!"

"He kicked you!? Who did?"

He pointed to me, and whined, "Her Daddy did! He kicked me just 'cause I touched one of his ole guns."

Aunt Venita's chin fell down into her pearls and her beautifully arched brows were all but lost under her perfectly coiffed hair-do. Mother started in, "Oh, those guns. I declare, if it isn't one thing it's another. Riley doesn't want anyone touching those guns, but it really doesn't sound like him, at all, to just up and kick somebody. There's no excuse for that and I just can't imagine—"

Grandma was quietly looking on. I took a deep breath and stood up, ramrod straight, but quivering, and stared at the liar. I said, "Aunt Venita? Daddy gave him a sidekick because he pointed a gun at Willy and clicked the twigger twice and he didn't even know if it was loaded or not! Guns are weapons, not toys!"

Willy made a face at me and James started sing-songing, "Tattle-tale, tattle-tale, stick your head in a garbage pail!"

Aunt Venita twisted his ear and promised him what-for later. Aunt Katie was laughing and said, "What was it he clicked, Toot? The twigger?"

Grandma patted me on the arm and poured me a cup of hot tea and milk and said reassuringly, "That's alright, Honey. Your Auntie Katie used to get her words twisted up, too. But, you got the message across, as straight as an arrow, and right on mark."

Aunt Katie gave me a big piece of fudge and Mother lectured her nephews.

"Well, I was sure in my own thinking that your Uncle Riley must have had a very good reason, if he did, uh, kick you, for he won't ordinarily even raise a hand to his own children, even when they need it and they do get ornery at times. That Alf is such a tease, although he's never given us a minute of serious trouble and he's as dependable as the day is long. That Marj is as stubborn as a mule and too sly for her own good but she minds her manners and Loralee's just as sweet as she can be but my, can she be mischievous! Of course, Toot and Josh are always into something, but, they'd never, a one of them, even think about doing a thing like that with a gun! Heaven forbid! Why, if one of my children did a thing like that I'd get out the razor strap!"

James and Willy rushed out as Mother took a second wind. Grandma whispered to me not to eat any more candy and to come to her room for a few minutes. She made the rounds of the remaining relatives and told everyone how nice it was to see them again, hoped they had a happy new year and do be careful driving home.

The sleet had warmed to a fine drizzle and the soupy slush dampened the spirits as well as the boots and socks of those who had to ply through it to their cars, but they called cheery good-byes as they slipped and slid and waded and stomped their feet and cautioned others to *be careful— look-out—don't splatter me—hurry up and get in—Bye! See you next year, ha ha—thanks for everything—nicest time ever—come and see us, ya hear?*

We stood shivering on the front porch, waving, until the last car was down the lane. As we went back into the house Dad was complimenting Mother on how good the dinner was and how capably she managed it all. Mother laughed, "Well, it's nice having all of the family in, but, would you just look at this house? It looks like a cyclone struck!"

I never knocked on Grandma's door. She had showed me how to softly thump my fingers so that the sound carried nicely, was more than adequate to be heard, easier on the knuckles and much more pleasant than a common knocking racket. So, I thumped twice. She called for me to come in. She was sitting in her reading chair, already dressed for bed. A book, her spectacles and a beautiful big orange were on the nightstand. There was also a little china plate, a coupla of napkins and Grandpa's pocket knife.

"Toot, I know this is probably silly. We have certainly had enough to eat. But, I've been looking forward all day to share an orange with you. Would you like that? Pull up the footstool there."

Grandma opened the mother-of-pearl handled pocketknife that had been Grandpa's, and began to peel the orange as thinly as possible, just the way Grandpa had done so many times in the past. I said, "Grandpa used to say the white part's good for you too, and makes the orange last twice as long."

Grandma's eyes were shiny and twinkled as she sliced the white off. She divided the orange into sections and raised her first slice in toast, "Here's to your Grandpa."

I raised mine, too, and repeated. "Here's to Grandpa." I didn't know what to do with the seeds so I just swallowed them. Grandpa and I used to spitball the seeds into the fireplace. Grandma had a seed in her piece of orange too. She took it out of her mouth and put it in her eye wash glass. It looked so funny I giggled and then put the rest of the seeds I found in it, too. I told her how Grandpa and I used to blow them into the fireplace. She laughed and said, "I know, Honey. You and your Grandpa were quite a pair. He'd have been proud of you this evening. I was. I don't want you to be bothered by James' idiotic taunting."

"He's a liar, Grandma, and dumb, too."

"No, Honey. True, he told a story and he acted dumb, pointing that gun at Willy, but, you must not label him just on the basis of one foolish act. He's young, yet. Old enough to know better, but he hasn't been taught properly about guns or apparently, about being truthful, either. How old is he?"

"Same age as Alfie."

"My, my. Why, he can't hold a candle to Alf. There's no comparing them. Alf isn't any taller, but he has the demeanor of manhood. And you, little lady, six years old, and you spoke up for the truth."

I beamed in the praise. Everyone knew Grandma didn't lavish compliments ever, but she had a way of saying something or maybe just lifting an eyebrow, so that you knew whether you were on the right track or not. We sat in silence for a moment. Somewhere in a distant part of the house a radio was on with Bing Crosby singing "White Christmas". Grandma sighed, smiled, and said, "We've certainly had a white Christmas today."

I told her about riding horseback with Dean and his Dad and brothers down through the woods. She smiled, "I saw you, Honey. I saw you making angels in the snow, too. Why, they were so pretty, I could almost hear them singing. And I saw Dean ride up on that Chestnut. Is that a new horse? I don't recall seeing it before."

"It was his Christmas present. He said he would give me the second born foal. His big brother gets the first one."

"Your Grandpa and I grew up on neighboring farms."

I said, "Dean thinks I'm his kid sister."

Grandma laughed, "Yes. His Mother told me he'd claimed you. Sometimes, a friendship can grow into something deep and very special." Grandma gazed off into a land of memories. I sat quietly, waiting. She sighed again, smiled and said, "Your Grandpa loved Christmas-time. He'd go to any lengths to surprise me with some gift that he knew I'd treasure but would never have suspected."

"Like the four-leaf clover?"

Grandma laughed and got up from her chair. She moved over to the dresser and picked up the lovely brooch that she had worn earlier and looked at it fondly.

"Yes, I think of all of them, this must be my favorite. I used to find four-leaf clovers without even looking for them. Your Grandpa would search and search for them and he never did find one. It was kind of a joke between us. Then, on Christmas, in 1910, he tied this on our Christmas tree."

"It's so pretty, Grandma. Those diamonds look like they have fire in them."

"Yes, they're brilliant, alright. There's six, you see. One for each baby."

"Six babies? But, there's just Dad and Aunt Katie."

"We had four babies born dead, Honey. Only your Dad and your Auntie Katie survived. I suppose that's one reason your Grandpa was so foolish over babies. He thought they were a miracle, and, for us, they truly were."

Grandma sat back down in her chair, put her glasses on, and studied the brooch. The four leaves were each perfectly formed and gracefully shaped with tiny raised veins running the length of them. Three diamonds were clustered in the center and three were situated down the curving stem. Grandma handed it to me. I help it under the light and watched it gleam and sparkle. She smiled and said,

"That's the only one in the world, Toot. Your Grandpa had it especially made for me. He found a goldsmith in St. Louis and told him about me always finding four-leaf clovers in the yard and the fields and how he wanted to give me one of gold with a cluster of six diamonds, one for each baby."

"Were you surprised?"

Grandma laughed and her eyes glistened as she said, "Oh yes, I'll say I was. And, your Grandpa was so pleased. He laughed all day 'bout how he'd bet I was the only woman in the whole world to find a four-leaf clover on her Christmas tree."

Tears brimmed, spilled and ran down Grandma's cheeks. She put the pin back in the box, wiped her eyes and said softly, "I'm sorry I'm giving in to my emotions here. I didn't intend to, but, I really miss him. This is the first Christmas in over forty years that we've been apart."

"I'm sorry, Grandma. I really miss him, too. I thought maybe he would see the angels in the snow."

Grandma nodded and smiled through the tears, "I know you miss him, Honey. And, I do believe he saw you making the angels in the snow. But, it is good to remember the good times. And I'm so thankful that we were able to share a Christmas orange. Now, I have already told your Daddy and Mother that I want you to have this pin someday. That's why I wanted to tell you about it, so you would understand it has a very special significance."

"I understand, Grandma. It's the only four-leaf clover in the whole world to ever be found on a Christmas tree."

Grandma laughed, "You sound just like your Grandpa."

8

🕊 THE HOLY DEVIL

There was an epidemic of the old fashioned red measles in the late spring. So many students were absent there was talk of closing the school. Our second grade class dwindled until it was so small it was temporarily absorbed into the third grade. Thus, I was introduced to Geography. I loved it. I loved the word, the subject, the teacher, and the maps and the new old names of rivers, mountain ranges, states and capitals. Memorizing the oceans and continents was child's play and I would frequently ask permission to stay in at recess in order to pore over the 'extra reading' books on other cultures in other lands. It was a whole new world to me. Other subjects were time consuming necessities but Geography made the world go round. I loved the magical sounding names of Czechoslovakia, Yugoslavia, Moravia, Prague, Salzburg, Fontainebleau, and I would bubble with enthusiasm to Dad, who would fire questions that would send me scurrying to the encyclopedias and newspapers for answers. What country borders Czechoslovakia on the east? What about the sell-out to Hitler? Name three great composers from Salzburg and don't ask your Grandma. Who built Fontainebleau? Which major Protestant faith grew out of the English founder's contact with the Moravians and don't ask your Mother. What was the name of the great German clergyman who founded a leading protestant church?

The measles attacked me about a month after I had been 'promoted' to the third grade. Days passed in a blur in the darkened bedroom. The doctor had come and said it was definitely measles and a classic case at that. Mother would look in from time to time to rub me down with cornstarch or to raise or lower a window. Grandma kept me equipped

113

with water, tea and juice, and Dad bought me a radio to keep me company. Grandma would sit with me and tell me stories of her childhood and when I got well enough that the light did not hurt my eyes she would read to me.

One fine morning I awoke feeling quite well and antsy to leave my room. I was ravishingly hungry and everyone seemed to have forgotten about me. I got up, opened the draperies, pulled on the blind and let it spring clear to the top. I opened the window wide. The birds were chirping lustily outside and above their merry din a mocking bird was running through its repertoire. I was fascinated and amused with its musical antics and was trying to locate it when Mr. Aiken came hurrying up, hollering,

"Hey there, Missy! How 'er the measles?"

"Almost gone."

"Almost gone, huh? Well, it's 'bout time. Seems ya've had a spell of 'em. Ya hear that mockin' bird?"

"Yes sir. But I can't see it anyplace."

"He's up yonder in the top of that there walnut tree. Just a warblin' for the whole world to hear. Mighty purty! Well, now, ya take keer of ya'self, ya hear? Measles ken be seerious."

He moved on to tend to his gardening. I watched him for a while, remembering how I used to be so afraid of him. Now, it was Joshua that he would tease, and, true to form, Josh would go screaming into the house. Weird. Kinda funny, though, in a way.

Grandma came in carefully carrying a rumpled, much used brown paper sack and a breakfast tray. She seemed surprised to see me up at the window.

"Good morning, Honey. Isn't that mocking bird cheerful? I'm glad to see you're feeling so much better. Looks like the blind got away from you."

"I think I'm well now, Grandma."

She laughed as she glanced at my face and arms.

"You won't be well, until all of that rash is gone. But, look here. Mr. Aiken brought you a present this morning."

I sat up straight with curiosity and reached for the sack.

"Mr. Aiken brought me a present? Why, we were just talking while ago and he didn't say anything about it."

I gingerly looked inside the sack and an "Ohhh" issued from my throat as I saw the elaborately tooled silver jewelry box.

"Oh, Grandma. It's the prettiest thing I've ever seen."

She was looking on, smiling her approval. She said, "Open it."

I held it carefully and slowly, cautiously raised the lid. A delightful, clear, happy melody tinkled out from the red velvet interior. I was transfixed in rapt concentration. As it began to wind down I became aware of the little turnkey on the bottom. Grandma cautioned me to use care in turning it and not to wind it too tight. I ran my fingers over the raised figures on the lid of a man and a woman in elegant costumes, sitting under a tree with dogs at their feet and flowers all about.

"Oh, it's beautiful. And a music box! What is the name of that song? It sounds like one you play."

Grandma nodded, smiling, "Fur Elise, by Beethoven, a German composer."

"Oh, it's so pretty. And Mr. Aiken gave it to me? Why didn't he bring it in himself?"

Grandma was smoothing the bed and fluffing up the pillows. She said, "He's awfully shy, Honey. But, he's fond of you and he was so sorry that you were sick. Why, he's asked about you everyday and yesterday, he asked me if it'd be alright to give you a music box. He told me while ago that he bought this for his wife when he was in France during World War I, and that it had been one of her favorite things. He thought you'd like it, too."

"Oh, I just love it. It's the nicest gift I've ever had. It's so pretty and I just love the music!"

"Well, why don't you write that down in a nice thank you note, after you've had your breakfast. And quit scratching, Honey, you don't want to make any sores."

"Grandma, do you think Mr. Aiken saw the Eiffel Tower in France?"

"Why, I've an idea he did. Why don't you ask him about it?"

"I'm going to go to France someday—and Germany and England and Scotland and Holland."

"Don't forget Wales: my father's home. I'll tell you what. You clean up your breakfast now, and then if you feel well enough to leave your room you may come down to the laundry room with me. We can talk while I do some ironing and mending."

The laundry room was in the basement and smelled of soap and bleach and steam. A basket was piled high with dampened-down dresses, shirts, blouses, aprons and smocks, bed linens and tablecloths. The huge white sheets and assorted tablecloths, made whiter and brighter by Little Boy Bluing, were expertly guided through the mangle, deftly folded and stacked in columns. The collars, cuffs and shirt fronts were dipped into a blue cold-starch mixture that made a ssissthth of steam when the hot iron glided over them drying then and stiffening them to a smooth board-like finish. I loved the huge old green overstuffed arm chair that one could snuggle up comfortably in and observe the weekly tasks and visit or read while being in the center of activity.

"Do you like to iron, Grandma?"

"Heavens, no! I can't imagine anyone liking it. It's a thankless task, but it has to be done. It's just one of the many household chores you have to learn to do perfectly, quickly and mechanically, so your mind can think about more important things while your hands do the work."

She put the finishing touches on a shirt and hung it on a hanger to 'set' before folding it. She laughingly recalled, "When I was a young girl, we had to heat the irons on a stove. I scorched a many a shirt before I learned how to gage them."

"You were born in that house out by the cemetery, weren't you, Grandma?"

"Yes. The big brick and stucco house that has the old oak trees all around it. My father built that, himself, before he married."

"And he came from Wales?"

"That's right. His people lived in Carmarthenshire, Wales."

"Where, Grandma?"

"Car-MARTH-en-shire. You can say it. Sing it. CarMARTHenshire!"

I repeated it in sing song and liked the way it rolled off my tongue.

"Were they gunsmiths, too?"

"No, Honey. The gunsmith's are on your Grandpa's side of the house. My father's father was a weaver. They had hundreds of sheep and men to tend them, but they had a lot of trouble with the British always trying to rake the cream off the top. You see, they had to pay tax money to the British, but that wasn't the worst of it. The British were determined to keep the Welsh right in their pocket, telling them what they could do and what they could not do, what they could have and what they could not have and even refusing to let them have schools for learning the basic rudiments of education. They insisted on dictating how they were to worship. There was no freedom of choice about anything and the harder a man worked, the more they taxed him. Father was named after his famous ancestor, Griffith Jones, who had been a great teacher and preacher back before the British realized that an educated Welshman wants to be a free Welshman or at least to have some say in matters pertaining to him and his family and his property. Father was a lot like him, in that he was knowledgeable and outspoken, and he was threatened with arrest because of it. So, when he told his parents he wanted to come to America, they agreed, although his mother cried for a fortnight."

"A fortnight?"

"That's just an expression meaning two weeks. But, they made the necessary arrangements and sent him here to live with his cousins, the Gore's, who farmed out around what is now Oaksville."

"How did he get here?"

0h, "He got passage on a cotton boat, and he claimed he sneezed all the way. They sailed across the Atlantic and down and around to New Orleans. Then he came up the Mississippi on a gunboat and made his way down here over land. He worked hard and never spent a penny without sleeping on it first. He soon owned a lot of land and had rich orchards and a dairy herd and sheep. He always kept a flock of sheep. He said they were good at clearing new ground, especially when it was too rocky or hilly for farming or for grazing cattle."

"What year did he come here?"

"Oh, he was a late comer in comparison to your Grandpa's people. Father was just a lad when he arrived here in the fall of '62. The War Between the States had everything in turmoil. All three of the Gore boys were off to war and he was bound and determined to sign up too, but Agatha Gore, who was a widow and trying to look after the farms, prevailed upon him to help get the crops in first, so, he joined the home guard, and spent the war mostly farming."

"Which side was he on, Grandma?"

"Honey, a Welshman, who had known such terrible oppression, could only be on the side that advocated freedom for all."

"The North?"

"Yes, the North."

"Mother says the North was wrong about a lot of things and it was the Yankees that burned her Grandma's home in Tennessee and stole all of the animals and jewelry."

"Your Mother's people suffered and they lost a lot. I'm not making any excuses for the crimes committed in the name of war by either side, for both the North and the South had their Holy Devils."

"Grandma? What exactly is a Holy Devil?"

"Well, Honey, it's hard to explain. Your Grandpa would say it was someone with ice water in his veins and fire in his speech and hate in his heart. We've had a lot of Holy Devils in history. They come in every race and creed. Sometimes they become a threat to the whole world. There's one on the rampage now in Germany, one in Italy, one in Russia, and of course, Tojo, the Japanese General who's terrorizing the South Pacific and even parts of Europe. Your Grandpa had quite a time with one here in our community a few years back, but we'll come to that later.

Father worked hard to keep the Gores' farms going and when they got back from the war they were mighty pleased and they paid him in land. He worked it, built his home and married Agatha Gore. Mother died of the fever when I was fourteen, so I had to forget about my schooling and run the house and keep the accounts. The Mason's land bordered ours and it was just taken for granted that you're Grandpa and I would someday marry. When I was seventeen, I contracted a fever and for a long time I lay in bed, scarcely able to move and there were days when I didn't even know anyone. The doctors said I had infantile paralysis and if I survived I'd be crippled for life. It was a long time before I could sit up in a chair and I had to learn to walk all over again. My hair had turned gray and my flesh had withered away until I was just skin and bones and my right leg was paralyzed. I told your Grandpa I wouldn't marry him and that he wasn't to come courting anymore."

Grandma had on a royal blue long-sleeved dress with lace at the collar and cuffs. It made her eyes look even bluer than usual. I thought she was beautiful and I knew from the pictures I had seen that she was a lovely young lady. There was no discernible limp when she walked, although she did use a cane in bad weather. I started to ask, "But, Grandma, how—I mean, you did marry Grandpa?"

Mother and Josh came in with tea and snacks. Grandma turned off the iron and sat down for a rest as Mother teased, "Your Grandpa Mason was a stubborn German if ever there was one."

Grandma laughed, "That's true. He said if I was going to be a spinster, then he'd be a bachelor—and that's the way it was for eight years."

I asked, "Grandma, why wouldn't you marry him?"

Grandma stirred honey in her tea and smiled. Mother said, "Oh, I'm so glad we came down here just in time for this story. I never get enough of hearing it. Here, Josh, you sit on my lap and listen to your Grandma."

Grandma sipped her tea and looked reflective. She began, "I didn't want to be an encumbrance and I didn't think I could be a proper wife. But, your Grandpa kept on trying to court me. Sometimes we'd go to church or to a social. Then, in the spring of '92, I'd taken the buggy and gone into town to get some supplies. I'd left a list and the buggy at the feed store and was walking, with my cane, down the boardwalk when a strange man stumbled out of the tavern and yelled at me, 'Hey, Miss Jones! You hirin' at your place?' I said 'No' and walked on. Well, he kept following me and pestering me. I told him my father did the hiring and he already had all the hands he needed. The man was dirty and drunk. He'd wait outside a store when I'd go in and then start following me and pestering me when ever I'd leave it. He was calling me 'Crip' and yelling about me being an old cripple and how he wanted to help."

"Oh, Grandma, that's terrible! Wasn't there anyone around to help you?"

"Oh yes. There were a lot of people who saw and heard him. Some of the men tried to restrain him and told him to leave me alone and he sulked off and I went on my way doing my errands. But, just as I got back to the feed store, he ran up from behind me and grabbed my purse and pushed me down in the mud. Carlton Gore drove me home and then he and Father and John, your Grandpa, went looking for him. They found him at the tavern. Father told him who he was and the man knocked him down. He was cussing and saying bad things about me and your Grandpa challenged him. Somebody called the sheriff but by the time he got there they were having a regular knock down and drag out fight. Your Grandpa was a big man, but the stranger was bigger and he was mean, too. When your Grandpa started getting the best of him, the man pulled a knife on him and sliced him through his left shoulder. Carlton wrestled him down but got cut bad on his thigh. They said later the man was stabbing at everyone. Father grabbed him from behind and the sheriff pulled a gun on him, but the man wrestled Father around in front of him and held his knife at his throat and told the sheriff to drop his gun. John had taken a little thirty-eight with him. He was weak from losing so much blood, but when the man waved the knife about threatening some of the other men who were trying to talk sense into him, Father broke away and John told the man to drop the knife or he'd shoot. The man lunged for him and John shot him."

It was hard for me to imagine my Grandpa, as I remembered him, in that situation. Grandma seemed lost in reverie and I wanted to know but was reluctant to ask, if—"Grandma? Did he—die?"

"Yes, Honey. He died instantly."

Mother said, "They never did find out who he was or where he came from, did they?"

Grandma answered, "No. Someone said he'd ridden in on the rails and was asking a lot of questions about who had the biggest farms when someone saw me and mentioned that we'd just hired extra help. He was given a paupers' grave."

I asked, "Did you ever get your pocketbook back?"

"No, I never saw it again, but he still had most of my money in his pockets. I did get that back."

My head was full of questions but I kept remembering how Grandpa used to put hot flannels on his shoulder a lot and I could almost hear him say, 'Never point a gun at anyone unless all else fails and you just have to use it.' No wonder he was so solemn when he'd say that. No wonder he, nor Dad, would allow foolishness with the guns. Mother seemed to be lost deep in thought. I asked, "Was Grandpa hurt bad?"

"He nearly lost the use of his arm. It was a long time healing, and then, he just wouldn't give up on it until it was nearly normal. Carlton had a deep gash and torn muscles that nearly cost him his leg. He limped the rest of his life."

"Was your Father alright?"

"Oh yes. Father was fine. He was bruised and sore for a few days but he was fine. And, Honey, he wouldn't give me a minute's rest until I agreed to marry your Grandpa. He and Carlton both kept talking about how John was such a fine man and how he had defended my honor and how he loved me and had waited so long and I ought to grab him and thank my lucky stars. And, so, I did just that. We were married after the harvesting in '92. People came from miles around and the church bells rang—my! How they rang! Oh, it was beautiful—so beautiful. Everybody teased us about being sooo old, and waiting sooo long, to get married, but, it was all in good fun."

Mother sighed, "And they lived happily ever after."

Grandma poured more tea and seemed to radiate with the happy memories. She laughed, "I won't deny that we were happy. After Riley and Katie were born and lived and grew, John used to say he had everything he could ever hope for."

I asked, "What was that 'bout Grandpa and a Holy Devil? Was that the mean man?" Grandma and Mother exchanged looks. Mother said, "He's a mean man, alright, I don't care if they did send him to Congress. He didn't get my vote or the vote of any other decent person that knows him for what he is. He just rode in on Roosevelt's coattails and it's no secret the only interests he represents are his own."

Grandma said, "This is someone else we are referring to, Honey. You see, your Grandpa did well at everything he did. And, it got so a lot of people looked to him for advice and counsel. He got involved in politics, not up front, but he had a lot of influence and just like anything else, when you're going up or are on top you sometimes step on somebody or they think you have if you won't let them use you and then they resent you just because you are what you are. One time this particular man was running for Congress and he asked your Grandpa to support him, but, John wouldn't do it because the other candidate was much more capable of the office. So, the man was defeated and he blamed your Grandpa for it, and he started picking at him trying to discredit him. We had seven tenant farmers then. One of them was a colored man that John had hired on the basis of his orchard knowledge. He'd given him and his family a little house as part of their pay and there were a lot of people that didn't like it. He'd also taken on a newly arrived German family who were experienced farmers. There were those who thought they were only good for the mines. They called them 'hunkies'. But John felt he could hire whomever he pleased and they were good workers, just needing a chance. But this man started misrepresenting things, telling people John was bringing in cheap help and talking about how he'd bought off justice one time when he'd killed a man in a barroom brawl. Well, it had been several years since it had happened and people tend to forget the facts. It got ugly. There were some vicious rumors and it really hurt to hear some of the bad mouthing. But, your Grandpa believed that the truth would prevail and we had a lot of good friends, so we didn't let it bother us too much. Then, one night, after we'd gone to bed, the dogs woke us up, barking and growling. We heard shots and then, wounded cries, and your Grandpa ran to see what was happening. There were about eight or ten men in sheets and hoods putting a big cross up in our front lawn. They were waving guns and cussing and yelling and carrying on like madmen."

"Were you scared, Grandma?"

"Scared? Honey, I was so scared I thought it was the end of the world."

Mother laughed, "That's not the way I heard it! Your Grandpa told me you grabbed a gun and said, 'If they come in this house it'll be over my dead body!'"

Grandma looked embarrassed and I giggled. She said, "Well, John was furious. He told me to ring the sheriff, and he went back to the bedroom and dressed. He took a shotgun in each hand and walked out the front door. They'd set the cross on fire and it was blazing fiercely. One of them yelled, 'There's the, . . . uh, lots of bad words, and you've never heard such a commotion. John fired in the air, and then he yelled, 'Jake, I don't want to hurt anyone, but if you don't put that fire out and clear out, I'll open up on you!' They milled about for a minute and then one of them yelled, 'We want to ask some questions!' John bellowed, 'I'm not answerin' questions for any yellow-bellied cowards hidin' behind sheets, terrorizin' my family and killin' my dogs! Now git!' and he shot over their heads and they high-tailed it out of there. Several of the hired men had come up. They put out the fire. The sheriff and his men along with David Joe Boone, the editor of the paper, and his two sons, helped bury the dogs and cleaned the mess up the best they could in the dark. The next day the whole truth of the matter came out in the papers. Then all of the people saw who it was that had just been stirring them all up with his prejudicial lies of envy and bitterness against your Grandpa."

Mother said, "Whatever did I do with that picture of you and Father?"

Grandma said, "The one that used to hang in the library? I think Riley took it to his office." Grandma laughed. Mother looked incredulous as she asked, "You mean he's hung it on the same wall with a picture of—?"

I sat waiting, impatiently, while the two ladies laughed at their secret. Grandma noticed me and said, "Honey, do you remember the big picture of your Grandpa and me with those puppies?"

I nodded with the memory. She said, "We never knew for sure where those doggies came from. Someone just left them at our front door one night in a big box."

"Was it one of the bad men who'd shot your other dogs?"

"Well, we never found out for sure, but we thought it was their way of saying they were sorry. Your Grandpa said those pups made the best bird dogs he'd ever had."

"Who was the man that was running for congress?"

Grandma hesitated. Mother chewed on her lip. Grandma said,

"Honey, I really think it best to let sleeping dogs lie. I wouldn't have told you any of this unpleasantness other then I wanted you to know the straight of it so you can deal with it if you ever are confronted with it. But, you asked me an honest question and it certainly deserves an honest answer. His name was Davidson. Jake Harold Davidson."

I couldn't believe my ears. I said, "Why, there's a picture of him at school! He's the one that lied about Grandpa?"

"He's the one alright. He drug a lot of people through the mud before he finally got elected this last time."

"Oh, Grandma, that's not fair!"

"No, it doesn't seem fair. But, don't you fret about it! You see, life balances itself out. I'm not saying we can always understand the rhyme or reason for things that happen, but I really do believe that things balance out."

"Grandma? Would you say Mr. Davidson is a Holy Devil?"

"I'd say he seems to fit the description."

Mother laughed to herself, and said aloud "We must get a copy made of that picture. I sure wouldn't want anything to happen to it"

I was reading and listening to the radio in the late afternoon, when I heard a whistle that brought me instantly to my feet. I raced to the window. Dean waved and grinned up. I call, "Come on up!"

Grandma brought a tray with cookies and milk, as she ushered Dean in.

"Hi."

"Hi yourself."

"How 're the measles?"

"Goin' away."

"You wish!"

"Yep."

"What are ya readin'?"

"'Bout Czechoslovakia."

"You say it nice—"

"I like the sound of it. Grandma says it's because I've got Welsh blood and the Welsh language is musical."

"Have you learned about Yugoslavia, yet?"

"Not much, but I love the name. I know Hitler just captured it last month."

"Invaded it."

"Same thing."

"When I was in the third grade I had to give a report on Yugoslavia. I got all flustered and said Yugoslober."

"What happened?"

"Everybody died. They kept teasing me. Mrs. Jenkins gave me an M, though."

"You always get M's, don't you?"

"Yep."

"Did you know Almeda's folks are from Austria?"

"I don't know Almeda."

"She knows you. She thinks you're cute."

Dean had sat down on the edge of the bed and was riffling through purple mimeographed papers and the arithmetic book while we were talking. He hit me on the head with the papers and "So? What else is new?"

I got up to get the music box and told him about Mr. Aiken giving it to me. We played it and he admired it and said, "That's nice—for a girl. From France?"

"Yeah. France, Fontainebleau, Paris—won't it be fun, Dean, to go see the Eiffel Tower and a real castle?"

"Be interestin'—"

"You gonna help me with the arithmetic?"

"Somebody needs to. When you skip a grade, ya have to work twice as hard."

"Will you show me?"

"I'm tryin'."

Late in the afternoon Marj came in my room, asking "Where's that music box everyone's talking about?"

"On the dresser."

She picked it up and opened it, listened to the music, admired it and set it back on the dresser. "It really is nice, Toot. Measles goin' away?"

"I hope so!"

"Don't scratch. That makes them last longer."

"Ohhh!"

She laughed and flounced out. Hot tears stung my eyes as I wriggled down between the cool sheets wondering if they'd ever go away. I remembered the grinning picture of Congressman Davidson, that hung in the hallway at school. I saw him as a personal enemy and began to imagine how I, as an avenging angel, could bring down the Holy Devil.

Long after dark I was awakened by someone lowering the window and turning off the radio. A cool, big hand, gently but firmly sought my wrist and held it for a moment and then rested briefly on my forehead. He leaned down and planted a soft kiss on my forehead and began tiptoeing toward the door. I mumbled, "G'nite, Dad."

He said, "Sweet dreams, Toot."

When the Japanese attacked Pearl Harbor, we were all caught up in the fire of patriotism and indignation that burned in our breasts and soared like a prairie fire across our beloved land. Three days later, when Hitler's Germany and Mussolini's Italy declared war on the United States, every red-blooded boy and man in town were rarin' to do their part in stopping the Holy Devils.

Alf, and three of his best friends, wanted to enlist immediately, but Dad insisted they wait until after they graduated from high school in June. Loralee, who was attending a Nursing School in St. Louis, wondered aloud if she should try to volunteer. Suppertime was sober as we all listened to the latest news reports on the radio.

Early the next morning Mr. Aiken was in the kitchen, twirling his hat in his big, work-worn hands, shuffling his feet and clearing his throat, trying to force out the right words to convey his thinking. Grandma poured him coffee and Mother urged him to sit and have some breakfast. He and Dad talked of the latest atrocities on the news. Finally, after many attempts, Mr. Aiken said, "Welp, what I've come to tell ya ain't easy, but I 'spect ya'll understand. Ya know I was in the Great War, 'n I thought there'd never be a'nurther 'un. But, it looks lak we're in ta it—I'm too old fur the fox-holes 'n marchin'. Guess I ain't much good fur nuthin', but I'se thinkin' 'bout the war fac'tries, 'n I figger I ken do weldin' 'n machine work 'n I ken ev'n work two shifts if'n need be, 'n since ya don't really need me, now, this time 'a year."

Dad said, "I understand and I admire you for it! I'm hoping I can get things squared away here and join up—if they'll have me."

Mother was unusually contemplative. She asked, "When will you be leaving, Mr. Aiken?"

He grinned sheepishly and said, "Welp, seein' as how hit's alright—there's a bus ta Chicago this afternoon."

Mother exclaimed, "So soon? I just don't know how we'll get along without you, but, I guess we'll manage. You've been so good to us over the years. We're really going to miss you, just like one of the family. Now, you've got to promise you'll write and let us know how you are and you know you're welcome to come back anytime you like. Un ummmh! I just don't like this war business at all! Heaven knows how we're going to miss you around here!"

Mr. Aiken drained his cup, wiped his mouth, thanked Mother for her kind words, shook hands with Dad, and facing Grandma spoke in a soft, low voice, that was full of sincerity and respect, "I ken never tell ya, Mrs. Mason, how indebted to ya I am. Ya gave me a new lease on life 'n I'm much obliged."

Grandma smiled and offered her hand to Mr. Aiken.

"You're a good man and a good friend. I wish you Godspeed."

Mr. Aiken put his hat on and opened the door. He looked back, his dark eyes sweeping the room. They lingered on me and he smiled and raised his hand in a salute.

"Bye, Missy."

I choked on the lump in my throat and ran to him, flinging my arms about his waist and sobbing how I would miss him and always remember him. He patted me on the shoulder and said hoarsely, "There, there, Missy. Don't fret. We gotta do what we ken to stop the Japs 'n that hateful Hitler 'n that mean ole Mussolini—so ya ken go ta France when ya grow up 'n see that Eiffel Tower ya'self."

I reluctantly turned loose of him and with tears streaming down my face, looked up at him and asked, "Will you come back someday?"

His face was wet too. He smiled a bit wobbly, nodded his head, tipped his hat, and went out the door.

Mother sat with bowed head, one hand over her eyes. Grandma and Dad seemed to be exchanging some unspoken message. Dad got up, grabbed his hat and hurried out, saying, "I'll give him a ride into town."

Grandma called after him, "Find out when the bus leaves. Tell him I'm making him some sandwiches."

Mother lifted her tear-streaked face and called, "And cookies!"

She rose quickly from her place at the table and began searching through the cabinets, gathering the things she needed and talking to no one in particular.

"Mr. Aiken just loves our chocolate-fudge cookies. Oh, I do hope I've everything I need. There's plenty of flour and cocoa and butter, let's see, eggs, yes. My, how we're going to miss that man! Sugar? Oh, good, there'll be enough. Thank you, Lord, for little favors. If they ration it like they've threatened to I just don't know how we'll manage, but, I'm sure we can make do. It just hadn't occurred to me that he'd up and go like that. Vanilla—Brown sugar? Yes, now—Oh, that horrible Hitler! And that terrible Tojo! They make me so mad I could cuss a blue streak! Why, I'd stand in line to get a shot at either one of them!"

Alf, along with most of the young men in his graduating class, tossed his mortarboard into the air, donned a khaki colored cap, and boarded a troop train for camp.

Dad talked about wanting to go, too, but Mother would give him no peace on the subject. She told him he was too old, too overweight and that there were lots of important things to be done at home, for, heaven knows, not every war is won on the battlefront. Dad would clinch his mouth and stalk out. One evening at supper he announced he had been accepted for a special assignment with the Home Reserves. Mother said, "Exactly what does that mean?"

Dad chuckled with pleasure, "Well, you gave me the idea when you were talking about the way Mr. Aiken is fighting the war. I went down to the recruiting center and told them I'd be willing to teach these young men about handling firearms on a voluntary basis. The Sergeant said they could use my expertise if they could find a uniform big enough for me."

Grandma nodded approvingly, "I'm proud of you, Riley. Those boys couldn't have a better teacher."

"Instructor, Mama. The only drawback is, I'll have to start out as a Lieutenant, at my age!"

We all laughed, although I didn't know what it was that was funny. Mother said, "Does this mean you'll have to go to some Camp?"

"Just for a week at a time, maybe about once a month. The important thing is, I'll be doing something beneficial. Some of these city boys have never even held a rifle and don't know the first thing about them, let alone how to use them. So, indirectly, I'll get some licks in, too."

Dad overlooked his duties as the County Commissioner but delegated as much as feasible to his eager deputies, on days he worked at the Camp. Of course, there were surprisingly a number of greedy and fairly wealthy "home owners", mostly a few that had businesses downtown, who expected to have their roads and, of course, their driveways, paved or blacktopped or at least graveled and brought up to par free gratis. They were not accustomed to being told that "other roads" must take precedence.

Letters from Alf were few and far between. He and Dad had worked out a code about money and stock so that we always knew where he was. Buying was latitude and selling was longitude. Arrivals and departures were borrowings and tradings. Dad would pull down the big map in the study and pinpoint exactly where he figured Alf to be. The thin, airmail letters, tightly written in narrow lines, were probably non-sensible to the censors, but they always brought a semblance of well-being to us at home and thus, an element of relief from the worry and tension that grew between the letters. Mother would read and reread the letter, while walking about from room to room, expounding on them and worrying aloud.

"Well, at least he's alive and fairly well, from the sound of things, as well as you could expect, any way, in that God-forsaken pest-hole, with those sneaking Japs creeping through the underbrush. Oh, it just makes me shudder to think what he must have to go through. That poor boy! And I well know, there's thousands of them. Freddie Andrews, Frank Oathout, Alf; the cream of our youth out having to fight those –yellow devils! Oh, God, keep them safe from harm! I couldn't bear to have a gold star in the window."

Dad had never cussed much, except when he would get angry, and that did not ordinarily happen, until the war. He would listen to the news broadcasts by Edward R. Murrow and Lowell Thomas and cuss under his breath and sometimes during supper he would use such descriptive phraseology that Mother would shame him;

"Riley, you shouldn't talk that way in front of the children. Their ears are tender and hard sayings here don't help those boys over there."

Dad would mumble something about growing up and facing reality or wish he was over there, ". . . doing something to help win the war like building roads with the engineers. Those boys are having to cut roads through those jungles where white man's never been. God knows it'd be a difficult job under ideal conditions but, God Almighty! Having to do it under such extreme circumstances—but, By God, they're doing it, and probably at such a toll of life and limb we'll never know the whole of it. It just haunts me to think I might be able to help if I were there. That's my job! It's what I'm trained for and I'm not as old as MacArthur and he's in the thick of it."

Grandma would talk of the importance of his instructing those city boys in the use of firearms and artillery and how important his work was as County Superintendent of Roads. She said, "I've heard from different ones that that new road out to the camp was ready in record time and all of the roads are being improved and kept up better than they ever have been before. These things are important in the overall scheme of things. Farmers are playing a vital role in this war, too. Mr. Swanson's men work around the clock; you can see their lights burning night after night. Ralph has expanded his fields and crops, but they have to have roads to truck on. It's all important work, Riley. It's just like the background of a tapestry. One sees the central figures and ohs and ahs over the lavish colors, but the background threads are of equal importance. If they were not strong and durable, the whole thing would fall apart."

Dad would grudgingly comply, and attack whatever job was at hand with a vengeance.

He took to going to the basement after supper and I would go with him. He had a pot-belly stove set up down there and we would melt down lead and pour molten ore into different shape molds. Dad would tell me about some battle of the Revolutionary War or the Civil War and inquire about my history lesson and elaborate on that. He made history come alive and would trace the events and ideas and dreams of years past into the actualities of our time, contrasting the lifestyles of then to the luxurious convenience we took for granted.

Dad knew firearms and their development and the integral role they had played in the history of our world, country and family. He would elaborate on how, "The early gunsmiths made every little piece by hand and would proudly put their name on the finished product. They learned by trial and error and from each other and our modern day warfare that's turned out by monstrous assembly line in huge factories has grown from the seeds of their labors. The factory perfect barrels and locks and firing pins of today had their beginnings in those early forges where the gunsmiths worked from sunup to sundown to make the best possible, dependable and sturdy firearm in their ability. They had nothing but raw materials to start with. Trees that had to be cut down, processed and dried. Ore that had to be dug from the hills, and somehow carried to the forge. Nothing was easy, and yet, some of those very guns are still as dependable today as they were when they were first made. And, they've made it possible for our country to develop into the world power that it is today."

I memorized battles and the warfare used, presidents and their platforms and the type of guns of their day. I argued with teachers when their versions differed from Dad's, and I suffered the consequences on one particularly raw occasion. Our history teacher, short, thin, bald Mr. Darian, was talking about the war and insisted on calling all weaponry, guns. I told him that in the army they only called artillery, cannon, or fixed or mounted pieces guns. He stared at me real hard and the tips of his ears got bright red. He sent me to the office for impertinence and gave me a circled "U" for the day.

The story spread quickly and there were lots of teasing comments about it. I was embarrassed and left for home as soon as the dismissal bell rang. I heard Dean calling me as he came running after me.

"Hey, Toot! Hold up."

"Hi, Dean. Don't you have practice?"

"Nope, not today. You walkin'?"

"Unless you wanna carry me."

"You want me to?"

"Don't be silly!"

"Heard you got sent to the office."

"Oh brother! I guess everybody knows it."

"Seems like it."

"I think I'll die."

"Tell me about it."

I told Dean of the sequence of events and his easy laugh made everything seem fine, even when he cautioned me about keeping on my own side of that "two-way street of learning."

On the fair weather Saturdays and Sundays that Dad was home we would set up for target practice. Hitting anything less than the bull's-eye was not good enough.

"Try it again, sight and pull easy, don't jerk. Lean into it, that way it won't kick so much."

I especially liked using the old muskets, measuring out the gun powder, tamping it down; "My gosh! They had to do this every time before they fired?"

I progressed to skeet shooting and then, at long last, Dad let me go hunting with him and some of his friends. I had no qualms about shooting small game or fowl. I basked in my success and in the hearty congratulations of the men. Mother did not approve and verbalized at length on the subject. Dad would ignore it and laugh with pride.

"She's as good a shot as any of us and it does me good to see her show up ole Doc, after his years of braggin'."

I practiced target shooting weekly. Dean would frequently compete with me and he always won, usually by the least margin in the last round. The targets, themselves, were various objects in different shapes and forms, but in my mind they represented the Holy Devils.

9

🐦 A GOOD DEED BANK IN THE SKY

I liked walking down through the woods and wading in the creek. It was wide and fairly shallow in my favorite spot. There was a stump one could sit on and watch the water bubble over the rocks. It was always cooler there under the canopy of the many branches intertwined amongst the huge old trees.

It was pied-a-terre for insects and spiders and tadpoles and frogs. Squirrels scampered through the trees and birds would sing and sometimes fuss at my intrusion. The musty woody smells and the occasional unexpected sounds of leaves rustling or a branch snapping or a fish jumping or a fly buzzing, were enough excitement to make it a fascinating place for me.

Dean would frequently come there, too, and we would talk or argue. He was terribly bossy; just like Alf used to be.

Mother forbade me to climb trees, but the big old willow was so inviting. I fought the drooping branches and climbed as high as I could, letting the weeping willows curtain me off from the path and from the whole world.

Marj was busy packing and planned to leave right after the graduation ceremony on Sunday. She already had her train ticket and was excited about joining Loralee and working at the defense plant in Chicago. I missed Alf and Loralee and I did not want Marj to leave.

We had not heard from Alf in over a month and tension reigned at home. The list of the honored dead grew every week. It now included three names of young men who had frequently been in our home. There were times when I cried myself to sleep at night. Our friends were the "big kids" that used to come to our home all the time. Billie, Gus, Charley, and Russell, who was taller than anyone else and used to always carry me on his shoulders, were all someplace overseas in the war now. Vern, Stanley, Freddie and of course, Alf, looked so grown up and different in their uniforms.

I checked the strawberries that Grandma had put in a little bag for me to be sure I had not crushed them. They were big and luscious and I plopped one in my mouth and marveled at the sweet, delicious juiciness of the ripe fruit.

Mr. Williams, the Negro man who had worked for Grandpa, had brought a dozen flats of big red strawberries to Grandma yesterday. They had tea and sat and talked for a long time about the farm and the war. He said his son had enlisted in the Navy and was someplace in the Pacific. He and Grandma had prayed together before he left. I had asked her,

"Grandma, why does Mr. Peters and all those other men bring us things all the time?" She had smiled and said, "Honey, one just can't out give God. You can be sure, when you do what is right and good, it comes back to you, in many ways."

She had sent generous helpings of the beautiful delicious strawberries to the Swansons and the Andrews and had made a shortcake for us for supper. This morning she was filling mason jars with jelly and preserves and making pastry for strawberry pies.

I saw Dean coming up the path with his fishing rod and catch, but he did not see me. I waited until he was right in front of me and giggled. He jumped and looked up. "Toot? What are ya doin' up there?"

"Nothin'."

"You get down right now! You shouldn't be climbin' trees down here by yourself. You might fall and get hurt."

"I will not!"

He held the weeping willow branches aside as I jumped down. I fell forward on the uneven ground and skinned my knee. I tried to pretend it did not burn or hurt as I tried to brush off the embedded cinders and dirt. Dean insisted on washing it off with some creek water and it did feel better. He tied his blue kerchief about it and fussed,

"Now you stay out of the trees. Punks aren't spose to be climbin' 'em!"

"I'm not a punk!"

"What were ya doin' up there?"

"Thinkin'."

"Bout what?"

"Oh –'bout strawberries. You want one?"

"Those were good last night."

"These are kinda mashed."

We savored the sweet fruit and I made mine last longer so Dean could have the most. He stood up and I looked up at him in surprise.

"You're gettin' taller!"

"Yep."

"Do you eat wheaties?"

"Nope! Do you?"

"No. I like puffed wheat."

"It'll make you fat."

"It will not!"

"Sure it will. It'll puff you up."

"What'd you eat for breakfast?"

"Oats."

"In the summertime?"

"Yep! If you eat a bowl of oats for breakfast you can work all day."

"Oats are for horses."

"They know what's good! Dad says Jennie will be dropping her foal any day now."

"Oh, Dean, can I watch?"

"Careful! You're gonna make that bleed more if you jump around. I better get you home."

"Can I watch, Dean?"

"Yep. I'll call you when the time comes."

My knee had bled through the kerchief and was burning. Dean helped me walk over the rough path. He insisted we go to his home since it was nearer than mine.

Mrs. Oathout washed and dressed my knee properly and said it would probably be a few days before the foal was dropped. She assured me they would let me know so I could watch. Dean rode me home on his old bicycle. The road was rough and it was hard to sit on the crossbar but Dean was big and strong and safe, just like a big brother.

He wheeled me up to the back porch and I jumped down. He said,

"Ya wantta go to the movie?"

"Maybe. Gene Autry?"

"Nope. Roy Rogers."

"I don't like Roy Rogers."

"He's King of the Cowboys."

"He is not! Gene Autry is!"

"Not any more."

"Dean! Gene Autry is King of the Cowboys!"

"You still have his picture?"

"Yes! And he's my favorite!"

"Welp—D'ya want to go?"

"OK. Josh will want to go, too."

"Dad'll drive us—'bout 1:30. See ya."

He wheeled off in a whirl of dust and I coughed and sputtered. He turned back laughing and I yelled, "Tell Jennie 'Hi!'"

He waved and grinned and I ran to the porch where Grandma was waiting and smiling.

The war seemed interminable and keeping abreast of the daily accounts of the European and Far East battle fronts dominated our lives.

At school, teachers urged us to buy war stamps with our candy money. Every Friday morning there was a keen competition between grades, classrooms and students to see who could give the most dimes and dollars. Students would line up waiting for the bell to ring entry to the building, counting their coins, naming them one by one as a Baby Ruth or a Hershey Bar or a pack of Juicy Fruit or a Dixie Cup. There was pride in giving up something we really liked in order to buy war stamps. It gave us a very real kinship to "the boys on the front", who, we believed were giving up "everything" to make the world safe for us. They were our heroes! The boys! We knew the names of the leaders and the generals who were in the news. Some we idolized: hung their pictures in our bedrooms, and fantasized about someday, maybe, if we were lucky, actually meeting them. Others, certain allies, we scorned as bloody, bungling, egotistical idiots, reflecting our parents' views, and parroting what we heard at home. But, our heroes were the boys: those who were brothers, fathers, uncles, cousins, our older sister's sweethearts and husbands and those good looking youth who had ridden through our town on the troop trains, waving and calling out from the windows of the long, long trains. Many threw out names and addresses and the pretty girls, all of the older girls were pretty, would wave and cheer and blow kisses and pick up bits of paper and anxiously read the names, whisper prayers and scrawl letters, enclosing their pictures and graphic descriptions.

We recited the Pledge of Allegiance promptly and properly each morning. No one would think of mouthing the words or slouching. We were proud of being Americans. We stood tall and straight, saluting with hand over heart, facing toward the flag, enunciating perfectly, and, By God, meaning every word we pledged.

Otto Hinesman sat next to me in music class and in orchestra. He was the best violinist in our school, but painfully aware of his German ancestry. He was vehement in his hatred of Hitler and the Nazies, but he was the victim of many a cruel joke on the playground.

Free time, during recess, was usually spent in war games and imitations of the goose-stepping Nazis and the slant-eyed buck-teethed

Kamikazes. Pencils, sticks, a bit of paper; anything that could be scrunched up between the upper lip and the nose, became a mustache and the more ridiculous the imitator of Hitler, the more we'd whoop and laugh. One day, when Otto had been teased unmercifully, I felt so sorry for him that I told him that I was part German, too. He did not believe me, so as we walked in to the cloakroom, I told him of how my father's people had come from the Northern Province of Hamburg, before the Revolutionary War. He said his parents had come to America after World War I, but still had family and friends there. He whispered that one of his uncles was a Nazi. I felt a pang of repulsion at knowing someone who had such close ties to the enemies. Otto's eyes brimmed with tears, and he turned quickly to hang his coat on a peg. I wanted to say something to make him feel better, but what can you say to some one who has a Nazi in the family? Why, they are killing our boys! The silence and gloom hung between us like a thick barrier growing with each second. I wished I had not taken his side in front of the others and I was tempted to run back outside, but he looked so pitiful with his head leaning against his coat. His knuckles were white from clutching it as though he had nothing else to hang on to. He was much taller than I, but his shoulders seemed to have wilted and drooped as he stood there with his face buried in his coat. I pulled off my wet gloves and mechanically unbuttoned my heavy coat, hung it up and sat down on the bench to remove my boots. I said, "You'd better take your boots off, Otto. They're making puddles."

He kicked them off and thrust his hands deep into the pockets of his dark brown corduroy, shiny-kneed, knickers, and walked over to the lone window of the cloakroom, and stood staring out at most of our classmates, who chose to brave the cold winds and icy drizzle in hot pursuit of the freedom of recess.

I remembered my Uncle David. Mother said it was not her fault if he owned a nightclub and folks should not think less of her for it because she wasn't responsible for what he did, "Although it would just kill Mama and Papa if they ever found out he was encouraging people in that kind of thing when they were so proud that he'd gone into law."

I said, "Otto? You are not responsible for what your Uncle does. It isn't your fault if he's, a, uh, well, it isn't your fault! You don't even know him, do you? Have you ever even seen him? My Mother says everybody's got a skeleton of some kind in the closet, but there's no point in being ashamed of it or worryin' about it."

Otto blew his nose loudly and then answered in a shaky voice. "That's kinda what my Mother says, too. She says Uncle Franz is a good Lutheran and wouldn't be a Nazi if he had a choice."

Wanda Smith came in shivering and looked at us suspiciously. Her thick red hair, escaping from her knotted cap in wispy tufts, framed her face with it's cold, apple red cheeks and shiny red nose and made her brown eyes and freckles stand out even more than usual. Her mittened hands clasped her wiggle stick tightly, and, as always, she looked both right and left and behind her, before laying the precious wiggle stick down on the bench, so she could remove her wraps. She continued to eye us with open curiosity as she called, "Hey! It's too cold to play, isn't it?"

I said, "Do you have a new wiggle stick, Wanda?"

She glanced at me and then fastened her gaze on it. She struggled free of her heavy wraps, hung them on their proper pegs, placed her wet and muddy boots under the bench, sneaked a cookie out of her sack lunch which was stored on the running shelf above the coat pegs, and sat down on the bench, nibbling on the homemade, oversized, sugar cookie, holding the foot-long stick in her right hand, staring at the brightly colored ribbons tied to the top of it. They wiggled and flipped and danced about as she manipulated the stick in a nearly palsied motion. I repeated my query. "Isn't that a new wiggle stick, Wanda?"

She brushed the crumbs from her mouth and off her dress front with her free hand. She darted a defiant glance toward me and pouted, "Johnny Jackson and Mark Hayes broke my wiggle stick yesterday and Mrs. Williams didn't do nothing about it. My Mom had to make me this new one last night."

"Didn't do anything."

"What?"

"Oh, nothing!"

She was such a big baby about everything. I had never known anyone to cry as easily or profusely as she. Grandma had said she was terribly high-strung for a child and it was best to just leave her be.

Otto was watching Wanda flip the stick about. Mrs. Williams had tried to keep her from using it during class time but Wanda would cry and pout and bite her nails until they bled and be so upset without it that Mrs. Williams had finally relented and had even threatened the rest of us with 'what for' if we teased her about it.

Wanda had visited with me at home several times. Mother and Grandma had speculated on her fascination with the wiggle stick and had worried if she were normal, but had concluded, after subtle cross-examination, that it was a harmless amusement and that she would probably outgrow it.

Dad had driven us to a Gene Autry movie one Saturday afternoon and had later chuckled as he teased me. You've certainly got some interesting friends, Toot. Does she always wiggle that thing in front of her nose like that?"

Mother had commented on how it was alright, she guessed, for just a few hours at a time, to have to watch someone doing that, but for me not to get any ideas about such foolish goings on, for if she had to watch someone doing that day in and day out she would soon go batty herself, and then she would have to go to the loony bin and get herself a wiggle stick.

Otto turned from the window and asked her point blank, "Why do you do that?"

Wanda wiggled her stick even faster when she got anxious or angry. Sometimes she would move it so fast her hand was a blur of motion. That was the way it was when she answered him in her most hateful tone, "I don't have to tell you nothin', you German Nazi, you!"

Otto started toward her. I jumped up and moved between them, angrily facing the overly sensitive spoiled brat whom we all had been cautioned to handle with kid gloves.

"You shouldn't say that, Wanda! He's an American, just like you and me!"

"He is not! He's got German blood and you can't even understand his Dad!"

Otto's face reddened with anger and humiliation. I felt sorry for him and angry toward Wanda and her dumb wiggle stick that she was waving fiercely in front of her face. Otto grabbed for it. She yanked it through his grasp and the brightly colored ribbons fell to the floor. She screamed and cried and jumped up and down yelling at the top of her voice.

"You broke it! I'm gonna tell! You're a Nazi! A nasty Nazi!!" I picked up the ribbons and took the stick from her and tied them back on. I said, "Wanda? Do you know I'm part German, too? Does that make me a Nazi? Boy, are you dumb! A lot of Americans have German blood, and not all Germans are Nazis! Where did your parents' people come from?"

Wanda sputtered through her tears and sniffled, "Why, we're Americans! They came from America, and they've always been Americans!"

"They had to come from someplace else, Wanda. Only Indians were here when the Pilgrims came. You're not an Indian."

Wanda pouted and examined the large amateurish knot I had made with a disapproving scowl. Others were straggling in and as the warning bell sounded a herd of laughing, cold and hurried boys and girls crushed into the cloakroom depositing their wet garments, trailing puddles of muddy slush and smelling to high heaven of wet wool, active sweat glands, enlarged adenoids and the ensuing snotty smelling breath. The cloakroom was narrow and intended to hold wraps, not young people.

We pushed and shoved each other good-naturedly, as we scrambled for the classroom and resumed our individual, designated territories. I sat in the front seat of my row of desks. Mrs. Williams was writing a math quiz on the black board. I put my new glasses on and raised my hand for permission to ask a question. The bell sounded and all activity: getting books, papers and pads from under the seats, sharpening pencils, the occasional threat or snicker, ceased. As Mrs. Williams turned to face the class, I raised my hand. She arched her eyebrows questioningly and nodded toward me. Anxiety propelled my questions on one long breath.

"Mrs. Williams, some of us were talking about what kind of blood we have and isn't it true that all of us came from other countries and wouldn't we be Indians if our families had always lived here?"

Other hands were waving in the air. Mrs. Williams put her book down on the desk, smoothed her reddish-brown hair back, fingered the bun at the nape of her neck and replied, "In the first place there are not different kinds of blood. I know you didn't mean that literally, but it is a misnomer and implies that different people of different races have different kinds of blood. Blood is classified into different types, but one's race or color or country of origin has nothing to do with the type of blood one has. What you are referring to is one's blood line, or family line, meaning ancestry. I am well aware that there is a lot of talk, now, about ancestry, and, unfortunately, there are those who are denying their ancestry for fear of being identified with our present-day enemies. It is true that Caucasians, referring to all white people, regardless of which country they come from, are relatively new to this country. The Indians, a red people, were the first known occupants here as you know. It is possible that some of your ancestors mingled their bloodlines, but, that is not for you to worry about. Who your ancestors were, is not nearly as important as who you are. True, we reap the results, either pluses or minuses, for our linage. You are, in a sense, the summation of many generations. No two of you are alike. You have different talents, different looks, and my, aren't you glad?"

Laughter and teasing taunts were allowed briefly. Then, Mrs. Williams continued, "There are five races of man, which you will be studying more thoroughly in the higher grades. Our physical features give a good clue as to our origins, but you can't be certain just from looks. America is called the Melting Pot, because, here, so many races meet and mix and blend, ideally, each with their own color and culture and creed. But, nevertheless, in this day and age, there are few Caucasians, in this country, who can claim direct decadency from only one country. Just for an example of linage; my Father's people came from Scotland. My Mother was born in Holland to parents of White Russian, Dutch and Austrian linage. My husband's people were English for many generations, but his grandfather had married a Cherokee squaw, not a princess; so, my husband's blood line is English and American Indian. Our children are a combination of both of our blood lines. Probably, most of you, could trace your ancestry back to many different countries."

Mrs. Williams paused for breath and glanced over the hands waving all over the room. She nodded toward Doug Ivy, a handsome, strongly built, blonde, blue-eyed lad, who seemed to excel in everything. He said, "My Dad says there's a lot of talk about Japs and Nazis and Deigos and kids call each other that when they're mad, 'cause they're kinda like cuss words, but it's wrong to hate people or try to hurt they're feelings just because of their race. He says everybody oughta be proud of their own kind and that all of us are Americans and we've all got to work together to end the war."

There were murmurings about the room. Mrs. Williams nodded assent, smiled, and pointed toward Johnny Jackson, a dark-haired, black-eyed boy, who was a model student in the classroom, but a holy terror on the playground. I hated him. He was such a bully. He enunciated, "My grandfather says Washington should be ashamed of the way they've treated the Japanese Americans. They can't help it because they're Japanese. He says they'd be as good soldiers as the Negroes."

Mrs. Williams walked around to the front of her desk, frowning. "It is unfortunate that some people are ridiculed and prejudged, just on the basis of their race. That is exactly what is going on in Germany. Hitler is trying to make what he thinks would be an ideal race: blond, blue eyes, muscular. Isn't it peculiar that he looks nothing like that? He is also trying to extinguish the Jewish people, for no reason other than he hates Jews, which is really strange, because some say his Grandparents were Jewish. Now, do remember, the Jewish people are not actually a race. They are a Religion.

"You and I and all the people of the whole world must learn from this horrible war. It is wrong and wicked. We must do everything that we possibly can here at home to help our boys who are over there. And, we must be very careful that such bigotry and hatred is never allowed to happen here, and is never again allowed to run rampant, anyplace, over people just because of their race or religion."

Eager students were waving their hands for permission to contribute their thoughts or questions or to repeat some hearsay. Mrs. Williams motioned for hands down, walked over to the windows that lined one wall, and raised one. She put a finger to her lips and shushed. We all strained to listen. There were the sounds of the wind and the rain. Off in the distance a dog was barking and a sound truck was urging people to get out and vote for the county election. The sound of someone's footsteps hurrying along the walk, sloshing through the puddles, brought smiles. The breeze was chilly and raised goose bumps as it hit us. Mrs. Williams lowered the window and turned to face the class with an expression that defied denials.

"I've heard many of you out on the playground yelling hurtful things to each other, even labeling each other as enemies, when, in fact, you are all citizens of this country, regardless of your ancestry. All of us stand here each school day morning and salute our flag and pledge allegiance to our country. How dare you, any of you, call another a Jap or a Nazi?

"You may ridicule Hitler and Mussolini and Hirohito all you wish as far as I am concerned. They are public figures and the leaders of our enemies, and, I know some of you give some hilarious imitations of them. That's as it should be. These men strip their own people of human dignity; they enslave them to serve in their godless aggressions and they train them to be mindless masses of puppets, who do not know what it is to be free or to enjoy liberty and justice as you and I do here in America. But, you must not deprive an innocent person of his dignity. You must not throw hateful epithets that cut so cruelly and maliciously that they wound the very hearts of the victims, ruin their reputations and kill their spirits."

Mrs. Williams eyes were bright with indignation and as they scanned the room it was as though we had each been drenched with a scalding scowling. The long slender red hand on the wall clock ticked off the seconds as Mrs. Williams walked slowly back to her desk. She picked up the class record book and cradled it in her arms as she walked around to the front of the desk and leaned against it in a leisurely manner. Her tone was softened but still had a note of reproach as she continued, "I have been so proud of this class. As you well know, we have been the top ranking class in buying war stamps and savings bonds for the last twenty-three weeks. None of us are rich people. I know many of you sacrifice to give as much as you do. But, there is one family that I know of, that really sacrifices in order to buy extra war bonds to help our country win this war. I will not tell you who they are, but, they are the ones who put our class on the top of the list. Would you accuse them of being disloyal?"

Otto was looking down at his hands, busily intertwining his fingers into a tight knot. Everyone knew that Otto always bought savings bonds while the rest of us usually bought a column of ten-cent stamps and dutifully pasted then in a little booklet designed to hold fifty.

Mrs. Williams casually asked, "How many of you know for certain that at least some of your ancestors came from England?"

Proud hands were raised about the room. She asked, "Any from Scotland? Wales? Ireland? Wanda, I thought surely you must be Irish, with that red hair, no? Well, any from the Netherlands, Russia, Norway, Austria?"

Wanda raised her left hand. Her right hand was shaking the wiggle stick furiously, right at the tip of her nose. The ribbons were fluttering in her face as she stared fixedly at them.

Mrs. Williams said evenly, "Some of you may want to raise your hands many times. Please do any time you know you've ancestry from the country I name. France? Poland? Denmark? Italy—No one— Germany?"

The room was absolutely still except for the belabored breathing from a few stuffy noses. I raised my hand, straightened my back and braced myself, as I turned to look around the class. Otto's hand was up. Slowly, one by one, others raised their hands. Wanda was shaking her wiggle stick and tears were streaming down her cheeks. She stared about the room. Fifteen hands were raised with attitudes varying from the shy to the defiant. Otto was smiling and shaking his head in disbelief. There was a loud gasp and a shuddering sob and I turned to see Wanda, holding her right hand aloft with the wiggle stick pointing ceiling-ward.

Mrs. Williams ignored the drama, and inquired, "Are there any countries I have not mentioned that any of you have ancestry from?"

Johnny Jackson volunteered French Canada; Almeda Sewardson beamed Sweden; Al Mickinick, the class clown whose father was the owner of the local greasy spoon, waved his hand wildly, leaning forward on his desk. Mrs. Williams nodded to him. He clattered to his feet, pointed a finger at her and admonished in a mock-serious tone, "Don't forget the Greece, I mean Greeks."

His antics drew gales of laughter. Mrs. Williams tapped loudly on her desk for order, and amidst the ensuing moans and groans ordered,

"You will now get out your paper and pencils, put on your mental blinders, look inside yourself, and write down your thoughts on this discussion, or on your heritage and how you feel about it. Write whatever you think as fast as you can. This is not a penmanship assignment. No talking. Begin."

She walked over to the window and stood staring out into the gray day. A newly sharpened red pencil was behind her ear. Ordinarily, she would be walking up and down the aisles, reading over our shoulders, correcting our errors or pointing them out to us. Not today. She stood there, staring out the window the whole time. The sound truck, urging voters to the polls, went by the school, causing a brief interruption of thought. I knew Dad was running again for office and that he was confident of winning.

Mrs. Williams called time and asked if there was anyone who would like to read aloud what they had written. Several volunteered. Otto sat quietly listening to the heartfelt expressions of his classmates. Wanda hesitantly raised her hand, stood, laid her wiggle stick down on her desk and falteringly read, "My Daddy says we are Americans and it's no one's business where his Dad was born. He hates the Germans and Hitler and gets mad when my Mom speaks German or worries about her folks who are still in Austria. He won't tell me anything about my Grandma or Grandpa because they are German but they farm in Wisconsin and someday I'll go see them and ask them all about my ancestors and what my real name is."

Mrs. Williams smiled, nodded and said our time was up, and instructed us to pass the papers to the front and get ready for the math quiz.

It was raining hard when school was dismissed. Mr. Swanson was waiting for Dean and called for Josh and I to ride home with him. We scampered into the car out of the cold wet weather. Mr. Swanson said, "I've been drivin' people to the polls all day. Everybody's votin' for your Dad—says he's done a fine job."

"Yes sir."

"He'll win easy."

Dean said, "How do you like your new glasses?"

"I only wear them to read."

"Let me see."

"You'll call me 'specs'."

"Nope! Won't."

"Everybody else does."

"So who cares?"

"I do."

"Ya shouldn't."

"Specs' and 'four eyes'. That's what everybody says."

"Do they help?"

"Yeah."

"Lemme see 'em."

I handed the black hard leather case to Dean. He opened and removed the round metal-rimmed eye glasses. He used the little pinked square of blue flannel with the optometrist's name imprinted on it, to go through the motions of cleaning them, before putting them on. Josh told him, "You look silly."

Dean peered through the glasses. He said, "Not much difference."

"They're just for eye strain."

"Readin' too much?"

"I guess."

"Eat lots of carrots."

Dean put the glasses back in the case and handed it to me. Mr. Swanson said, "Glasses aren't so bad. They sure make things a lot plainer. Lot'sa times young 'uns need 'em for a spell after the measles."

The windshield wipers were sashaying from side to side in a rhythmic flub-flub as they swished away the pounding, wind-driven sheets of rain. Josh was nodding his head in time to the measured beat.

We saw the lone figure walking on the opposite side of the road. He had his head down against the wind and the rain. A duffle bag was slung over his shoulder. Mr. Swanson stopped the car, turned it around and pulled up to the soldier and motioned for him to get in. He pushed the duffle bag in ahead of him, as Mr. Swanson asked, "Where ya goin', Son?"

The soldier said, "Heading for Peoria! I've got a three-day pass 'fore shippin' out."

"Ya plannin' to hitch?"

"Well—I got this far."

Mr. Swanson pulled out his watch and said, "There's a north-bound train due in at 4:10. It'll get you there a lot quicker and a lot drier."

The soldier acted embarrassed. He said, "Uh—I gotta hitch, Sir."

Mr. Swanson reached over and clasped him on the arm. He said, "It'll be my pleasure to see to it ya get home, Son. No point in ya bein' stuck down here when ya could use that time at home. I could drive ya, but the train'll be quicker."

We pulled up to the depot and Mr. Swanson and the soldier went in. We watched through the blurry windows as Mr. Swanson stepped up to the ticket window and then gave the soldier a ticket and something from his wallet. They shook hands and stood talking for a few minutes.

Mr. Swanson hurried to the car through the driving rain. He was whistling as he got in. Dean asked, "How many's that make, Dad?"

Mr. Oathout shrugged and smiled, "Don't know, Son. But he's one mighty happy boy. I'm glad we happened along."

Grandma had a pot of hot tea in the cozy and was spreading graham crackers with a rich hot fudgy icing. She stirred a bit of ginger wine into our tea to ward off a cold. Dad would tease her about the ginger wine but she would point out the Salvation Army would not sell it if it were alcoholic. She maintained it was medicinal and would chide him for knocking what had done him so much good. Josh and I told her about the soldier boy and about our day at school. He proudly showed her his graded papers before darting off for his radio program, imitating the announcer,

"The shadow knows, eh eh eh!"

I told Grandma about the big discussion at school and how Wanda had admitted she was part German. She said, "It sounds like her folks need to reconcile themselves to the truth. It's a pity, being so ashamed of one's people. I suspected something was bothering that child. It just isn't natural for a girl that age to be so overweight and fidgety and attached to a wiggle stick. It's right to hate the war and the cruelties of the war, but you can't fight within yourself over something you can't help."

"Did you go out in the rain to vote, Grandma?"

"Why, of course I did. A little bit of rain isn't going to keep me home from the polls. What's more, everyone I saw said they were voting for your Dad."

"I wish I could vote."

"That'll come soon enough, Toot."

"Did we hear anything from Mother today?"

"No, Honey. I 'spect she's busy with her folks. Her Mother's in such poor health now. But, I'm certain Martha will return as soon as she feels she can."

"I wish she wouldn't go away so often."

Grandma frowned slightly. "She isn't on a pleasure trip this time. It's our bounden duty to help each other, Honey, whether it's family that's sick or a stranger that's caught in a storm or a friend that's mixed up. The Bible tells us to give freely and 'the windows of heaven will pour you out a blessing that there shall not be room enough to receive it'."

"I think the windows of heaven are just pouring out rain today."

"It'll be good for the orchards and the crops."

Grandma was busy with supper preparations. I read an assignment and was answering the questions at the end of the chapter when Dad came in grinning. He mischievously untied Grandma's apron strings and said he had won handily, even though they were not through counting the ballots yet. The phone began ringing after supper, with dozens of congratulatory calls for him.

It was still drizzling the next morning. Dad drove Josh and me to school. Mrs. Williams was unusually short tempered all day. The whole class was aware of the strained atmosphere. We were as careful as if we were walking on a mine field. During the last hour of the day Mrs. Williams instructed us on an art assignment. I was the first to finish, but I knew it was well done. I took it up to her desk, as was the custom. She glared at me and said in a loud voice, "What do you want?"

I started to hand her the drawing. She bridled and squinted her eyes at me and said sharply, "You did not have permission to leave your desk!"

Everyone was staring. I hurried back to my desk and sat down. I raised my hand to ask permission, but she ignored me. Johnny Jackson raised his hand. She nodded toward him. He said, "I'm through with my drawing, Mrs. Williams."

She indicated for him to bring it to her and then addressed the class. "The bell will ring in about ten minutes. If you've completed your drawing, bring it here to my desk for grading. Then you may get your wraps and be dismissed."

Several rushed toward her desk, giggling and whispering excitedly about getting out early. I was feeling apprehensive about approaching her again as I stood in line waiting for my turn. Almeda was in front of me. Mrs. Williams took over long with her and the line dissolved as the mass of students crowded to see and hear what was going on. As Almeda stepped away, Mrs. Williams asked, "Who's next?"

I answered, "It's my turn now."

I lay the drawing on her desk. She glowered at me and slapped me hard on the face. She marked a big red 'S' right in the middle of the paper and rumpled it toward me as she snapped, "You're dismissed!"

My head ached and my ears rang as my eyes filled with tears. Everyone was deathly still. It seemed as though time had stopped. The humiliation was stifling; the frustration was cyclonic. I woodenly picked up the drawing and walked the length of the room to the cloakroom, which was a beehive of curiosity and speculation. Otto asked, "What happened? What did you do?"

I told him I did not know. He shook his head in amazement. Johnny talked about her being mad all day. Several marveled over the red finger marks on my cheek. I dressed for the outdoors as quickly as possible, met Josh and hurried toward home.

I imagined inventive retorts I should have made, but the "whys" plagued me. Josh was sweet and loyal and claimed he was going to beat her up. He would bam-bam and shadow-box for a few steps, flexing his six-year old muscles that were well padded in a snowsuit and rain slick, and make verbal threats in his amusing lisp. As we walked up our lane, the embarrassment of having been slapped welled up even greater than the indignation and seeming injustice of the actual slap. I felt an inexplicable guilt, as though I had committed some terrible offense. Josh darted in the house ahead of me, yelling, "Gram-ma! Gram-ma! Toot got slapped at school!"

I stood at the door reluctant to go in, ashamed to face Grandma, dreading to ever have to face anyone again. Grandma helped me off with my coat and told me to take off my boots while she poured the tea. Moments later she called, "Come on, Honey. Let's have some tea and warm you up. You can tell me about it when you get ready to."

I sat at the old familiar table sipping tea and munching on warm cheddar cheese cookies. The pressure cooker rattled on the range and Grandma adjusted the heat and released some steam. Josh kept up a good-natured dialogue about what he would do if a teacher "swapped" him. Grandma reminded him, "You just see to it that you mind your business, and you won't have to worry about getting slapped or spanked or stood in the corner. You go to school to learn; not to get into mischief."

Her gentle admonition washed over me in a tide of perplexing guilt. I drained my cup, took a deep breath, and looked up into Grandma's kind, warm, caring, patiently waiting eyes. My throat constricted as a wave of conflicting emotions engulfed me. Tears streamed from my eyes and my nose ran and I sobbed as Grandma embraced me and soothed me with her gentle philosophy. "There, there, it can't be that bad. My! That cry sounds like it's from a deep hurt. Let's spill it out and study on it, Honey, and see what we have to deal with. You're not alone. I'm hurting for you, but I'll just bet that a hundred years from now we'll have forgotten all about it."

I nodded my head, blew my nose, and wiped my eyes. Grandma listened thoughtfully as I told her of the chain of events, my humiliation, and the sense of injustice I felt at being berated and slapped so hard for no reason. I told her of my drawing and how it was not even graded on its merits.

"She didn't even look at it. She just scribbled a big sloppy red 'S' right in the center of it. She ruined it and it was good."

The injustice of the grading seemed to surmount the slap in the face. But doubts plagued me. I began to wonder aloud if I was wrong about the drawing being good. Maybe it was so bad, she got angry by just a glance at it. Grandma said, "Let's not jump to any conclusions. I just had an idea, and, if I'm right, then, her getting mad had nothing at all to do with you or your drawing. Run in the study and get this morning's paper."

When I got back with the paper, Grandma was talking on the telephone to Dad's secretary.

"Oh, yes, of course, Williams. Seems like a fine man. Too bad someone has to lose in these elections. Yes, well, I'm very pleased, too. Oh, by the way, could you tell me whether or not his wife teaches school? Oh? At Franklin Elementary? I see. Well, I'm much obliged for your help. Thank you kindly."

Grandma looked up the school's number and read it off to the operator. She glanced at the clock over the range and worried that everyone had gone home for the day. I could hear the periodic ringing at the other end of the line. After seven or eight rings someone answered. Grandma identified herself and asked to speak to the principal. She paused briefly and then said firmly, "This is a very important matter to me. I wish to speak to Mr. Edwards about it, now. Thank you. Hello, Mr. Edwards? This is Mrs. John Mason. My granddaughter was treated rudely and most unfairly by her sixth-grade teacher, Mrs. Williams, today. Oh? What version did you hear? Yes, that's exactly what I was told. No, the marks were gone by the time she got home, but the injustice and humiliation have hurt her deeply. Did you talk to Mrs. Williams about it? I see, well, I suppose that is up to you. Who did you say told you about it? I'm glad they did. You are aware that her husband was running against, uh, Yes, unfortunately, I suspect so. No, I'll reserve judgment on that until we've talked to Mrs. Williams. Oh, no! We don't discuss business with the children. Do understand that we have no complaint with her teaching, but I am terribly disappointed in her behavior today. Yes, I'll be here. Thank you kindly."

Grandma smiled at me and poured some fresh tea. She said, "Three of your classmates told Mr. Edwards about the incident right after school. He sent for Mrs. Williams, but she had already left for the day. He said he had just talked to her on the telephone. He also said to tell you he is truly sorry and hopes you won't be bitter."

I laughed shakily and shrugged. Grandma explained her theory and a wave of relief swept over me. "You mean, she slapped me because Dad won the election?"

"Not because he won, Honey; because her husband—lost!"

"But Grandma, that's not my fault!"

"Of course not. You're an innocent victim of misdirected anger and frustration. Life is full of injustices, Honey. This should not have happened, but, it did, so, the important thing now is how are you going to handle it?"

My cup clattered in the saucer as I looked up in surprise. "Me? What can I do?"

"Let's look at the facts closely, Honey, with our eyes wide open. You were wronged. You were treated rudely, shabbily, and shamed for no reason of your own doing. It would be only natural for you to feel bitterness and resentment and to want revenge, like Josh."

We both laughed. Grandma continued, "I'm not making any excuses for Mrs. Williams' actions today. She's an intelligent woman and knows better than to lash out at a mere child, just because of her own disappointments. But, everybody is subject to irrational behavior once in awhile. I suspect Mrs. Williams is well aware of the mistake she made today, and what the consequences might very well be."

"What consequences, Grandma?"

"She could be fired, Honey."

"Oh, no, Grandma! Why, I like her. Everybody does. She isn't mean or cynical like Miss Thompson: she's always slapping kids, or pulling their ears and saying mean things. I'd just die if I had her. Mrs. Williams is nice, really."

Grandma smiled and patted me on the arm. She spoke softly. "Tell me all of the good things you can think of about Mrs. Williams and all of the good deeds that you know of that she has done."

It was a challenge to verbalize good things and good deeds about someone with whom I still felt peeved. But, once I began, it grew easier and there were many things to cite. Grandma listened attentively, nodded appreciatively, smiling her approval, as I enumerated at length, instances of kindness, wisdom, and good teaching from my point of view. Then Grandma said. "Now, tell me all of the things you don't like about her, or that you think are wrong." There were only the disquieting, hurtful actions of today.

Grandma said, "Now, hold up your hand like a scale. Pretend you've all of the good things and good deeds in one hand, and all of the bad things and bad deeds in the other. Which weighs the heaviest?"

I held my hands up and went through the motions of seeing which was the heaviest; the good deeds and the good things or the bad deeds and the bad things. Finally, I let one hand fall much lower than the other. Grandma laughed when I tried to act like it was really heavy. Then she asked quietly, "Which weighs the heaviest? The good deed side or the bad deed side?"

I grinned sheepishly, and conceded. "The good side."

Grandma reached over for my hands and clasped them tightly as she spoke in her soft, clear, but firm voice. "I know it was an embarrassing and hurtful experience for you. But, now that you know you were not at fault, how do you feel about it?"

"I don't know. It hurt, Grandma. It really hurt! It rattled my brain and made me dizzy. It made my cheek burn and she ruined my drawing. And everybody stared."

Grandma released my hands and sat back in her chair. Her eyes were twinkly and she smiled conspiratorially as she half—whispered, "A wound to the pride can become a festering sore, unless one does the hardest possible thing."

"What's that?"

"Forgive and forget."

I felt betrayed and it must have shown on my face as I stammered, "But, shouldn't she at least, maybe, say she's sorry?"

Grandma looked thoughtful.

"Ordinarily, when one wrongs another person, the proper thing is to make amends by apologizing. But, this is really awkward. A teacher wrongs a student in front of the whole class. Should that teacher apologize in front of the class? Would that heal the hurt? Or, mightn't it prolong a matter best left alone? You see, honey, the more something like this is talked, the bigger it gets, and the more likely it is to scar. If you can bring yourself to do it, I'm confident the best thing would be to take comfort in that you were not at fault, so you really need not feel any shame or remorse. You're in a position to show mercy and compassion, but the good will be undone if you talk about it. That's why it is important to simply forgive and forget. It will help to think about all of the good things. Don't even think about the unpleasantness. Just forgive and forget."

"Should I tell Dad?"

Grandma feigned surprise. "Tell him what?"

I frowned, "You know—?"

Grandma gave me a sidelong glance as she began removing the tea things from the table. I understood and laughed. "I forgot!"

She smiled approvingly and said, "Honey, my father used to say there's a special bank in the sky for good deeds. It pays better returns than you can ever anticipate: ten times over what you give and then some. I hope that's especially true for you. I'm very proud of you."

After supper Dad and Grandma were in the study for a long time. Dad was talking on the telephone when I went in to get an Atlas. He did not say much while I was in the room, but I could tell he was stalling, waiting for me to leave.

Dad shook me awake the next morning with a note of excitement in his voice. "Toot? Toot! Wake up, Toot! There's a telephone call for you."

"For me? Who is it? What do they want?"

"Come see. Hurry up, he's waitin'."

I shielded my eyes with my hands against the bright lights that blinded my sleepy eyes as I hurried downstairs, wondering aloud who was calling me so early in the morning. The kitchen smelled of coffee perking. Grandma had on her robe and was smiling as she lay my heavy coat on a chair. I picked up the phone and cautiously said, "Hello?"

"Toot?"

"Dean!"

"Jennie dropped her foal while ago."

"Ohhh!"

"Ya wantta come see?"

"Yes, I'll be right there!"

Dad was chuckling as he pulled on his hunting boots. "I'll run you over there, Toot. Dress warm."

The sky was just beginning to lighten with the promise of a new day when Dad scrunched the car to a halt at the barnyard gate. I jumped out and ran over the frozen churned up mud to the open door of the stable. The pungent tang of hay and muck and the lingering warm animal smells assaulted my nostrils as I hurried toward the stall where Mr. and Mrs. Swanson, Dean, and several of the hired hands, stood admiring the new foal.

A sense of awe enveloped me. I stood staring at Jessie cleaning the spindly long-legged chestnut foal. Everyone was talking and laughing but I stood, unheeding, completely absorbed in the marvelous spectacle. Dean said, "It's a colt."

"He's a beaut."

"He's yours."

"Oh, Dean, I love him."

"Mighty handsome."

The colt wobbled about trying out his legs. Jessie nuzzled him and he emitted a whinny. Mr. Swanson happily fussed about losing so much time to "that little Jinx," and so the whinny, beautiful, little wobbly chestnut foal was named.

Dean and I watched the delightful, awkward antics of Jinx as he would explore his new world and then clumsily fold his long legs and curl up for a snooze. We stroked Jessie and got her oats and speculated about how many hands high Jinx would grow.

Dad said we had to hurry to get ready for work and school. Reluctantly, I waved to the sleeping Jinx and promised to be back as soon as possible. Mr. Swanson teased, "Now, if you don't want that little Jinx, there's a good many here who do."

"Oh, Mr. Swanson. I want him! I want him more than anything. He's just perfect."

He laughed and rumpled my uncombed hair. "He's a dandy, alright! Won't be long 'fore you and Dean can start trainin' him."

"Oh, I can hardly wait."

I was eager to tell everyone at school about Jinx. We had a substitute teacher. She said Mrs. Williams was ill, but would be back the next week.

10

🐦 THE KING OF NILESVILLE

Dad was highly respected for his work "out at the camp," and for his expertise on guns and the history thereof. Some claimed he was a "walking encyclopedia" on the subject. A famous novelist, historian and gun collector came to see him one day and they spent hours in the study talking and laughing. Dad even showed him some "pieces" that he usually kept locked up. Some reporter had interviewed the man at his hotel and reported in the paper that the visiting dignitary said Mr. Mason's gun collection was the most complete and authenticated collection that he had ever seen. Mother had a fit, claiming, "Well, now, that's all we need. Broadcasting what we have all over the papers, so all the robbers and thieves will know where to come to get what they want."

Dad's friends would come out on Saturday and Sunday mornings and they would drink coffee and talk about the war and cuss out their frustrations and then compare their dogs, ready their shotguns and go hunting for quail or cotton-tails, they would return after a few hours, stomping their feet against the cold and laughing about the antics of the dumb bitch, Fanny, that Dr. Matthews insisted on taking along. She was terrified of birds and gunfire. The men would laugh and tease him, claiming that every time anyone fired a shot the trembling bitch would cower between Doc's legs and try to climb into his pocket. He would snuffle and clean his glasses and mumble apologies about how she was really such a prize and not to be faulted since he just had not had the time to train her. He would stroke her on her throat and she would purr and nuzzle against his leg amidst the envy tinged taunts of, "Damn bird dog thinks she's a lap dog!"

"Purrin' like a kitten."

"Just a poodle at heart."

"Ya hand feed her, Doc?"

Dean and I would frequently go with them on Saturdays. Mother insisted I attend church on Sunday mornings and objected to me going hunting at all. But Dad was proud of my bearing and Dean was as good and as careful a shot as any of the men. Dad maintained it was necessary for us to "weed out" those pesky rabbits, and from time to time there would be quail or pheasant. Grandma would nod and smile approval on whatever I bagged.

There were times the men would set up the traps for shooting and Grandma would bundle up and come out to watch. She didn't care for shooting rifles or shotguns but she was deadly accurate with her little revolver. She never seemed to take aim but she always hit the target; even a quarter on a fence post at thirty paces. Doc had claimed he couldn't even see it. Mr. Swanson would watch her carefully and then marvel that she was so accurate without seeming to take aim. Dad would chuckle with pride and urge her to, "Tell 'em how you do it, Mama. They wouldn't believe it, if I told 'em."

"Why, I just point the pistol the same as I would my finger."

Mother was expecting and held that very obvious fact over our heads in order to have her way about everything. She fussed at Dad in private and in public and in front of his friends. And she laid down the law to me. "I just don't like you wearing pants all the time and going out with the men and the boys like that. It's just no way for a young lady to behave."

"But, Mother, I like it! It's really thrilling to go out and pitch wits against the game and compete with the men in skill and expertise. Tomorrow we're going quail and pheasant hunting with muskets just like the pioneers did."

Mother quipped, "The pioneers wouldn't have wasted their precious shot on quails."

"Why, Mother! How'd you know that?"

"Humph! I haven't lived with your Father for twenty-five years for nothing!"

"Mother, I really like hunting and shooting and going out with Dad. Besides, he says I'm really good. There's nothing for you to worry about and I'm sure Dad would tell you that too."

"Well, I've got a surprise for you. You're going to be too busy to think about hunting or riding or shooting. You, muh deah, are going to take dancing lessons."

"Mother!"

"Now, that's all there is to it. I've already enrolled you and I laid down good money for it, too. You start tomorrow afternoon and I expect you to be nice about it. We'll have to go shopping in the morning to get the things you need."

I hated the ballet class. I was one of the oldest students and a head taller than any of the rest. I was also awkward, clumsy and given to fits of self-conscious giggles. Fanny and I had a lot in common. I was as out of place in the ballet class as she was on the hunting field, but I didn't have a pocket to climb into.

We did not hear from Loralee or Marj very often. Their letters were brief and usually about a month apart. But they sent postcards from time to time and would call on special occasions. They were both working in the same war plant and sharing the same apartment. Neither had divulged much, if anything of a social life.

When the Western Union car pulled in to our lane we all gathered about the door: Alf was still overseas. Telegrams never brought good news. Mother accepted it hurriedly, tore it open and said, "It isn't Alf— It's—I don't believe it!"

A bombshell would not have created more shock, confusion or havoc. Loralee was married. Mother read, reread and reread the telegram. Each time she found something more to comment on. They were arriving here on the train on Saturday; no, they were arriving here on Thursday evening, and would have to leave early Saturday morning. He was a soldier, a Sergeant, a Chicagoan, a Polish boy, a Polish Catholic boy! Mother was on the horns of a dilemma. She was also big with child and distraught over her delicate condition.

"Oh, Loralee would do this to me at this time. Why, our oldest daughter just going off and getting married like that, and, Oh Lord— heaven knows, the world is so full of nice Protestant boys, and here she's married—actually *married*, a Catholic! A Polish Catholic! I wonder if they are the same as Catholics here in town?"

Mother wandered about the house carrying the telegram bemoaning the fact that they were to be home such a short time and wondering aloud if she should plan a reception or just let things happen, come what may. Grandma convinced her it was best not to plan on having people in, since Loralee could always call the ones she wanted to see if she so desired.

Grandma asked me to help her with a few things. She cleaned and aired Loralee's room and made a lovely arrangement of Helichrysum and locust pods and pencil cattails and autumn leaves. The Helichrysum had been hanging upside down in the basement and the beautiful oak and maple leaves had been soaking for weeks in a glycerin solution. She called the arrangement, "An Everlasting". She telephoned the jewelry store and had them bring out a tiny little gift wrapped box.

All through supper and on into the evening Mother fussed and fumed. She said she guessed she didn't mind having to serve fish on Friday because fish is good brain food and we all should eat more of it than we do, as long as we are careful to eat the right kind of fish, that is those with both fins and scales, but— "What if he expects Polish sausage for breakfast on Saturday? I'm not serving pork in this house for anyone, I don't care if he's the King of England!"

Dad emitted a long sigh from behind the newspaper. Mother shuffled off to the kitchen, where Grandma was baking a cake and preparing pastry for pies. When Mother returned a few moments later her eyes were bright and her lashes wet and her nose was shiny red. She said, a bit wistfully, "Well, I'm sure he must be a good boy. Catholics are usually close family people, and Loralee has always had high values. Unless, you don't suppose she just got swept off her feet? Oh, my goodness! Surely not, Oh no! I just can't see Loralee, of all people, as a poor Mother loaded down with ten kids. Oh, it just makes me shudder! You know what they say about Catholic men; they want their wives barefoot, pregnant and in the kitchen!"

Dad slapped the newspaper together, folded it and slung it down on the table.

"Good God, Martha! Do you hear yourself? They were just married this morning and here you've got them with ten kids! Can't you trust her judgment? Loralee's twenty-two years old. You could look the world over and you wouldn't find a saner or more level-headed, beautiful, young lady. You can be sure she had the pick of the bunch. Why, there were any number of fellas around here who would have been serious contenders if she had ever given them any hope!"

Mother chewed on her lip and drew herself up to her full height of five feet, one and a half inches, and stood profiled in front of the huge gleaming mirror over the buffet. She moaned, "Just look at me. Here I am in this condition. Some Mother of the Bride!"

Dad said with quiet desperation, "They were married this morning. They are only coming for a short visit so we can meet him. Their time is precious! I think it remarkable that they want to spend some of that time here with us."

Mother pouted and snuffled and Dad began reading his paper again. Mother was buffing the silver service and muttering to herself. I was sitting at the table chopping pecans for Grandma, and Josh was busily hulling out walnuts. Mother began, "Well, I'll tell you, I'd be a lot happier about it if I'd had some kind of a warning. It just hadn't occurred to me that she would up and do something like this without even consulting her own Mother. And, what's more, I heard a preacher on the radio say that Catholics are the anti-Christ! They do such strange things and the way they believe, uumm ummph. I never could understand how supposedly intelligent people could believe that the bread and wine actually become the blood and body of Christ! It sounds so paganistic; like a bunch of cannibals! And those beads they use to pray with , and, you know, they don't pray to God. They pray to the Virgin Mary. Do you 'spose he. . ."

Dad took off his glasses, threw the paper on the floor, put his glasses in their case, snapped it shut and exploded. "I don't give a Goddamn who he prays to or how he prays or even if he prays at all! And I don't give a Goddamn for any chicken-shit radio preacher, who'd put down another's faith. Who's he to call someone else anti-Christ? God Almighty? Why do you listen to that bull shit? Let alone babble it."

"Riley! Your language! Olivia, take Josh and put him to bed."

Dad said, "I'll take him! Come on, Son. Let's go outside for a minute, and look at the stars!"

Mother hurried into the kitchen and started bustling about. Grandma had gone to the basement for another basket of apples. Dad stopped at the door, hesitated and said softly, "Martha? They'll be here tomorrow. He must be an exceptionally fine boy for Loralee to love him. You just forget all of that nonsense you've heard about Catholics! I know you're pregnant and upset, but you've been raving like a lunatic all evening and you've got all of us on edge. You must bridle your tongue! How in the name of Christ Almighty can Toot and Josh look on him fairly, after all of the bigoted harping you've been doing? He's already our son-in-law, whether you like it or not, and no amount of bitching's going to change it. Now hear me! I don't want one unpleasant word, so help me, God, not one unpleasant moment, while they are here in this house! Give him a chance! You may even like him."

The door clicked determinedly. Mother stared at the closed door and sighed, "I just don't know what gets in to him anymore. He didn't use to ever talk to me like that. He'd never say barnyard words in front of his Mama. And, here I am with child, and at my age. Why, I could be a Grandmother in less than a year! Oh, I just don't know what this world is coming to. All the nice Methodist boys, or she could have married a Baptist, but, oh, no! She had to go off up there and marry a Catholic, a Polish Catholic, for heaven's sake. Olivia! Go get the 'P' Encyclopedia. I'd better learn something about Poland."

I hurried to get it for her and then went outside to be with my Dad.

Dad held both Josh and I tight against him as we shivered and huddled for warmth on the front porch steps looking up at the night sky. It was cold and clear and the stars hung like precious twinkling gems in the blue-black field of unexplored space. Dad said, "You children mustn't pay any attention to your Mother's windiness. She doesn't mean it the way it sounds. You've both got a new big brother now. I'm sure you're gonna like him fine, and don't be bashful. Let him know you like him. Loralee's a fine girl. See the big dipper up there, Josh? Toot, look at that; absolutely brilliant."

A tall, broad-shouldered, dark-haired man in an olive-drab soldier's uniform with chevrons on his sleeves bounded down from the train. He swung Loralee down and held her briefly to him before they turned to greet us. His azure eyes were warm and friendly and he was more handsome than any movie star. He exuded confidence, authority and an unaffected charm that was winsome and magnetic.

"Dad! Mom! Oh, Grandma! This is Steve!"

Dad and Steve simultaneously extended and grasped hands in a firm handshake.

"How do you do, Sir?"

"Welcome—Son—Loralee!"

I thought I had never seen such a handsome man as Steve or such a radiantly beautiful girl as Loralee. They were so much in love; so obviously perfect for each other. He was affable and fun and from the very first hour we were all captivated by him.

Steve was fascinated with five-year-old Josh and he told me he had always wanted a kid sister. His parents had died when he was very young and he had been reared by his older brothers and sisters.

At the supper table he looked around at our family gathering, put his arm around Loralee and let his eyes linger adoringly on Grandma and said in an awed tone, "I thought I was the luckiest man in the world to win Loralee; but now, I know for certain, I really am, for she has brought me a whole family."

Early Saturday morning we gathered around the breakfast table in a subdued but congenial attitude. Steve said he felt more gratitude than he could ever express for "Dad and Mom" accepting him so readily and he expressed a hope that, after the war, Grandma would favor him with "some time for catching up" since he had never known his grandparents. Mother smiled sweetly and Dad assured him we were happy to have him and hoped it wouldn't be long before the war was over so he could be home for good. Grandma poured more coffee and gave Steve the gift and told him it was from his new family with love.

He was touched and surprised and said he was not accustomed to receiving gifts.

His big hands, with the shiny gold wedding band on the third finger of his left hand, seemed to dwarf the tiny, elegantly wrapped gift as he held it in the palm of his hand, smiling in self-conscious anticipation. Gingerly, he tugged at the bow and carefully removed the heavily embossed paper. A dark blue, velvet box was revealed. He opened it and stared and tears brimmed his eyes. He lifted the silver chain with the silver crucifix, touched it to his lips and slipped it around his neck. It clinked against his dog tags as he rose to embrace Grandma. Dad had his cold blue eyes fixed on Mother, who sat quietly, smiling sweetly.

Steve cleared his throat and said, "I know the sentiment is real, and the mode of expression is beautiful. Thank you, more than I can ever say, thank you!"

When train time came for their departure we were all so saddened to see them go. Although it was unsaid, we were all especially concerned for Steve, who was returning immediately for Europe. Mother hugged him and said, "Now I've got two soldier sons. One in the Pacific and one bound for Europe."

Steve put an arm about her shoulder and said with gratitude and affection, "And now, I've got a "Mom" to pray for me."

On Saturday, before Christmas, Mother had to go shopping for a few last minute items. She was very methodical about her shopping and had compiled a list which was guarded with much ado, shrouding it in secrecy while waving it before us temptingly with fanfare and teasing us that we had better be good for it was a list for Santa. Josh would get giggly and so excited he could hardly contain himself and we both enjoyed anticipating the good things, the fun surprises, that were bound to come from that long, carefully planned list.

Mother never signed the presents she gave us children at Christmas. They were always pretended to be from that unknown entity, Santa Claus. For us, anticipating what Santa would bring was as much a part of Christmas as the Candlelight Service on Christmas Eve and the actual opening of presents on Christmas Day.

Mother did not approve of children going to the stores. Only on rare occasions did we accompany her. Today, it was a matter of logistics. Dad had left early for the office. Grandma was visiting and shopping in St. Louis and would not be back for another day or two. Marj and Loralee were not coming home until Christmas Eve. Josh could not be left alone and I was needed to carry the parcels.

Josh pranced about and promised for the nineteenth time that he would not peek as Mother waggled a finger at him and gave him a playful threatening glance for the nineteenth time; called a taxi, and bundled her heavily corseted protrudence into her full-length stone-marten fur coat and griped that she looked like a brown barrel and Dad knew she preferred mink but one coat is as good as another as long as it keeps you warm. She tied a red scarf on her hair and pinned a stunning gold Christmas tree with red and green jewels on her lapel. She pulled on fur-lined boots, fur-lined leather gloves and tucked her well-kept list into her brown alligator skin purse.

There was a gay festive air about the city streets. The beautiful Christmas tree on the courthouse lawn dominated the town square. We stopped to read the list of honored dead and Mother noted that Dad's car stood alone in the county parking lot. We hurried on in the biting breeze, cheerily exchanging greetings with friends, neighbors and complete strangers.

Mother insisted that Josh and I stand just inside the entryway of the stores so she could shop unhindered. After three or four such stops and increasingly longer waits at each, I was loaded down with packages and Josh needed to use the bathroom.

Mother told me to put the parcels in Dad's car and to take Josh in the courthouse to the restroom there. She said she would meet us at Walgreen's for a nice treat. Josh drooled in anticipation of a cherry phosphate and excitedly darted ahead of me toward the courthouse. I hurried after him, dodging the bustling friendly folk who crowded the walks, and weaved between the cars parked double on both sides of the street. Josh helped me deposit the sacks and boxes in the back seat of Dad's car. We were both very careful not to peek or feel too closely. He was doing a free imitation of an Indian Rain Dance by the time we got inside the courthouse. The quiet courthouse halls were awesome in their austerity and the interior was as dark as a deepening dusk. Our footsteps echoed loudly and Josh's rubber galoshes squeaked on the gray marble tile. I told him to tip-toe or he'd wake the dead. He grabbed his private parts and jiggled all over while grimacing and making either laughing or crying sounds in his throat. I did not know where a light switch was, but Josh's need superseded his fear of the gloom. I told him the nearest restroom was in the basement, just to the right at the bottom of the stairs. Daylight from the street door paved the way and he ran for relief.

Dad's office was on the first floor of the south wing, near the street door. We had entered from the east wing so I walked the length of the corridor to the center of the building. As I turned into the south corridor I saw a woman framed in the open doorway to Dad's office. The light from his office served as a spotlight cutting a swath of soft light across the brightly polished, pearly marbled floor. She was laughing and stepped backward into the hallway. She had on a tight deep-rose pink skirt with a lighter pink sweater and she was standing as though she were showing off or posing like a Betty Grable or Rita Hayworth Calendar. Both hands were on her hips, her head was tilted slightly forward and to one side. There was a wide cinch belt about her waist and the pretty pink skin-tight sweater was accentuated by a strand of pearls that hung gracefully between her breasts. I had never seen anyone look or act like that outside of the movies. She tossed her chestnut colored coiffure about and flashed a bright, fushia smile to someone inside the door. She pivoted about on her high heeled shoes; then turned back toward Dad's office, bent forward with palms outward at shoulder level, emphasizing her full, well-rounded bosom and the long strand of pearls dangling between the soft pink mounds. She pursed her lips, as though for a kiss, shimmied, laughed, waved saucily and tottered off. Her tight skirt seemed to be alive with round moving objects. It was fascinating how one person could move so much in so many different ways at one time. Her unrestrained buttocks, in this day of corsets for ladies, seemed to vie for the eye as they moved the pink wool into ever-changing moon-like crescents.

She kinda looked familiar in a way. Kinda like one of the ladies I had seen on the Society Page in the paper. But, what was she doing here? At Dad's office? Why was she strutting around like that?

I heard Josh come running up the stairs and hurried to stop him. He made such a frightening racket just walking in the deadly quiet hall. I shushed him angrily and he demanded why. I was not sure why, but I knew I did not want Dad to know we were there. Goosebumps crawled on my flesh as I tried to quiet Josh so we could leave unnoticed. I coaxed him in whispers that bounced off the walls, to quietly hurry because Mother was waiting to buy us treats.

Mother was sitting in a booth with more packages piled beside her. She seemed to know everyone and people kept stopping at our booth for a chat. Christmas music was playing on the jukebox and Josh sat on his knees on the seat of the booth in order to reach the double straws of his cherry phosphate float.

A Santa's helper created a round of laughter when he came in on his coffee break and removed his beard to eat a piece of pie. Josh eyed him suspiciously, but Mother offered reassurance. "Oh, it's alright, Josh. That man's just one of Santa's helpers. He's not the real Santa Claus."

An older man in the adjoining booth took a great interest in Josh and began talking to him about Santa Claus. Josh announced that that man's beard wasn't real or he couldn't take it off like that. His new friend said,

"Well, I don't know, Son. Things aren't always like they seem. It'd be mighty hard to eat a piece of pie with all that fuzz around your mouth. Why, sometimes when I'm eating my teeth get in the way and you know what I do? I just take them out! See?"

He pushed his false teeth out and Josh yelled and then broke into nervous giggles. The man cackled, sputtered, and coughed. Mother was speechless. I was caught in a spasm of laughter which was only intensified when the man's wife stroked her index finger in shaming him for scaring that child. Others were looking at us as though they were wanting in on the joke.

Several of Mother's lady friends came in and spoke in friendly confusion. One of them, a Mrs. Rushing, leaned over Mother and whispering, inquired after Loralee and her new husband. Mother said distinctly and a bit too loudly that she could not be more proud of her new son-in-law; such a nice, good-looking young man and we could not be more fond of him. Mrs. Rushing's mouth oh'ed and she whispered again, "Is it true that he's a Catholic?"

Mother's eyebrows raised ever so slightly. She answered in an easily heard, but confidential, mellifluous tone, "Yes, he was reared Catholic and he was educated in private Catholic schools. They have to pay tuition, you know."

Mrs. Rushing said, "His people must be monied then?"

Mother smiled sweetly, as though with secret pleasure, and replied, "We couldn't be happier for Loralee and Steve. They are so much in love and such a striking young couple!"

Mrs. Rushing went hurrying off to rejoin the other ladies. Mother called a cheery "Merry Christmas" and under her breath added, "you old bats."

She got her slightly crumpled list out and guarding it against our inquisitive side-long glances, proceeded to check off a series of items. I said enthusiastically, " I know something Dad would really like to have!"

Without looking up, Mother asked, "And what's that?"

"An arquebus."

Her pen stayed in mid-air as she thought quietly for a moment, then looked at me with wide-eyed interest, "A what?"

I enunciated, "An AHR-kwee-bus! I heard him and Doc talking about them and Dad said he'd give anything to get his hands on an arquebus."

She said disgustedly, "It must be a gun."

Something went off in my head and in a flash I saw Dad's eyes: as Mother rebuffed his thoughtful gifts time after time; as they'd twinkle with merriment over some dumb gift we'd give him; as they darkened with disappointment when Mother hounded him about the guns or hunting, and as they hooded in sadness at her tirades. And then there was the pink lady laughing and posing. I blinked my eyes and drummed up all of the facts I could muster, "It's a small cannon that men can carry, Mother. It was really the first gun that they could carry into battle, like back in the fifteenth century. They're really museum pieces but there might be one someplace for sell. They had to car—"

Mother shook her head and frowned. "There's enough talk about battles and wars without you dragging up the fifteenth century! This will be the second Christmas that Alfie has missed being here at home. That poor boy! out in that God-forsaken hornets' nest like that. There ought to be a law against keeping them away from home for so long."

"Do you think he's got our package yet?"

Mother sighed, "Oh, I hope so! Some Christmas! In a foxhole."

Josh was making slurping noises with his soda straws as he tried to get the last of the froth from his nearly empty glass. I tried to get back to the subject of a gift for Dad without aggravating Mother too much. I used my sweetest tone, "Mother? You know how Dad always gives us such nice things? I wish we could give him something that would really surprise him."

Josh piped up, "Let's give Dad a cannon! Boom!"

Mother was annoyed and shushed him, frowning darkly. I knew it was a lost cause but I kept talking as a peculiar sense of desperation gnawed at me. "Mr. Wilkerson said he knows a man who's got a German Luger—maybe we could get him to get it for us. Dad would like that and it would surprise him or maybe we could get Dr. Matthews to let us buy his old blunderbuss. Dad's been trying to get that from him for years or maybe we could buy him a brand new gun! Oh, please, Mother, I know he'd really like a Winchester, or a Remington. Let's get it for him for Christmas! Please?"

Josh was squirming with excitement as he urged, "Put it on your list, Mom! Let's get him a gun. Dad likes guns! Put it on your list."

Mother gave me a reproachful look and scolded, "I wish you would show as much interest in your music as you do in those guns. I declare, I don't know what I'm going to do with you. The way you carry on, it just isn't natural for a young lady to be so taken with guns and such."

Discretion flew the coop. Begging was demeaning; wheedling was despicable and Josh's support was not helping matters any. The older man and woman in the adjoining booth seemed to be taking great interest in our conversation and I could feel my cheeks flush but a sense of urgency bade me press on.

"I know he'd really like it and I really wish we could do it, just this once, Mother, please? It doesn't have to be a special one. We could get one for not very much and I know he would like it!"

Some teenagers were looking at us as though they wanted our booth. Mother told them we were leaving very shortly and began helping Josh with his coat. The old gentleman cleared his throat and spoke to Mother in a voice anxious with hope. "'Scuse Me? Uh, I heard you talkin.' Just thought I'd mention I've got an old gun my Daddy left me—it's not a modern one, but it's in good shape to be so old. You can have it for ten dollars, if you want it."

Mother acted flustered and annoyed. She said sharply, "No, thank you! She was just talking out of school. I've no intention of buying anything like that. Thank you, anyway."

Josh begged, "Let's get Dad a gun for Christmas!"

Mother wobbled his head from side to side as she pulled his ear flaps down tight to fasten them under his chin. She cooed in honeyed tones, "I've already bought Daddy a couple of nice white shirts. Your Dad's just like I am. He isn't hard to please."

Mother glared at me as I implored her to talk to the man and see what he had to offer. She said, "It's just out of the question. I can't afford anything like that and I wouldn't be inclined to if he were asking ten cents, let alone ten dollars. Besides, I told you, I've already got a gift for him and it's the thought that counts."

Josh and I were waiting for Mother to pay the bill when the highly rouged, chestnut haired lady, wrapped in a soft brown cashmere coat, glided in. She looked at Mother and half smiled, as though she would speak. Mother looked right through her, as though she did not exist or was not worthy of recognition. I wanted to ask who she was but something in mother's demeanor stopped me.

Another lady, one of her Bridge Party friends, greeted Mother warmly, cheerily and cautioned her about not overdoing, "Or you're liable to get that baby for Christmas."

Mother laughed a shade too brightly and wished her, "Merry Christmas to you and yours!"

We plunged into the increasingly crowded walks. Santa's helper, beard back in place, was busily distributing red and white striped peppermint sticks to kids from one to ninety. A Salvation Army worker was ringing a bell at his collection pot and Josh clamored for coins to drop in. Mother fished some out of her purse for him and then held her hand to her head as people pushing by looked on with concern. I said, "Mother? Are you alright?"

She clamped her lips tightly, grimaced and then held her head high with an air of defiance and determination. She said, "I have bought everything I came after and then some. But, I really should get a few things at Kroger's while I'm here close by. We'll call your father from there. No point in me paying a taxi when, he's not 'spose to be working today anyway. I do hope things won't be too picked over. I swear, this town is growing by leaps and bounds and I don't see it as any improvement, either."

On New Year's Day, Mother gave birth to a son. It was the custom for the first male baby born in the new year to be hailed as the King of Nilesville. Merchants gave him gifts and there was a long write-up on the first page of the town newspaper.

Mother stayed in bed for three weeks and was completely isolated. She did not want to see anyone. Friends, out of town relatives, neighbors, even the minister were turned away without her seeing them, or without being allowed to see the baby.

Grandma was gracious and hospitable to those who called and expressed regrets that Mother did not feel like receiving them.

Miss Quinn, a tall austere nurse moved about the house in low-heeled white shoes. She wore a starched white uniform and white hose and Josh was terrified of her. I went to great lengths to avoid her, too. She never spoke to me and I could not interpret her looks. I resented having her in the house, but there were days when I did not even see her.

One afternoon when I got in from school, about a month after the baby was born, Grandma told me Mother wanted me to hurry right up to her room. I was a bit apprehensive because she had been so different since she had been in bed. It was strange seeing Mother with her hair down. It was long, to her waist, and wavy, but she had always worn it done up in a bun and I did not like it down. I had seen her a few times since the baby was born. Each time she had been either sleeping or absorbed in her thoughts and did not notice me.

The door to her room was wide open. Mother called to me cheerily, "Well, it's about time, young lady! Come in here and let me see you. My, you look nice today. Is that the skirt Marj gave you for Christmas? It looks like quality. Sit down! I've been waiting all day to talk to you. Since you've grown so much and what with us having a new baby I thought it high time I was warning you about the Curse of Eve so it won't creep up on you unaware. Mama didn't tell me anything and I'll tell you it really gave me a start. I thought I'd bleed to death. Of course, back then such matters just weren't talked openly."

Mother rattled on and on. She insisted on telling me about the birds building nests and singing and the bees humming and buzzing about from flower to flower and I really, God help me, couldn't put my mind to what she was talking about. But she was enjoying the telling of it and was unusually animated as she belabored the habits of the birds migrating and building nests and how the daddy bird goes out to search for worms to feed the baby birdies and there's only one Queen bee and she's the biggest and best and sometimes she has to fight tooth and nail, knock-down, drag-out, but then, it's all a part of God's great plan and that's where honey comes from, too.

I heard her voice drone on and on but the words just did not register. Miss Quinn had brought the baby in, laid him on the bed, and quietly left again.

Such a strange looking baby. I had never seen many babies, but, this one, was . . . so different. I had heard Miss Quinn telling someone on the telephone that he looked like he'd been hit with an ugly stick.

I realized Mother was through with her soliloquy. She was smiling patronizingly, "Do you have any questions?"

"Well, I was wondering, did I look like that?"

Mother was flabbergasted. I knew Dr. Matthews had been there nearly every day and each time had tried to tell her about the baby, but she had refused to listen to him. Dad had told her and she had tuned him out. She still refused to receive friends or well-wishers, insisting it was too soon. and, now, inadvertently, I had asked for a comparison; an opinion. I had caught her completely off guard. Mother looked all about the room, avoiding me and the baby. He lay, listless, on the bed. She ran her hand through her hair pulling it around over one shoulder and twisting it so that it hung in one long curl. She sat up, smoothing her bed jacket's lacy ruffles, and peered at the baby. She did not offer to pick him up. She frowned and looked at me, cocked her head to one side and observed, "Oh, well, now—as a matter of fact, uh, I, uh, but—"

Pain played across her face and I felt my own eyes brim with tears. Mother saw and exclaimed, "Why, Olivia! Are you crying? Did I frighten you with that silly talk about the Curse of Eve? Why, it's perfectly natural, Honey, and, it's nothing to be alarmed about."

I said, "I understand, Mother."

I considered telling her about the wonderful things Loralee had told me at Christmas time about "Loving" and "Caring" and "Fulfillment" and how marvelous the relationship between husband and wife can be, but I sat mutely, staring at the baby, and anxious to leave.

She sighed a smile and said brightly, "Well, then, if you've no more questions?"

Words sprung from my throat: a question I knew the answer to. "Mother, Josh didn't look like that, did he?"

She took a deep breath and chewed on her lip. She picked the baby up and cradled it awkwardly in her arms. She turned the little blanket back and seemed to scrutinize him. He was oblivious to all that was going on. She looked from him to me and off into the distance. When she spoke her voice was soft and wistful and seemed to come from far away. "Josh was such a pretty baby. Each of you were healthy and pretty and . . . The doctor's always bragged on our babies. And you twins, oh, words cannot express . . . how beauty . . . So much fun and laughter . . . we've never been so happy as . . . Billy was perfect! I swear that's why God took him . . . he was just too perfect for this world!"

She looked at the baby in her arms, and a shudder of revulsion shook her and she put him down on the bed as bitter tears coursed down her cheeks. She blinked her eyes and cleared her throat and forced a bright cheerfulness, "But, then, no two babies are alike. I mean, after all, each is poured from a different mold. Michael David, poor little thing, won't win any beauty prize, but he's still the King of Nilesville!"

Mother used the hem of the sheet to wipe her eyes and then leaned toward the baby cooing, "Yes, you are—you may not know it yet—but you are the King of Nilesville. It looks like we're just going to have to be your slaves."

She sat back and said to me, "He can't help it about his skin and hair and the way he looks, but I think he will improve in time. His little eyes have some kind of infection. I don't remember what the doctor called it, but his medicine will clear it up in no time."

I asked hesitantly about friends coming to see "the King of Nilesville", for there were many asking to come and see him merely because of all of the publicity. Mother's voice was brittle as she snapped, "No! They shouldn't even ask such. We're not in any condition to be having a houseful of people in. What if one of them brought in a cold germ? Or, maybe something worse? No, now, you just tell your friends that you are sorry but the baby isn't well and you are not allowed to have company in now. I know they're curious, I mean about him being the King and all, but they'll just have to wait until a better time to see, uh, to come and visit. He'll soon be better. Just as soon as the medicine can take effect. But, in the meantime, I don't want anyone outside of the family in this house. Do you understand that, not even Dean or Kathryn or any of your so called friends!"

I do not know when, where, or how come, but Dad hit the ceiling over the dumb title. I suspect that the irony of it was too much for him. Mother used it repeatedly, for the first six months. But, then it was dropped and seldom referred to again.

I missed having friends in to visit after school and on weekends, but I soon learned at Grandma's heeding, to fill the empty hours with music or reading or painting. She suggested interesting books, not just classics, but biographies and novels of history, romance and suspense. There were times when she would surprise me with a new song book or a sheet music of a popular song or a spicy fiction or a light fantasy from the public library, because, as she would smilingly say, "Variety is the spice of life and your Dad's library is a bit heavy for one so young."

We would browse through the bookcases at home and she would give a synopsis of one of her favorite books or volumes and they soon became my favorites, too. Her tastes were as varied as a spice rack, and she laughed that one should nurture the mind just as one feeds the body; a bit of nourishing meat, a tasty vegetable, a little broth, something crisp, and a nice dessert.

She was partial to Shakespeare, Edgar Allen Poe, the Bronte' sisters, F. Scott Fitzgerald and O. Henry. She confessed that she had never liked Chaucer or John Bunyan or Robert Burns and that Grandpa had teased her about her lack of appreciation for his favorites. She would reminisce about how she and Grandpa would sometimes sit up all night reading when they first got electricity. She would talk about how they would laugh and marvel about how much brighter and cleaner the electric bulbs were than the candles or the oil lights or the kerosene lamps.

"Why, even if electricity were not good for anything else, we thought it was well worth the price just to have it to read by."

Books replaced friends. We left them laying all over the house and would read several simultaneously, depending on which room we were in or what subject we fancied at the moment.

Grandma began asking me to read aloud to her as she sewed or ironed or prepared the meals. She liked the short stories in the kitchen. Sometimes I would feel a little self-conscious reading aloud about unseemly, shocking things. When I was reading her Aldous Huxley's, "*The Nun's Luncheon*", Grandma would insist I read with expression and enunciate and try to sound just like Miss Penny telling it so matter-of-factly. I tried. When I got to the climax, where the woodsmen found the toothless nun in the shack and thought her daft, Grandma was laughing with delight and beaming with mischievous pleasure. I really didn't think the story was funny but I got tickled at Grandma. Neither of us noticed Dad in the doorway until he said, "What's so funny?"

Grandma said, "Have you read, 'The Nun's Luncheon'?"

He nodded a sober yes. Grandma nearly lost her composure laughing. Dad looked on helplessly. He gave me a questioning look and said, "Mama?"

Grandma murmured, "Miss Quinn."

Dad began a low chuckle, caught a breath and roared with laughter. It sounded so good!

The reading of a novel or a story was only the beginning. Grandma would ask who wrote it and when and why and what did I like about it? Were the characters real and was there a free flowing continuity that swept one along like a tide? We would discuss them at length and sometimes reread favorite passages. Our all time favorites were biographers such as Bruce Catton and Carl Sandburg, whose works were sheer pleasure to read. We would talk about Washington and Lincoln at the supper table as though they were old, much-loved friends. Dad approved wholeheartedly and bought any and all volumes that we showed even a nodding interest in.

The baby did not cry for the first several months. I would not see him for days at a time. But, there were times, terrible times, when Grandma would be heartbrokenly sad. I heard her and Miss Quinn talking one day in hushed tones, and I didn't really understand exactly why, but it scared me when Grandma said she had lived too long, too long.

Dad usually had to go to some meeting after supper. On the rare occasions when he stayed home we would go to the basement and melt lead for musket balls and talk until bedtime. He would take Josh up on his lap and tell us some outlandish tale of Teddy Bear. Of course, the bear always got the best of the hunter or any other animal and usually ended up in the artichoke patch happily munching on artichokes. The end of the tale seemed to coincide with the fire going out or sleepy eyes beginning to close. Dad would be so pleased when Josh would giggle and react and he would sometimes say, "Alfie used to laugh at that, too, just like I did when I was a boy. But, I'm afraid your baby brother will never understand it."

Mother refused to acknowledge that anything was wrong with the baby. One day I heard her telling someone on the phone, "Why, I've never had a better baby. He's eight months old and he just lies there and sleeps. He's never once cried at night and he seldom makes a sound during the day. Oh, he's fine. Dr. Matthews gave me a different prescription for him but it hasn't had time to take effect yet. Oh, I let Miss Quinn go. She wasn't doing a thing except drawing her salary!"

The real reason Mother let her go was no secret. Miss Quinn had tried repeatedly to explain to Mother about Mongolism being a congenital mental deficiency, and the fact that there was no cure for such. She had pointed to the obvious physical signs: the rough yellowish-tinged skin, the small head with the flattened forehead and the weak slanted eyes, the wiry hair and the protruding tongue and lop-sided jaw, the tiny arms and legs and the spade-like hands. She had boldly stated that he could never be more than an idiot or an imbecile at the most and that he should be placed in an institution where they could give him the proper care and perhaps even teach him as time went on, to do some things for himself.

One day, Mother crossed her arms, cocked her head to one side with a wide eyed stare and said with child-like innocence, "Why, Miss Quinn! I can't imagine why you persist in telling me such things. My baby's just fine. And now, I want to thank you for the good service you've given me and I'm sure you can find another position without any trouble. We'll be fine here on our own."

Grandma did everything about the house and meals. Mother was irritable and restless. Her tone assumed a bitter resignation to "her plight", which she adamantly and constantly claimed to be "God's punishment". She railed against any suggestions of putting Michael in an institution, insisting that she would care for him, but delegating the actual tending of him to Grandma or me. Dad would assume the duties at night and in the early morning.

Mother laughed that we were all "slaves to the King".

11

❡ HIS EYE IS ON THE SPARROW

On a cool rainy day in April we received word that Mr. Aiken had died of a heart attack while walking to his second job of the day. For nearly three years he had held two jobs, working a full eight hour shift daily and nightly at two different plants. He had lived meagerly and had invested every dime over living expenses in US war bonds. In his coat pocket were several letters and cards from different ones of us, his 'family'. We suspected that he had some idea of his impending doom for he had left a will. In it he expressed fondness and familial ties to all of us, regrets that his own children spurned him, his desire that all of his earthly earnings and holdings be divided evenly between the Red Cross and the USO, a wish that his body be cremated and his ashes scattered in some out of the way place.

Grandma had had a black wreath hung on the front door. Mother wondered aloud if she should put a gold star in the window for him. No one of us doubted but what he qualified by having died in the line of duty.

I wasn't hungry at suppertime. My insides ached. I stayed in my room and lay on my bed and played the beautiful silver music box and reread the three Christmas cards with their brief hand-written messages that Mr. Aiken had addressed to me. I remembered how he had teased me, threatening to cut off my ears, and then later, how funny it was when he would tease Josh. Grandma had said many times that she had never realized how much he did until after he left and there was no one to do the hard work.

The music box ran down. I rewound it and the happy lilting tune of *Fur Elise* tinkled out filling the room with sunshine and birds singing and flowers coaxed to perfection and the wind turning the leaves before rain and dark wooly worms predicting winter and a big red juicy apple, warm with the sun, right off the tree and a deep friendly voice booming up, "Did ye hear the mockin' bird?", and then as the music wound down a hoarse low voice, comforting, "There, there, Missy. Don't fret. We gotta do what we ken to stop the Japs and that hateful Hitler and that mean ole Mussolini, so ye ken go to France and see that Eiffel Tower fer yerself."

The music stopped and as I rewound the turnkey the setting sun burst through the clouds, momentarily bathing the yard in a bright glistening golden light. The brightness and the memory of a familiar figure whom I would never see again teared my eyes. I hoped Mother would put a gold star in the front window for him. He would have liked that. After all, he was kinda a member of the family. The music slowed again and then stopped. I opened the box and studied the mechanism closely. If there were only some way it could rewind itself while it was still in motion so it wouldn't run down, then it wouldn't stop. I wound the little turnkey and watched the tiny wheels activate the brass cylinder with its needle-like notes rotating it round and round. The precisely placed needles played like delicate fairy fingers on the tiny shiny keyboard. The music slowed and was about to stop. There was no way I could keep it going. The way it was made, it had to stop. It wasn't intended to go on and on. There was no way to keep it going. There was nothing I could do about anything. Hopelessness and despair mingled with grief. It wasn't fair, to die on the street like that, all alone, just like a . . . vagrant. He had worked so hard, for so long. Working in the war plants was his way of fighting the war. It was almost as though he had died in battle. He did, in a way, so he was a hero: Yes, by cracky, a hero, a real flesh and blood war hero. Just as much as MacArthur, by God! He used to say he was just a Missouri mendicant, beat by the depression and too tired to fight. Mother said he was a bitter old man thumbing his nose at convention. Grandma said she thought he might be an 'angel unawares.' I bet he never thought anyone would call him an angel. Oh God!

I was awakened sometime later by Grandma tucking a quilt about me. She had put the music box and the Christmas cards back on the dresser. She patted me on the arm and whispered softly.

"It's alright, Toot. Mr. Aiken and your Grandpa will get along fine."

"Grandma? Someday I'm going to go to France and see the Eiffel Tower with my own eyes."

The war was taking a heavy toll from our small corner of the world. The fresh black ink seemed to emphasize the most recent names added to the growing roster of honored dead. Old men, withered with age and worry, would stand in front of the hastily erected, but now permanently fixed, bulletin board that had been placed on the courthouse lawn. Four spotlights shown on it at night. They were placed in the front at four intervals so the entire board was bathed in light. No one name stood out over the others. Each was illuminated brilliantly. The men may have begun life unequal in birth and opportunities, they may have begun their military service unequal in rank and responsibilities, but they had each given their ultimate in defense of their country. They were equal in their death. We were careful to honor them equally.

Hoards of people paused in their shopping to read the names, to remember the faces and to retell the old familiar stories of childhood pranks, teenaged antics and the battlefield or oceanfront heroics of our boys, our heroes. Laughter, evoked by sweet memories, would turn to sob as the hometown folks shared their sorrow, their grief, their bitter losses, and they wondered aloud when would it ever end.

I could never remember when I first heard the voice. It seemed to be a part of the countryside. It was at one with the wind that blew up from the woods, or on the gentle breeze that swept across the fields. Sometimes I would hear it as I lay in my bed at night waiting to drift off into sleep. It usually seemed to be coming from a far off distance; other times, it would be so near I could distinctly hear every word, every note, every nuance.

The voice was a clear soprano, light, lilting and true in tone. The songs were patriotic or canonical or popular sentimental ballads that were somehow, peculiarly personalized. *When Freddie Comes Marching Home Again, My Country Tis Of Thee, America The Beautiful, Dona Nobis Pacem* (Give Us Peace), *I Know Whom I Have Believed, Give Of Your Best To The Master, Now Is The Hour, Oh Freddie Boy . . .* and a hauntingly beautiful song that Grandma used to sing, ". . . *sing because I'm happy . . . sing because I'm free . . . for His eye is on the sparrow . . . and I know He watches me . . .*"

As the days went on and the voice continued, I would frequently walk or run toward the woods or the open fields in order to hear more clearly. Some said it was a crazy woman. Dean told me it was Mrs. Andrews, a widow, whose only son, Freddie, had been killed in action in the Philippines. He said that she lived in a small cottage in the woods, just on the side of our property line, and that she was a very nice lady, whom they had called, 'Singing Sally.'

Money matters, per se, were never discussed at home. I never knew how much Dad made or what the expenses were. When Mother received her inheritance it was not a matter of conversation as to amount, but rather her dismay that her father's estate had dwindled so and that her own brother had cheated her out of most of it.

Mother claimed that she did not like to keep books or bother with accounts, but her records were meticulous. I marveled, on the rare occasions that I saw her record books or bank books, at the neat and tidy columns and the systematic detailed accounting. It was a paradox that her papers could be so precise and her speech pertaining to such so vague and absurd. But it was a serious matter with Mother. "*It isn't nice to talk about money matters. A lady never discusses her expenses or discloses her income.*"

Repeatedly she alluded to our "*dire straits*" and of "*the wolf knocking at the door.*" It was her ability to "*get by on a shoestring*" or "*squeeze Abe until he shrieks*" or knowing how to "*rob Peter to pay Paul*" that kept us out of the '*poor house.*'

If one expressed real concern about a financial need Mother would equivocate, "*Oh, we'll manage to scratch it up*" or, "*Well, I just don't know how we can afford another penny for anything extra, but I've never denied you a day in your life so you needn't worry about it now.*"

The high school had a new cafeteria. School lunch money was a daily source of contention as the dimes and quarters and sometimes half-dollars were doled out with advice on how to spend them sparingly and an admonition on how hard they were to come by, "*because quarters don't grow on trees you know but I know you have to eat or at least you think you do so I'll get by somehow. I always have and it's sure a good thing somebody around here cares enough to be saving or I'll tell you, there wouldn't be a penny for anything.*"

Mother considered the practice of giving allowances to one's children as an insult and a sin. If we broached the subject she would get huffy and render a scorching tirade against the sinfulness of gold-bricking: "*I'm not rearing you to be a malingerer and if you get it in your head that you're going to get something for nothing than I've failed miserably for there's nothing in this world that's free and nobody owes you anything. Now if there's something you need or anything you want, you know I'll be glad to get it for you and you've not a thing to worry about. I know you like to have things the other children have. But I've got eyes to see and ears to hear and I know for a fact that you've got more than most. But you can just get this allowance business out of your heads. I'm not going to have any shirkers around here and that's all these weekly allowances, as you call it, is good for, and there's no use in talking to your Dad about it. I hold the purse strings in this house and it's a good thing I do. Why, if it was up to your Dad he'd spend every last cent on guns and there wouldn't be milk and bread money let alone anything else. Those guns don't pay the light bill and here that new preacher had the gall to want me to raise my tithe. Why,*

I've tithed all my life for it's the right and proper thing to do and I know they have to budget and know what they can plan on but that's a horse of a different color and I don't want another word about allowances. But now don't you ever hesitate to tell me if you need something, Honey. Why, I wouldn't have a one of you in want for anything and you know I'll do without myself, if necessary. I've always put you children's needs before my own and I'm not going to stop now, but I'd be derelict in my duty if I encouraged you in thinking you can just live free and easy on some allowance."

If one tried to enumerate the merits of "learning to budget" the quick response of *"Now don't get your dander up!"* or a hurt reproachful, *"I just don't know what to think. I just can't believe you'd doubt my judgment and after all I've done for you children. It just goes to show the more you do, the less it's appreciated."*

Grandma never alluded to Mother's refusal to me of a weekly allowance. But she called me to her room one Sunday evening and said, "It has occurred to me that a certain young lady should have some practical experience in budgeting to go along with those pretty pillow cases in her hope-chest."

She handed me a small ledger and a five dollar bill. "I'll forward you five dollars each Sunday evening. You don't need to give an account of it to me. But, just for your own edification, keep track of your expenditures. See there where you list your credits? That's money coming in, and, of course, debits, is the money going out and here's for listing what you save and what you donate."

I thanked her and as I was leaving. She said, with twinkling eyes full of understanding, "Perhaps we should not voice this about. We'll see how things are in a month or two."

Our family had always been involved in the community activities. We children were in Scouts and 4-H and attended the Epworth League and went to church camps. The church had pot-luck dinners and Vacation Bible School programs for parents and ice cream socials. Mother griped and fussed over preparations for such functions although it was Grandma who nearly always actually prepared the foodstuffs. Mother's concern was for her recipes.

"I can't take a cake or a salad to anything without some nosey woman, whom I don't even know asking me for the recipe! Can you imagine the nerve of some people to just walk up and say 'How'd you make that icing?' Why, I just feel like telling them to go jump in the creek and one of these days they're going to get me at the right moment and that's exactly what I'll do. It's no one's business how we make

*icings or anything else for that matter and if we tell them then they'll
be doing it too and then how can you have anything special if everyone's
doing it?"*

Grandma would quietly, obligingly, copy down some recipe and tell
the recipient to enjoy it in good health.

Grandma never disagreed verbally with Mother. She was careful not
to belittle or undermine her in any way. She never argued. She never
seemed to be bothered by Mother's oft-times escapism in totally self-
engrossing, seemingly mindless rhetoric. The prattle in itself could be
tuned out and was not overly distracting. It was akin to a radio playing
constantly; sometimes you listen but ordinarily you don't.

Grandma would quietly pay the milkman and the delivery boy from
the grocery store and give them tips because we lived so far out. They
loved her. If it happened that Mother answered the door they'd have to
wait for her to check over everything, *"I can't afford to pay for
something I don't get"*, question something, bemoan how much it'd
gone up and wait while, *"I'll just have to see if I can find that much,
I'll tell you, it's just something every time I turn around and the way
everything's getting so high it's just about to price me out of house and
home."*

She'd count out the cost to the penny and thank them kindly. The
travesty was demeaning and the men resented her tight-fistedness and
her detaining them with her distrust and unfounded suspicions of being
overcharged. And, of course they talked, and speculated and wondered
aloud. In a small town such eccentricities can be bantered about and
clucked over until they become not a matter of concern, but rather,
just another tidbit of general knowledge.

There was a strong bond of affection between Grandma and Mother
that was evident in many ways. Mother gave her love, respect and honor
and held her opinions in high esteem. Grandma brought out the best
qualities in Mother and she cultivated them and tended them and took
pride in her abilities and frequently attributed Mother with thoughtful
deeds and acts of kindness that were in fact her own. Grandma's
personality was like a fresh mountain stream that stems from a deep and
steady source with sweet refreshing nourishment year round. Mother
was more like a bubbling brook that goes dry in the heat when you need
it most or becomes a raging torrent during a storm, beating relentlessly
at your very foundation.

Grandma was thoughtful and contemplative: Mother was opinionated
and chattered like a magpie.

Grandma was like a thermostat that controlled the emotional climate
of her environment. Mother was like a thermometer that hung out in the

elements registering the extreme temperatures, ranging from an aloof cold-shoulder indifference to a fevered frenzy of activity and verbalization.

Mother was mercurial, quick-witted, volatile and changeable. Grandma was a metronome: steady, sure, dependable, and always supportive.

They were not competitive. They never criticized nor demeaned each other. Mother was glad for Grandma to do for us children. She claimed to be totally absorbed with the "baby."

Grandma had a steadying influence on Mother. She also served as buffer between Josh and me and the churning, chilling, unpredictable acts that grew out of Mother's obsession with Michael David.

My social life centered around school and church. The fact that Josh and I were not allowed to have friends at home affected us differently. I had always had friends visit me after school and on the weekends. They liked to come to our home. It was larger than most and it had the added advantage of being in the country. To suddenly quit a common practice had created a lot of mystery, speculation and inquisitiveness. As time went on, even good friends made cruel comments about us having such a nice big place but never having any parties or friends out. I learned very quickly that if one does not reciprocate in small social niceties, one is soon dropped. When I tried to discuss it with Mother she said it was of no consequence: that they didn't like me anyway, they just wanted to use the house and, more than likely, were just curious about the baby, and she wasn't going to have them nosing about for any reason.

Josh quickly grew accustomed to going to his friends homes for play. When his friends came to our house, they had to wait at the door for him and then they would go out in the woods or down by the creek to play. Grandma and Dad had fixed up a playroom in the basement so he could have friends down there on a rainy day or during wintry weather. He had been yelled at on occasion when one or more would start to enter the house from the front door or want to go to the kitchen for a drink, or run upstairs to use the bathroom if the others were busy. Mother was a terror against those she saw as *intruders.* We had not celebrated a special occasion with relatives in since Michael David's birth. Mother was too busy to discuss it whenever the subject came up or would suggest someone else have it this year. Grandma always stayed home to care for Michael David. She said Mother needed to have a nice time and to get out and visit with her folks. She would tell her to relax and have a good time. So, Mother would spend the entire time talking about Michael David and her hard life.

The year I was a high school freshman, Dean was a senior. He was a good student and did well in all of his studies. He had little interest in the extra-curricular activities, but he was very popular and had many friends. Several of the junior and senior class girls had crushes on him, and everyone knew that Dean and I were neighbors and friends.

Many of the clubs and groups that I participated in required extra hours of meetings or practice after school. Every time we performed, Dean was there.

One evening, after a grueling, but fun, performance of *Rio Rita*, Dean had come back stage and waited for me to take me home. Marcia, a beautiful soprano who had played 'Rita', saw Dean waiting for me. The next week she started pestering me to tell Dean how much she liked him and begged me to get him to ask her to the Senior Prom. She was so pretty and popular and had never even talked to me before. It made me feel kinda important and I told her I would tell him.

Saturday morning I ran across the pasture that separated our properties and found Dean in the barn.

"Dean! Hey!"

"Hey yourself, Toot."

"What're you doin'?"

"What's it look like?"

"Muckin' out."

"It's part and parcel."

"You goin' to the prom?"

"Nope!"

"Dean—I know somebody who'd like to go with you."

"Can't take a freshman."

"Oh silly! I don't mean me. She's a senior."

"Who?"

"She's pretty and smart and she'll go if you ask her."

"Who?"

"She's liked you for a long time."

"Who?"

"You sound like an owl!"

"Owls don't say 'who', they hoot. Sometimes it sounds like 'Toot'."

"Does not."

"Yep."

"She's very nice, Dean."

"Most people are."

"She really wants you to ask her. She really likes you a lot."

"Welp! Ya gonna tell me who?"

"Marcia. Marcia Williamson."

"She's pretty."

"Um umph, and she likes you."

"She said so?"

"Um umph. You goin' to ask her?"

Dean stood in front of me looking at me intently. His tone changed slightly as he asked, "Ya want me to?"

I felt a pang of something. It was not clearly defined, but, I suddenly had doubts about him taking Marcia, or any one else to the prom. He stood within two feet of me. It was almost as though I hadn't really looked at him before. Six feet of tanned muscle and those piercing blue eyes and that . . . kind of feeling. . .

"You're very handsome, Dean, and, you're getting so tall and muscular."

"Ya want me to ask her?"

"Well, . . . I thought it was a good idea, . . . I mean, she asked me to ask you, . . . to ask her. Ohhh."

"Toot? If a senior could take a freshman, would you go with me?"

"Why, of course I would!"

Dean grinned and threw a forkful of hay in the stable.

"So, why try to push me off on someone else?"

"Dean! You know Marcia's a senior and she, . . . she's begged me all week to tell you to ask her. . ."

"I'll wait for my girl to grow up."

"That's not funny. If you don't ask her she's gonna be really mad at me and she'll probably think I didn't tell you what she said and we were just getting to be friends."

"Toot? If I'd wanted to go, I'd have asked someone 'fore now. I'm not bashful, ya know."

"Dean?"

"Yeah?"

"I'm glad you're not going."

"I figured you would be."

"Guess I'd better go home. I've a lot of lessons to get."

"Ya wanta go for a quick gallumph?"

"Oh yes, let's!"

I really liked school and I tried to devote all of my energies to studying. Mother had started delegating more and more of the care for Michael David to me. Either Grandma or Dad would usually intervene and tell me go on and do my lessons.

When I won a contest in speech and drama and was asked to give a Shakespearean speech on the local radio station, I ran all of the three miles home to tell Mother and Grandma.

Mother said, "Well, how nice."

Grandma was so proud and happy for me. She made tea and asked me to recite it for her, and that night at supper she told Dad and I recited it again.

The day of the broadcast I was beset with anxiety and feeling nervous about being on the air. What if I forgot? What if I got a frog in my throat? Grandma shushed my fears and said,

"I'll be sitting right here in the study listening. Just pretend you're talking to me."

I did, and it was so easy. Later, Grandma complimented me on it. Mother was so sorry she had forgotten to listen. I was disappointed that she had not heard me, and I asked, "How could you forget?"

Mother answered off-handedly, "Oh, it doesn't matter. I've heard you practicing and knowing you, you'll probably be on again sometime. Besides, I had to feed the baby and you know how long that takes. But, there'll be another time, you can bank on that, and it wasn't that I don't care for Shakespeare, although it's no secret I've always thought he was nothing more than a dirty old drunken Englishman who just happened to have a way with words."

Mother forgot to listen. The big moment for me, and Mother forgot to listen. Dad had heard me on his car radio. Josh's teacher had the whole class listen and he had beamed with pride as he told me of how everyone thought his sister did a good job and that his teacher said so too. But, Mother forgot to listen.

Grandma and I were tidying up in the kitchen following supper when Dean came riding up the lane with Jinx in tow. Grandma said, "Here comes Dean, Honey. My, that boy has grown so, and he's so handsome. You go on. I'll finish up in here."

I went out on the back porch. Dean swung down and called,

"Shakespeare would've been proud!"

"Did you hear me?"

"Yep, wouldn't have missed it."

"Did I really sound OK?"

"Couldn't have been any better, Toot."

"It was so much fun. I think I'll try out again next year."

"You'll probably get it. I'll be up at the university then, but, I'll listen."

"I don't like to think about you leaving, Dean."

"Ya gonna miss me?"

"Oh, you big lug! You know I will, just like a tooth ache."

"That didn't sound very Shakespearean."

"Mother didn't even listen to me."

"Hey, come on! Mom and Dad both heard you. They thought you were great. I'll bet your Grandma did too, didn't she?"

"Yeah. I pretended I was talking just to Grandma. It kept me from being nervous."

"Toot?"

"Yeah?"

"Do me a favor?"

"OK."

"Next time, pretend you're talking to me?"

"Ohhh, alright. You'd be as easy as Grandma."

Dean sighed and rolled his eyes. He moved over to adjust the straps on Jinx's saddle and said gruffly, "If ya wanna go for a ride you'd better go get changed."

"Oh, I do, Dean. I'll just be a minute."

"I'll be right here."

12

A WHITE HORSE – A BLACK WREATH

It was a mild spring day. A delicious cool breeze bearing whiffs of new life; fragrant flowering shrubs, freshly cut grass, and upturned soil, was welcomed into the house through wide open windows. I could hear the steady hum of Mr. Swanson's tractor in the South field. The old oak tree was alive with the happy chittering and the bustling activities of the newly-mated birds building their destined nests of promise in preparation for their young.

It was hard to concentrate on my history term paper. Dean and I had been going horseback riding on Saturday mornings for many months. But Mother was still peeved at me for making Jinx rare up on his back two legs while Josh was riding double with me. Josh told her he had begged me to do it. Anyone could see he was thrilled with it by the way he giggled and begged me to do it again, "... just like Gene Autry." But, Mother only saw inherent danger in such antics: *"What if you let him fall? Why, he could be crippled for life! That horse could fall over backwards and squash you flatter than a pancake. Now, I'm not going to have you jumping that horse or making it do any of those foolish things. If you can't just sit on it and ride gentle like a lady then you just don't need to ride at all!"*

She had forbid me to go riding this morning because of the impending due-date of my term paper. She had harangued on, *"... first things first ... work before play ... you can't learn any younger ... keep your nose to the grindstone. . ."*

I knew not to argue with her. I reluctantly acquiesced to her heeding that I finish the assignment, "now."

181

I had completed the research and writing of the assignment and was ready to try out my newly acquired typing skills on the typewriter Dad had given me for my birthday. But, I had a clear view of the horses from my window. I never tired of watching them or of admiring their sleek coats as they grazed and milled about the pasture of sweet clover. The pastoral scene was so conducive to day-dreaming and sketching and the slightly chilly April breeze felt so good right in front of the window and the horses seemed to be posing for me, so, I eagerly reached for my sketch pad and chalk.

Sometime later I heard Grandma's voice, excited and curious, calling Mother. She was at the dining room window which was just below mine. "Martha! Martha! Look at that horse! It's going to take that fence!"

Mother's voice floated up from the kitchen window, "Where, Mother? What horse?"

"That big white mare! What a beautiful animal! Oh, look at that! It sailed right over that fence just as smooth as silk! Who does it belong to? Why, it looked like my old Nellie."

Mother's placating voice queried, "What horse, Mother? I don't see any white horse out there."

"It was right there in the pasture, Martha. A big white mare, but it jumped the fence and went in behind those trees. 'Minds me of Nellie. Such a beauty. . ."

There were seven horses in the meadow: four that were primarily black with white markings, two that were brown with black markings and one chestnut. There was not and had not been a white horse in sight. None of the horses had jumped a fence.

A sense of alarm shot through me numbing the very core of my being. I raced downstairs. Mother was standing by Grandma's chair. Her voice had an anxious note of concern that belied her calm query, "Are you feeling alright, Mother? You're looking awfully pale."

Grandma's face was blanched white with blue veins straining on her smooth forehead. She clutched her chest and seemed to be struggling for a deep breath. Mother told me to get a wet towel and ran to phone for the doctor.

I held the towel to Grandma's forehead, feeling awkward and presumptuous. She tried to smile her thanks and then, with great effort, asked, "Honey . . . did you see . . . that . . . beautiful . . . horse . . . jump . . . that fence?"

I could feel and hear the awe in her voice and as Mother hurried back with a blanket, I answered, "I wish I had, Grandma."

Mother wrapped the blanket about her and said the doctor was on his way and that Dad's secretary was going to get word to him to come home as soon as possible.

Grandma lay her head back but seemed oblivious to the wool cocoon. She seemed to relax a bit and tried to smile but her facial muscles wouldn't comply. Her speech was slurred and seemed to require great effort, but she continued talking about what she had seen.

"So beautiful . . . must have been sixteen hands . . . of grace . . . good breeding . . . My Nellie . . . why . . . that's been . . . sixty years."

Tears clouded her eyes and she caught quick shallow breaths of air. Mother wondered if we should carry her to her room, but Grandma chided her for making such a fuss and insisted she was comfortable there. She began breathing easier and mused, "Surely that wasn't a messenger of death. Such a beautiful white horse. Strange, neither you nor Toot saw it."

Mother kept looking signals to me expressing how worried and anxious she was, but to Grandma, she acted calm and as though there was nothing to worry about. She said, "Now, Mother Mason, don't you think things like that. The doctor'll soon be here and everything'll be fine. I imagine I was just too slow getting to the window and Toot had her nose in her books, so, you don't worry about us not seeing it. It's possible Mr. Swanson got a new horse or maybe he's keeping it for a friend."

Grandma sighed wearily. Her earnest efforts bore convincing, though barely audible, whispered words on unsteady wisps of breath.

"So lovely . . . I . . . see . . . Trust. . ."

I had been sitting on the floor at Grandma's feet while Mother held the wet towel against her forehead. Grandma's eyes seemed to be looking far into the distance, questioningly.

She spoke softly, "John?"

Grandma slumped forward, unconscious. Mother held her in the chair, enveloping her in loving words and soothing tones interspersed with orders barked to me. When she realized that Grandma could not hear her she gave vent to her own anxieties.

"Put that window down, that breeze might be too chilly. Why, there wasn't a white horse out there! Will you hurry up? Just push on it! Hard! Bring me a hassock! My back's about to break. Messenger of death, indeed! Why, Mother Mason never believed in superstitions. Where is that doctor?"

I dragged the heavy hassock from the study and placed it for Mother. I stood quietly, feeling helpless and close to tears as Mother tucked the blanket tighter about Grandma and crooned, "Now, you listen to me, Mother Mason, you're going to be just fine. Why, you haven't been sick or had any warnings of anything serious. This must just be a fainting spell. I'm sure that's all it is. Olivia, go turn off the oven and take those pies out before they burn up! Put then on the wire rack; I don't want the counter-top scorched! Where is your Father? Is that the doctor's car? What's taking him so long? Did you turn off the oven?"

Michael David had awakened from his morning nap and was howling for attention. I did everything Mother said, running from place to place, each time hoping Grandma would revive, wake up, and be fine by the time I got back. Mother's tone grew more impatient as Michael's incessant howling tore through the house.

"Oh, I wish that child would shut that up! He sounds like a wild animal! Will you go see about him? He's probably crapped all over everything and you'll have to wash his eyes again! Make him hush that insane howling! Good-for-nothing spoiled brat!"

I hurried to tend him; dreading the sickening mess, repulsed by the strong odor of feces and urine, repelled at having to clean and wash a boy of six who still lived in diapers and required cleaning several times a day.

The logistics were physically straining. Michael weighed over sixty pounds. he still had to be lifted in and out of his crib. He was not at all toilet-trained. He could not yet stand up-right by himself, and would, upon awakening, sit up and scoot about his crib. Usually, as on this occasion, a diaper change also meant sheets and blankets had to be changed too. When the feces was thin and soaked through the padding to the rubber sheet, it required an immediate cleaning and airing, or the room would be permeated with a dead mouse smell.

I resented having to clean him. The revolting smell gagged me. The smeary, pasty feces was spread all over his buttocks and groin and thighs. It was smudged on the sheets and blanket and caking on the legs of his diaper. Involuntary retchings tore from my throat as I went through the necessary motions of cleaning him; steeling myself against the unpleasantness by repeating in my mind, *Don't think about it; just do it.* Aloud, I cooed, "Don't cry now. It's alright, now. Shhhh. Don't fuss. He's a good boy."

His little watery eyes were nearly glued shut with the habitual yellow discharge. His oversized tongue protruded from his lower jaw that was jutted forward in a peeve. The howls had subsided to a guttural growling, interspersed with gleeful sounds.

He liked the soothing tones. He also liked being cleaned and washed and would giggle idiotically whenever the groin area was cleaned. But he hated having his eyes cleaned and always fought it. He was double-jointed and would flop his hands and legs about in such bizarre positions that one had to be constantly alert to keep from being unintentionally hit or kicked. I had reached my full height of five feet, five inches and weighed about 108 pounds. Tending to Michael was a mammoth task in every respect. I nearly always had bruises on my arms and legs from him.

I heard voices downstairs. I knew both Dad and the Doctor had arrived. I was worried about Grandma and hoped that Mother was right that she had only had a fainting spell. I wanted to go downstairs and find Grandma well and laughing about some little pleasantry. But, Mother had told me to tend Michael and that meant doing everything that needed to be done. I dressed him, bundled up all of the soiled things, put fresh sheets on his bed, adjusted the air wick, placed him in his playpen, gave him a bottle of milk, tried to brush the wiry hair on his unusually small head into some semblance of a combing, turned the radio on to some music, mixed more boric acid and boiled water so it would be ready for the next time, and then, fraught with exhaustion, anxiety and apprehension, I made my way back downstairs.

Mother was standing in the doorway to Grandma's room, her shoulders heaving with silent sobs, her hands covering her face. Dad stood at the side of the bed as the doctor pulled the sheet up over Grandma's face.

Dad walked over to the window and stood looking out. Scalding hot tears streamed down my face and I choked on sobs that wrenched up from my innermost being. I seemed to be engulfed in a reddish-orange world that was spinning crazily. I heard someone screaming, "No! No! She can't die! Not Grandma!"

The doctor was waving ammonia under my nose as I coughed and sputtered and gasped for breath. Dad was half-holding me in his arms. I saw the hurt, fear and relief in Dad's eyes and heard Mother exclaiming, "Why, I've never known that girl to faint before. It must be the grief. She and her Grandma were just about inseparable, but, I'd never have dreamed she'd just faint dead away like that."

Dad carried me to a chair. The Doctor patted me on the arm and said he was sorry about my Grandma but that it was really better this way because she wasn't in any pain or having to depend on someone else.

Mother told them, almost ver batim, about Grandma seeing a white mare jump the fence, and how she had looked and there wasn't a white horse anyplace about and Grandma had said that maybe it was a death messenger.

Doctor Matthews stroked his chin. "Humph. A death messenger. That's interesting: most interesting."

Mother acted flustered. She said, "Now, Doctor, you mustn't get the wrong impression. Mother Mason wasn't superstitious. Her eyes must have just played some kind of trick on her."

Doctor Matthews adjusted his glasses, cleared his throat and fixed Mother with a benevolent look. "Well, Martha, I'll tell you. I used to be quite skeptical of such stories, but, I've heard some very convincing ones over the years. I don't doubt for one minute but what she actually saw, exactly, what she said."

Mother chewed on her lip deep in thought. Dad and the Doctor went into the study to call about arrangements. Michael began howling again. Mother looked nervously toward the stairs. I stood up on my wobbly legs, amazed at how weak and dizzy I had become. Mother said, "Do you feel like tending him for awhile? We've got to call Katie, and, oh, what a shock it'll be for her! I just hate having to tell that poor girl her Mama's gone. And there are so many others to be notified. Of course, we'll have her laid out here, and then, the service, I don't know . . . she never did join the Methodist Church . . . still kept her membership in that little Calvin Presbyterian, even after all of these years. My, she was generous with them, too. Of course, she'll want to be buried down there next to. . ."

Michael David seemed to be getting louder and louder. My senses seemed numbed, but my ears were roaring and a feeling of nausea cramped my stomach. I said, "Mother, I've got to go lie down. My head is splitting."

Mother looked from me to the stairs and back to me. She looked incredulous and her tone was mocking. "You've got to go lie down? Your head is hurting? Well! I've got news for you, young lady. There's no time for that kind of foolishness. If you've got a headache then take an aspirin. Now I know you think you don't feel well, but there's nothing wrong with you but grief and the best thing for you to do is to keep busy. You can go tend to Michael so I don't have to worry about him. Maybe when Joshua comes in from his ball game—oh, what a shock he's going to have. Umm umph! One just never knows. He'll help you when he gets here, but for now go quiet that poor baby. It just isn't respectful, him carrying on like something out of the wild."

"I wish you would let Dad put him in an institution. He'd be happier and so would we."

"Now that's enough of that! I've got enough to think about without you starting in on that. People will be coming in here in spite of everything. Oh, I don't know what to do first. I'm so glad she baked those pies. I must order a black wreath. I'd better go right now and call Anderson's so they can bring one out. Oh, how I hate those things! Is that the hearse here already? Go make him be still! And see to it that you keep that door closed. I don't want anyone nosing around up there!"

I watched from the window in Michael's room as the long, black hearse pulled away from the front porch and slowly made its way down the lane. Dr. Matthews followed in his black Chevy coupe. Within a few short minutes Dad's black Buick sedan shot down the lane swirling dust crazily behind it. I could see Mother talking animatedly and pointing toward the pasture. A sense of desolation swept over me suffocating me with its intensity. I wanted to cry and scream. I was inexplicably afraid and angry at being left so alone.

Michael was content. The gentle midday breeze stirred the mobile over his play-pen. He was staring intently, as though fascinated with the Mother Goose characters that were turning about.

I wandered through the house; a sense of anxiety gripped me every time a board creaked or my scandals squeaked. It was so quiet, so empty, so desolate. There were reminders of Grandma in every room. An open book and her reading glasses were on the library table. I picked up a few yellow blooms that had fallen from the spray of wisteria that Grandma had arranged a few days earlier. The aroma of the freshly baked pies that she had baked that morning permeated the kitchen and dining room. Tears stung my eyes as I entered Grandma's room. The bedspread had been thrown back and left in a tumble. Mechanically, I straightened it. An unfinished letter to Aunt Katie lay where she had left it on her writing desk. It looked to be akin to a page from a penmanship exercise book. The letters had been perfectly formed with a fine-tipped pen dipped in blue-black ink. I leaned over the creamy white sheet of linen stationary that bore Grandma's initials embossed in gold in the upper left corner and read:

"*Friday evening, My dear Katie,*

How very sweet and kind of you and Ralph to invite me to make my home with you. It is very tempting. Perhaps, in a few months, I shall be able to. But, for now, I feel I must do what I can to ease the burdensome worries and cares that weigh so heavily upon the hearts and minds of those whom we love so dearly, here.

I trust that in time Martha will accept the inevitable and place this pitiful child where he can receive the proper care. You must not worry about my health. It is fine. Do give my love to Kenneth when he calls you. Thank God he will soon be home now. I hope and pray his wounds heal quickly. We have not heard from Alf for over two months. Steve is a Captain now. He said in his last letter that he thought it would be over soon. Please tell Sharon I am sorry I could not attend her birthday party. But I am delighted she likes the suit. Your Father always loved that shade of blue. . ."

I wondered if Dad or Mother had seen it. It was written to Aunt Katie. A pang of guilt stabbed my consciousness at the realization I had read it uninvited. I opened the top drawer of the writing desk and found a matching envelope. I took Grandma's long, slender, black and gold pen from it's holder, dipped it in the ink well and wrote across the envelope in my best script, "Aunt Katie."

I folded the unfinished letter, slipped it into the envelope, sealed it and propped it against the inkwell. I thought it strange that Grandma had not finished it. She always wrote her letters before retiring. Had she been ill or in pain? She was not a complainer, but, then, too, she did not lie and she had written that her health was fine. Yet, she had sometimes sighed that she was *"bone-tired"*. I had seen her, after she had been tending Michael David, sit down with her hand on her chest, breathing deeply. I had asked her if she was alright. She had answered with a sigh, *"I'm just tired, Honey. That boy's almost too big for me to grapple with."*

"I'll change him, Grandma."

"I know you would, Honey. You do more than your share. I'll be rested in a moment."

My head was throbbing with a dull ache. I pressed my hands against my temples. The pain and the grief were too acute. Tears streamed down my face and hollow sobs wracked my body as I collapsed on Grandma's bed.

After the wave of grief was spent I became aware of a light flowery fragrance. I inhaled deeply and felt a sense of calmness. The smell of Grandma's cologne seemed to linger about the bed. The mattress was soft and yielding as I snuggled on it. I let my fingers trace the raised intricate maze-like pattern of the snowy-white heirloom bedspread. The pattern seemed to go on and on and following it with my fingertips was confusing unless I looked at the whole segment. The same pattern seemed to be in turn, a snowflake, a flower or a maze with no obvious solution. It all depended on how you looked at it.

I remembered Grandma talking about the tapestry of life: *"each stitch is important; each day is valuable."* I traced the patterns as far as I could reach without having to shift my position. A snowflake, a daisy, a snowflake, a daisy. God! Why did she have to die? The desolation of death seemed to enshroud me in a dense fog of gloom. Yet, the sweet light fragrance lingered, and I remembered another time when Grandma had commented on death:

"Honey, death is natural. It is just another side of living. You can't keep snow from melting or flowers from fading. There's a time for all things. That's nature. But, you must remember that the snow becomes water and the flowers live on in their seeds. Our souls live on, too. It is all a part of God's plan."

The guttural ululate broke my reverie. Anger and resentment burned in my chest. I stared at the ceiling and, aloud, asked the space above me,

"Why? Why didn't you take him instead of Grandma? Grandma's good and kind and wonderful. He's not even human! He's disgusting and sickening and putrid. Why didn't you take him? All he does is drink and pee and eat and shit and tear every body's lives up! Why do you let him live?"

The howling grew louder, more demanding. Reluctantly, I lifted myself up from the comforting bed. A red-orange world whirred about my head as I bent over to smooth out the wrinkles I had caused on the bedspread. A feeling of heaviness pressed upon me. My head felt too heavy to hold up. There seemed to be a vise-like grip on my chest. My legs were rubbery and the room seemed to be spinning. I stood at the foot of the bed, leaning against it for support, trying to calm the inner turmoil, fearing the consequences of losing control.

The angry yowling persisted. I knew he had either wet his diaper or the mobile had run down. I wondered if there were any new batteries in the house as I methodically plodded up the stairs to tend the needs of the living.

The hall clock chimed the time of two o'clock. The sun hid behind the now threatening rain-laden April clouds. The breeze grew chilly and blustery. As I went from room to room to lower the windows I would look at the clocks, wishing the time away. Where were they? What was keeping them so long?

Does it really take such a long time to make "the arrangements"?

A car scrunched slowly up the long graveled lane. I walked out onto the front porch as old Mr. Anderson lifted the black wreath from the back of the old station-wagon that he used for deliveries. I shuddered involuntarily with a chill.

"Hello, Mr. Anderson."

"How are you, Miss? Looks like it's gonna blow up a shower. Yer folks here?"

"No sir. They've gone to. . ."

"Mighy sorry 'bout Miz Mason. Yes, it's a mighty sad time. She was a grand lady. My wife made this special."

He held the black wreath for me to see the fullness and the mastery of placement of the preserved materials. A wide black satin ribbon was intertwined about the wreath and topped it with a large double bow. I said, "It was very kind of her."

"I'll put it up for you."

I tried to brush the goose bumps off my arms as Mr. Anderson secured the black wreath to the front door.

He stepped back to check the symmetry, adjusted the bow, and, then, turned to go. I thanked him. He hesitated, cleared his throat and asked, "Don't know when your folks'll be back?"

"No, sir. Anytime, I hope."

"You here alone?"

"Yes, sir."

He seemed to be looking inside the front door. I realized then that technically I was not alone, for, Michael David was in his room. But, for all practical purposes I felt alone. Mr. Anderson cleared his throat again and started down the steps. "Tell your folks to let me know if I can be of service to 'em. I 'spect they'll be needin' some things."

"Yes, sir. I'll tell them."

I started to say "Thank you" but I remembered Grandma's graciously warm expression of gratitude. I said, "Thank you kindly. We're much obliged."

Mr. Anderson stopped, tipped his hat and said, "I'm glad to be of help."

His long strides carried him quickly across our newly-greened lawn. I watched him climb into the old stationwagon. Bracing myself with a deep breath I turned to face the hated black wreath. I looked closely at it and was amazed at the perfectness of each item and the loveliness of the design. Strange. I had seen many of these symbols of mourning, but I never really looked at one. I had thought them morbid; to be dreaded for their gruesomeness. But this black wreath was exquisite in its' beauty. The dark brown magnolia leaves had a soft velvety texture. The clumps of black bell-like blossoms shone with a brilliance and were rubbery to my touch. Tiny dew-like droplets of glycerine hung like accents of jewels from the miniature, but preciously preserved, petals.

I felt a scant trace of the glycerine on my fingers and automatically rubbed them together, relishing the familiar soothing feel of the commonly used preservative, medicine and skin-care agent.

Josh and I had frequently helped Grandma gather autumn leaves for preservation. She had taught us how to carefully trim the clusters and then submerge each one in the "Magic Mixture" that would nearly fill the old blue-enameled roaster pan. We would turn the clusters biweekly and add water to replace what had evaporated. Josh and I had both been fascinated with the growing changes in the colors and feel of the leaves and branches as they slowly but surely responded to the "Magic Mixture." Grandma had been patient with Josh's determined but unorthodox attempts to measure the amount of water that evaporated between the turnings. He had insisted on trying to measure it with a yardstick as well as counting the number of gallons needed to bring the solution back up to the original line.

"Whip 'er will, whip 'er will, whip 'er will."

The soft whistle-call roused me from my reverie. It came from the roadway and I turned and looked with eager anticipation for company. Emotion welled within me when I saw Dean hurrying up our lane. He waved and I ran out to meet him.

"Dean!"

"How ya doin', Toot?"

I was so glad to see him. He seemed to emanate strength and a comfortable presence. A feeling of relief crumpled my composure and tears gushed from my eyes. Dean put his arm about my shoulder. He smelled of horses and fields and woods. He was a head taller than I and his shoulders seemed to be as broad as a wall. The wide raveled brim of his old straw hat caught and pulled strands of my hair as we walked toward the house, but he did not notice and I did not care.

"I heard your Grandma died. Don't cry, Toot. Death isn't the end."

"Who told you—about Grandma?"

"Singing Sally. I was mending fences out around the West field. She told me she had seen the hearse here."

We stopped at the front steps. The black wreath seemed to dominate the entire front of the house. I questioned the beauty I had seen in it earlier as I felt anew the heavy weight of grief in my chest. Dean said, "It's a pretty wreath. Toot, I'm sorry about Mrs. Mason dying. I really liked her, a lot. Mom and Dad did, too."

We sat down on the steps in the shrinking shaft of the afternoon sun. I said, "I never thought about Grandma dying. I already miss her. . ."

"Yer folks go to the funeral parlor?"

I nodded, and griped, "They've been gone forever. I hate being here alone!"

"Do you want me to stay with you?"

"You know Mother!"

"Yeah . . . Are ya havin' to watch the boy?"

I nodded again. Dean leaned forward resting his elbows on his knees. He frowned and said in a low disapproving voice, "They shouldn't leave you here alone . . . especially now! Where's Josh?"

"Ball practice. He doesn't know yet."

The weight of all that had happened since Josh had left that morning seemed to press upon me. The tears of tiredness, grief, confusion, frustration and remorse began again. Dean's eyes were brimming, too. He took his hat off and twirled it in his hands.

"Don't cry, Toot. Death isn't the end."

"How do you know?"

He shrugged, shifted his position and stared off into the distance as he answered on a sigh.

"Sometimes ya can't explain, at least, not like a math problem where there's only one right answer."

"You mean it just depends then, on what you believe, whether it's true or not?"

"I didn't say that. . ."

"Do you believe in premonitions?"

"I'm not sure. I've heard some pretty convincing stories. I think I've read every book in the school library on dreams and superstitions and psychic phenomena."

"All twelve of them?"

"Big deal! Ya must have looked yerself if you know how little is available, but, that stuff doesn't appeal to me as much as the Bible and the Discipline."

"You've read the Discipline?"

"Didn't you?"

"No, I didn't think anyone did, 'cept preachers."

"Well, you're just a little kid. What would you know."

"Dean!"

"Why did you ask about premonitions? Did you have one?"

I told him about Grandma seeing a white horse jump the fence just before she had the heart attack and how she had been so positive about it, but neither Mother nor I had seen it and we both had looked.

Dean listened intently. He told me of incidents he had heard of and mentioned several reasons why he believed that physical death was only a transfiguration to a higher form of life.

". . .just like a caterpillar sheds it's skin and comes out a beautiful butterfly. Our spirits just shed the skin at the time of death and live on in some heaven-like state."

"You really believe that, Dean?"

"Seems like a lot of things point to it. Why, I'll bet your Grandma is watchin' us right now, like a guardian angel. You know, always lookin' out for ya, 'cause the love and the caring live on just as the spirit lives on."

We sat in companionable silence for long moments. I heard Michael David begin to howl. I groaned and stood up and Dean got up as though he were going to leave.

"Dean? Don't go! Oh, I wish you could come in. I've got to see about him. Please, wait for me?"

He sat back down on the steps.

"I'll be right here; visiting with Mrs. Mason."

I laughed as fresh tears filled my eyes, "Oh, you're spooky. Would you like an orange?"

"Sounds good."

The beautiful black wreath swayed gently as I opened the door to go in to tend to Michael David.

"Dean? Thanks for waiting for me. Do you think he knows . . . about Grandma?"

"He knows, Toot. Maybe not the concept of life and death, but, he probably senses something is wrong. Be kind."

13

🔫 EVERYBODY OUGHT TO KNOW

Mother was at loose ends after Grandma died. She went off in all directions at once like a bazooka gone berserk or a loaded cannon spinning wildly on a broken pedestal. When her wrath was spent she would flounder like a rudderless ship lost at sea. One could not be near her without feeling dread or guilt, pity or shame. She used words for ammunition to capture and hold and command. But there were times, pitiful times, when phrases, and poorly thought and less well-expressed concepts, would be mouthed in a sea of befuddlement that was attributed to tiredness and worry. The rantings and rages would dwindle to the bemoaning, "*I just don't know which way to turn. I've nothing to hang on to. I feel like I'm drowning in troubles and no one cares enough to toss me a raft. I wish there was someone who cared. I just don't know what I'm going to do. The whole world is going to pieces, and no one cares.*"

Alf had tensions of his own. After four years in the Jap and malaria infested jungles of New Guinea and the Philippians, Alf was just another member of the Secret Shell-Shock Society who had a double-whammy as well: Malaria; complete with the night sweats and the uncontrollable trembling chills when he would be wrapped in an army-issued green wool blanket, even on steamy hot and humid days and nights. There were times when his skin would be a yellow-brownish color and the whites of his eyes would be yellow and red. The turmoil of our home life compounded his adjustment to peacetime.

Michael David had the characteristic appearance of the mongoloid child, which was in itself strange and pitiful. It was especially hard for Alf to deal with after his years in hell fighting the Japanese in the Pacific.

The blood-curdling howls for attention from the 'pampered and spoiled idiot' would frequently begin around three-thirty or four o'clock in the morning, awakening Alf from his nightmares, catapulting him from one battlefront to another. He would pace the floor unable to go back to sleep. He grew even more gaunt and nervous and started drinking heavily.

Mother could not understand why he let every little thing bother him. She thought it unseemly for one to be so touchy and sensitive and lectured him dutifully on that and every other subject.

Alf could not stand the confines of a building or being in close proximity with strangers. He did not want help, or what he construed as pity, from anyone. He could not understand what had happened at home, and would lament. *Why has everything changed so? Why is Mother so bitchy? Why don't they put that idiot in an institution? Why doesn't Dad do something about it? If only Grandma were still here."*

He would drink himself into a stupor and express his frustrations in monosyllabic oaths.

I learned to live in a state of ambivalence. As a means of keeping my sanity I developed an armor of stoical indifference. But it wore thin quickly as I was torn between loyalty to my own "hero" and to the much-preached, blind respect due one's elders.

I idolized Alf, but he would turn on me with a blistering pent-up wrath when I would try to explain or make excuses for Mother's behavior or Michael's condition. It was a red-orange world of love and hate. I would try to find a balance: measure the good against the bad; think of beautiful things; do what you have to but let your mind soar to a higher plateau. Feed the slobbering idiot; be gentle and kind as you try to teach him to use the spoon. Listen to Caruso and Evelyn McGregor and Thomas L. Thomas. Think on beautiful things. Let your hands do what they have to, but let your spirit soar. Praise him, praise him; who? Michael David of course, for his remarkable accomplishment of finding his mouth with a spoon. Speak cheerily. Don't fret about the dropped food or he will grow sullen and refuse to try. Clean it up as quickly as it is dropped and don't let him get discouraged. After he has tried a few times then hand-feed him the rest. The motions are mechanical; think about the music.

One evening, Alf stopped in the kitchen on his way out, to watch. "How can you stand to do that?"

"Someone has to."

"Why? Do you get a kick out of it? Do you like playing nursemaid to an idiot that doesn't even know his mouth from his ass hole?"

"He's learning, Alf."

"Shit! He's learning like hell. Where do you get off thinking you can teach him anything? Are you trained to work with idiots? Is that all you're going to do for the rest of your life?"

"He has to eat."

"Why? Tell me why, Goddamit!"

Michael David had had one fit right after the other all afternoon. His jaw jutted forward and to one side. He stuck his tongue out and began to chew on it and began a low guttural growling As usual, when he started getting upset about something he began to flail his arms about. The fact that his arms and hands were double-jointed made it even more likely that one would be hit and that accidents and spills would happen. I tried to grab the plate, but he knocked it from my hand onto the floor, where it landed upside down. I said, "Oh, what a mess. Well, at least the plate didn't break."

Michael David was staring at the mess on the floor and jabbering. I said, "It's OK. We'll get some more."

"What's OK about it? You're going to fix him another plate of food, fit for a King, when he doesn't know how to appreciate anything? Why? Just so he can throw it on the floor again?

"Alf, please!"

"Oh, alright! I'm leaving. I've had a belly-full just watching you try to feed that spoiled bratty imbecile. And I think I feel a puke comin' on."

Alf had started toward the back door. "God, Toot. How can you stand to do that?"

Tears of self-pity streamed down my face and uncontrollable sobs wracked my body as I tried to explain, "I have to, Alfie. You know how Mother is. It makes me sick too, and I hate it, but I have to do it. I don't know why: I . . . I . . . just . . . have to."

I so dreaded having to clean up the mess and start all over again. I put my hands over my face and without realizing it murmured, "God help me."

Alf stopped for a few seconds, came back to my chair and pulled me up. He wrapped his arms around me so tightly and held my head against his chest. "God, Toot! I'm sorry. I don't mean to hurt you. For Christsake! You're just a little kid, yourself. I just feel so Goddam helpless. I know Mom's got a thing about tryin' to shove him down our throats. I know, too, that she's really rough on you. I wish I could protect you, Toot. I just feel so helpless. You shouldn't have to be doing any of this caring for him."

I fought to stifle the shameful crying. Michael was howling again, louder and began a piercing siren-like wailing. Alf cursed. Mother came rushing in on a tide of words. "Why, what in the world is going on in here? Such a racquet! Whatever did you do to the poor boy? Did he get choked? I've told you time and again to be careful not to give him too big of a bite. He just can't handle it."

Alf kissed me on the forehead and turned toward the door, as I hurriedly started cleaning up the mess on the floor. Mother looked at Alf and then back to me and said, "What in the world is the matter with you? Why, you ought to be ashamed of yourself! A great big girl like you crying like a baby. There's absolutely no excuse for your behavior. You're old enough to control yourself. Now clean up that mess. And get him another plate of food. You'd think I could trust you to just feed the baby without creating some crisis!"

Alf had stood quietly by, watching and listening. He said, "Shit! Mom, that's no 'baby'! You ought to put him in an institution where they have people trained to handle him. It isn't right for Toot to have to take care of him."

Mother feigned indignation and whined, "Why, Alf, he's alright. It's no trouble caring for him. I'm the one who sees to him. There's no one else around here who ever bothers with him. I'm the one who tends him night and day."

I was struggling to lift Michael out of the chair so I could finish cleaning up the mess. He had gained so much; he weighed about eight-five pounds and it was all in torso. Alf offered to get him. I stepped aside while he lifted him down. He whistled, "Whew, God, he's heavy! Mom, Toot shouldn't have to be lifting him. He's as big as she is."

"Why, it doesn't hurt her to help once in awhile. She's as big as I am, but then, it stands to reason, no one cares about me."

Alf stared at her, shook his head in exasperation, and said, "Shit!"

Mother caught her breath sharply, as he stormed out the door. Michael sat on the floor, staring expectantly at me. I got his glass of juice and knelt beside him, holding a towel under his chin as he drank. Mother looked at us in disgust. "Put him back up in the chair. You're getting so you treat him like he was some kind of an animal. It doesn't hurt you to help with him and I'd better not hear you complaining about it again, young lady, or you're just liable to find out who has the last word around here."

Mother had no patience with Michael David, but she was adamant that he not be placed in an institution. She blamed Dad for his condition as well as his birth. He would try to appease her but she rejected all supplications. He suggested having help for him at home, but she steadfastly refused to have anyone in, maintaining he was her responsibility and she would see to him. She usually referred to him as *"that poor baby"*, but we all heard her yelling at him that, *"You're just like a pig wallowing in your own filth! You don't have the sense God gave a goose! Stinkin' up the whole house! Oughta keep you out in the shed, and if you don't start using the throne that's where you're going to go!"*

One never knew what would tick her off, so Josh and I tried to be careful not to disturb her. I helped him with his homework and in daily matters that had previously been done for both of us by Grandma. As I did for him, Mother noticed, and began adding duties by wheedling,

"Honey, if you don't mind, that just looks so good and I haven't had a thing all day, or even a chance to think about eating; why don't you just do that for all of us for supper?"

I would iron my things and Josh's pants and shirts. Mother would wonder aloud, *"Since you've got the iron hot, perhaps you'd like to iron those shirts for your Dad. I just don't have time to get them done. Oh, there's a couple of housedresses you might touch the iron to. You don't have to be too careful with them, since they're just for me and it doesn't matter what I look like around here. If you want to do those pillowcases and tablecloths I sure won't stop you, for they've got to be done."*

Mother hated housework and simply would not do any. So, my Saturdays became housework days for me. After awhile friends quit asking me to do anything on week-ends. Mother's demands were endless.

She griped that cooking was a thankless task; a drudgery that no one appreciated. So, I began cooking, baking and preparing full meals. It was taken for granted that I would tidy up the kitchen. If I needed to go to the school or church for an evening, she would say, *"Well, if you don't get it done before you go, you can just count on it waiting for you until you get back."*

The washing of clothes was done on a Maytag wringer washer. I was terrified of the huge wringers that the clothes had to go through before and after being rinsed. Mother had told me horrendous tales of people losing their arms in them and I had nightmares of getting caught in the wringer. Josh would try to help me with the weekly wash and thought me daft when I would yell him away from the arm-eating monster.

Completed tasks were never mentioned again; no show of appreciation, no sign or word that it had been done. If something was not done properly, after it had been mentioned or suggested, the ensuing scolding would begin with, *"If I've told you once, I've told you twenty times, that you've got to. . ."*

Dad made *good money* and was *generous to a fault*, according to Mother. He gave her over and above what was needed for household expenses and shopping, but he did invest in guns. It was a constant source of contention that caused painful bitter bouts of arguing that would usually lead to a discourse on how he, and he alone, was responsible for Michael David's condition. The accusations would bounce back from the walls and the pervading guilt-laden gloom intimidated us. Josh and I were ashamed, embarrassed and confused. We tried harder to please her, to amuse her, to help her, but our hearts went out to Dad.

Mother was a champion at thrashing it out with raillery, badgering, haranguing, harping, prattling, sermonizing, moralizing, ranting and raving with innuendoes and accusations rife with blame, censure and reproach. She never cussed or used bad words. She never cried and only seldom raised her voice above normal conversational tone. It was the constant fusillade that was nerve-wracking.

Josh and I discovered, after the first few 'attacks,' as we came to call them, that she followed the same pattern each time. It was like playing a record over and over. Somehow, the repetitions, being able to anticipate what was coming next, tended to lend some respite. Comments or responses were not expected or wanted nor was time allowed for them. Mother talked non-stop. Josh and I would send little eye signals to each other offering encouragement. It was a matter of survival and concern for each other. There was nothing we could do for Dad, and Alf avoided any confrontations with her.

Dad was a gentleman; a man of compassion and great patience. His eyes showed the pain of her piercing, berating attacks. At times his shoulders would sag, he would rest his head on his hand as though bedazzled, bewildered and caught in a web in a corner of hell. But he never complained about Mother. He would sometimes pat us on the head or the arm and say sorrowfully, "I'm sorry, Toot, Josh. I sure wish things could be different."

He always encouraged us to, "Mind your Mother now. Do what you can to ease her."

There were times when he would apologize for her, asking us to be understanding.

"Don't let this bother you. She doesn't mean it against you. She's sick with worry. She doesn't mean to hurt you."

As time went on, Dad began leaving the house during stormy attacks. Mother would be incensed and pout and plan and talk to herself about how he was going to pay for his escapades. Then, he began leaving when he sensed the storm clouds gathering. But, Mother would not be denied. She would flay him mercilessly at breakfast with a barrage of words that tore and pierced and shattered the ears, hearts, minds and very souls of us all.

In a first hour English class one morning our teacher, Mrs. Dawson, became thoroughly aggravated with the drowsiness of some of the students. She began talking about the merits of a good breakfast to wake one up and make one more alert. She asked, "How many of you had breakfast this morning?"

Only about half of the class raised their hands. She then asked, "What did you have?"

There were various responses of, "Eggs and grits."

"Shredded wheat."

"Pancakes."

I had raised my hand signifying I had eaten, but then I remembered I had not had a thing. Mother had had one of her fits and the bickering was not conducive to eating. I had only sat at the breakfast table.

The list of new words and their meanings, that we had been assigned the day before, were still on the blackboard. I read, 'Polemic: of or involving dispute; controversial; argumentative; an argument or controversial discussion; a person inclined to argument.'

Mrs. Edwards asked, "Olivia? What did you have this morning?"

"Polemics."

Her eyes widened. She smiled and said, "Over the funny papers, I hope?"

I smiled back. She asked if the class had understood what I said. There were murmurs and groans and an occasional horse laugh. I felt more relief than I had known in a long time. What was it Grandma had said? *A merry heart is better than medicine?* Try to find some humor in every situation. How can you find humor when there is nothing funny? 'Polemics' for breakfast: I bet Dad would smile about that.

When school was out for the summer, Josh and I conspired to toilet-train Michael David. We watched him constantly and rushed him to the bathroom periodically for the ritual we had decided upon. Modesty took a back seat as we did what we had to do. Michael David was afraid of the commode at first. We cajoled and coaxed him and held him steady until he overcame his fears and began to understand and respond cooperatively. It took weeks of constant surveillance, but he eventually mastered recognizing the impending need and would rush to the bathroom in time to avoid soiling his clothes.

Josh taught him how to stand and hold himself to urinate. He could not manipulate a belt buckle, so we had him wear suspenders to simplify letting his pants down for a bowel movement. After using the commode he would point and jabber, shaking his finger in the air as though scolding, adjust his clothing, carefully push the lever on the commode, and wobble his head about, laughing as he watched it flush and refill. He would lower the lid, step to the basin and proceed to wash his hands. He would lather them until they were white in thick soapy suds and hold them up for our approval. He would laugh as he held them under the running faucets watching the suds swirl away. He would carefully dry his hands on his towel, refold it and place it on the rack. He would look in the mirror, pat his hair, shake his head in congratulatory greeting, turn off the light, and carefully place the door in a half-open position.

It was a milestone. It eliminated the dreaded, smelly, laborious tasks of cleaning him and changing his clothes repeatedly. Josh and I congratulated ourselves. Dad bragged on us. Mother griped because he continued to wet the bed at night.

Marjorie came home from college for her summer vacation. She was absorbed in her newly acquired religious activities. She seemed to view Josh and I as nuisances and made no attempt to conceal her disdain for Michael David. Alf called her a fanatic. Mother fussed that she was loafing; wasting good time when she should be working if she wanted to go back to school in the fall.

Marj asked repeatedly to have meetings, Bible studies, or parties at home. Mother refused; angrily denying her such a privilege and threatening to order out any and all outsiders who dared step through the door.

In mid-August, Marj invited me to go to a tent revival meeting with her. I was excited about being included and could hardly wait for the evening to come.

There were hundreds of people in attendance. Dozens of young people milled about before the service. Marj seemed to be the center of a large group who were laughing and planning dates for afterwards. The camaraderie before the service was as infectious and fun as the evangelist was repulsive and confusing.

The service began with an hour of song: congregational singing interspersed with special musical presentation. The music was well done and impressive. But the informality and inane ramblings of the evangelist were obnoxious and disgusting to me. I thought him unclean. He began the service by bragging on the fine mess of catfish he had eaten for supper and thanked all the fine folk who had been feeding him so high on the hog all week. Yech! No wonder he was so fat and red-faced.

All during the sermon he kept talking about what the Gospel says, or the Bible says. I wondered why, if he knew the Bible so well, would he eat scavengers when the Scriptures specifically said not to? I remembered Grandma laughing about the old preacher who had been asked to say a table blessing over some abominable church supper. His flock had strayed from the food laws. They turned a deaf ear to his admonitions and teased him that he was old-fashioned. They flaunted their disregard and insisted that times had changed; the old food laws did not apply to modern times. The old preacher had stood with his right hand raised in blessing. He sighed heavily and prayed, "O God, if Thou canst bless, what Thou has cursed, then bless this roast pig."

I smiled remembering the incongruity of it. Marj nudged me and frowned. The evangelist was talking about people being hard-hearted and laughing at wickedness. I flushed in embarrassment.

Marilyn, an extremely large person, sat next to me, oozing a suffocating smell of sweat, Tabu and peppermint. She sat quietly, eyes closed, hands folded across her massive stomach. I had never seen anyone so fat. I wondered how much she must have to eat daily to be that big: probably enough for five or six people. She was not tall. Her hands and feet were quite small, actually. How could such tiny feet support all that bulk? Where would her center of gravity be, or, more appropriately, her center of mass? What would be her specific gravity? It would take an awful lot of water to find out. I must ask Dad about that.

The evangelist was red-faced and sweating profusely. A vein stood out dangerously on his forehead as he moped his brow and coaxed and scowled and pleaded into the microphone, "Won't you come right now, brother, sister? This may be your last chance. Come now! Kneel at the altar. Confess your sins and Jesus will save you! Hallelujah! Come now!"

The long altar was soon lined with people crying and praying. Little groups of people stood all over the assemblage, pleading with some unwilling person, some sinner? to take that first step on the road to heaven. The choir kept on singing, repeating the same song over and over. I watched the tiny knots of people as they formed and dissolved and gravitated toward the altar. Marj leaned toward me and whispered, "Do you want to go to the altar and confess your sins?"

I jabbed her with my elbow and whispered, "I don't have any sins!"

I felt an arm about my shoulders and smelled the pepperminty breath. I turned to see Marilyn's little pig eyes beneath a frown that contorted her face into a mask of joyous fanaticism. She spoke softly but forcefully. "Olivia, listen to your sister! She has you on her heart. She loves you and wants you to be saved just as she has been. You may not understand it, but you are at the age of accountability. You need to confess your sins and ask Jesus to save you."

Her tone was solicitous and her expression conveyed patient concern and longsuffering fortitude. She wiped her eyes with a wet handkerchief, popped another peppermint into her mouth, clinched her eyes tight and prayed aloud, "Jesus, touch her heart, right now! Don't let her harden her heart, Lord."

I tried to shrug away from her. I was painfully aware that some, God! several, people were watching with keen interest. I could feel the embarrassment, the anger, the humiliation reddening my face. I looked around wondering how I could leave without making a spectacle of myself. I whispered to Marj, "Let's go!"

She looked surprised. "To the altar?"

"Home!"

"Shhh. We can't leave yet."

I heaved a great sigh, clenched my lips and wiped my sweaty palms on my skirt. Marilyn began pleading, "Won't you let Jesus come into your heart? Don't you want to be a Christian? Jesus wants to save you, if you'll just confess your sins."

"I don't have any sins."

"Everybody has sins. We're born in sin. Even tiny babies need to be saved. All are sinners and must confess their sins if they want to be saved."

"Bull!"

Mildred tightened her hold on me. I looked to Marj for help. She said, "Honey, I know you are a good person and you haven't done anything wrong, but, as I understand it, you still have to go to the altar to be saved."

Marilyn soothed, "Don't be afraid. Have faith. Jesus will save you. Everything will be so much better. Come on now, You'll see."

Marilyn was half-pulling me toward the aisle, toward the altar, toward being saved. I was so accustomed to doing as I was told. Inwardly, I wondered if there was something to the mysticism. God, anything that would make things better would certainly be worth trying. I let myself be led to the altar and obediently knelt down. Marilyn eased her heavy frame down next to me and began praying aloud for my redemption. Marj knelt on the other side of me. I felt suffocatingly hot. The hard-packed dirt hurt my knees. The smells of body odor, Tabu, and peppermint made my head swim. I listened to the joyful sound of others who had been saved. They seemed so happy, so thrilled, so caught up in a display of religious ecstasy unlike anything I had ever seen or heard. The evangelist was walking up and down the platform above the altar. He stopped in front of me and demanded, "Do you want to be saved?"

I raised my eyes to get a good close look at him. He straightened up and stepped back with a strange, wide-eyed expression. He frowned and said quietly, "Don't be defiant, Miss! Confess your sins! God wants to hold you in the palm of His hand."

He moved on to the next repentant. I honestly could not think of any sins, but the idea of God holding me in His hand intrigued me. I liked that, but, I would rather climb up on His lap. Wouldn't that be nice, if there were a great big lap one could crawl up on and be held snug and comfy and safe? It would have to be a man; a great big man with a bushy brown mustache and kind of a sloping stomach and big shoulders so one could lay back against him and nuzzle his soft leathery throat and feel the coarse bristliness of his jaw line on your head just so, and he would smell of tobacco and gun oil and maybe we would share an orange. I felt so alone, confused, frustrated and tired. Tears ran down my cheeks. A sense of desolation and a yearning to be accepted, to please, to have peace, swept over me . . . *Peace . . . What the hell is peace?* I cried and prayed and felt a great sense of relief and light-headedness. Marj and Marilyn hugged me and congratulated themselves on getting me "saved." Marilyn proffered a roll of peppermints and talked of having a star in her crown for every soul she won.

The service was ended after a fervent prayer by the evangelist, who thanked God for the dozens of converts and dedicated us, ". . . to a life of service and glory and fellowship in Christ with such fulfillment and enrichment as the world can never know and to peace that passeth all understanding and the secret power that can say to a mountain, 'move', and it will move, if we just live by the simple recipe that Jesus taught us; the secret recipe that only God's children can understand. The only way to true joy: Jesus first, others second, yourself last. Yes, thank you, Jesus, for showing us the way and make it possible that we all come back tomorrow night and make us all fishers of men, Lord. Let each one bring one and give us souls for Thee. Amen and amen."

People exited in all directions. The tent flaps had been raised for air circulation. Night bugs swarmed about the lights as untended youth climbed about the platform, and a crowd of worshipers pressed about the evangelist. Marj was talking with one of the recently returned soldiers who was still in uniform. She seemed to have forgotten about me. I stood at a discreet distance watching and listening as the small clusters of conversationalists grew and dissolved as the people moved about greeting each other and happily making plans for meeting at some home or restaurant for refreshments. The older boys and girls seemed to pair off as others looked on in unabashed envy.

Marj's friend put his arm about her shoulder and propelled her toward his car. I felt a cold chill at being forgotten, but could not find my voice to call to her. I watched as they climbed into his shiny maroon Chevy coupe and saw her snuggle up to him as they drove off amidst the many departing vehicles. A sense of desperation seized me as the few remaining people moved towards their cars. The lights in and around the huge tent were turned off and the night closed in. I felt a tremor of terror building in my embarrassment and humiliation. I clinched my arms tightly about my waist and fought back hot tears that threatened to spill at all thought of having to walk home in the dark, alone. I wasn't exactly sure where we were. I knew it was on the opposite side of town from where we lived. It was so dark and everything was so strange.

The light dew that was settling over the grass made by bare toes squish in my scandals as I started walking toward the road. I heard voices coming from the far side of the parking area. One sounded familiar and I grabbed at the hope, the possibility, of getting a ride. I saw Marilyn's massive outline in the small group that was standing by a car in the nearly deserted parking area. I ran toward her asking if shewould please give me a ride home. She looked annoyed and hesitated before asking, "Well, don't you have a ride? Who'd you come with?"

I was nearly breathless with dread of being left alone at the dark desolate looking campgrounds and flushed with the shame of having to ask a near stranger for a ride. I forced my voice to answer her.

"Marj and Helen."

"Why don't they take you home?"

"Helen took a bunch to some restaurant and Marj left with some guy."

Ellie, an older plain looking girl, snorted, "Some guy! She latched on to Bill!"

They exchanged looks and Marilyn sighed, "That's way out of my way, but I guess we can't leave you stranded here six miles from nowhere. Come on."

I climbed into the back seat and scrunched into the corner as Ellie, Clara and Mary crowded in. Bernice and Anne sat in the front seat next to Mildred's ample form. The old prewar vintage Ford sedan squeaked and groaned in protest at it's heavy burden as Marilyn grinded the gears and lurched along the rutted dirt lane toward the hardroad.

I was so relieved to be with them. The fear and dread of being left alone in such a strange, desolate place had been much more frightening than my embarrassment at being regarded as a bother. Yet, guilt and shame burned my face as Marilyn griped about having to drive so far out of her way, being low on gas, and worried that a patched tire might go flat.

Talk turned to the service, the marvelous speaker, who was, unfortunately, married, the fine choir and who paired off with whom. They speculated on where "they" would go and what "they" would do and whether or not anything would come of it. Bernice and Anne kept cracking jokes about Marj coming home from school and snaring Bill. Sometimes they would whisper real low and giggle.

I began humming a new chorus I had just learned that evening. Ellie began singing the words and others joined in, in harmony. Marilyn added an enchanting descant. The effect was so pleasing, we sang it over again and again, striving for perfection.

"Everybody ought to know, (Everybody ought to know)
Everybody ought to know, (Everybody ought to know)
Everybody ought to know, (Everybody ought to know)
Who Jesus is, (Who Jesus is)
He's the lily of the valley
He's the bright and morning star,
He's the fairest of ten thousand,
Everybody ought to know."

We congratulated ourselves on how well we sounded as Marilyn pulled the aging rattle trap into our long lane. She ignored the slipping clutch and the stripping of the gears and talked of us providing the special music for a service sometime. I was flattered to be included, anxiously agreed, and ran inside happy with my new-found friends and at peace with my religion.

I waited up for Marj, eagerly anticipating a continuation of her big-sisterly caring and counsel. I was excited about the possibility of being a part of a singing group and was anxious to tell Marj about it. I sat in my room trying to concentrate on reading the Bible, confident that was what a newly born Christian should do.

Dad's Bible had a complicated cross-chain reference. One subject could require reading in several different books of the Bible. I was quite fascinated with it and was thoroughly engrossed in my research when I noticed the headlights of a car pull into our drive. I heard the gravel of our long lane crunching as the car slowly approached and swung round in a semi-circle ready to head back out.

I felt Marj would be pleased to find me reading the Bible. I posed in a variety of ways in front of my open, inviting door. I waited. My correct reading posture melted into more comfortable lines as the minutes stretched endlessly on. The Bible seemed to grow heavier as the time grew later. I slung my legs over the arm of the chair, propped the Bible in my lap and with my chin on my chest, I earnestly pored over the Scriptures, the same ones repeatedly, losing my train of thought as I strained to hear sounds of Marj coming into the house. My eyes grew heavy. The bed was so tempting, but the Bible was big and bulky and seemed to hold me in the chair.

The draperies were open and the curtains billowed in the chilly night air. I nestled down into the chair for warmth and put all of my effort on concentrating on the Word of God.

Another car scrunched into our lane, accelerated and screeched to a noisy halt. A car door slammed and steps could be heard hurrying towards the house. I sat upright in my chair and assumed an attitude of intent studying. A distant door slammed shut and Alfie's heavy steps came plodding up the stairs. I felt his eyes on me as he staggered by the door without speaking. Tears stung my eyes and deep in my heart I prayed for God to help me to help Alfie.

"What the hell do you think you're doin'?

Alf was standing at my door. He steadied himself with one hand on the doorsill. His droopy eyelids nearly concealed his bleary, red-shot eyes. His mouth was clamped in it's perpetual sneer around a Lucky Strike. The corners of his mouth seemed to be lost in the deep furrows that extended from the side of his nose down to his jawline. It looked like the face of a much older man; one experienced in suffering, one who had met and been scarred by stringent tests of endurance and survival under extreme circumstances, circumstances such as I could only guess at; one ravaged by malaria, whose eyes and skin still had a slight yellowish tinge. I knew there were still hot summer days when he would be wrapped in a wool khaki colored army blanket fighting chills and fever as well as a hangover. I had tried repeatedly to let him know I cared and wanted to help. Each overture had been met with such scorn and contempt, such harsh cussings and hard looks, that I had actually become afraid to speak to him at all unless he spoke first. Then I would be so anxious to please I would gush or giggle or muff my words or say something stupid that would being on such a torrent of swear words and hard icy glares from hate filled eyes that I would cringe inside and yet, try harder to be letter perfect in everything so he would not have anything to criticize me for.

I looked at him now in a new light, not with fear, but with compassion. He was ten years older than I, but I felt we were, somehow, on an equal footing. I replied, "I was just waiting for Marj to come in so I could ask her what this means."

"What what means?"

I pointed to the passage I had been reading as he came nearer to see.

"Is that Dad's Bible? Does he know you have it?"

"I'm sure he wouldn't mind."

"The hell he wouldn't! Look at the way you're holdin' it! For Christ sake, that's not the way to hold the Bible. Can't you show a little respect for it? You're gonna break the back openin' it up like that!"

He grabbed it away from me and stood, swaying, caressing the leather cover of the Bible. I prayed silently, "God, please help me to say the right words. Please don't let me make him mad at me again."

Aloud, I said, "You're right. I should have asked Dad if I could use it. . ."

He glared at me and blustered, "You're Goddamn right, I'm right! It seems a hell of a contradiction to sneak someone else's Bible so you can act goody goody and read it."

"Dad's always said we could read anything we wanted to in the library."

Alfie took quick steps toward me and clamped his big right hand in a vise grip on the top of my head. His fingers dug into my scalp and I could feel my cheeks wobble as he roughly shook my head and leaned over me grinning menacingly, and yelling, "What have ya got in there, huh? What have ya got between yer ears, huh? Sawdust? Huh? Is this the library, Stupid? Huh? Is it?"

I did not want to fight him and I did not want to let him know how much he was hurting me, although I thought he was going to shake my head off. My neck hurt and the room was swimming. I willed my eyes to stay dry and said as calmly as possible, "Alf, please!"

I had put both hands up to my head. He released his grip and patted me on the head, saying, "Oh, 'scuse me, your ladyship. Did I stir up the sawdust? Mustn't hurt that little empty head."

I smoothed my hair and brushed off the ashes that had fallen on me and tried not notice as he crushed his cigarette out on my gold-trimmed dresser tray. I mustered up the courage to testify to my new found status and blurted out, "Alfie, I was converted this evening."

"So? You want a medal?"

"I just wanted you to know. That's why I was reading the Bible."

He started toward the door, stopped, took the Bible out from under his left arm and seemed to weigh it in his right hand as he cocked his head to one side and seemed to measure me with his own eyes' standards. I obviously did not measure up to par. His scathing glare made me doubt the urging of the preacher and Mildred to "tell the whole world what the Lord hath done for you."

"So! Now I know! Ya gonna be a holy roller?"

"No, of course not."

He mouthed a roll of words that sounded like so much gibberish ending in the familiar auctioneer's spiel for Lucky Strike cigarettes. I laughed and he actually smiled at me as he took out a cigarette. Thoughtfully, he tamped it against the pack, lighted it and blew a stream of smoke toward the ceiling. He sat down on the edge of my bed and leaned forward, propping his elbows on his knees, and asked,

"Don't ya have a Bible of yer own?"

"Not exactly."

"What do ya mean, 'not exactly'? Either ya do or ya don't"

I hastened to explain, "I have a little New Testament with the Psalms; one that was given to me at Bible School when I was in the sixth grade."

He seemed to be thinking, remembering. The lines on his face softened and his voice changed, mellowed, as he said softly,

"Yeah. I carried one like that for four years."

"I didn't know that, Alf."

"Well, so ya didn't know; so what else is new in the land of paradise?"

He rubbed his hands over his eyes and sighed heavily. "There's a lot ya don't know, Toot. And there's a lot I can't tell ya. Don't need to anyway. Wouldn't serve any purpose."

We sat in silence while he drew deeply on his cigarette, picked a piece of tobacco off his tongue and let the smoke curl crazily around him. I ached to tell him of my feelings: love, concern, pride, pity—no, not pity. He didn't want that. But, pride, yes, and gratitude. How does one convey such feelings without being met with a wall of defiance and rejection? How do you say to one who has been through hell and come back that you really care and that you feel an indebtedness, a gratefulness, an appreciation that is centered deep in the inner fibers of the heart and yearns for expression, but it gets hung up on inadequate words with multi-meanings and it is choked off by doubts and fears of rejection that plague the spirit and wreck havoc with the mind? How can a kid-sister say to her big brother that she feels he, personally, won the war and preserved the peace just for her? And that she feels grief and regret over the torturous years that he spent trudging through the hell holes of the primeval rain forests of New Guinea and the Philippine Islands where every engineer had a machete extending from one hand and a Tommy-gun from the other and checked his ammunition more carefully than his C-rations and wished he could aim the fiery farts at the Japs as accurately as the pygmies aimed their poisonous darts. And, Oh God, the remorse! How can one empathize with another in the tortures of his soul as he relives the battles, the personal encounters, the kill or be killed, the pursuit of the Goddamned yellow devils, and the suspicion that, Oh God—they're people too? How can one who has been safe in the confines of home and sheltered even from the grossness of the worst of the bloody news, claim to understand anything of the living nightmare, the oppressive heat, the sickening stench, the deafening roar and the nerve-shattering staccato of gun fire, the never satisfied pangs of hunger and the unquenchable thirst, the never-ending demands on one's physical and mental stamina and the persistent buzzing and biting of flies, mosquitoes, leeches and the hoards of unnamed parasites? Can one living in an antiseptic home in a peaceful and clean community in a nearly shock-proof society really claim to be able to imagine the filth, the stench, the screams of piercing pain, the groans of the dying, the silent mask of death and the ever-present need for being alert: listening, watching, hoping, God!, and praying and feeling a sense of thankfulness in the midst of the living nightmare that one is still vitally alive, actually surviving a passage through hell?

Alf stood and stretched broadly, making a fist and playfully jabbing it toward me. I said, "Alf, if you'd ever like to talk, I'd be glad to listen."

"Ya would, eh?"

"Yes, really. I'd like to hear about who you were with and what you thought about and . . . mostly, I, well, I just want you to know that I appreciate. . ."

Alf raised his hand and said, "Whoa, hold it right there! You can't appreciate anything! You don't have the least idea of what it was like and I'm not agoin' to tell ya, 'cause those little green, wet ears of yers are too delicate to hear about the blood and thunder."

"I went to the movies every week to see the newsreels and I read the papers every day and we always listened to Lowell Thomas and Edward R. Murrow. . ."

"Well, bully for you! So ya get an 'A' in current events!"

I pounded the arms of my chair with my fists and moaned, "Oh, God! Why do I always say the wrong things? I don't want you to be mad at me, Alfie."

"Then leave it alone, Toot. Just leave it alone. I wish to God I could."

He laid the Bible on the night-table, took off his windbreaker, stretched, yawned, looked out the window, swore softly and pulled the curtain back for a better look. He murmured, "For Christsake! Looks like our sister's doin' some holy-rollin' from the way that car's rockin'! Christ Almighty! Some people have all the luck. Don't you look, Toot! You're too young for such as that!"

I had jumped up to see what he was talking about. He put an arm-hold around my neck and scuffled me away from the window and toward the door. I was laughing and pleading with him to let me see. He pushed me into the hallway and said, "Go make me a sandwich! A Dagwood, OK? I'm starved. Mom doesn't fix much anymore, does she?"

"Well, not like Grandma did. But, there's some coleslaw and fruit salad and chocolate bread pudding. Do you really want cheese on your roast beef?"

Alf nodded and smacked his lips nosily as he gave me a gentle push toward the stairs. "And pickles and lettuce and tomatoes and sandwich spread about an inch thick on both sides of the bread and horseradish mustard on the roast beef! Um umh! Fit for a king, I mean the King of England, of course. I'll be down in a minute. I gotta go take a pee . . . I mean . . . 'scuse me, mam . . . number one."

14

GOD, GUNS AND GRANDMA

"*A woman's hair is her crown of glory*" Mother used to quote as she would urge Loralee, Marjorie and me to brush one hundred strokes each night. Her hair was shiny brown and longer than her waist; but very thin and very fine. It always looked elegantly done, braided and coiled into a chignon or wrapped around her head with soft waves in front. She would never allow any hairs to hang loose and considered such as being "*unkempt.*"

One Saturday morning Mother awoke me at six o'clock chirping. "Rise and shine! The early bird gets the worm! Get up now; I've got a lot to do today. You can't lay in bed all day just because it's a Saturday, and don't get any notions about going anyplace or reading anything because I need you to help with a few little things around here. I just can't do all of this work myself and I needn't to with a great big girl like you just laying there getting her beauty sleep. Now get dressed and see if you don't like that new Hoover. Why, it makes vacuuming so easy and it's no work a'tall! I do want the windows done today. They're so dirty you can't see out of 'em. Josh can hold the ladder for you but don't be lettin' him climb up on it! That boy's as awkward as a colt. You can use that bundle of rags down in the basement but don't throw any of them away. They've got a lot of good use in them yet. Do remember to get the streaks off! I always say a job worth doing is a job worth doing well. And that silver needs a good going over. Why, it's so tarnished it's a crime! And while you're in there you might give that chandelier a lick with a cloth but I don't want Josh climbing up on that table for he'd be sure to fall off and break an arm or a leg and I don't want any of those prisms broken either, so you be extra careful and take your shoes off."

"Are you going someplace, Mother?"

"Why, yes, matter of fact, I am! But that's none of your concern. I want you to watch the baby and see to it that you change him as soon as he wets or soils. Your Dad's changing him now. That poor baby's got blisters as big as your fist and I don't know what I'm going to do with him. Nine years old and still in diapers. I'm tempted sometimes to put him out in back in the barn."

"Dad says that place at Anna is really nice and M.D. might be able to learn to do for himself."

Mother was dressed in a stylish maroon suit of wool with a white lacy blouse peeking from under the tailored jacket. A small pill box hat with a half veil turned back was placed squarely on the top of her head. Black shoes, a black purse and white gloves completed her outfit. I had sat up in bed and listened and watched as she primped in front of my mirror and planned my day for me. She said, "Your brother is not going to an institution as long as there is breath in my body."

"He doesn't seem like a brother at all. He doesn't even know about anything other than just. . ."

Mother walked to my bed and yanked the covers back angrily. "You just shut that up. I've told you and told you that it is our lot in life to be his slaves. There's just no way around it, and we should not question what God has planned."

"Mother, that "slave" crack just isn't funny, and I do not believe that God has anything to do with it."

"Well, what do you know, especially so early in the morning? Now, get up and get dressed. You're getting to be so lazy."

She twisted and turned admiring herself in the mirror. I ventured a guess at the obvious.

"Are you going to St. Louis?"

Mother eyed me with a mischievous grin. I said, "You look nice and pretty, Mother."

"Thank you, muh dear. Now you get up and at 'em! Are my seams straight?"

She crossed over to the door and turning back chattered happily, "I've got to catch the seven-ten but I'll be back 'fore bedtime. You'll want to fix a nice supper for your Dad and Josh and don't neglect the baby. I'll have a nice surprise for you when I get home." She laughed, " I'm going to surprise everyone!"

Mother laughed and clickeyty-clacked off down the hall. I traced my fingers along the intricate stitching of the brightly colored quilt that

Grandma had made and reluctantly, but, obediently, rose to meet the work waiting for me. What choice did I have? There would be hell to pay if I didn't get it done.

First thing every morning Dad would change and clean Michael David. He had already fed him his breakfast, bundled him up and carried him outside on the porch for their daily outing. He was sitting beside him in the porch swing, pointing to the trees and the squirrels, trying to get M.D. to notice them and to listen to the birds, feel the nice breeze, smell the flowering lilacs. Michael David's eyes were dull but he would chew on his tongue and grunt with pleasure if not understanding. His attention span was indeterminable but he was usually content as long as someone was with him. We knew readily when he tired of something. His lower jaw would protrude and he'd begin a low guttural growling. If one didn't immediately determine what he wanted he would begin flailing his arms about and howling at the top of his lungs.

Dad had patiently and consistently sought to find some spark of intellect. He read medical journals and every book he could find that dealt with the retarded or the mongoloid trying to find some explanation or help of some kind. He learned there had been an Englishman , almost a hundred years earlier, who had studied the subject and decided that the uniqueness of the situation made it an evolutionary throw-back to an inferior being with very limited intelligence. Thus, it was called "Down's Syndrome." He offered no hope for any improvement.

M.D. was beginning to learn to walk but his weak bowed legs would give way after a step or two and he'd plunk down on his bottom and scoot about, babbling idiotically. When he'd scoot up to a chair or a piece of furniture and could go no further he would wail and howl. One of us would sit on the floor with him and try to demonstrate how to go around it. There were times when he seemed to understand and we would praise him and think we were making some progress. Other times he would hit his head against whatever was in front of him in a steady thump, thump until one of us could hurry to him and lift him bodily and turn him in another direction.

Dad was always trying to advise me, and Josh, on what to do and how to do it, as Michael David grew heavier and stronger and more difficult to deal with. Dad cautioned us on being very careful to guard ourselves against injury, because M.D. was getting to be terribly strong, and the resulting scratches and bruises, that friends and teachers were always commenting on, were terribly embarrassing and impossible to cover up in warm weather.

Dad never criticized Mother but would frequently say, "I wish she'd let me put him in a hospital where they know how to give the proper care to children like Michael. He might be able to learn to do for himself if he only had the proper training. He's just too big for Martha or you children to have to carry or lift. You shouldn't have to do it at all."

On this particular late April Saturday morning as I joined them on the porch I asked, "So . . . is Mother going to St. Louis just for shopping or for something special?"

Dad answered, " I don't know, Toot. She wouldn't tell me what she's up to but I guess she's going shopping. She kept saying we'd all be surprised this evening."

He said he was going to take Josh with him out to the mine if he wanted to go but would be home by noon. He sighed and said apologetically, "I heard your Mother telling you what you are to do today."

I was feeling dejected with the weight of the workload. A sense of hopelessness had gripped me and I dreaded the repercussions of it not being finished as much as I dreaded doing it. I was not going to ask Josh for any help. I had determined that, even before Dad said he was going to take him with him. I knew Josh would rather do anything than work about the house and I didn't think it fair for him to have to do housework at all.

Michael David's blabbering cut through my gloom. I watched as Dad tenderly wiped the slobbers away and then tucked his big white handkerchief into M.D.'s hand and was patiently trying again to teach him the motions of drying his mouth and chin. He would allow Dad to manipulate his arm but would not or could not even try to do it himself, in spite of the coaxing. Dad would praise his every gesture or small accomplishment, as did we all. I got up to go in the house. Dad said my name quietly. I hesitated; he took a deep breath and said, "What a beautiful day! Toot? What would you like most to do today?"

I took a deep breath too, of the invigorating fresh spring air and stretched expansively and gave flight to fancy and answered with exuberance, "Gee whiz, now let me see. As Grandma used to say, "*If wishes were horses we'd all ride*". But, actually, if I could do anything I wanted to do, I think I'd go horseback riding this morning down in the woods and shoot skeet this afternoon and maybe go to a movie tonight."

Dad laughed, "Now that sounds like a good day!"

We heard the train tooting off in the distance. Dad took his watch out, looked at it and held it up for Michael David to look at and listen to. He said, "Seven-ten. It's right on time . . . Tell you what, Toot. There's been so much gloom around here . . . for such a long time . . . seems like. God! . . . it's been two years . . . next week, since . . . Mama died . . . God!

. . . she tried so hard . . . to keep things, on an even keel . . . It plagues me that the heartbreak . . . and the hard work . . . God knows I wish I could have spared her from all of this. . ."

He looked at Michael David and sighed, "Christ Almighty! It's been nine years."

Michael David showed no interest at all in the big gold watch that Dad was holding in front of him. Dad put it up, ran his hand through his dark wavy hair that was beginning to show gray around his temples and then said decisively, "I want you to do exactly what you've wished for today. That'll be good for you!"

I stammered, "But, Dad . . . I can't . . . Mother told me. . ."

He interrupted, "Yes, I heard. But I'm not going to have you climbing around on a ladder. I'll have Mr. Swanson send a couple of his men over to do the windows. They're always glad for a little extra work. Maybe Mrs. Hawkins can come and do the house this morning. I don't have to go to the mine, matter of fact, I'll call Alf and see if he wouldn't like to join us . . ."

I said, "I really miss him. I wish he'd come back home."

Dad gazed off into the distance and said, on a sorrowful sigh, "We sacrifice our best, for what?"

He shook his head and continued, "He really had a hard time of it, more so than we could ever understand. And then, coming back here, with everything so different . . . But. I can certainly understand. He's not to blame for any of it. He has a nice place . . . in there. . ."

I knew what Dad was alluding to. Alfie had griped to me about Mother pestering him to death about everything. He resented her constant nagging; "bitching" he called it, and her interference in his own affairs. He had rented a room in town and seldom came home. When he did it was usually only for a few moments at a time.

Dad was trying to get Michael David to stand. "Here, Son, see? Put your feet together like this—Whoops-there, now you've got it. That's a good big boy! Why, you can stand up fine! Come on now, let's take a step, alright? There you go, that's the boy. I'm holding you. Here now, move this one—good boy! There you go. Move this one now. You can do it. That's the way. Good boy! Move this one, here, lift it, see? There you go! Shhhhh. It's alright. You're doing fine. Come on now."

Michael David had taken several steps before he finally balked and began fighting and howling. He stopped as soon as Dad picked him up. He continued talking to him about how he could walk. I held the door for him as he carried M.D. inside. Dad said, "You'd better eat a good breakfast, Toot. I want you to have a good time today. I'll set the traps up and ask Alf and Doc and Pete to come out. Josh oughta have a hand at it too. That boy's got a good eye and a steady hand."

I said, "Dad, what about M.D.?"

He put him down on the floor where he began a rocking motion. Dad started toward the phone.

"I'm calling Miss Quinn right now."

"Dad, she's a nurse!"

"Well, he needs a nurse! Who else would know how to care for him?"

Two minutes later he hung up; satisfied with the accomplishment. Miss Quinn was on her way.

He called Mrs. Hawkins; woke her up. She hesitated. It was a Saturday. Dad talked about how much there was to be done,

"It'll really be a full day's work, but, of course, I'd be happy to pay you whatever you think it's worth. No, Martha's, uh, visiting. Thank you, that'll be fine. We'll see you soon then."

Dad looked at me with an elfish grin and chuckled, "I woke her up. She's liable to charge me extra. Maybe you better make a list of what's to be done."

He called Mr. Swanson who agreed to send someone over to do the windows and then, turning to me, Dad motioned toward the phone and said, "It's all yours."

Dean was always eager to go riding. He seemed surprised and pleased to hear from me and he said he'd saddle up and be right over.

Dad had taken M.D. to his room. I ran for my jodhpurs and boots; tied my hair back in a ponytail, tidied my bed, woke Josh and told him it was going to be a fun day and got downstairs just as the staid old sourpuss, Miss Quinn, arrived. She rang the front doorbell. I opened it, smiled in greeting and said, "Oh, Miss Quinn, I'm so glad you could come!"

She gave me an incredulous look and I blushed with the realization of how I must have sounded. The awkwardness made me stammer, "Really, Miss Quinn, we really are glad, I mean, Dad and I . . . we . . . I'm really glad."

A smile broke lines in her face and it was as though a light bulb had come on in her eyes. They were such a sparkling blue. She removed her wrap and asked, "Are you going riding?"

I answered, "Yes Mam. Dean Swanson and I are going riding on the trails down in the woods."

She smiled again! and said, "I used to like to ride. Watch out for the low hanging branches! Is that Dean now?"

Dean was riding up the lane, with Jinx in tow. I started to go out, but, something, made me run looking for Dad. I called, "Dad? Dad?"

He answered from the study. I ran in, flung my arms around him and wordlessly hugged him. He patted me on the shoulder and said huskily,

"Go on now. Have a good time. Thanks for making the list. Alfie will be here this afternoon."

Kathryn, Wanda and I went to see a good mystery that night. Dad drove us there along with Josh and two of his friends and then picked us all up afterwards.

We were home. Miss Quinn had left. M.D. was asleep. Mrs. Hawkins had the house spic and span clean. The windows even gleamed in the dark. Josh had The Grand Ole Opry on the radio and we were laughing at some ridiculous tale of Minnie Pearl's little brother when Mother came in. She was looking at us all anxiously. She removed her hat. Dad caught his breath. I said, "Mother? Did you cut your hair off?"

She sniffed, "I had it styled. Do you like it?"

I gushed, "Oh, it's lovely, Mother. It looks very nice."

She looked at Dad. "Well?"

He said, convincingly, "It's very nice, Martha."

Josh had become interested and wanted to know what it was that was different. Mother fluffed the ends of her hair with her fingers and said, "Well, can't you see? I had my hair cut and permed."

Josh said, "Why'd you do that, Mom?"

Mother looked in the mirror and began patting the wispy static-laden strands of hair into place. She said, "Why, I thought you'd be surprised."

The whole world seemed to shift gears; jerking from a grinding but safe, comfortable low speed through dependable and predictable terrain found in the relative sameness of schedule and activities from day to day, to a high gear on a dangerous road of events, people and happenings, over which I had no control and very little understanding. There was no roadmap, no compass, no directions given, no road signs warning of dangerous curves or tricky turns. No shoulders to pull off on to reorient one's self, no shoulders to cry on.

It was just a matter of accepting whatever came up around the bend or over the hill, trying to dodge the obstacles that were hurled from unknown factors while hitting all of the pot-holes and constantly threatened with plunging from a sheer cliff on one side or crashing into an impeding high rock wall on the other side.

The strain on the nerves began to be evident in my physical reactions and appearance. I had always been slim but athletic and healthy. Now, I was thin, dizzy-headed and had little if any time for games or fun and no inclination for them and there was no one to notice or care, or even to comment, *"all work and no play makes . . ."*

Dad was frequently gone and transportation was nil. I discovered that I liked walking the three miles in the early morning. It gave me time to think, to memorize, to remember, and the peace and solitude I felt in those humbling walks gave me some respite, brief as it was, from the constantly threatening volcanic eruption of emotions and conflicting wills that had become a festering caldron in what had once been, such a short time ago, our happy home.

During the long solitary walks I began to address God as a friend and confident as I would ponder the perplexing problems that seemed to have no solution: formulating them into words and turning them over in my mind to see what they were made of, constituted a kind of prayer life, a one-way conversation, a meditation, a release of pent up anger and frustration. Of course, I did not talk aloud, but my thoughts were focused and just analyzing deeds, words and situations seemed to clarify them and make them more acceptable or durable.

God, why do things have to change so drastically? Why do babies like Michael David have to be born? It can't be because of Dad's girl friends, as Mother claims. Dr. Matthews says it has to do with chromosomes and the simple fact of Mother being too old and in the menopause. Why does she get so mad about the facts? The simple medical facts show that never in medical history has a woman under thirty-five given birth to a Mongoloid child. Dr. Matthews said that is a fact, a truth. Why won't she believe it? Does she just want to blame Dad for it? It is almost as if she hates us all and is using Michael David as a whip of some kind to punish us. God, why won't she listen to any of the other doctors she's gone all over the country to see? They have all told her the same thing. Dr. Matthews tries so hard, but, then he's no match for Mother. She just tunes him out and then talks about this latest expert that she wants to bring over from England. I hope he's not another one of these Pentecostal Healers that'll just want a lot of money for his holy hokus-pokus, and then claim he can't do anything because we waited too long to ask him, or even worse, when he claims that we don't have enough "faith" so it isn't "his fault". They give me the creeps. God, can you heal Michael David? How could you possibly "heal" one who simply did not have the where-with-alls to begin with? Can you heal our home? Can you heal me? Can you help me? Can you show me how to find some answers? Do you even care? Does . . . anyone . . . care . . . ?

Mother says we must never tell anyone, especially the nosy busy-bodied gossips, anything about Michael David or anything about our home. But, people are always asking. I don't know what to say. Is it a lie to say, "Oh, everything is just fine, thank you very much."

I was well aware that our home, Mother and Michael David were juicy subjects of gossip and looked on as curiosities. Michael David was never out in public, and few, aside from the family had even seen him. But he had been born under rather unusual circumstances, the first male child of the year, and the resulting publicity, along with Dad being so well known, fueled people's interest. His "condition" had been a popular source of gossip. Dr. Mathews said M.D. was the first Mongoloid baby he had seen in over 40 years in medicine and that he did not personally know of any others.

Mother had steadfastly refused, since his birth, to allow Josh or me to have any friends at home. She did not have any in either. But she talked to anyone who would listen, expounding on her trials and tribulations and her dedication to her responsibilities in spite of adversity and harassment and the family all against her.

Total strangers would ask me about that poor child that I was not suppose to acknowledge and remark about what a wonderful woman my Mother was. Some were even so bold as to rebuke me for not helping my poor sainted mother.

Mother would never have out and out lied about anything; but she had a way of inferring that left people to draw their own conclusions. She was explicit in her vagueness. She knew how to turn a phrase to her own advantage: to twist the truth until it no longer resembled the facts.

Mother catered to "the baby" with her words but she directed whomever was at hand to see to his immediate needs, such as changing his diapers, cleaning his eyes, feeding him, or just quieting him. She talked constantly, whether there was anyone in the same room with her or not. Her voice had taken on a whining, plaintive tone that grated on the ears and mind like a discordant note. She wallowed in self-pity, enjoying it, slopping it about, splattering it on any one who happened near, refusing to be coaxed out of it, and refusing to be ignored. She seemed to rejoice in a pathetic religious conviction that we all must be "slaves" to "that poor baby" and it was her lot, her burden, her cross, to see to it that we would suffer it through.

Mother played the role of the martyr to the hilt. Reality was lost in her martyrdom. Her reasoning was lost in self-mortification. She began dressing strangely in bizarre get-ups; a striped skirt and a floral blouse or a faded housedress with an old smock. She had always worn hose, but now she started wearing Dad's old socks that were sizes too large for her. The heels would stick out half way up her legs and the absurdity of men's socks with ladies' scandals was mortifying. Her hair hung limp and straight and completed the disheveled appearance. If we suggested she change or freshen up, she would whine that we were ashamed of her or claim that she had nothing else to wear or she would take umbrage and in child-like innocence demand to know, *"Why, I can't imagine what you think is wrong with this. I know you're the fashion expert around here so you just tell me what you think is wrong with what I've chosen to wear today! It's clean, isn't it? Your Dad threw these socks out but they don't have a hole in them and you tell me why I should give them to poor people when I can get the good out of them just as well as they. See? They're perfectly good! And this dress is fine, don't you think? Well, I like it and I'm the one wearing it and if you don't like it you can just lump it. I don't know who you think you are to criticize the way I dress anyway. What is it with you? Why, these sandals are just as comfy as house slippers and, now, I know they may not look so good but I'm just slaving here at home and there's nobody to see me so what difference does it make? Or are we having the King and Queen of England for supper? Did someone forget to tell me? I wouldn't be one bit surprised! Nobody tells me anything around here. Oh, I know what you think; but you're wrong! Someday you'll know how wrong you are but then it's going to be too late. Oh, the saddest words on human tongue are those, 'Too late, too late'! But there's nothing I can do about it. I guess the good Lord knows how much a body can take and I know He's not going to give me more than I can bear! Oh, there you go! You just can't stand still for a minute can you? Haven't you the common decency to excuse yourself from the presence of an elder? Oh well, I'm just your Mother, I know I don't count for anything. You're just like all of the rest of them. Nobody cares what I do so what difference does it make what I wear? I'm not going to a tea party! And I surely can't have one here: you know I can't have anything here! Such a great big beautiful home like this, with everything so well done and we're all just stuck here . . . just slaves . . . to the King of Nilesville!"*

Mother worried about money and talked of never having enough to make ends meet. She began hiding wads of bills about the house and then claiming Dad wouldn't give her anything for expenses.

"But that's just fine. I'll show him I don't need his old money."

She put an ad in the paper for ironings and people—curious people, prying people, nosey people, amused people—called on the phone with inquiries and brought their ironings in bushel baskets, laundry baskets, cardboard boxes and paper bags, to the Old Jackson Place; the big white house on the hill out on the West hardroad, for Mrs. Mason, wife of a county official—*"Having such a hard time, poor thing"*—to do their ironings. Mother delighted in it. She greeted them graciously at the door as though they were there socially and she would talk as long as they would linger. It didn't matter who they were to her as long as they had a willingness to listen to her sad story. And she who hated ironing, who refused to iron for her own family, began ironing for strangers, taking meticulous care in order to please.

Dad was humiliated, furious, shamed and fed up. Mother was *"just as pleased as punch"* with the nice response to her little ad and simply couldn't understand what everyone was making such a fuss about.

"Why, I'm just doing honest work for honest money and there's nothing wrong with that."

When we'd urge her to teach school if she wanted to work she'd say, "Why, you know I couldn't leave that poor baby with a stranger all day. And I don't care anything about teaching anyway. There's nothing to be ashamed of with ironing. Why, those poor colored women do it all the time and I'm in the same boat with them. Besides, I've got my life to live just like the rest of you and what I do is nobody's business but mine and if you don't like it that's just your hard luck and you can have that for supper too."

I never knew the particulars of Dad's leaving. He went up North to see about a job and he did not come back. Each week a letter would come from him but Mother claimed they were addressed to her and were for her eyes alone. I never saw them.

Mother had several sets of china and sterling silver flatware as well as silver-plate and the stainless steel that was for kitchen use. One evening I decided to cheer things up by using the "best" for setting the table. When I lifted the lid from a serving bowl I was amazed to see it was full of bills with large denominations. Mother was in the basement ironing. I took it to her. "Mother? Did you know. . .?"

She sat the iron down on it's heel and with her hands on her hips, defiantly said, "What were you nosing around in there for? You have no business being in that china closet! If I've told you once, I've told you twenty times there's no use in using those good dishes for just us here at home. They'll only get broken for nothing. Why, of course, I know that money's there! What do you think I am? Some kind of a dummy? It's mine, isn't it? But that's none of your concern. Now, my legs are killing me and I don't want to have to go up those stairs unnecessarily, so you march right back up there and put that where you found it and forget all about it! Do you hear me? Not one word!"

"These are the happiest days of your life", Mother would tell me repeatedly. *"Now you just go on and enjoy yourself, I'll be fine here."*

I liked school and the extra-curricular activities were the highlight of my life. I was in concerts, plays, and operettas. Mother always refused to attend any event I was in, even when I had a leading part. It was a common practice to have a tea or reception for the parents of the participants and teachers would question me as to why my parents did not attend. It seemed that all of the mothers were always there, except for mine.

Mother had many imaginative excuses. Everyone of them centered around Michael David. He had a cold—he might have a cold—no point in buying a ticket if one can't go. She seemed to enjoy making herself sound so sacrificial. *"There'll be plenty of people there; no one will miss me."*

"Well, I've heard you sing; I don't have to buy a ticket and go to the school to hear you sing."

"Oh, I know the Messiah's nice but I'll hear Christmas music at church or on the radio. You just go ahead, I'll be alright here with the baby."

"Now don't go planning on me attending. I never did care for that play and somebody's got to watch the baby. I can't afford to have someone come out here to baby-sit. Why should I pay someone to do something I can do myself? He's my responsibility and I'll see to him."

"My, you do look grown-up in that gown of Marjorie's and your pink costume for the dance number is so cute, although I'm not so sure it was worth five dollars for Mrs. Hornsby to make it, because I know sewing that little thing up didn't take that long but you had to have it and I understand although I don't think it's right for the school to expect me to pay for something like that but what's done is done and I'll get by alright but there's just no point in expecting me to go for as much as I'd like to, I just can't leave that poor baby alone of the evening and besides you don't know what it is to have to stand and iron all day. I'll tell you, little girl, it's hard work. I'm earning every cent I make and I'm not going to waste it on some ticket to some school show. No, thank you! When you get to be as old as I am you'll see that these things aren't really important. Oh, I know you think they are now but you just tell them I'm busy with the baby. That's a good enough excuse for anyone! It's nobody's business whether I go or not and I tell you it's getting so when night falls I need my sleep for tomorrow's another day and you never know what the day will bring, although, I swear, it's getting so some mornings I don't know if it's worth getting up or not. But beggars can't be choosers so I get up and at 'em."

It was mid-November: cold but clear with a raw Northerly wind blowing the last of the autumn leaves from the trees. Mallards in their

'V' formations were a familiar sight as they followed their migratory path south to Horseshoe Lake.

It was the kind of day when one walks briskly to keep warm: the cheeks sting and the books seem heavier and more awkward then usual because the fingers, though gloved, tingle and smart and numb with the weight and the cold and when one stubs a foot or turns an ankle on the rough gravel it hurts and the cold exaggerates the pain.

Cars whizzed by hurling stinging flurries from Boreas and I thought of him as he was depicted in Josh's reader with big gray cheeks puffing out the North wind.

The long climb up our rutted lane meant just a few more steps now; warmth and food awaits. I was eager to do my homework and get it over with. There was a big French test to prepare for tomorrow. Operetta practice tonight with a full dress rehearsal. That'll be so much fun.

Charlie's picking me up at seven. He's such a creep but he has a good voice and a car, and he's one of the few who isn't overly inquisitive about Michael David or always wisecracking about the baskets of ironings sitting right in the front hallway.

The house seemed unusually quiet. No lights were on. The kitchen was gloomy. A dirty diaper smell was emanating up from the open basement door. Mother would not carry Michael David's soiled things down to the wash room. She tossed them down the stairs and left them laying wherever they landed. I closed the door, dreading to have to go pick them up and put them in to soak.

Open cereal boxes were standing on the countertop, breakfast dishes were piled in the sink, some bowls had crusty cereal caked on them, others had brown soggy foul-looking gobs swimming in a milky residue. The tea kettle was cold and empty and greasy with spatters.

Michael David's baby bottles were standing about: some empty with dried slobbers all over the nipples of the hard rubber tops. Some with an ounce or so of juice or milk, "*Waste not, want not*"—cold toast was still in the toaster.

I dropped my books and wraps on a chair, poured a glass of milk, stirred chocolate in it, glanced at the clock and bet myself I could have the kitchen cleaned up in three shakes of a lamb's tail: uhh, make that a dead lamb's tail.

I cleaned the tea kettle and put it on for tea so it would be ready when Josh got in. I washed and dried the dishes and put things away and cleaned the crumbs off the bare table. God? Whatever happened to tablecloths? I measured out the tea in the little metal strainer and poured the boiling water directly over it just like Grandma used to do. She always said that was better than letting it steep. I tucked the cozy around it nice and tight, set out the honey and a mug and sandwich makings for Josh, gathered my things and went upstairs to my room.

I had heard Mother moving about upstairs. A radio was on, as usual, in Michael David's room. I called, "Mother?"

She answered from my room, and, I sensed in the instant before I saw, that something was wrong.

My room looked as though a tornado had struck. Clothes from the closet were thrown haphazardly on the bed. Wool skirts and slacks were on top of starched, and perfectly ironed, blouses. Drawers were pulled open and under-things and sweaters were bunched in suitcases. My typewriter had been put in its' case and was sitting on the floor by the door with my radio and alarm clock stacked on top of it. I asked, "Mother, what are you doing?"

She crammed another handful of my clothes into a suitcase and forced it to snap shut. Her appearance was startling in itself. Her hair was un-brushed and hanging in limp strands about her face. Glasses magnified her eyes and gave her an owlish look. Her mouth was clamped in a tight line. The faded summer housedress was soiled and wrinkled and strangely out of kilter for cold weather. Mother did not seem to notice my perplexity. She said, more to herself than to me, "I heard you come in. I knew it was time for you to be home and I figured you'd come hurrying in here any minute wanting to get to your books so you could go rushing out again for one thing or another but I've just had more work than I could shake a stick at and I've got that ironing down there calling me and I've been trying all day to get through with this."

"Mother! What are you doing?"

She looked at me as though she had not seen me previously and grimaced with indulgence and cajolery. "Why, Olivia! How would you like to go live with Loralee and Steve? Now, won't that be nice? They've such a nice little house and although Marjorie is living with them since she got that nice job up there, they still have an extra bedroom and no children and probably never will have any. I called her and she said, 'Why yes, we'd love to have Toot,' and you know how much you've always enjoyed visiting with them. They'll be here tomorrow night to get you and I told her I'd have your things all ready although I suspect they'll wait until Saturday to make the drive back. I just didn't think you could manage all this on the bus."

The torrent of words amidst the havoc and the blatant violation of my domain seemed to suck me into a whirlpool of emotions and confusion. No one would treat someone else's things like this. My precious keepsakes were tumbled about on the floor. Even my Bible and Gene

Autry's autographed picture and the bookends made from my own coppered baby shoes were jumbled with other things on the floor. I fought to control the surmounting anger. The desecration was appalling and Mother was talking, talking, talking; rationalizing, as she called it. God!

I saw with my eyes and heard with my ears, but I could not understand. My thoughts were on matters of great importance to me; the French test tomorrow, full dress rehearsal tonight, it will be such fun, Charlie will be here at seven.

The whole world began spinning even faster as my mind rejected what my senses were telling me. I was suddenly so tired and frightened and bewildered: I felt myself being submerged in a sea of red-orange mist, and my knees were rubbery, but I stood, transfixed, in the doorway to what had been, and to what I had assumed would always be, my own personal private room: my refuge, my own world, a place of comfort and rest, of studying and dreaming, of security and stability. I tried to ask her what happened to cause this sudden decision. She was evasive and preoccupied and rambled on about how, " . . . Nothing's easy in this life and if you want something you just have to dig in tooth and nail to get it for you can bet your bottom dollar no one's going to give it to you.

Now you've been riding so high and mighty here all your life and I'm just doing the best I can but one gets to the point where they just can't take anymore. My Papa, God rest his soul, used to say you've got to take the lumps life hands you and if you don't grow with them then you deserve the licking you're sure to get so you can just stick that in your bonnet and see how it fits."

I could not understand it. I was being sent away? From home? From school? What about the operetta? My classes? My friends? The football game tomorrow night? What about the reading I am to give on the special Thanksgiving radio program? What about the birthday party? My French test tomorrow? The operetta next weekend? I could not fathom it! Did I do something wrong? What did I do? Why do I have to leave? Are we really broke? What about the money in the bank? Aren't we still receiving dividends from the trust and stocks? I don't need any money. I can skip lunch and I don't like Cokes anyway. May I stay if I don't need any money? I'll do more to help. I won't ask for anything and I'll try not get in your way. Can't I finish school? Why do I have to leave?

Mother batted the questions like fly-balls in a practice session. She had an answer for everything, but it was all nonsensical to me. It was non-sequitur. Nothing perturbed her. Nothing I could say even phased her. She was dogmatic and obstinate. There was no point of view worthy of consideration aside from her own. Her wordiness was like a wall of relatively polite phraseologies and colloquialisms that had little if any meaning in themselves, but it was impossible to penetrate that fortress. Questions deemed "*too personal*" or, "*not of your concern*" or "*nobody's business but my own*" bounced back to frustrate, thwart and checkmate any further attempts at understanding.

I slumped down on the floor: my knees would not hold me any longer. Her voice spun on and on like a record that never stops. The words, the phrases, the inflections, were all strung together with barbed jabs.

Mother was looking at the suits and skirts Loralee had given me the last time she was home. She wadded them in the suitcase angrily. "Um-umph! She buys the best doesn't she? These don't even look worn! She never did care a snap for money. It just goes through her fingers like water. But, I guess that's none of my business. I'm just her Mother. What I think doesn't matter to her one iota. It isn't enough for some people to have everything: they're not content unless they rub your nose in it. Here I am having to iron day and night just to keep body and soul together and all you can think about is school and singing and being on the radio just as though that's all there is to do. They don't pay you for it, do they?"

She picked up an old pair of brown and white Oxford saddle shoes that had run down heels and holes in the soles. With a sardonic smile she held them toward me.

"Just look at these shoes! And you say you don't need money for anything! Just how do you think you're going to pay to get these fixed? Are you going to sing them a song? Ha! Or give them a reading? Ha, ha. Why, the way you're so hard on shoes it costs a mint just to keep you in shoe leather and I've got more important things to worry about than your shoes."

Mother dropped them in the suitcase on top of a white blouse and continued in a wheedling tone, "Now I'm sorry but I'm doing the best I can and that's all anyone can do. I know for a fact there isn't anyone else, who, standing in my shoes, would do any different or could do any better, and most wouldn't even do half as well. I know you like your school and you're always involved in a lot of things and you have a lot of friends, in spite of your pestering me to let you have them here, as though it's my fault we can't have people in, but you'll find out a friend in need is a friend indeed. I've had a lot of friends in my day but there's not a one of them that's been worth spit when I really needed them. But you'll soon make friends up there and you'll soon get used to the school. Why, they've a much larger one than here so you know it'll be nicer and you'll soon make lots of friends and I understand that's important for your age. It isn't as though it's the end of the world! Marjorie has been staying with them for over a year now, ever since she quit college. You'll be fine once you get used to it. Of course, it'll be strange for you at first but you're young, you'll survive!"

I heard Josh downstairs. Mother snapped another suitcase together, banged the drawers of the dresser closed, picked up a good wool scarf and dusted the black, cow-hide grained suitcase. She griped about letting me use her good luggage and told me to dump things out as soon as I got there and she'd have someone bring them back to her for they were too good to get banged up and Loralee never took care of anything.

"Doesn't even know how to appreciate what she has. I'll tell you if you ever have to scratch around for chicken feed like I'm having to, you'll learn to appreciate it when you're well off."

"Mother?"

"Mother this and Mother that! Why can't you say '*Mom*' like everyone else does? Oh no! You're too high-falutin' to say just plain ole '*Mom*.' Why, I never called my Mother '*Mother*' a day in her life. I always said '*Mama*' and let me tell you if that poor baby could talk he'd be glad to say '*Mama*'."

She chewed on her lips and stared at me owlishly, expectantly.

I knew there was no point in arguing with her and she would consider anything I said as arguing. Usually, when she assumed that hateful kiddy tone we all just left her alone, but now, everything was at stake. God! How can one reason with someone who is not reasonable? What can I say to offset whatever I've done? Should I apologize for something? Does she want me to grovel? What did I do to make her so mad? I tried to keep the exasperation that was choking me out of my voice, as I said, "Mom?"

She snapped, "That just makes me as mad as a wet hen!"

I drew a shaky breath and plunged on, "Does Dad know?"

Mother crossed the room in a flash and stood over me. She punctuated the fresh barrage of words with a wagging finger and spoke between clinched teeth. "Your Dad has nothing to do with anything and there's no point in you bringing him up or thinking it'll change anything because it'll only make matters worse. It's just like mucking out; the more you stir it, the more it stinks and it's better to take things one day at a time and just do the best you can. You won't learn any younger that your Dad isn't what he's cracked up to be. You ought to know how selfish . . ."

Michael David was howling. Mother darted a frown at his door and hurried back toward the center of my room." Now look what you've done! You've got him to howling! Why, he slept all day just as good as gold and you're not in the house anytime until he's howling like a wild animal. Go see to him! There's not time to just sit around like you were the Queen of England and had nothing to do but twiddle your thumbs. He's probably soaked everything and you'll be lucky if it's not worse."

That night, before rehearsal, I told Mr. Smythe that I had to move away and would not be able to be in the operetta. He was livid with rage and paced up and down the stage yelling that there wasn't time for anyone else to learn the part and that I was inconsiderate and irresponsible. He bit his fingernails and harangued on how he had never in twenty years been treated so shabbily or had a student who was not honored and grateful for a chance such as this.

I was besieged with questions I could not answer. The "mystery" caused much speculating and there were a couple of girls that were in the chorus that I hardly knew who were giggling about me being in "trouble" and I did not realize the connotations. Mr. Smythe's indignation seemed to fire the entire cast. Animosity hung in the air as chilling as a cold wet fog. Even Charlie kept a distance as though he didn't want my humiliation to taint him. There were three sopranos anxious to do my part and any one of them would do well.

Mr. Smythe told me pointedly I could leave since I was no longer a member of the cast. Charlie stood looking down at his feet. I walked out into the cold dark night feeling utterly friendless and wishing I were dead.

It was a long cold walk in the dark. There was no moon; no street lights once I left the city limits. Only the occasional car lights that would zoom up and sometimes slow down to give the occupants a better gawk at the lone figure walking on the graveled shoulder of the hard-road. It was scary when they slowed down like that. I wished I had a little handgun. I'd feel safer with some means of protection. Grandma always said, *"GOD HELPS THOSE WHO HELP THEMSELVES."*

I dreaded having to face Mother when I got home. I wished I could talk to Dad but I didn't even know how to get in touch with him since he'd taken that job up North. Mother wouldn't even let us have his address. Everything had gone downhill since Grandma died. God, how I wish I could talk to her just one more time. She'd know what to do. She had a way of making things right. Tears streamed down my face and my nose ran and common sense dictated; it is too cold to cry.

It kinda sounded like Grandma. *"THE WETNESS WILL CHAFE."* I tissued my eyes and nose and walked through the cold and the dark on uncertain ground thinking of things Grandma had told me over the years. *"CRYING OVER A WRONG IS AS USELESS AS CRYING OVER SPILT MILK." "TEARS ARE GOOD: THEY CLEAN THE EYES:*

BUT BETTER TO SHED THEM OVER AN ONION THAN SOMETHING YOU CAN'T HELP."

"NEVER PUT ANYTHING SMALLER THAN YOUR ELBOW IN YOUR EAR." I never did understand that one. What are you 'spose to do when your ear tickles, or when you have water in it? God, mine are freezing. I should have brought that scarf anyway, even if Mother did use it for a dust-rag.

"THERE IS AN INNATE DESIRE DEEP IN THE HEART THAT CRAVES FOR GOD."

"HE CONTROLS THE TIDAL WAVES AND THE RISING AND SETTING OF THE SUN."

"HE CARES FOR THE SPARROW: HOW MUCH MORE HE CARES FOR YOU."

God! Are you there? I can't see a damn thing down here. How about a little moonshine? Oh, that's funny. I'm freezing cold, too! How about a little sunshine! I dare you! Did you put your sparrows to bed? Thanks a lot! How about sending a chariot to carry me home? God I'm scared . . . and who the hell cares? Everyone hates me. . . *"SARCASM IS BITTERNESS SURFACING. IF YOU GIVE VENT TO IT, IT WILL TEAR YOU APART LIKE A PACK OF WILD DOGS."*

That's all I need now, Grandma! A pack of wild dogs to really scare the puddin' out of me. God, if I heard an owl I bet I'd die on the spot. Mother looked so owlish; so bizarre and pathetic. I don't understand her at all. Why is she making me leave? God, why is she so mean to me? What did I do to make her hate me so much? Why. . . ?

"The quality of mercy is not strained. It droppeth as the gentle rain. . ."

"TRUST IN GOD. YOU CAN'T SEE AROUND THE CORNERS."

Wouldn't it be fun if there was some kind of a periscope that could see around the corners of the future? But right now I need eyes to see in the dark, like an owl's. Forget it. I don't ever want to be like Mother. Why does she make everything so difficult? She really seems to enjoy tearing people up or putting them down . . . especially . . . me.

"FORGIVE AND FORGET." "DON'T DWELL ON THE UNPLEASANT . . . THINK ON BEAUTIFUL THINGS." "LIFE IS WHAT YOU MAKE IT". "THE GOOD OUTWEIGHS THE BAD". "THINK ON GOOD THINGS AND LIFE WILL BE SWEET."

God, Grandma was beautiful. She was so kind and good and always seemed to know the right thing to do or say. I'd like to be like her.

"DO THE HARDEST POSSIBLE THING: FORGIVE AND FORGET."

Gee, Grandma, I never thought of you as being preachy but when I think about some of the things you said I do believe I could make my own set of commandments just by concentrating on your piecemeal advice. Of course! I'll call them Grandma's Commandments. Or does that sound a little sacrilegious? Maybe, Grandma's Guidelines? I'll keep them separate from God's commandments and that'll give me two sets of good, proper, tight rules to live by. And I'll give a copy of each to Josh. Gee, how about that? If I have God and Grandma . . . and . . . maybe a gun, umm? just to have, as a reminder of my stock, oh, that's a good one.

"TRY TO FIND SOME HUMOR IN EVERY SITUATION." "LAUGHTER RELAXES YOU AND THEN YOU CAN THINK MORE CLEARLY."

"THINKING BEFORE SPEAKING IS AS IMPORTANT AS AIMING BEFORE FIRING."

I wonder if maybe Dad would let me have that little Smith & Wesson .38 with the ivory handle that Grandma always used and, of course, I'd like a musket; one really rich in history. That Duris Egg with the spectacular silversmith work on the barrels is a real work of art. Much nicer than the one he gave Mr. Jackson for the house. I need a good rifle, for target practice; maybe a Winchester "Classic," 30.30; or a Remington 700, or that old Marlin with the octagonal barrel. God! I'd never seen Dad so happy and excited as he was when Grandma gave him that old British tower pistol. What a surprise! God, he acted just like a little kid. He was so thrilled and elated and kept admiring it and reading the paper of authenticity to all of us and Grandma was just sitting there smiling and Mother kept asking how much. . . ? No, I'll only think of good things. How about my birthday party, God? Let's see, a Browning "Sweet Sixteen" would be most appropriate.

Tears started rolling down my cheeks and it was much too cold to cry. I forced myself to quit crying. One cannot give in to emotion. One must think objectively. I mustn't think about the party. It doesn't matter. It really does not matter. A hundred years from now I'll never know the difference. I don't have any friends that would come anyway. Not after tonight. I wish Dean were here. But, *"IF WISHES WERE HORSES WE WOULD ALL RIDE ."* Oh, God, that's almost funny. I would really miss Dean not being at the party. But, there won't be a party, so, don't think about it. Wonder if I'll get to come home for Christmas? Can't imagine Christmas without Dean and being home.

The wind was so cold. My face felt numb. My feet were wooden as my shoes tapped out a fast clipped beat upon the frozen ground. *"FORGIVE AND FORGET!" "HIS EYE IS ON THE SPARROW: HOW MUCH MORE HE CARES FOR YOU". "FAITH, HOPE, CHARITY."* God! Charity? I could use a little charity myself! *"FORGIVE AND FORGET." "LIFE'S TAPESTRY MUST HAVE DARK THREADS*

AS WELL AS THE BRIGHT." "KEEP YOUR PRIORITIES STRAIGHT: THINGS WILL FALL INTO PLACE."

I could see the Swanson's home in the distance. They had the big glaring outside lights on that lighted up the barnyard. My mind dwelt on Dean. He really was my very best friend. Seemed like he could always make things better. Seemed like he was the only friend I had in the world that really knew and understood me and our crazy family situation. I thought of Dean so far away at school, and I longed to see him, to talk to him. He had such a level head on his shoulders and could see all sides of a problem. Maybe he could make sense of this bizarre situation, but, even he, could not do anything about it. I kept my eyes on their lights and walked as fast as I could. Only one more mile.

A car was coming up the hard-road fast behind me. I moved over as far as I could on the shoulder. It screeched to a halt and voices were calling my name. Charlie jumped out, opened the back door and yelled, "Hey! Toot! Come on, get in! We're all meeting at Walgreen's."

The car was full of cast members. Friends. Charlie cranked the car around and headed for town. They all talked at once about what a beast Mr. Smythe was and how he'd been so cruel and hateful and everyone was terrified of him and they were sorry I was leaving.

I asked how come rehearsal was over so early and they laughed about all of the confusion on stage when Elizabeth, my replacement, persisted in upstaging and overacting. All of the chorus and dancers had been dismissed early. So they had hurried to catch up with me.

Walgreen's was full of my friends. Tables and booths and every stool at the counter held my friends. Some were still busily blowing up balloons, and they had draped crepe paper over the mirror on the back wall. We ate and talked and danced in the crowded aisles and sang with the juke box. Others came in as the word spread that there was an impromptu party at Walgreen's and everyone was reluctant to leave. Mr. Shelby, the proprietor, shooed us out long after closing time, and, as he said, "Only because there's school tomorrow. Don't want you kids gettin' in trouble. Olivia, we're gonna miss you, but I do hope you'll enjoy your school up North, and that you'll have lots of wonderful surprises. Now, you kids be careful goin' home."

Everyone had a million questions and lots of good wishes and promises to write.

The moon was shining brightly and the countryside seemed bathed in a magnificent splendor as Charlie grinded his car up our lane. Kathryn said, "Gee, it's all dark! You don't 'spose you're locked out?"

Wanda said, "If you are, you can spend the night with me."

I said, with a confidence I did not feel, "Oh, I'm sure the back door is open. We never lock it."

Charlie maneuvered the car so the headlights would cut a path through the dark shadows under the trees. The door was unlocked.

I waved and called my thanks and watched as the tail lights disappeared from view. The lights were out at the Swanson's.

Dean had given me strict orders to take Jinx out for a "*Gallumph*" as often as I could. I wished I could see Dean before I left. Surely Mother will let me come home for Christmas! Maybe she will have changed her mind by morning. Maybe I won't have to leave.

I heard Singing Sally's sweet soprano voice come wafting over the frost covered fields. She was singing of the majesty and awe of God's creation and love and care. The stars looked as brilliant as diamonds in the night sky as I stood listening, marveling, wondering. Dean's probably right: there must be a Creator . . . such order . . . such magnificence . . . it could not have come about accidentally. It is too perfect for that. There are laws that govern, control, and guide the stars, the tidal waves, the seasons. What about me? Am I just a puppet being manipulated? What about free will . . . ?

Dean says "*it is free will that sets man apart. The freedom of choice.*" Grandma said "*it is innate in man to look to God.*" Singing Sally looks to you, God. She is so nice, and she has such a beautiful voice. Does her son really hear her? God! It's been five years since he was killed. Does he hear her? Please let him hear her. A rush of cold wind chilled me and I moved toward the door to return to my crazy mixed up world. God? It's so cold. Keep Singing Sally warm.

Administrators, teachers, classmates and friends bombarded me with questions and were chagrined, disgusted, disbelieving and overly curious. The one kind adult was my Speech and Drama teacher, Miss Marks, who "*regretted*" that I wouldn't be able to "*represent the Department again this year.*" Perhaps it was because she reminded me of Grandma, but, for whatever reason, Miss Marks had been my favorite teacher from the first day I met her. She was also the most demanding. But we were en rapport.

For the first time ever, I confided as much as I dared to her of the crazy, confusing circumstances. She listened quietly, sympathized, and insisted we should look on this as a much needed rest and an opportunity for a marvelous new beginning. She assured me she would talk to Mr. Smythe and the other teachers and urged me to remember Portia's speech that I'd done the year before, from Shakespeare's, *Merchant of Venice*: "*The quality of mercy is not strained. It droppeth like the gentle rain . . .*" God! Grandma.

15

🦃 IGNORANCE IS NO EXCUSE

The months I lived with Loralee, Steve and Marjorie were filled with contentment, peace and fun. Steve took on the role of surrogate Father and thereafter I always thought of him as my second dad. Loralee and Marj and I were very close. We were friends as well as sisters. We shared clothes, secrets, jokes and good times. Marj was happy in her work and took a keen interest in my schooling. Loralee was gracious and accomplished and I relished having new found friends in her home. The school work was child's play for me. Even the more demanding subjects were easy and required little work outside of school.

I learned to play tennis and golf and to dance the Polish Polka. In the spring we'd go sailing on weekends. A few times Loralee led us girls in a conspiracy to surprise Steve with outings to ball games or to the race track.

We would go shopping and to concerts and shows and movies. We would eat in the best restaurants and then seek out the home-made ice cream parlors in an on going search for the "thickest" milk shakes. Marj would arrange double dates and Steve would pass judgment on the young men before letting us leave the house with them. If he approved of them, he'd tell us to have a good time. If he was dubious of them, he would insist we be home early or suggest we spend the evening there playing bridge or canasta or crazy eight; whatever they were familiar with. He teased us in a playful big brother manner, but his love and concern for us and his pride in us were evident in everything he did and said.

I thrived physically, spiritually and mentally. Dizzy spells and blackouts were a thing of the past. The red-orange world had become one of

235

clarity and security. We seldom talked of 'home', but the circumstances of home followed us.

By the first of the year Mother had begun writing us long desperate sounding letters of how she needed me at home. Loralee talked to her on the phone for hours, finally convincing her to at least let me finish the school year without another interruption.

Loralee was haunted by the possibility of giving birth to a Mongoloid baby. Her love for Steve and her maternal nature craved fulfillment, but, her dread of bearing a baby like Michael David overshadowed Steve's bright hopes and eager plans for beginning a family. Steve made no demands on her. His respect, admiration and concern for her seemed to supersede even his love for her. He was such a big bear of a man: she was so petite, so dainty, so sweet-natured, and they were totally devoted to each other. She thought the sun rose and set with him. He thought the whole world spun about her. His greatest pleasure was in pleasing her. She expended all of her energies in "doing" for him. Everything seemed to be perfect in their world, except for that one little matter.

He wanted a baby; a son, a daughter, a house full of their children. Loralee wanted a family also, yet, she was terrified of the unknown aspects of the babies she might bear. She felt she could not chance disappointing Steve. She would do anything to keep him from being hurt or shamed or humiliated. She would not, could not, impose such a burden upon the one she loved more than life itself. But neither would she worry him with the details, such as the many methods of contraception that she tried on the QT. On one occasion, when all else failed and she found herself pregnant, she scheduled an expensive 'shopping trip' to Chicago.

Abortions were illegal. Even under the best of circumstances, it was a more or less dangerous procedure. Nature, as well as the law, revolted against the termination of the procreation process.

The secrecy and the guilt that enshrouded the abortion: the sorrow and grief for the life that might have been, and the bitter disappointment that accompanied her belief that she had no choice, were never evident in the cheery disposition she manifested for Steve.

Loralee wanted Marj and I to go with her. She thought it would be more convincing if the three of us went during my spring vacation. Marj agreed, and made the reservation for the train and hotel. Loralee called a long distance number from a pay phone in a public phone booth.

Steve took us to the train station. We kept the pretense of a happy shopping trip until we were safely on the train. Then, each one of us were, in varying degrees, guiltily preoccupied with private thoughts.

The three of us climbed into the back seat of a taxi. Marj gave the driver the address and answered his many friendly attempts at small talk with polite banterings. After what seemed to be an interminable drive, the driver stopped the taxi in front of a small two-story brick house that was surrounded by a wrought iron fence. There was a brass plaque with a doctor's name on it directly under the house number. He said, "Why, this is a doctor's office. I hope none of you pretty ladies is ailing?"

Marj laughed, "Oh, no. We're just visiting an old friend."

She paid him quickly and nudged Loralee and me to hurry out of the cab.

The fence and brick wall were lined with tidy evergreen shrubbery. The small square lawn was green and had a manicured appearance. We debated whether to ring the doorbell or just walk in. Marj asked Loralee,

"Are you sure you want to go through with this?"

"Do I have a choice?"

"You could take the chance. Chances are it would be normal."

"No, Marj. God help me, I'm not going to have a Mongoloid! I'd rather die than give Steve an idiot like Michael David. You know it might be hereditary. It's so unfair. But, I just can't. . . "

"Did you bring the money? They say it has to be cash."

"Yes, thanks to you."

Marj opened the door and we crowded into the small antiseptic smelling waiting room. A woman in a crisp white uniform asked if we had an appointment. Loralee said she did. The woman frowned at Marj and me and brusquely told us we must, "wait here."

Marj whispered, "At least it looks clean!"

Loralee smiled weakly as she turned to go through the door the woman was impatiently holding open for her.

Marj and I waited with shuddering sighs and nervous anxiety. The latest magazines lay untouched as we sat lost in out own dark thoughts.

A few people, obviously patients, entered the office, went into the inner chambers and left again. We waited on. The woman in white appeared from time to time to answer the phone or to usher someone in or out. She seemed to take no notice of us.

Our apprehensions grew as the minutes became hours. I asked, "Marj, what's taking so long? Do you think she's alright or has something really bad happened?"

Marj shushed me. "It just takes time. He's 'spose to be good. She'll be alright. Some women do this all the time, for no good reason."

"Really? Why would they get an abortion without a really good reason?"

"Toot, some women just don't want babies. Loralee really would like to have one. It just doesn't seem fair that we should have to have that goddamned idiot hanging over our heads! Still, all of the doctors claim that particular thing only happens to women who are older and maybe in the change of life. I wish there was some way we could know for certain. The whole goddamn thing just makes me sick!"

"Marj, if I ever got married and, maybe, someday, had a baby . . . do you think I might have one like . . . him, too?"

"How the hell would I know? But, I would hope not. I wouldn't wish that on my worse enemy."

Fear and dread permeated my very being. I shuddered with the horrible thought of having to repeat the nightmarish days and nights I had been through having to care for Michael David.

The minutes ticked on. Marj was turning through a magazine. Suddenly a thought occurred to me. I started turning it over and over in my mind. Dr. Matthews had said that a Mongoloid child had an extra chromosome. What did that mean? Where did it come from? How could one know? If one could determine whether or not an unborn baby had an extra chromosome, then they could know for certain whether or not the baby would be normal or mongoloid.

Marj threw her magazine on the table, and said, "Well, shit! I just hate this. I hate everything about it. It isn't fair to Steve. It's hell for Loralee. And it's so goddamned unfair to that poor baby that'd probably be my perfectly healthy nephew!"

I said, "Marj, I think I'll be a Doctor, or a Scientist."

Marj was taking a cigarette out of her purse. She looked at me as she tapped it against her lighter. She seemed to be weighing me as she lighted the cigarette, took a deep drag and blew the smoke toward the ceiling. "Toot, you have a lot of talent. You can draw. You can paint. You can sing. You can play the piano, the violin . . . not the French horn."

We both laughed with the knowledge that my attempts at playing the French horn had been disastrous. Marj tapped the ashes from her cigarette and looked at me intently as she asked,

"Toot, you can be anything you want to be: but, why the hell would you want to be a doctor?"

"I'm not sure, Marj. But, Dr. Matthews said something about chromosomes. I don't understand it, but apparently it makes a difference whether the baby is normal or not. I would like to learn what the difference is. I would like to be able to help people so that no one would have to have an abortion because of being afraid of having a monster. God! We shouldn't have to do an abortion without knowing for certain whether it's necessary or not! There must be some way to know. Then, one could make an intelligent decision, and not have to live in fear of what might be. There has to be an answer out there someplace. It just seems like ignorance is no excuse."

"Well, don't get all worked up. Don't look so worried. You're going to have wrinkles before you're twenty, if you don't learn to relax your countenance. Don't you remember how Grandma used to say, 'You mustn't frown. You only make wrinkles and hurt yourself'."

Marj and I both laughed. I tried to relax my countenance. I even picked up a magazine and thumbed through it, but my eyes kept turning to the door that had closed behind Loralee.

It was nearly noon when Loralee reappeared. Her face was drained of color and she seemed to be too weak to stand without support.

The woman called a taxi for us and seemed to be anxious for us to leave.

Loralee was strangely quiet. She seemed to be in a daze. Her step was faltering as Marj and I led her to the waiting taxi. I felt a sense of relief that we were leaving that horrible place behind us.

The noon hour traffic was heavy: the driver drove in spurts with jerking, jolting stops. He kept one hand on the horn and honked at pedestrians as well as motorists while cursing them under his breath. He braked to a screeching stop at our hotel and sat dumbly at the wheel while Marj and I helped Loralee out of the cab. His mouth fell open in disbelief when Marj gave him her sweetest smile and a nice tip in addition to the charges. Belatedly, he opened his door as though to get out and assist us, then slammed it shut and sped off into the flow of traffic.

I had not realized how long the lobby of our hotel was. Loralee was so weak, yet, trying to walk normally. The elevator seemed to stop at every floor to discharge or envelope more slow moving people. Loralee was as white as a sheet by the time we reached our room. She collapsed on the bed in tears. Marj and I stood helplessly by, as she sobbed, "I feel like a baby murderer."

Marj said, "Now, that's ridiculous! You can't murder something that isn't even living, or even formed yet."

"But it could have lived if it had had the chance and Steve wants a baby so badly. Oh God, if he ever finds out what I've done he'll hate me. I know he will. I hate myself."

Loralee covered her face with her hands and gulped great heart-wrenching sobs. I felt a sense of terror and helplessness compounded by an overwhelming guilt. In my mind's eyes I kept seeing babies: a beautiful baby in a lacy white christening dress, a baby in pink laughing in a cradle, a baby in blue being pushed in a buggy, and a precious much loved baby being cuddled by its' adoring parents. But, then, Michael

David came to mind and I shuddered involuntarily and began crying at the sheer injustice of such a threat.

Marj stood up quickly, scraping her chair backwards on the floor. "Now, shut up! Both of you, just shut up! Goddamnit, Loralee, you've got to stop torturing yourself like this. You did what you thought was best. Only God knows whether it would have been a healthy baby or a goddamn monster! But, one thing for sure; it is not a baby until it is born. It has to leave it's Mother's body, have the umbilical cord cut and begin breathing on it's own before it is an actual individual."

Loralee's face was flushed: her eyes were swollen and red. She stared off into the distance, gasping dry sobs.

I remembered Grandma telling me of her babies that were born prematurely and stillborn. What was it she had said about the one that looked so perfect but could not draw the breath-of-life? Can it be that "breathing" is what determines the time that life begins? Is that when the soul enters the body? I remembered Loralee comforting me after Grandpa died: telling me about how the soul is like the breath we breathe and that when the soul leaves the body, the body dies. But, if a baby never breathes, than it has not had "life" at all. Perhaps it could have. Perhaps it could be 'perfect:' if only one could know for sure.

Loralee grimaced and doubled over in pain, holding her folded arms tightly against her abdomen.

"Oh God! I'm flowing like a river. And . . . it hurts like hell."

Marj finished packing our few things and snapped the suitcase closed. She nodded for me to carry it and addressed Loralee. "We've got to get you home."

"What can I tell Steve? We haven't done any shopping, and the way I am . . . he'll know something's wrong."

"Go freshen up. Put on a double Kotex. We'll just tell him you've got women's problems and had to come home to see a doctor. Now, hurry up, we've just time to get to the train station."

Steve never seemed to question our non-productive trip. After a few days, Loralee was fine and was busily planning fun evenings and weekends full of surprises. Steve worshipped Loralee and doted on her. If he thought it peculiar that there should be no baby in the making after their many years together, he never revealed it.

Summertime came much too soon. I dreaded going home. I had missed Josh and Dean and Jinx. I had thought of them often, but I dreaded going back to hell after such a delightful time in paradise.

Mother welcomed me home with the same complacent regard she would show to one who had run an errand to the store and back. I had been gone for eight months. Nothing had changed, except my point of view. I saw things in a clearer light and I felt I understood Mother's actions a little better. I had had a much needed rest. I had been on the hilltop and I had looked down on the valley with a new, broader perspective. It wasn't quite so frightening at a distance. I was back now, full of vim and vigor and hope. . .

Josh went home with Steve and Loralee for the summer. He was excited about the visit and I was happy for him. I knew he would have a rich growing experience and the best time of his life. He had griped of how Mother had been pressing all sorts of hideous duties on him, but was too stingy to let him go to the movies.

It was strange at first with only Mother, Michael David and me in the house. Michael David had learned to take several steps at a time but still resorted to scooting about on his bottom as a regular means of locomotion. His gait was unsteady as he swayed his bulky frame from side to side taking giant steps with his feet pointed at angles. But he could walk! He had also learned to feed himself. I praised him on it and asked Mother when he began wielding the spoon and even a fork so well. She replied off-handedly, "Well, there was no one to do it for him so he just began doing it himself. I was just fed up with having to put every spoonful in his mouth. He had to learn sometime so I just sat his plate in front of him and told him there it is, now eat it and every time he'd start to use his fingers I'd take it away. He learned mighty quickly to use the fork and spoon."

I noticed how much he'd gained and said, "It certainly doesn't look like you denied him any meals. He looks like he's gained twenty or thirty pounds, all around the middle."

"Why, he'd eat all day if I'd let him. I'll tell you he really knows how to shovel it in. But he still chokes a lot and does that ever make him mad. I mean, watch out when he gets choked because he has a regular tantrum; throwing things and banging his fists on the table or anyone that's near by. That's why I'm still buying baby food for him; it's so much easier than taking a chance on him choking."

I asked, "Is that how you got those bruises on your arms and forehead?"

Mother turned away annoyed. "Now, don't you start!"

I asked, "Has he made any progress in toilet training?"

Mother rolled her eyes to the ceiling and shrugged, "Progress? Now there's a good word. I'd forgotten it. Seems like I've been going backwards for so long I don't know what it is to go forward. But, yes, to answer your question, he has progressed. At least as far as number one is concerned. Some days I don't even put a diaper on him but I'm not so sure it's worth the mess when he just out and out craps all over everything. Those jeans are so hard to clean and wash and I get so sick and tired of the whole stinking mess."

Mother looked as though she had aged years. Wrinkles were prominent, she looked physically exhausted, and she wore a worried expression. I said, "Mother, I think it is absolutely fantastic how much you have achieved with him."

"Pshaw! One just does what one has to. After you took off there wasn't anyone to see to him. I'm so sick and tired of being tied down and never knowing where the next cent is coming from."

"Mother, I know Dad sends you money all the time. There is no reason for you to do ironings or anything else if you don't want to. How much do you have in the bank?"

"Not enough to shake your fist at! How do I know how much I'm going to need for that baby? Why it cost me nearly three thousand dollars just to have that quack from England come and look at him. He didn't even spend ten minutes with that baby and then he talked so hoity-toity I could hardly understand him."

"What did he say?"

"Well, what do you think he said? 'Put him in an institution'—That's all anyone knows to say! 'Put him in an institution'."

I sighed, "Mother? If it would be the best thing for him, then why not do it? I'm sure it would be the best thing for you and all of the rest of us. I don't like to see you so worried and tired . . ."

"Oh, I'm alright. It just burns me up when I think of that so-called expert acting so high and mighty and coming in here like he was something on a stick, craning his neck about, gawking at everything and then saying there was nothing he could do. But he sure knew how to take my money and had the gall to pretend it was just for expenses! Some fancy expenses! And then he stood right there and counted the money after I'd already counted it out for him."

"You don't mean you gave him cash?"

"Why, yes, what's wrong with that? It's better than a check any day of the week and I just thought I'd use up some that was laying around here not doing anyone any good."

"Mother! Will you please use some of that old money that's just laying around here on yourself? Why don't you go shopping and get some new things to wear. Have your hair done. See a good movie."

"Humph! Been so long I wouldn't know how to act."

"It has been too long, Mother. You have done everything over and above what could possibly be expected for Michael David. You know there is no cure for Mongolism. You've had doctors all across the country and now even this fancy one from England tell you the same thing. He can never be normal. He will never be able to understand any better than a one-year old baby. They might be able to train him to do some things if you put him in an institution. They're trained in techniques that we don't know about."

"Now I'm not asking for your opinion. You don't understand; no one understands! You're just a child yourself and there are some things that just hurt me too much to talk about them. I don't understand either but Lord knows he's here and I'm not going to put him away in some institution and if I have to live the rest of my life with him about my neck . . ."

I started laughing at the preposterous mental image of Michael David about Mother's neck. She began laughing too, but then grew thoughtful, "Your Dad used to say I'd never be satisfied with anything, not even the moon on a string to wear about my neck. Fat lot he knows! I sure never thought he'd give me anything like this! But then he never did care a hoot about me or any of you children. All he ever thought about was guns and guns and guns. 'They're an investment' he'd say; 'they're our heritage', 'they're better than money in the bank'. Bull! Why, I can see right through him and some days I have a good mind to just sell every one of them myself. They're not doing a bit of good just laying around in there or packed away in boxes. Of course, he took some with him for his hunting pleasure, and I'd sure give the world to know what else he's doing for his pleasure but I'd bet my bottom dollar he's living high on the hog and never gives a one of us a thought."

"I had several nice letters from Dad, Mother. Don't you hear from him every week?"

"That doesn't mean a thing. He just discharges his duties like he does his bowels. That doesn't take any thought."

"Mother! You didn't use to talk so earthy!"

"Well, when you have to live in it you get to recognizing it for what it is."

My head began to throb and I pressed my hands against my temples in an old forgotten gesture. Mother was agitated. "Now don't tell me you're going to start getting a headache! I thought you said you didn't have them anymore! Why, you haven't been home twenty-four hours and here you are holding your head."

I couldn't remember the things I was going to say. All of my plans, so carefully formulated, were going haywire. I had come back home determined to not get mired down in the ruts of the daily grind; confident that I could convince Mother of the unreasonableness of her attitude toward Dad, money and Michael David's condition. What was it I had planned? The way she twists everything around is so confusing. What was it that seemed to be such a clear solution? Truth. Truth! And humor. Find something to laugh at. *Laughter relaxes you and then you can think more clearly*. Something to laugh at. . . ?

"Mother? Did you know . . . uh . . . Steve has such a marvelous sense of humor. He was always telling us Pat and Mike stories and Polish jokes and relating humorous things he'd heard. Uh—Did you know the first tribute to Mother is Scriptural? Who said, 'Mother, you know I love you, but the way you're raising Cain is just killing me?'"

Mother looked puzzled. She folded one arm across her waist, rested her elbow in her hand and smoothed her forehead with her fingers as though deep in thought. She queried, "That's scriptural?"

I grinned, "Well, kinda."

"Cain? Cain and Abel? Oh, Abel!" She laughed with abandonment.

Michael David came scooting into the room imitating the laughing sounds and drooling all down the front of his shirt. I got up to wipe his mouth. Mother repeated the question and laughingly planned to tell the preacher. She said, "See there how he's laughing at that joke? You can't tell me he doesn't understand what's going on."

"I'm sure he understands the emotions or the feelings or the pulsations; but the words themselves have no meaning to him."

Mother began chewing on her lip and nervously twiddling her thumbs as she sat with her shoulders stooped, staring at the floor.

"Loralee and Marj gave me several tubes of lipstick and all kinds of make-up, Mother. Would you like to look through it and see if there's something you'd like to try?"

"Why, I never have worn much make-up. Never did wear lipstick. I always thought that was for hussies."

"Oh now, come on, Mother, you used to say a little paint never hurt the old barn."

Mother laughed, "But I never thought of myself as that old barn."

"You know I didn't mean that! But I do mean it when I say I want you to go someplace or do something just for the sheer hell of it. Just for fun! You are way over-due, Mother. Now, where would you like to go? St. Louis? Florida? New York? You name it!"

"Don't tempt me, Child. You know I can't afford. . ."

"Bull feathers! The truth is you can easily afford anything you want. Now isn't that the truth? Honestly, Mother?"

Mother stammered, "Why, I don't know whatever gave you such an outlandish idea! And here I am slaving away at ironing for a living, nearly killing myself with trying to care for that poor baby. . ."

"He is not a baby, Mother! True, his comprehension is no more than a baby's, but he weighs as much as you or me. He is not a baby!

"True, you do seem to be trying to kill yourself. But isn't there an easier way to go? Are your legs still bothering you? Are those veins getting worse? Can you tell me why you are doing ironings, Mother? I mean the truth! Is it just to shame us all? Is it to make Dad look little and foolish? That's what everyone says. Is that true?"

"Why, Olivia! It just isn't nice to talk to your Mother like that. I just can't believe you're pumping me for information that is of no concern to you at all. What lies between your Father and me is of no consequence to you children. I'm not surprised that you girls, being together like that, have speculated on things. And I know each one of you would choose your Dad over me any day of the week, but I can't help that. You can think what you want to. I'm just trying to do the best I can with what little I have to work with."

"Mother, that's exactly what I'm trying to find out. What do you have to work with? How much is in the bank? What do you have on hand? How much does Dad send you each week? What do you get in dividends from the co-op? What were the profits from the crops? Don't you see what I'm saying? You don't need to punish yourself doing other people's ironings! You always said you hated ironing! Why hurt yourself doing it if it isn't necessary? If you want to work, teaching school would be a lot easier."

Mother brushed her hair back from her face and seemed to be weighing what I'd said. I looked around at the deteriorated condition of the kitchen. It looked as though it had not been cleaned thoroughly in months. Mother followed my gaze and laughed, "If there's one thing I hate more than ironing, it's doing housework."

"I'll tell you what, Mother. You go visit Aunt Katie for a few days while you think about where else you would like to go! I'll watch Michael David and have the house all cleaned up when you get back."

"You'll do that?"

"It'll be good for you, Mother. Why don't you call and get an appointment to have your hair done this morning? Then stop in Taylor's Shoppe and buy a new dress. I dare you! You'll feel like a new person."

"Well, I don't know. I've got to finish Mrs. Taubman's ironing and she always brings more when. . ."

"I'll tell her what to do with it, Mother."

She laughed, "Sometimes I'd like to! You know she looks down her nose at me! It's like she gets a kick out of me doing her ironing. She acts like she thinks she's better than I am."

Mother sighed and chewed nervously on her lip and talked more to herself than me as she imitated a patronizing nasal tone, "'Now Martha, be very careful with this blouse for it's very expensive and these ruffles must be starched and ironed so they stand up.' I felt like telling her she was too big to wear ruffles, that old bat! I could buy and sell her twice over any day of the week if I took a notion."

"Do it, Mother!"

"Why—do what?"

"Buy her! Sell her! Show her up! You'd feel better and it could be fun!"

"Why, Honey? Such a thought! Why, I can't waste good money. . ."

"It wouldn't be a waste, Mother. Have some fun with it! Put it to some good use! What could you do that'd be spectacular in a quiet way?"

Mother looked thoughtful and seemed to be enjoying herself as she recounted, "Well, let's see now. The preacher was wanting money to send some of the needy children to church camp and he's always wanting money for something about the church; the basement needs work and he wants to fix up a recreation room for you young people and . . . Do you want to go to Church Camp this year?"

"No. I hadn't even thought about it. After being away so long I don't much care."

"Well, you can if you'd like. Maybe I'll just give him ten dollars for some needy child."

"Give him a hundred, Mother."

"What?"

"Give him a thousand and tell him it's a memorial!"

"Well, now . . . I don't know. A memorial. . . ? Who to?"

"Mrs. Taubman's ironing?"

Mother laughed and giggled like a school girl. She fluttered her eyes and stretched freely, "Oh, you silly girl! My, it is good to have you home, but I don't have time for this foolishness if I'm going to get my hair done and I do need to do some shopping. You won't be afraid here by yourself if I leave for a few days?"

I asked, "Why should I be afraid?", and thought to myself—I have God, guns and Grandma.

Mother teased, "You used to be afraid of the ghost in the attic."

I said, "Thanks to Marg and her scary stories."

Mother giggled indulgently and I asked, "Is that rope still hanging in the attic?"

We both laughed with memories of happier days. She said, "I haven't touched it. But it seems to have gotten awfully frayed", she suddenly saddened, ". . . just like my dreams. . ."

I was determined to keep things light, and more daring than I'd ever been before, I said, "You do have a way with words, Martha! But you know what the Bible says about dreams—any fool can have them but it takes a man to make them come true."

Mother gasped and stared at me in puzzlement, "If I didn't see you with my own eyes I'd think you were your Grandma talking! It doesn't say that in the Bible does it?"

"Yep! Same place it says to vote Republican!"

"Mother Mason always quoted Proverbs and Philippians'. You know, about a merry heart and thinking nice things. I don't know if they were her favorites but she certainly adhered to them."

Mother was animated and excited about going shopping. She went upstairs to bathe and dress. I called Alf. The phone rang repeatedly, was fumbled off it's cradle and a sleepy sounding voice said, "'Ello?"

"Hi Alf! Did I get you up?"

"No, you smart ass. I had to get up to answer the phone! When d'ya get back?"

"Yesterday."

"Well? D'ye have something in mind or d'ye just call to wake me?"

"I need help, big brother."

"Aww hell, Toot! It's too early for violins . . . What kind uv' elp?"

"It's a virtual jungle out here; the grass is knee high to an elephant and there are weeds all over the gardens."

"Shit!"

"That's piled up in here."

"Well, get somebody to clean it up."

"Hi, Somebody!"

The silence grew heavy. I asked, "Alf?"

"Yeah. What's Mom doing?"

"Getting ready to go shopping, I think."

"I'll get Tom and Guy and Harold. We'll be out in a little bit."

"I'll have some coffee ready."

"Naw, I'll bring some beer."

"You better bring a machete!"

"Shit."

I made two more calls. Mr. Swanson said he'd send a couple of men over to do the windows since they were just watching the crops grow. Mrs. Hawkins was glad I'd called and said she'd bring her daughter to help with the housework.

Mother was excitedly planning her own day and was oblivious to the plans I was making and left in a taxi just minutes before Alf and the "crew" he'd enlisted pulled up.

I started cleaning in the kitchen and inventoried sandwich makings as the steady hum of the mower provided background orchestration for the amiable, though coarse, calls of the yard crew, who'd chucked their shirts in the humid heat of mid-June. They'd plop down in the shade from time to time to have a beer and swap yarns and war stories and off-color jokes which they made a big deal about not letting me hear.

Mrs. Hawkins and Maud arrived and the three of us cleaned and mopped and waxed and washed the walls and polished furniture. Michael David was excited and fascinated with all of the hub-bub. He'd sit rocking back and forth in the house for a while and then go scooting on his bottom out to the porch, babbling incoherently to himself, enjoying all of the activity. Every time someone would call something to him —'What do you think of all this, boy?'—he'd laugh and croak idiotically. The boys had dubbed him 'the Sergeant' and he quickly imitated their salutes.

Mrs. Taubman drove up the lane in her post-war Ford. She lifted a basket of ironing from the trunk and carried it up to the front door. I stood at the screen door smiling sweetly, ignoring Michael David who had come scooting up to see who had come to the door. She stared at him. He sat on the floor staring back, his oversized tongue protruding from one side of his jutted out mouth. Disgust and repulsion showed in her expression. Michael David felt it and continued staring at her sullenly. I realized she had not seen him before. Mother always kept him out of sight. I felt a temper of defiance but I tried to be dignified and gracious, realizing the incongruity of the situation and the contrast between M.D. and me.

I said, "Good afternoon."

She stared at me in confusion and stammered, "I've brought . . . are you. . . ? Is Martha here?"

"Mrs. Mason is out now. May I help you with . . . something?"

"Why, I brought my ironing. And she's supposed to have some ready for me."

Mrs. Taubman had opened the screen door and was trying to put the basket down inside while she was talking. Michael David saw the door open and started scooting through it to the porch. She stepped back quickly and gave him a wide berth. I pulled the door shut as she stood there still holding the laundry basket, looking at M.D. as though he were contaminated. I said through the screen, "If you'll wait one moment, please? I'll see if I can find your . . . things!"

She had been straining to look past me. Mrs. Hawkins was nosily wielding the vacuum cleaner and Maud was washing the wood work. Alf was busily trimming the evergreen shrubs around the porch and taking a keen interest in our exchange. Tom and Harold were pulling weeds and hoeing and from out in the back the mower whirred it's path through the overgrown lawn. Mrs. Taubman set the basket down and stepped to the railing, craning her neck to see the man up on the ladder washing windows.

I scampered to the basement feeling giddy with mischievousness and wondering how I'd ever know which things were hers. But a frilly over-sized blouse caught my eye. It was hanging with other freshly ironed blouses and shirts. A laundry basket with un-ironed things stood near. I gathered them all up and carried them to the door. Mrs. Taubman seemed to have regained her composure and complained haughtily, "But . . . they're not all done!"

I smiled, "These are your things?"

"Well, yes . . . but, she didn't iron them all! Where is Martha? Is she here?"

"Mrs. Mason is out."

"Well, will you tell her I've got to have these. . ."

"Mother will not be doing any more ironing for you, Mrs. Taubman."

"Wh—She's been ironing for me for months. Is she sick?"

"Oh no. Mother is fine; thank you."

Mrs. Taubman was rattled. Alf was watching with amusement. She said, "Well, who can I get? I don't like to drive down in nigger-town."

I replied, "I neither know nor care. Will you excuse me please?"

"But, I owe you, or . . . Martha, uh, Mrs. Mason, for these things. . .Will a dollar be enough?"

"No mam! You keep your dollar; for the inconvenience."

Her face reddened and she was perspiring profusely as she stood there holding the ironing on hangers in one hand, her purse in the other, and the two baskets of laundry at her feet. She acted flustered, and inquired, "Are you . . . is it . . . Olivia?"

My face seemed to be frozen in a tight smile. I inclined my head slightly as I had seen Grandma do so many times.

Mrs. Taubman sized me up from head to toe. I was glad I had on the designer shorts and blouse that Loralee had given me. I knew they screamed quality. She smiled syrupy, "I've heard so much about you."

I did not respond but wrapped myself in dignified silence.

Michael David made a rather rude sound that could have been interpreted in different ways. She looked at him with raised eyebrows and asked, "Is that, uh. . ."

"He is my brother!" I turned to Michael David and said, "Michael? Would you like to say "How do you do?' to Mrs. Taubman?"

His little round head bobbed and his gooey slanty eyes were enveloped in folds of flesh as he grinned broadly. He threw his hand up in an attempt at a salute; the double-jointed little finger was nearly touching the back of his stubby hand. He grunted, "Uhh!"

Repulsion was written on her face as she took a step back and then, ignoring Michael David, and looking all about she asked, "What are you doing?"

I said, "I beg your pardon?"

She stared hard at me and repeated, "What are you doing? Cleaning?"

"Yes."

"Are you going to be staying here now?"

Defiance and resentment toward the overstuffed and overbearing matron fought with my anger and shame of Mother. But I did not mean to be rude when I asked, "I beg your pardon?"

She caught her breath and narrowed her eyes and repeated as though I were dense or deaf, "Are you going to be staying here now?"

Again, I inclined my head. She looked at me for a moment and said, "Well, Martha's bragged on you a lot but I never . . . My, you're nothing like your Mother, are you?"

"A Dieu ne plaise que."

She stared and said sharply, "What did you say?"

"Excuse me please! I've much to do."

Mrs. Taubman murmured something under her breath as I stepped away from the door. She turned to Alf with a sharp commanding tone and ordered, "Can you put these things in my car?"

I heard him drawl in a voice reminiscent of Mr. Aikens, "Wahl, yas, ah can in that ah'm able ah reckon. But ah tak muh orders frum the sergeant there! What d'ye say, Sarg? Ye want ah should 'elp th lady, er, uh, woman?"

Michael David croaked and grunted, "Uhh".

Mrs. Taubman waddled with quick little steps to her car, as Alf obligingly carried the two laundry baskets and sat them down next to her car, in the freshly cut grass. He sauntered back to the shrubs and saluted M.D. who laughed idiotically. She was obviously angry as the large clumps of matted grass clung to the wicker baskets of her un-ironed clothing and to her sandaled feet.

I walked away from the door feeling more guilt than pleasure. Perhaps I should have been more civil? Mother can fight her own battles. Mrs. Taubman isn't to blame for hiring her work done. Mother probably asked for the put-down, the way she tries to milk sympathy from everyone. But that old bat should not have reacted to Michael David like that. Staring at him as though he were an object of disgust instead of a person with feelings. Looking at him so mean and repulsed. He knew what she was thinking, or feeling. I didn't handle it right. What would Grandma have done? It isn't right to hide him away from people; especially here in his own home. But she hurt his feelings. It was so obvious. He was happy until she came and then that look in his eyes when she drew away from him with such a show of revulsion. God! I was too nice to her. But, maybe it was the first time she had ever seen a Mongoloid child. Maybe it was just the ignorance. She was probably afraid of him. Maybe she thought it was catching. God? Do we really get back ten times over what we give out? In feelings as well as deeds? What about ignorance? Are the ignorant excused from class? What about good manners? Good manners dictate kindness. *Be ye kind one to another.* Should I have been kinder to her? Shouldn't she have showed some kindness to Michael David? God! I wonder what Grandma would have done.

I had hurried to the kitchen and poured a big orange soda for Michael David. It was his favorite drink. I took it to him on the porch and sat by him, holding the drink for him and telling him what a good boy he was. He babbled and chortled contentedly.

By five o'clock the lawn was neatly manicured; no trace of new cuttings. The flower borders had been weeded and the fresh turned-up soil encouraged the perennials to new life.

Grandma's peonies lifted their heavy heads in thanks as the choking weeds that had smothered them into near oblivion were gently removed from around their roots and through their branches. Even Mr. Aiken would have chuckled with approval at the battle those "vets" had fought and won on that lawn that day!

I had no qualms about dipping into the China Bowl to pay for the housework and window washing.

Mother arrived home heavily laden with dress boxes and shoe boxes and a hat box. She came in the door talking, "Well, I just can't believe my eyes. I told the taxi driver we must have the wrong house! How did you ever manage to get that yard . . . Why, you even . . . ? What in the world did you do? Wave a magic wand?"

We had a light supper and chatted about the happenings of the day. I put Michael David to bed and had a leisurely bath. I was reading in my room when Mother came in with a worried expression on her face and a handful of receipts.

"Do you know how much we spent today?"

I said, "Now Mother! You had a good time and we got a lot of work done. Let's not think about the cost."

"That's easy for you to say! How much did you pay Mrs. Hawkins?"

"She brought Maud with her and they both worked hard all day. I didn't give her too much."

"But what I'm wondering is, if she works like that several days a week, she must be doing alright."

"I hope so. She is a very nice lady."

Mother toyed with the jars, bottles and tubes of make-up on my dressing table. She wound the music box and held it up, admiring it as it tinkled out it's merry tune. I turned the radio off and braced myself for the impending storm that seemed to be brewing; the storm that always seemed to follow in the aftermath of our spending money. I made a stab at deterring it.

"Your hair looks so nice. I wish you'd wear it like that all the time."

Mother looked in the mirror and agreed,

"Yes. Charlotte does a good job, but I don't think I can afford a dollar fifty every week just to have my hair done. Do you think maybe you could do it?"

"I can try, but it won't be as much fun as going to the beauty shop and hearing all the gossip."

"I don't need gossip. I do wish you hadn't been so blunt with Mrs. Taubman. There's no telling what she'll be broadcasting about. Not that I care, but it's just the idea."

"You said you didn't like the way she makes you feel, Mother. So why punish yourself by dealing with her? It isn't necessary."

"Do you know how much I spent today?"

I answered in sing-song, "My Mother told me it isn't nice to talk about money!"

Mother smiled and sighed. I said, "You bought some lovely things, Mother. I wish you'd just enjoy them. That hat is so pretty on you."

"You really like it? You may wear it sometime if it isn't too old for you. Your Dad always liked my hats. Oh, he'd tease me about them being silly, but, I know he liked them, nevertheless."

Mother was dabbing some rouge on her cheeks. I watched as she smoothed it to near nothingness.

"Try that pink tube of lipstick, Mother. It's a nice shade for you."

She put it on carefully and blotted it on a tissue and stared at the results. I said. "That's very becoming."

She said, "It reminds me too much of Shirley Zimmerman."

I asked, "Who's that?"

She began wiping her face and said disgustedly, "She's one of your father's old girl friends; a painted hussy, if there ever was one."

I wondered if she was the lady in pink I'd seen so long ago. I asked, "Does she have red hair?"

"She dyes it red. It's really a mousy brown. How did you know?"

"Oh, I used to see some red-headed woman in town once in awhile. She was always made up more than most."

"It was probably her. She lives up North someplace now but she's down here frequently. Her father was a preacher! She married young, but is divorced now."

Mother got up and walked about the room. I still had unpacking to do. She unbuckled a suitcase and went through the contents without comment. I turned the radio on and the lovely strains of *Sweethearts* sung by Jeannette McDonald and Nelson Eddy filled the room. Mother sat down on the edge of the bed to listen. After awhile she spoke in a far-away voice, "I just don't know what to do. Sometimes I think we ought to get a divorce and be done with it; nothing can ever be the same again. There's just been too much said and done. But I've never believed in divorce. It just goes against the grain! Not that I don't have grounds; that is, Scriptural grounds; but I just don't like the connotation. I just can't bring myself to do it."

I asked quietly, "Mother? Can't you forgive and forget?"

Her voice was hard and brittle as she snapped, "That's easier said than done, little girl! How can I ever forget as long as I've got that poor baby on my back as a constant reminder?"

God! Find something to laugh at . . . humor . . . God, help me!

I said, "Mother, I do wish you could have seen how Michael David was enjoying all of the attention he was getting today. The boys called him 'Sergeant' and taught him to salute and he'd just laugh and get so excited. I really think it was good for him to have a lot of people around. He really enjoyed himself. And he even held his glass of pop without spilling it."

She looked at me suspiciously, "Were they making fun of him?"

"No, Mother! Not at all! They were all wonderful with him! Why, Alf helped him walk out on the grass and he even sat under the tree with them for awhile."

"I hope he wasn't out there when Mrs. Taubman came."

I was quiet; hoping she wouldn't want a response.

"Was he? Did she see him?"

I told her of the sequence of events. She listened intently, opening her eyes to their widest and taking a sharp intake of breath when I described how Mrs. Taubman had reacted to Michael David. When I told of Alf's asking the 'Sergeant's' permission to carry the laundry baskets, Mother began laughing.

"Oh, I wish I'd been here to see that! Alf used to always be such a cut-up. My goodness gracious! Here I've dreamed of her getting her come-uppance and then I miss it."

Mother began chewing on her lip and looking worried. She mumbled, "I hope she doesn't tell everyone but I know she will. One just can't keep a secret for long in a small town."

"Everyone knows about Michael David, Mother."

"Well, yes, I know they do. But they haven't seen him, or, that is, very few have. I'm not going to have him a topic of ridicule! You know how children and even grown-ups: people who ought to know better, try to imitate and make fun of one who's retarded. And they know! They know people are making fun! And it's bound to hurt them even if they don't know how to express it. It hurts me so bad! I get all torn up inside and I just don't know what to do about it."

She looked so vulnerable; as though every nerve were exposed. I said, "Please, Mother. You know you mustn't let other people's attitudes bother you like that."

She continued, "I know, I know that. I'm not responsible for what they do or how they think or how they act but it still hurts! Why, even Josh got so mad at me because I wouldn't let him go to a movie last week."

"He told me about that. He said all of his friends were going."

"I know that! But I'm not going to spend my money on a ticket for some movie where the so-called comedian does nothing but act retarded. I think he's sadistic and cruel and I hope to God he gets back every pain he gives out! What I can't understand is why people allow it. Why do they go to see it? Why do they pay their money just to see some idiot who's just poking fun at the poor unfortunates of this world?"

"It's just a movie, Mother. It's supposed to be funny. I'll bet Josh didn't even relate it to M.D."

"I'm not blaming Josh for wanting to go. It's only natural for a child to want to go to something that's 'spose to be entertaining. But I do blame Hollywood for pushing such a base and vile joke on the public. Some joke! Some star! Why, I've got more talent in my little finger than he shows with his parody of the handicapped! I sometimes think it'd serve him right to be permanently palsied and to lose all of his faculties. Then he could see how funny it isn't!"

I'd began doodling on my drawing pad and answered without feeling, "If he lost all of his faculties he wouldn't know what he was doing anyway. But, as it is, he's a big star and probably laughing all the way to the bank."

"I'll bet you he isn't laughing when he reads my letter."

I asked with interest, "You wrote him? Did you ever see him in anything?"

"I saw him on TV while I was in New York and yes, I certainly did write him and believe me, I told him a thing or two."

"Egad, Mother! He's a big star!"

Mother rose from the bed and slowly walked over to the window that was open wide to the cool night air. She stood looking up at the night sky and spoke softly but with intent feeling, letting her voice build in a crescendo, "No, Honey. He isn't a 'star'. He's vermin! A star is lofty and ideal. A star brings out hope and offers beauty and excellence as a shining example. Oh, I've seen 'stars' on the stage and in the movies and they can make one's spirit soar or cringe in a fanciful flight of imagination. And there's a place for satire, when it's done in good taste, but this . . . this little turd of a man only imitates the poor unfortunates who can not help themselves. And, so help me God, I hope he reads my letter because, I told him a thing or two that ought to open his eyes if he has any conscious at all."

Mother turned away from the window with a short laugh. "Oh, listen to me ranting on, as though anyone cares what I think."

I said seriously "You've made a good point, Mother. But maybe he's just ignorant."

"Ignorance is no excuse in this day and age! He is deliberately exploiting the poor innocents for his own selfish gain! It just isn't right, regardless of how you cut the cloth!"

Mother looked with curiosity at what I was working on. I turned so she couldn't see and busily scratched with the charcoal. She lifted some garments from the suitcase and hung them in the closet as she continued,

"I think I'll go to the Met next week. It's been such a long time . . . and if you can watch things here. I do hope Josh understands. Why, I wouldn't deny him a movie or anything else ordinarily. You know I enjoy a good movie myself. And there's nothing more entertaining than a good comedy. Why, we used to laugh ourselves sick at some of those films. I've no quarrel with slapstick or someone acting a clown or a dunce or even being a bit risqué, but this . . . I do hope Josh understands. I tried to explain but he gets to acting as bull-headed as his Father."

"I'm sure Steve can explain it to him, Mother. He expressed very similar sentiments to yours about that guy, only he said it in stronger terms!"

Mother beamed with satisfaction. "Isn't that nice? I'm so happy for Loralee; I hope she realizes what a fine man she has. Did she say anything . . . about whether . . . she's changed her mind . . . on having a baby?"

"She said she never would. Too risky."

Mother turned the bedspread back, fluffed the pillows and folded the top sheet back neatly, smoothing it wrinkle-free as she had done, how many times? Thousands, probably, if one considered the care and attention she had given us all over the years. God! I felt a surge of love and appreciation. Her movements were mechanical; her thoughts far away, as she automatically did the work at hand. Some announcer was auctioning off his wares. I turned the radio down and added a touch of shading to my caricature. Mother sighed audibly, "I've tried to tell her it is NOT hereditary!"

"She knows that, Mother."

"Well, then, I guess there's nothing I can do about it! Sometimes, though . . .if Billy had lived why, the way you are . . . My! I'll bet he would really have been something! I'll never understand . . . He was so perfect . . . and now. . ."

"Mother?"

I started laughing with the exaggerated vision before my eyes of a very fat woman in a frilly blouse shrinking away from a tiny roly-poly, grinning likeness of Michael David with his hand and it's prominent pinky extended in a half-salute. The fat woman wore an expression of abhorrence and fear. I had captioned it, "Is it catching?"

Mother looked at me, her eyes bright with anticipation. She held out her hand and I gave her the cartoon as I collapsed on the bed, doubled over with a spasm of giggles. She studied it; holding it at arm's length. She began to smile, then a low chuckle emerged and grew into a merry, "aahahahah, gasp, whew!"

She carried it over to the lamp and holding it under the shade, said, "That really looks like Mrs. Taubman. You've captured the likenesses of both of them. Did she really act like that?"

She studied the cartoon thoughtfully.

"Mother? You don't think I'm making fun of Michael David when I do something like that, do you?"

"Oh, no. Honey! My! When you're on the inside looking out you have to laugh to keep from crying—Do you mind if I keep this?"

"It isn't that good."

Mother laughed, "Well, it's the next best thing to being there! By the way, muh deah, I think you might be interested to know that after we'd talked this morning I checked my records and found exactly what I've earned from that woman's ironing. I'd been doing it for nearly six months and it came to a total of sixty-seven dollars and ten cents. Such a pittance for all the grief she's caused me! So I gave it to Reverend Miller this afternoon and told him to use it for Church Camp."

I sat up in disbelief. "Mother! You gave . . . ? Why, that's fantastic! But . . . ? Such an odd amount! Why didn't you round it out?"

"Why, it doesn't make any difference. He was glad to get it. He said that'd send six and two-thirds children."

"Six and two-thirds? Egads. You should have given him enough for the other one-third."

"Oh, he'll get it. My, I've spent so much today! And I'm sick and tired of having to call a taxi every time I want to go someplace."

"Dad offered to get you a car."

"I don't want anything from him!"

I laughed, "You probably wouldn't drive it anyway."

She bristled good-naturedly, "It's no laughing matter to have a drunk driver chase you right off the road. Now that just scared the puddin' out of me."

"Mother, that was twenty years ago."

"I remember it like yesterday. He came straight at me! If I hadn't swerved into the ditch he'd have had me sure. No, I'm just not the type to drive. But I guess you could! Maybe we should see about that. Yes, I think that would help. What do you think?"

"I don't have a license, Mother."

"Why, you don't need a license just to go back and forth to town! I've never had one."

"It's the law, Mother. They're required."

"Well, how much is that going to cost ? And since when is it law?"

"I don't know when it went into effect. Probably after you quit driving."

"Well, I certainly never knew it was necessary. Why, I'd just get in the car and go. Don't you think, maybe, blue, would be nice? A big sedan, maybe, two-toned, light blue above and dark blue below and all blue inside. I think that'd be nice! Don't you?"

I yawned sleepily, "Sounds good, Mom."

Mother stood at the door as I slid under the sheets. She said, "Are you sure you need a license? Do you want to get one tomorrow?"

I said, "Well, I uh. . ."

She laughed mischievously, "Mr. Adams is bringing the car out in the morning!"

She switched off the light and closed the door chuckling softly to herself. I lay in the comforting darkness, exhausted from the long day's heavy work, pleased with the accomplishments and hopeful. God!

I awoke from a horrible nightmare drenched in sweat. I had dreamed I was lost and wandering in a terrifying maze of high shrubs. Ghostly mocking faces kept appearing before me threateningly. A great weight was on my shoulders and I was fighting to free myself of it as it growled and howled with the most unearthly sounds.

I got up and walked to the window. The cool breeze brought goosebumps to my bare arms. I could hear Mother cooing to Michael David,

"That's alright. We'll get you changed. You just had too much to drink today, didn't you? You want to go see if you can do something in the potty? See, if you use the potty, then you won't get your bed all wet."

I called, "Mother? Do you need any help?"

She answered, "No, Honey. He just tried to drown himself, but I've about got it cleaned up now. You go on back to bed."

The hallway clock downstairs struck the half-hour; but what was the hour? Two? Three? Four? I turned the radio on. There was static and a buzz as I fumbled the dial until I found KXOK and the announcer's voice boomed out. "It's three-thirty a.m. and time for a brand new record that's sure to make the top ten. From the latest movie of Hollywood's hit comedy team, the smooth mellow voice of. . . "

I flipped it off, hoping Mother hadn't heard. I just loved his voice and the songs he sang. I would have liked to have heard the record; but, his partner was contemptible and you can't support one without the other.

16

🐦 "DID HE TELL YOU YET?"

It took Mother three days to prepare for a two week trip. Alfie moved back home so I wouldn't be alone. He had his friends out frequently and we never attempted to 'hide' Michael David again. The ice had been broken: he was out of the closet of fears, frustrations, shame, emotions, ignorance and denial that had prevailed ever since he was born. Seemed like nearly all of us had 'pet' names from time to time; so, Alf and his friends started calling Michael David 'M.D.' or 'Sarg' and I did too from time to time.

Old friends accepted my invitations to them to come and visit and after the first few awkward moments they accepted Michael David in their individual ways. There were those who ignored him as they would have ignored anything in poor taste; some looked on him in the same vein as a house puppy; a few accepted him as an individual. Some confided laughingly of the *'queer old bird'* in their family closet or the great-aunt with *'bats in her belfry'*. It seemed everyone had or knew someone who was a bit *'off'* or *'nuts" 'zany'*.

M. D. enjoyed having lots of people coming and going. We began to notice that he was much better behaved and had fewer accidents when company was about. He had his favorites and would observe them closely and try to imitate their gestures and laugh whenever they laughed.

Tom Smeely, one of Alf's friends, took a special interest in M.D. He would encourage him to try to walk and taught him to sit on a chair in the living room. M.D. giggled happily with the accomplishment.

One evening Tom brought a little toy drum out and proceeded to teach M.D. how to play it. He would watch him and grunt but refused to try it himself. Alf picked up the sticks and said, "Here, Serg! Like this!", and beat out a 'rat-a-tat-tat'. M.D. chortled with glee. Alf put the sticks in his hands and guided them in a like sound. M.D. sobered and leaned over the drum with the intensity of a surgeon at an operating table. He touched the stick to the drum, 'tap'. We all applauded and laughed as he chortled and carefully did it again, and again, repeatedly.

Tom assumed a Napoleonic stance and quoted, "If a man does not keep pace with his companions, perhaps it is because he hears a different drummer. Let him step to the music which he hears, however measured or far away."

Alf called, "I'll drink to that!"

M.D. chortled and 'tap-tapped' again as though in response. It was so incredulous we were convulsed in gales of laughter.

Johnny Reece held his glass high and announced, "I want to propose a toast."

Tom laughed, "You want to do what, John?"

He wobbled and said, "I want to propose a toast; to the man who thought of the drum and to the only fool I know who'd try to correlate Napoleon and Thoreau."

Alf yelled, "I'll drink to that!", and again M.D. responded just as though he understood every word.

Alf had his friends out of the evening. I had mine out during the day while he was at work. There were times when the hours would overlap but we usually respected the tacit agreement.

Kathryn and Wanda were frequent companions of mine as they had been for many years. They competed with each other in everything from dress to anecdotes. They were good-natured and fun-loving; good students and good looking. They adored the handsome older vets who looked on us as 'kid sisters'.

Almeda and Janie Lynn came over one afternoon with the year book from the previous school year and spent hours bringing me up to date on the inside dirt; recounting the grind and the crime of Mr. Darion's history class and the comical as well as embarrassing antics of the bedeviled Mr. Smythe, and the whispered confidences of the hallway and locker room. By the time they left I was beginning to feel a tingle of excitement about being back and returning to school in Nilesville for my Senior year.

Dean rode over early one morning while the dew was still on the grass. I heard the horse's clop-clop, clop-clop and I ran out the door to greet him as he rode up on Jinx, my Jinx, my favorite chestnut. He called, "Hey there! Welcome home!"

"Hi Dean! You're a little late. I've been here nearly two weeks."

He jumped down with ease and grace and let the reins hang loose as the horse nibbled at the grass. I stroked Jinx's neck and he nuzzled me when I asked him if he remembered me. Dean said, "Jinx missed you. Tell her you missed her, boy."

Jinx raised his head and neighed and I told him I had missed him, too. Dean secured him to the back fence and said, "I just got in late last night."

I asked, "Four H'ers?"

"Yeah. We had a good camp."

"How'd you like being a counselor?"

"More work than fun."

"You've grown taller, Dean."

"Yeah. And you're prettier."

"And you're full of baloney."

"Mom told me you'd grown up, but I can't see it!"

He looked me over approvingly and grinned. I said, "Thanks, friend. Come on in. I'm feeding, rather, watching Michael David."

He hesitated and then followed me in. It was the first time since Michael David had been born that I had asked Dean in. He said, "Your Mom's letting you ask people in now?"

I explained, "She's gone right now. She's visiting. Alf has moved back here with me while she's gone. I hope he'll stay even after she gets back! As for us having people in, it just kinda happened. Mother wasn't here at the time but she didn't seem to mind."

"Dad told me about your clean-up crew. I wish I'd been here to help."

"So do I!"

Alf had already left for work. M.D. sat at the table manipulating the spoon with careful concentration. I said, "M.D. this is Dean. Can you say 'Hi'?"

He laid down the spoon carefully, looked at Dean, raised his hand in the awkward looking, palm out, pinky doubled back salute and said, "Uhh."

Dean stepped up to the table and leaned across extending his hand for a handshake and said, "How're you doing, boy?"

M.D. stared at Dean's hand. He weaved from side to side and slowly reached his little stubby hand out to meet Dean's huge, strong callused hand. Dean gave his hand a firm grasp and shook it a time or two. M.D. snorted with pleasure and babbled. I said, "I think that's the first time he's ever had a hand shake."

Dean said to him, "You did a good job!"

Michael David bobbed his head and grinning, chewed on his tongue. I told him to finish eating and asked Dean what he was up to.

"Oh, I just thought I'd say 'Hi' to my girl and see if everything's OK. We really missed you, Toot. Christmas was terrible."

"It was strange not being home, but I had a nice time with Loralee and Steve. Marj is there. You know Josh is visiting with them this summer. He'll probably stay and go to school there, too, if Mother will let him"

"You're not going back then, are ya?"

"I don't think so. Actually, I had a wonderful time there. It was so peaceful and fun and I loved the school and the teachers and met some nice friends. But, then, Mother started having a fit for me to come home. So, here I am. But, you know how changeable she can be."

Dean was leaning against the kitchen counter twirling his hat in his hands. "I'm glad you're back. We kinda missed havin' ya around here. Did ya have any "special" friends?"

"Who, me? Why, of course, lots of them. Everyone is "special" in my book, even you."

"Gee, thanks. Is your Mom gonna be gone long?"

"She's due back next Wednesday. Alf says he's going to have a party every night while she's gone."

Dean grinned and asked, "What do you do when he has his friends in?"

"Nothing. There's two or three of them that give M.D. a lot of attention. But I usually put him to bed by eight and read in my room."

"There were still a bunch here when I got in about two o'clock this morning."

"Really? Well, I'm not surprised! He's making up for lost time."

I laughed thinking of some of the capers Alf had been threatening. "Yeah, he's been having a lot of fun. At least, I really hope so. Dr. Mathews finally found a medicine that helped him. He hasn't had any attacks for quite awhile."

Dean said, "Well, it's about time! How's your Dad doin'?"

"Fine, I guess. He was under the impression that I wanted to go to live with Loralee. I don't know what Mother told him."

Dean walked over to where I was standing and put his hand on my shoulder.

"Toot? You didn't ask her if you could go, did you?"

I looked up at him and flipped some suds in his face. "Are you kidding? I begged her to let me stay right here at home. I thought I was going to die. I even had to miss out on my part in the speech competition. I still don't know why she sent me away. Why do you ask that ?"

"We were told you wanted to get away from here."

I was washing the glasses from the night before and turning them upside down on the drain-board to dry. I looked at Dean, probably the best friend I had ever had. He was always right there. Something in his voice . . . I gathered M.D.'s breakfast things and said, "You know, I never even thought about what Mother might have told others. But, that would explain some of the rather strange comments I've heard from a few. . ."

Dean said, "Welp, yer here now. That's the important thing. Would you like to go riding, when you get through with that?"

"I'd love to, Dean, but I have to watch Michael David."

"You want me to watch him while you go take a quick galumph?"

Dean pulled a chair out from the table, turned it around and sat astraddle it with his arms resting on the back. Michael watched him, widened his little slanty eyes, cocked his head to one side and blabbered, "uh wuh wuh wuh wuh." Dean said, "Is that a fact?" and Michael blabbered again. I said, "I don't think he's ever seen anyone sit like that."

Michael stood up still jabbering. Dean asked, "Do you want me to turn your chair around?" and moved it for him. He helped Michael straddle it and placed his short stubby arms on the back. Michael rested his chin on his arms and chortled with pride in his achievement. He sat there contentedly while Dean and I talked about things that had happened over the past several months. He told me about counseling at camp and about the silly giggly girls that always had some crisis they just had to see the counselor about late at night. I detected a slight pang of jealousy and wise-cracked, "They were probably all madly in love with you."

He said, "Ya think so? I should be so lucky!"

I looked at him closely. He was so much taller. His shoulders were so broad and his arms were tanned and muscled. His eyes were even bluer than I remembered and he had the nicest smile I'd ever seen. He was really handsome. "You are taller, Dean."

He grinned, "Yep. Taller than Dad. He says there ought to be a law against it."

He asked me if I'd dated anyone in particular 'up there'. I told me about Steve's 'test for approval' and how embarrassing it had been a time or two. He laughed and said he thought it was a good idea, "'Cept I guess I'd never pass that one."

He pushed his wide brimmed hat back on his head and wiped his brow. The sun was blazing through the windows with the threat of a beastly hot day. I finished up the breakfast things while Dean talked of mutual friends and neighbors, horses and crops and college. We argued over the merits of the University and the small church-related college I'd selected. Dean was going into his third year and thought I should apply there, too. He enumerated the many reasons why it was superior to my choice and we bantered the subject about as old friends do when each feel they are right and the other misinformed. Michael watched Dean constantly. He tried to imitate his gestures and seemed to be fascinated with his hat. Dean plopped the old straw hat on Michael's head and he bounced and giggled and waddled his head with glee. I laughed, "He likes you, Dean."

"Yep. Most people do."

"Boy, are you conceited!"

"Just tellin' it like it is."

"Whatever happened to modesty?"

He looked askance at my brief shorts and blouse and said, "You've got enough of that for all of us." I threw the wet towel at him. He caught it and tossed it easy to Michael who deliberated soberly and then tried to toss it back to Dean and chortled excitedly.

The hall clock struck nine o'clock. Dean stood and said, "It's gonna be hot as hell in another hour. Do you want to take Jinx out? I'll watch the boy."

"Oh, Dean! I'd love to! You don't mind?"

"Well—maybe I'd rather watch his sister."

I ignored him and moaned, "It's too hot for jodhpurs."

"You need pants on and you're not going without boots! Jinx is feeling his oats and those tennis shoes can't grip."

"Well, I'll go change. I'll just be a minute."

"We'll see about that."

Dean was encouraging Michael to touch the horse when I rejoined them in the yard. He gave me a boost up and I rode off into the quiet still air cutting through it with the abandonment of one who's seen the light at the end of the tunnel. Jinx was sure-footed and anxious for a good run. I turned his head toward the woods and relaxed the reins. He knew the path better than I and within a few short minutes we were following Crazy Creek as it paralleled the path deep in the woods. God! It was good to be out on Jinx. I'd missed the woods and the peaceful solitude they offered, but my mind lingered on Dean.

He had changed in some indefinable way. He looked the same, but more so! His blond curly hair was always tousled. His face was tanned and getting a bit weather lined which seemed to only emphasize his good looks. His eyes were a clear dark blue and they were teasing and thoughtful and always kind. He was taller and bigger, more muscular. So? He'd always been around. . .

We came to the clearing by the narrow part of the creek where the water was so clear you could see the fishies and it made it's own music as it bubbled over the rocks. I could hear Singing Sally coming up the path. I reigned in Jinx and waited. She was singing the happy song about how God watches over the sparrows.

I called, "Hello, Mrs. Andrews!"

She waved and made her way toward me. "Olivia! You were gone a long time!"

"I'm glad to be back."

"Did he tell you, yet?"

"What?"

She stroked Jinx on the neck affectionately and said, "Why, even Jinx is happy you're back." She reached for my hand and gave it a squeeze as she said, "Oh, my! You are so pretty and so grown up. The difference a few months can make. Have you seen Dean yet?"

"Yes, mam. He came over and brought Jinx this morning. He's watching Michael David so I could come out with Jinx for a little bit."

"Dean is growing up, too, such a handsome young man, so good-hearted, really excelling in school—Only one more year until he gets his degree. Ruth says they have to fight the girls off with a stick."

She laughed, and then sobered as she looked off into the distance toward the sound of a mourning dove. "We've all missed you, Toot. Are you home for good or are you just visiting?"

"Oh, I hope I can stay here for my senior year. Mother was wanting me to come home, so, I don't think I will have to leave again."

"I surely hope not, Child. Dean was home for his Christmas Break. He told me it just wasn't the same without you. He said he missed you so much it hurt. I told him he should write you and tell you how he feels but he said your Mother told him you really liked the big city life and were dating lots of boys up there."

"Oh, no, Mrs. Andrews, that simply isn't true. It wasn't like that at all."

"I suspected not, Child. I told Dean I knew you better than that. You are both so dear to me. I have watched you both grow up and I love you like my own. My prayers are always with you, Toot, and with Dean."

I reached my hand and she took it in both of hers and touched it to her lips. "Thank you, Mrs. Andrews, for your prayers and for your beautiful music. It always makes things better."

"Your Grandma used to tell me the kind things you said about my music. Of course, I always sing to Freddie. But, sometimes, I'll find a new hymn and I think maybe Toot needs this."

Her eyes were twinkling. She spoke quietly, hesitantly, as though undecided, "I know I shouldn't say anything, but, I just feel so compelled."

"What, Mrs. Andrews?"

"Did he tell you yet?"

"Tell me what?"

Her eyes were twinkling and she whispered melodiously,

"He loves you."

I caught my breath, and stupidly said "Who? Me?"

She nodded and smiled. I said, "You mean Dean. . . ?

She nodded and laughed. I said, "We've always been friends, but, I hadn't thought about, I mean, I hadn't exactly thought about . . . Wow."

Mrs. Andrews had her hands clasped as though in prayer but was smiling widely as she stepped aside so I could turn Jinx toward home. I called, "Thank you, Mrs. Andrews," and told Jinx, "Let's go home, boy!" and gave him his head.

Dean and Michael David were sitting on the front porch steps as Jinx and I approached in full gallop. Dean hurried out into the yard as I reigned up. He held his arms up and I slid into them. He caught his breath and held me tightly against him. My arms went around his broad shoulders and fastened about his neck. His eyes were searching mine, questioning and then his lips were on my lips in a long hard kiss that left us both breathless. Jinx was whinnying and Michael was babbling and the birds were singing more sweetly than they ever had before.

Dean murmured, "God, Toot! I've waited so long for you . . ."

He kissed me again and I was aware of nothing under God's blue heaven but Dean's strong muscular arms holding me against him: Dean's sweet bruising searching kiss breathing new sensations into the innermost parts of my being; Dean's caring, caressing, loving.

I had assumed that 'love', if and when it came, would be in the far distant future. I had doubted that such was for me at all. I had not been looking for it or even thinking about it. To suddenly encounter it in the eyes of an old childhood friend, to hear an old familiar voice take on new nuance and to feel the urgent precious loving embrace of the old friend I had thought I knew so well, struck a chord on my heartstrings and stirred the embers of my soul into dancing flames and the transition from friendship to the plateau of lovers was an easy beautiful climb that propelled us into what seemed to be a preordained togetherness of loving, caring and sharing.

Psalmists, poets and lyricists have tried since the beginning of time to express the all consuming passion; the rampage of conflicting emotions and the delicious delirium of ecstasy that constitutes the marvelous world of discovery in one's first romance.

We were inseparable for the remainder of that summer. Friends, neighbors, strangers on the street, remarked on our 'young love' and how 'perfect' we looked together. Alf called it 'puppy love' and claimed Dean was robbing the cradle. Mother was strangely quiet.

Dean talked of marriage and the prospects of building a home just down the road. I'd nestle in the comfort of his arms closing my mind to the dark forebodings of such a future. I could not bear to express them. He was so sure of himself, so confident, so sturdy and safe, so dependable and comfortable. I would never hurt him or disappoint him. But I could not think of 'marriage'! I could never live the rest of my life 'just down the road'!

Dean had said something—a question? I hadn't heard. I mumbled, "Comme il vous plaire."

He dug his fingers into my shoulder and turned me to face him, "Au contraire, mon un cher ami."

The soft light from the window fell across his face, reflecting in his eyes as he looked with piercing insight. "You've been avoiding giving me a direct answer for the last three days. What's wrong, Toot?"

I stammered, "I—Dean . . . I really . . . God! I was going to, to, to—"

He grinned, "You've got your tooter going", and hugged me close to him. His tone changed and he asked, "Have I assumed too much? I know you well, my sweet! When you start hiding behind your French—and what's this 'please yourself' bit? You better not tell me that again."

Dean pulled me close to him and kissed me and I yielded to him, hating myself for wanting more than life with him could offer. My heart sang Dean is enough, enough; his love is sufficient; my mind said, or should be, surely it would be? He loves me! That's all that matters. We don't have to even think about "having children," for pete's sake. Weigh the balance—be fair minded. But it is still two years off; maybe I'll know for sure by then. But know what? A lot can happen in two years. Why do we have to think about getting married? I don't want to hurt him. But I can't get married! Why can't we just go on like this? We have been so happy except for all of that getting married talk. I could never live 'just down the road'. And, then, what if we were married, and then . . . someday . . . had a. . .

Tears squeezed through my eyes and I pushed away from Dean and doubled over with fear and pain and dread. He was solicitous and I cried harder. I hurt more than I had ever hurt and I did not know what to do or say. He held me upright and looked exasperated as he said, "God! Toot—What is it? Please tell me. I love you so much. I can't stand to see you hurting like this. Please forgive me if I've hurt you in any way, shape or form."

I sobbed, "Oh, Dean, I love you too, too, too. . ."

He grinned and kissed me on the tip of my nose, "There's that tooter again."

We laughed and I found the courage to say, "I don't ever want to hurt you, Dean, in any way. I've always loved you, even though I didn't have sense enough to know it for such along time. But, I just can't bear to hurt you or disappoint you. I love being with you and I probably shouldn't even tell you this. Actually, I can't even begin to tell you, how much I miss you when you're gone. It isn't just once in awhile. You are always in my thoughts, my dreams, my plans, my conversations. My whole world revolves around you. But you know, I have to go to college, Dean, and I must travel some. I've wanted to see England and France and Germany and maybe Japan. God, Dean! Don't you understand? Dean, don't look like that. Please don't be hurt, can't we just go on, for now, being together?"

Dean had leaned back against the back of the porch swing and gazed off into the night. He released his hold on me, patted me on the shoulder as though comforting me, and sighed heavily, "I guess I've known, especially the last day or two. You never once flat out said, 'Yes, I'll marry you.'"

"Dean!"

"Toot, I've loved you, seems like, all my life. Whatever happens, I'll never forget the first time I got to kiss my girl or the first time I saw love in your eyes."

He put his arm about me and pulled me to him. His voice was soft and low and full of awe. "When you slid down off Jinx into my arms, it was as though you were a gift from heaven. All of my dreams and plans and prayers, right there in my arms. If I live to be a-hundred I'll never have a greater, more exhilarating moment!"

I snuggled against him and kissed him on the cheek. He leered at me comically and said teasingly, "That may be an overstatement. Do you want to see if you can help me improve on that?"

We laughed and talked as old friends do and loved as lovers do and the pain of parting cast a pall about us and we were too honest to deny it; too full of love and hope to recognize it; too young and too happy to know the very heavens were crying for what should be but would never be.

Dean returned to the University. Josh called begging to be allowed to remain with Steve and Loralee for the school year. Mother reluctantly agreed. She seemed to be happier and more content than she had been in years. Alf didn't say anything about leaving and continued to have his friends out frequently.

Michael showed considerable progress in many little ways. Dean had let Michael have his old straw cowboy hat. Michael would wear it about the house or keep it near him at all times.

Dean called me long-distance early one evening. In spite of Mother's long inquisitive glances and constant mumblings, we talked longer than she thought appropriate.

Later, after I had tidied the kitchen and put Michael to bed, I was sitting on the front porch listening to the radio, savoring the rich, sweet romantic mood created by the beautiful duets of Thomas L. Thomas and Evelyn MacGregor.

Mother came out to join me. She sat down in the swing and held her hand up to the light admiring her new ring; a large blue sapphire with fiery diamonds surrounding it.

"You shouldn't be sitting out here all alone like that."

"I was listening to the music, Mother!"

"You look sad."

"Why, I'm not sad at all."

I tried to laugh convincingly while trying to think of a safe subject to steer toward.

"What a beautiful ring, Mother. That sapphire is exquisite. Where did you get it?"

"New York. Black, Starr and Frost on 5th Avenue. Isn't it pretty? It certainly should be! They had some larger, of course. But, believe me, this is the biggest one around here. See how it picks up the light? Um umph! I've always been embarrassed over that tiny solitaire your Dad gave me for an engagement ring. This makes up for it."

I didn't want her to start in on Dad, so I quickly changed the subject.

"I was just thinking about school. I'm glad I don't have to walk in of the mornings now."

"Walking is good for you. But I know it isn't very pleasant in bad weather or with all of the books you have to carry. Heaven knows I didn't buy that car for Alf, but it sure looks like he's taken it over."

"It's alright, Mother. His doesn't run half the time."

"I wish he'd settle down and get married and have a family."

I was trying to listen to the beautiful music as Thomas L. Thomas and Evelyn MacGregor blended their voices in a popular love song. Mother said, "Now you've just got to pull yourself together and stop this moonin' over that boy! I know you're thinking about him."

I sighed, "Well, yes. He's always in my thoughts, but, . . ."

Mother interrupted me as she stood up suddenly and half yelled, "I knew it!"

She started pacing back and forth delivering the diatribe. "I could see it coming from the first time I saw you together last summer. I thought to myself as sure as the night follows the day that girl's heading for a fall. I was hoping you wouldn't but I knew it was bound to come. I can't understand for the life of me how two people can be so similar in so many ways and still be as different as night and day. But you are! You can see the difference. Why, he's blond and blue eyed and likes to work out in the sun. You're dark haired and dark eyed and would stay up all night, every night, reading and writing and drawing. Can't you see it? He's a worker; you're a dreamer! You'd never make it. Why, you'd end up just like your Dad and I have."

"We've always been friends, Mother. But it is much more than that now. He is very special to me, but he's gone. . ."

"Oh, he'll be back at Thanksgiving if not before. . ."

"No, he can't come home. He just called to tell me he has a good part time job."

"Well, sooner or later, you'll be seeing him and he may persist but I'm telling you it's for your own good to forget any foolishness about marrying him! There's too much to life and living for one so young to even consider such. You've got to kick up your heels and have some fun while you can! Why, you always said you wanted to travel and see the world and you'll never be content until you get that out of your system. And, who knows, you may meet somebody or even a lot of some bodies before you meet Mr. Right-for-you. There'll be plenty of time for that after you've finished your schooling and seen the world. I just hope and pray you haven't sacrificed your pearl of great price because I'm telling you, you've only got one and it's to buy a happy marriage when the time comes and if you squander it on just any Tom, Dick or Harry, then when you need it, you won't have it and you'll just be left in the lurch!"

"Mother, for crying out loud!"

"Oh, you'll just never know how it scared me so bad when I got home and saw how you two children were so lovey and carrying on like there was no one else in the world and to think you'd been here alone all that time. Why, I don't believe in placing temptation in front of children. I'd never have left if I'd so much as an inkling of you getting a crush on somebody, let along the boy next door!"

"It isn't a 'crush', Mother. I love him and he loves me."

"Yes, I know. I know you think you do but you're so young and I'm trying to tell you, if you'd just listen, there might be someone a lot better for you just around the corner or over some mountain or maybe even across the ocean. And Dean may meet some girl his own age at the University who'd like to be a farmer's wife. I just hope you didn't do anything rash! Life's a one-way street and once you've spent your ticket, that's it. I should never have left."

"I know you had a good time, Mother. You looked so rested and happy when you got back. I hope we can keep you that way now. Don't worry about me, OK? Dean has another year before he gets his degree. And I've got to get my mind on my science assignment."

I stood and stretched and breathed deeply of the honeysuckle in the cool still night air. A mocking bird was singing his heart out and as we listened we could hear another voice, far off in the distance, sweetly singing of God's love and care.

Mother laughed, "There's old Crazy Sally. I don't think she ever sleeps. Just walks and sings to the trees day in and day out and half the night."

"She isn't crazy! She's a lovely lady."

"And you're as daft as she is. I do wonder how her voice can stay so nice and clear! She's been doing that for years, in all kinds of weather."

"Her son was killed at Okinawa."

"I know that. But it's no reason for her to go off her rocker like that."

"Mother? Speaking of 'crazy'—did you call those other ladies to cancel out on that crazy ironing business?"

"That isn't a very nice way to talk to your Mother, but, yes, I did. I just got to thinking there's no sense in me punishing myself when if the truth were known I probably have more in the bank than any of them. Why, it's an irony of ironies for me, of all people, to even consider doing someone else's ironing."

School life was challenging and a lot of fun. Even Mr. Smythe welcomed me back into the music department without any reference to my ignoble departure that had left him in such a tissy. Classes were interesting and especially meaningful in the light of college pre-requisites. Grades were important to me and I worked hard to excel. Friends and a social life took a back seat to my studies. I loved learning and there was so much to learn.

Mother was finding a life of her own in renewing old friendships, and was beginning to take an interest in things outside of home.

One evening after supper we were having coffee and talking about Michael David learning to string beads. Alf had bought him a set of large wooden, brightly colored beads that he was learning to put on a yard long twine that had a knot in one end and a hard rubber threader at the other end. Michael's coordination was improving and he would sometimes succeed in getting two or three on at a time before losing interest.

Alf asked, "You thought any more about that institution, Mom?"

Mother toyed with her cup and said, "I've been studying on it for a long time now and after seeing how that child's improved so much and responded so well to you children having a lot of people in, well, it just makes me wonder if, maybe, he'd like to go to a home or that is, an institution, where they'd have the trained personnel to teach him better than I can."

Alf said, "I think it would be the best thing for him!"

Mother chewed on her lip and mumbled, "Well, I just don't know. I don't want everyone to think I'm just putting him away so I don't have to bother with him."

A thread of hope for normalcy seemed to be dangling in front of my eyes, or was it the elusive "carrot" of trickery? I knew I must not let my voice betray how much I wanted it. Seconds passed as I sipped a drink of the strong black coffee. Alf and I exchanged glances, but I forced myself to use a non-committal but reassuring tone when I spoke, as though I were not directly involved, but rather just reading a part in a play. I said, "Mother, no one would think that of you. Everyone knows you have given him the best care and you've certainly spared no expense in consulting experts. We've already taught him more than they thought we could, but I do believe he would be better off in an institution with those who know how to teach and train him. I'm sure it would be the best thing for him!"

The next morning Mother announced she had decided on an institution. She completed the paperwork, mailed it to Dad for his signature and began packing Michael's clothes and "must-haves". The next week he was admitted.

It was good to go home after school and find the house alive with friendly banter and gossipy chatter. Mother had invited a missionary circle to meet there on Thursdays and she frequently had her old cronies, as Alf fondly called them, out for bridge and dessert.

Our home was once again a center for social activities. Friends came and went all hours of the day and night. Alf had his friends out freely and Mother took delight in their banter. I had study sessions, after-movie parties and slumber parties. Alf would tease us girls mercilessly and Mother would ply us with fudge and popcorn and cider. All of my friends marveled at how she had changed and was so much fun to be around. They loved her and talked openly of how they wished their mothers would be as nice as she.

After the first big frost we invited the youth group out from the church for a hayride and bonfire. Some of the boys played guitars and one had a banjo. The whole countryside rang with laughter and music.

Mrs. Hawkins came in regularly to do the heavy work.

The kitchen seemed to miraculously produce little surprises of tasty treats, and the French marigolds and sturdy chrysanthemums surrounded our home in a bright cheery golden frame throughout the long mild-weathered autumn.

17

🦅 LOVE CAME DOWN AT CHRISTMAS

Winter came suddenly, with a fury, during one late November night. An ice storm spindled the big oak and broke lesser trees in half. The freezing rain clung to the tree limbs and to the blades of grass and coated the countryside in a bright shiny brilliance that snapped and cracked like glass under the weight of the raw cold wind. The electric wires that bore heat and light broke under their heavy burden and the house grew as cold and desolate as a tomb.

Mother wore her fur coat about the house, huddling in it's warmth as she went from room to room, upstairs and downstairs, peering out the windows, pulling blinds down and drawing draperies, trembling with fear and dread of the winter ahead; beset with worries of what might happen next.

I stayed in bed, warm in my cocoon of homemade quilts and comforters that Grandma had made for me. I looked out upon the old oak tree, stripped of its autumn splendor. Huge branches that had cradled countless nests of birds and on which the pesky squirrels had scampered yesterday, had been torn from their mother's trunk and hurtled down to the ground by the icy blast of Boreas. They lay entombed in ice. A few stubborn red leaves clung to their branches and blazed in fiery hues through the ice-coated tangle, refusing to submit to the bluster of the elements. The stately evergreens, dripping with icicles, looked as though they had been sculptured in near perfect symmetry.

The roads were impassable. No horses or cows were in sight; even the birds had taken refuge from the storm. I snuggled down in the warmth of my bed and thought, ah well, as Grandma used to say, "*All things come to pass*". I guess the sun's shining someplace. Surely, Jinx is safe in the barn along with the other horses. It is such fun to ride horseback in the snow, but you can't do anything on ice except skate. Dean skates so well. I hope the pond freezes over so I can practice. Only twenty-three days until he'll be here, and everyone's going to be home for Christmas. Maybe it'll be like it used to be, before M.D. Everything has been so nice and normal for the last few weeks, since Mother had him committed. And, of course, he really seems to like it there with all of the different people, and he is learning to do some things. I wish Loralee could understand it isn't hereditary, but, God! I would be terrified, too.

Alf came in rubbing his hands and blowing on them and shuffling about. "Hey, Toot! You awake? Come on 'n get up. Let's go build a fire!"

"In the fireplace?"

"Where else, Dummy?"

"It hasn't been used since last winter."

"Well, now's the time. Come on!"

"You go ahead. I'll come down when it get's to roaring."

"A roaring fire's no good. It all goes out the chimney. Come on, I'll show you how to build one right. There's more to it than just putting a match to it, you know."

"Helps to have a log."

"Ya gotta have more than a log, Dummy. Hurry up. Mom's freezin'."

"You don't look over-warm yourself. Go on and get started, I'm coming."

Mother and I huddled in front of the long unused fireplace in the study as Alf expounded on the merits of fire and how all of civilization stemmed from man learning to make and use it. When Mother told him to hurry up and start it, he lectured on how one cannot start a fire; one must build it and he demonstrated with the slow deliberation of one who is thorough and confident and enjoying himself.

He laid the kindling and the little bits of wood just so and allowed them to burn down to red-gray glowing coals before placing a few small branches and very narrow-spliced wood on top. As these burned down from bright orange flames to a steady low blue-orange hue, he arranged them, raking them together and added a huge log to the back of the glowing embers and nestled smaller logs in them. It was a masterpiece! And he was warmed by our praise as we were warmed by his fire.

We stayed in the study all day; reading, talking, playing cards and feeding the fire. Alf carried the old Victrola up from the basement and we played dozens of the old thick records, cranking the old Victrola and marveling at the clear tones.

Late in the afternoon, the phone jangled. Alf jumped for it as Mother thanked the powers that be that phone service had been restored and hoped fervently that the electricity would be back on before nightfall.

Alf was unusually subdued as he listened on the phone. Alf signaled for something to write on and I hurried to get him paper and a pen from Dad's desk. He jotted something down and dropped the receiver, heavily, into place.

He said in a low, barely audible voice, "That was Dr. Matthews. They've been trying to get us since last night."

Mother said, "Well, what is it? Is something wrong? Why would he be trying to reach us?"

"It's Dad. He's had a heart attack. Doc said the lines were bad but he understood Dad's holding his own. He's in a hospital. Here's the address and phone number."

"How come they called Doc?"

"Our lines were down, Mom. The doctor up there called Dr. Matthews because he couldn't reach us."

Mother looked like a statue, unmoving, momentarily frozen in place, unblinking, as her eyes stared into space.

The fire crackled and radiated its warmth. But it could not penetrate the spine-chilling fears that held us in their grasp.

Alf called for more information and was informed that Dad was resting comfortably but would be required to stay in the hospital for ten to fourteen days before coming home for recuperation.

Mother nervously twisted the spectacular sapphire on her finger and wondered if she should go see him but thought the weather prohibitive.

I talked with Dad on the phone and he sounded reassuring, as though it were just a slight inconvenience that was nothing to worry about.

Mother took him at his word and speculated that, "… it's probably just indigestion. Gas can cause chest pains. There's no telling what he's been eating up there and he always did eat too much for his own good. Oh, I know, he's a big-boned man with a big appetite and he appreciates his meals but I'll bet you he's been eating seafood and pork and no telling what all they put out in those restaurants and fancy clubs and I'm not going to worry about him. If he wants to eat like that then he can just pay the consequences!"

Alf brought Dad home. He was only a shadow of his former self both in appearance and spirit. He was rail-thin and his six-foot frame was noticeably stooped. His thick black wavy hair was superseded with an iron gray. His face bore an unnatural pallor and he seemed to have retreated into himself.

Mother was close-mouthed and her fingers were ring-less as she went about her duties. She wore a worried harassed look and muttered and

mumbled to herself but refused to discuss anything with us 'children",
as she insisted on calling us. Alf and I worked hard to try to bring Mother
out of her dark mood. Our attempts at humor were either ignored or
rebuffed.

Alf cleaned up his jokes so he could tell them at supper and I'd try to
tell of comical things that had happened at school. Dad would chuckle
appreciatively but Mother would only dish out gloom. One evening I
was chattering about some of the antics in the lab class. I said, "We
looked at blood under the microscope today. We were comparing human
blood and frog's blood."

Alf grinned and raised his eyebrows, assuming a simpleton's
expression, "Was there any difference?"

I said, "Yes. One was green."

Dad chuckled. Mother looked at us with incredulous disbelief. She
threw her napkin on the table and stood glaring at us.

I said, "I was only joking, Mother. You know, green? Frogs are green?"

Mother whined in a hurt tone, "Alright, I know when someone's
poking fun at me, I'm not stupid! And if you think for one minute you're
going to get away with it I'll just show you all you've got another thing
coming."

Dr. Matthews came out several evenings and he and Dad would talk
for hours. Mother no longer had friends in nor would she take any interest
in going anyplace.

Early one morning, in mid-December, Alf and I sat at breakfast
watching the birds scurry for bread crumbs beneath the sun glinting off
new snow. Mother came hurrying down the back stairs, dressed for going
out and carrying her coat and a shopping bag of gaily wrapped presents.
Alf teased her about looking too pretty to be Santa Claus. Mother pooh-
poohed him and said she was going to see Michael David and would
ride in to the train depot with us. She said she planned to stay over night
and would probably return the next day but, "You don't need to bother
about meeting me for I'm not sure what time I'll be in."

After supper the next evening a taxi pulled up our lane and slowly
wheeled it's way right up to the back porch. I was amazed and heartsick
to see Mother coaxing Michael David from the car as the driver stood
by, holding the door, looking askance.

Mother was defensive about her actions and adamant in her decision.
She insisted, ". . . he's home to stay. Why, they weren't feeding him
properly. That poor baby's just wasting away to nothing and here it is
soon to be Christmas and it just isn't right for him to be all alone like
that. They just weren't feeding him at all. You can see how much weight
he's lost. Why, do you know here it is winter time and there was a fly in

his room and I thought if they have a fly in this weather then what must it be in the summertime and that fly probably crawled on his food and he wouldn't even know to brush it off! Why, they weren't teaching him anything and I just couldn't sleep nights if I'd left him there to be treated like some animal that doesn't have any feelings."

M.D. was proudly showing me a piece of clay that he had finished and a finger painting. I said, "Mother, look at these. These are great. They are teaching him some things."

She said, "He can do that here at home. You can show him that as well as they can. I'm telling you that baby's home to stay!"

Dad's health did not seem to improve. He read most of the time and seemed preoccupied when I'd try to converse with him. Mother was depressed and constantly harried and nagging. Any attempt at 'being positive' was met with rebuke and ridicule.

References to Christmas were turned aside or put off with some sarcastic rejoinder. Loralee called saying that they would all be home for Christmas Day. Mother fretted and fussed about all of the cooking and slaving that would be expected of her and harangued on the expense. She would reject my offer to help in words but then began compiling lists of things for me to do of the evening or suggesting I bake a few things "Just to have on hand if the children do decide to come."

I asked her if she'd like for me to get a tree and she said, "No, now, we're just not going to have one this year! I've given it a lot of thought and it's just too much trouble. I told you all I would like to just forget Christmas this year and I know the only reason Loralee and Steve and Marjorie and Josh are coming home is just because your Dad is here. But I'm laying down the law now on this Christmas tree business. They just get needles all over the carpeting and I'm the one who has to pick them up. Besides, we're all grown-ups except for that poor baby and he doesn't know what it's all about anyway and he'd be sure to hurt himself on the angel hair; you know how that can itch! It's a lot of foolishness anyway, carting a tree in the house like that."

Alf brought a beautiful eight foot Balsam Fir tree into the house after supper and yelled, "Hey! Mom! Where do you want it planted? The living room?"

Mother gushed, "Oh, Honey, you shouldn't have done that. My! Isn't it beautiful? Why, I suppose we can put it up in the living room. Won't that be the best place for it?"

Alf stood there holding it, grinning, "Whatever you say, Mom!"

Dad had already rearranged the furniture and had a huge tub of sand and rocks to steady the tree. Boxes of decorations had been brought down from the attic and were laid out in the order they should go on the tree.

Mother had followed Alf into the living room and looked about at the arrangements in surprise. She said, "Riley, did you know he was getting this tree?"

Dad chuckled, "I can't say I knew he was getting that tree."

Alf said, "Mom! Aren't you ever gonna learn who Santa Claus is?"

Mother supervised the decorating of the tree as Dad and Michael looked on.

We were almost through when Dean came in. It was the first time we'd seen each other since summer and my doubts and anxieties faded into the background as he held his arms open to me, and, I, oblivious of Dad in the armchair, Michael on the floor, Alf by the tree, Mother talking in the doorway, rushed to him, and it was Christmas and the angels sang and it was the Fourth of July and there were fireworks and it was Eastertime and a new beginning.

Love and peace and happiness walked in with Dean. Dad beamed with pleasure and shook his hand and called him 'Son'. Michael chortled excitedly while Mother talked about the University and how much it had changed in thirty years.

Alf and Dean and I hung the last of the balls and mementoes and threw silver icicles on the tree that was garlanded with gold tinsels. Alf plugged in the lights and dozens of multi-colored bulbs glowed on the pine branches casting a magical spell that transformed the whole room into a pine-scented softly-glowing roseate world of romance and dreams.

Alf left for a date in town. Dad retired early and Mother said she would put Michael to bed. She thoughtfully clicked the door shut behind her.

The span of time had not diminished our caring but had enhanced our yearning and we clung to each other with the sweet surging urgency of expressing our love and we found an even deeper love and peace and wonderment than we had ever known.

We talked and laughed and Dean held me close as the hallway clock struck away the hours. The fire in the fireplace died down but the beautiful lights on the tall, perfect tree glowed on.

Dean talked of his part-time job and of school and dormitory living. He casually mentioned that campus life had changed a lot for many of the upper classmen were vets who'd had their schooling interrupted by the war and that several of them were married.

"You'll be graduating here in another six months, Toot. With what I'm making we could rent an apartment and both of us go to school next fall, together! We could be married in June, right after you graduate, and live... Toot? I'm asking you again! Will you marry me?"

I snuggled my face against his throat and raised my eyes to his and knew that nothing else mattered to me but being with him. He read my answer and pulled me closer yet and smiled a radiance that warmed my very soul.

"Say it! I've got to hear you say it."

"Yes, Dean, yes! I want to be with you. I love you more than I know how to say."

Dean's eyes darkened and a frown creased his forehead. He gazed into my eyes, his lips only inches away from mine.

"I know you love me, Toot. You know I love you. I want to marry you! Say you will marry me."

"Dean?"

"Yes?"

"I don't like the word!"

"What word, marry?"

I nodded and he laughed and snuggled me tight, his arms and hands pressing me against him. He mussed my hair and said,

"Tell me then, why don't you like it?"

"I'm not sure! It sounds old and stagnant and ignominious. I don't like 'marriage' either."

He whispered, "The state or the word?"

"The word."

Dean held me tightly without speaking or moving. A terrifying dread began building in me and I thought, God, if you're there, don't let me hurt him.

His voice was low and he sounded worried as he asked, "What can I do? I don't understand your reluctance to say you will marry me. "Are you still thinking of traveling and seeing the world?"

I answered quickly, anxious to make him understand what I did not know how to put in words.

"No! I mean, yes, I'd like to go to many places, with you, someday. But I would not want to go anyplace without you. I know that right here is the most exciting place in the world as long as I am with you. Oh, Dean! I love you so much! Why don't you, why can't you... ? Oh, you big lug! Don't you see? You always think you know everything! Why can't you understand?"

I pushed away from him and walked over to the fireplace staring down into the graying embers. Dean followed me to the hearth, enfolded his arms across my waist and rested his chin in my hair and drawled, "Well, let me see. There's more than one way to skin a cat, and there's lots of other words, I guess. How bout, will you give me your hand, and all that goes with it, in holy matrimony? Will you be my bride? May we tie the nuptial knot? Why don't we just elope?"

I turned to face him and put my arms about his neck. He held me close and whispered, "I want you, all of you; morning, noon and night. I want to hold you against me while we sleep and see you first thing when I wake. But it's no good unless you want me, enough to marry me, and be my wife!"

"I do, Dean."

He grinned and said, "Say again."

"Oh, I do. Really, I do!"

He swung me around and kissed me soundly and sighed, "Oh! That's music to my ears!" He hugged me tightly to him and whispered softly, "Thank you, God."

I said, "What?"

He put his hand under my chin and lifted my face to his, "I've been so afraid I'd lose you. Everythings been going so well, but, it doesn't really mean anything to me without you. I want to share my whole life with you."

"Dean? Did you . . . I mean . . . have you ever . . . uh . . . Am I really . . . uh, Do you believe in monogamy?"

Dean's eyes twinkled merrily as he tightened his arms about me pressing me to him. His voice rang with surety. "One mate for life? You better believe it! That's why I waited for you to grow up!"

Hot tears stung my eyes and I batted them away, determined not to cry. I turned away from him and feeling a sudden chill, hugged my arms tightly about me. I walked over to the Christmas tree and stood looking at the small nativity nestled in the cottony snow under the tree. I knelt down to straighten some of the figures. I traced my finger over the tiny baby in the manger and sat back on my heels.

I said, "I think I'd just die if I ever had a baby like Michael."

Dean's voice came down from across the room. "You know the facts. It is not hereditary."

His breath caught on the words. He crossed the room quickly and knelt beside me.

"Is that why you were so hesitant to say you'd marry me?"

I nodded, and the bitter tears spilled down my cheeks.

"God, Toot! I know it was hell here for you for years with Michael David, and I know you've been concerned for Loralee's fears, but, I didn't realize . . . I mean, you know . . . Oh, Toot. I'm so sorry. You never let on. . . "

He stood and ran his hand through his hair. He laughed shakily, "And I thought I knew you. You had me believing you preferred travel over marrying me."

"I do want to travel someday."

Dean took my hand and pulled me up, saying, "We will!"

"I don't want to hurt you, Dean. I don't want to disappoint you, or burden you."

He cupped my chin in his hand. His eyes shone with tenderness and patient caring. His lips brushed my hair and my cheeks as he breathed utterances of assurance. "My sweet Toot! My love. My Girl. My Bride-to-be. Don't be afraid. I do understand, now. But I promise you this; I'll do everything I can to make our marriage happy and perfect and beautiful! And, hear me, Toot! It might be awhile before we're ready to have babies. But, when we do, our babies will be perfect. Believe me. Perfect!"

His words were as a healing balm to a deep wound. A wound caused by a horrible fear and a haunting dread in spite of the medical facts. A wound so terrible and so deep I had not been able to face it alone; the intimidating, plaguing horror that I might have a Mongoloid child. Medical facts were embroiled in emotions and daily frustrations, compounded by the greed of many medical doctors who had offered false hopes and created greater strife. It is hard to trust medical facts if they are akin to medical men. The sickening dread of inflicting such pain upon Dean, whom I loved more than life itself, had magnified my interest in travel. It was the obvious conscious answer to my subconscious fears; a running away. We looked at the situation honestly, examined it closely, cauterized it thoroughly, and soothed it with loving promises that we would not harbor such fears but would face the future, whatever it held in store for us, together.

We talked and planned and bantered and embraced in the light of the Christmas tree. His kisses were tenderly asking, searching, seeking and grew harder, finding, demanding. His hands knew me well and we were as one as we readily gave and gratefully received the ultimate gifts of our love-fulfilling exchange.

We vowed our love and pledged our troth and the angel in the top of the tree looked down in a silent benediction.

Dean and I did the things we had done so often during Christmas vacation, along with relatives and friends. We rode horse-back through the snow covered fields, writing our names in cursive over the acres by the horse's hooves cutting a path through the new snow. We ice-skated on the frozen pond and we walked around the gaily decorated town square, window shopping, meeting friends and calling season's greetings. But it was different. Everything was intensified. The lights were brighter, the music more beautiful, the senses more acute. Dean was more handsome, more caring, more considerate; I was enraptured.

The old timers called us 'love birds' and asked when we were 'getting hitched' and would cackle with hints of marvelous memories when we would confide "in June." Friends exchanged knowing glances and teased us about what they were planning for our charivari.

Dean and I attended the Christmas Eve Candlelight Service and as the minister spoke of how love came down at Christmas, it seemed as though our love was part and parcel of that love. As we knelt at the altar for Holy Communion the minister paused in front of us and whispered, "You look so happy! God bless you!" and Dean slipped his arm about my waist and the candles burned more brightly as we partook of the bread of life and the wine of sacrifice.

On Christmas morning Dean placed a solitaire ring on my finger and we selected a plot of ground that was on a rise near the woods for our home site.

Marj played the piano and Mother played the violin and we all sang and clowned and harmonized. Our home rang with music and laughter and good times.

It snowed nearly every day and the weather was crisp and invigorating. But inside it was warm and cozy. There was an air of excitement and anticipation and a peace and contentment that only love can generate.

New Year's Day dawned cold and gray with snow flurries. Dean had classes the next day and decided to leave earlier then planned in order to have daylight for driving. We fought the melancholy of the departure and our kisses were rich in memories and full of passionate promises for our life-time of togetherness.

I could still feel the impression of where Dean's lips had lingered on mine when Mr. Swanson rang the doorbell.

There were words—empty words—disjointed words—words with a terrible meaning.

His face was creased in sorrow. His eyes were red and swollen with crying. Grief and despair were written there. His voice was choking, trembling, breaking; "... semi-trailer—crossed into his lane—jack-knifed—decapitated—straight stretch of road—slick—snow—never knew what hit him—!"

His trembling hands covered his face as his shoulders heaved. I saw Dad's tall stooped frame move quickly to embrace him, support him, hold him, as he cried with him. I heard Mother's voice speaking words; terrible heart-rending words of tragedy, sympathy and sorrow. It was a dreadful dirge of words of . . . ! My mind refuted them; rejecting their message even while my very nerve fibers screamed thousands of whys.

Through the red-orange haze I saw Mr. Swanson opening his arms to me, felt him crushing me, heard him sobbing,

"He loved you so!"

Dad's eyes were grief-stricken in empathy; offering solace though helpless to assuage the pain.

Alf's red-rimmed dry eyes and worried concern belied his philosophical pragmatism.

Michael David had Dean's old straw cowboy hat on his head. He sensed the sorrow and sat slouched on the floor, his hands slack in his lap, and glumly chewed on his tongue.

Mother's voice echoed through the gloom, "She'll be alright. She's in shock. It hasn't hit her yet."

"You'll be alright. You're just in shock. It hasn't hit you yet."

Sleep can be oblivion. It can also be evasive. Think on the good things. Don't think at all. The room is dark. The draperies are closed as added protection against the cold raw wind that screeches through the splintered oak and rattles my window. The conductor pipes groan under the floors as the hot air is forced through them in a steady combative vein that assaults the registers, making them creak and crackle as they belch forth their comfort-giving burden.

The sun was hiding behind a gray sky as I trudged through the snow in mid-day to the Swanson's home. Cars were queued up and down their lane and on the shoulder of the road. A black wreath hung forlornly on the front door. I walked around the house and entered by the back door as friends and family always do.

Mrs. Swanson's eyes were red and swollen as she moved about the quiet crowded room. She was carrying a portrait of Dean and talked freely of him; as a baby, as a child growing up, of his likes and dislikes, his antics and accomplishments, and his untimely . . . She repeatedly professed a faith and trust in some Divine Plan that mere mortals could not understand as she gazed at the portrait with tears streaming down her face.

The portrait was a true likeness of Dean. I had one just like it.

I made my way through the press of people; mutual friends, neighbors and Dean's relatives. They offered condolences and I moved, unfeeling, in a red-orange numbed state where one does what one has to do without thinking about it. One does not have to think to nod, smile and be pleasant.

The words are devoid of meaning and life is as empty as its words. Hackneyed expressions, stereotyped phrases, and commonplace idioms swim about my head in an oppressive sea of red-orange.

"Time heals all wounds."

"You're young: you've got your life ahead of you."

"Sorrow is but a shadow that moves over the sea of life."

"You'll meet again; beyond the curtain."

"Seems the good always die young."

"You must be brave; he'd want that."

"Be thankful for the time you had together."

"He's just beyond the veil."

"When your time's up, you've had it. Don't matter where you are."

"Such a pity. God only knows. . ."

Their eyes speak volumes of sadness, sorrow, empathy; they are dulled with grief, dark with despair, tearing in pathetic fallacy.

The portrait tugged at my heart as I saw it from across the room. Dean's sun-streaked blond hair was a bit tousled as usual. His dark blue eyes were twinkling under slightly quizzical brows. His nose was straight with a bit of a shine and his shy smile showed strong white teeth set in a square jaw-line above a muscular neck set firmly on broad shoulders. I could not take my eyes from it.

God! The portrait: it's just of his head! Doesn't anyone else notice? Don't they see? The horrible implication. . .

A wave of nausea swept over me and I begged to be excused. I must not make a spectacle of myself. Mind over matter. God!

The cold is reviving! Be one with the elements. Don't resist the wind; let it blow right through you purging the very pores. Nothing matters. A hundred years from now you'll never know the difference.

The morning sun was beaming through the carelessly drawn draperies, glaring in my face. I blinked my eyes against the brightness, annoyed that it had awakened me. I rolled over and buried my face in my pillow and wished I could stay in bed. Thoughts of the wake flooded my mind; words offered in kindness and consolation intruded on my consciousness pelting it with the reality, the finality, the actuality of. . .

"God!" I moaned, kicking the covers and flinging them away from me as one fighting for life. The static cling of my pajamas was irritating. Michael's radio was blaring some inane gospel music that grated on my nerves. I yelled, "Michael! Turn that thing down!"

The clock was ticking, ticking. The icicles hanging from the window pane were dripping, dripping. My bare feet were cold and I was drenched in a clammy sweat. I stood still, waiting for the room to quit spinning. My reflection in the mirror stared back at me—looking like death washed over. Strands of hair were plastered to my neck and clung about my ears. My eyes were swollen and the skin on my chin was still rough and wrinkly from Dean's whiskers. In my mind I could hear him saying, *"I want to hold you against me while we sleep and see you first thing when I wake."*

I touched the rough place and let the tips of my fingers linger over it.

"Did I do that? It looks like a burn! Does it hurt?

"Toot, I don't want to hurt you, ever, in any way, shape or form."

I raised my face to the nothingness and tried to remember the pressure, the intensity, the rapture of Dean's kisses. They say that hair continues to grow even after . . . But it probably isn't true if the head has been. . .

Mother burst into the room with a flurry of forced cheerfulness and a glass of juice.

"My goodness! You were sleeping so soundly I just couldn't disturb you, but the time is getting away from us, Honey. Are you going over to the Swanson's before the funeral? I've been baking and frying chicken and making salads for I know Ruth doesn't have time to think about things like that. Did you try on that pretty black dress I bought you yesterday? I'm sure it'll fit you nicely although you're awfully young to be wearing black."

"I can't."

Mother was straightening the jumbled-up sheets and comforters, flipping them about with a fury, accenting her words with whacks at the pillows and long sweeping strokes that smoothed out the ripples of the linens.

"You certainly can! You should have worn it last night! Black is for mourning. People will think you don't care if you flaunt convention. I know you're still in shock and it hasn't hit you yet but you must give some regards to others. You're not the only one suffering! Why, Ruth and Ed were crazy about that boy. He was their youngest and there's always a special regard for the youngest. Did you hear Bob and Frank talking last night about what they were planning for your charivari? Why, they were going to make Dean push you around the Court House Square in a wheelbarrow—right after the wedding!"

"There won't be a wedding."

"Well, I know that! I'm just trying to get you to realize that you're not the only one who's lost him. Why, Bob and Frank doted on him just like Ruth and Ed did. 'Course they're older and they've got their own families to think of, but that doesn't make Dean's death any easier for them; not by a long shot."

"Mother, I've got to get dressed."

"Well, I'm not stopping you. I put some fresh towels in the bathroom. Aren't you going to drink your juice after I carried it upstairs for you? What is that on your chin? Did you burn yourself? Why, that looks terrible."

I grabbed my robe and Mother's voice followed me as my bare feet padded down the hall.

"I wish you'd put your slippers on. You'll catch your death of cold walking around here bare footed. It's going to be cold at the cemetery so you'd better wear . . ."

The bolt on the bathroom door clicked into place. I leaned against it, grateful for its protection from the painful practical preaching. I felt suspended in time; caught in the throes of memories of Dean, our love, our plans, our promises, and the horrible reality of . . . I will not wear black! I will wear—brown; just like a little brown sparrow. God? You still watching over the sparrows? So, . . . ! Why weren't you watching ov—

It was quiet. I couldn't hear Michael's radio. I should not have yelled at him. He'd been so glum, so sad, as though he knew... I opened the door and hurried to his room. He was sitting on the floor by his bed looking dejected. The radio was barely audible. A stack of magazines with brightly colored pictures lay untouched in front of him. Dean's old hat was hanging on the back of a chair. I made myself sound as normal as possible, "Hey, Boy! How ya doin?'"

He looked up and smiled and grunted, "Uhhh."

His eyes were a mess; clumps of matter hung in the lashes, and they were red-rimmed and runny. I poured some boric acid solution and said, as cheerfully as I could make it sound, "Now you know this hurts me more than it does you."

Michael nodded his head and obediently held it back for me to cleanse his eyes. I crooned, "He's a good boy. There, now, doesn't that feel better?"

He grinned and nodded his head and spoke, "Uhh uhh uuh."

I brushed his hair and apologized, "I'm sorry I yelled at you, Boy. Michael's a good boy! Want me to turn it up for you?"

I raised the volume and Michael started rocking back and forth happily grinning and babbling. The hat was hanging on the chair; I knew it was there, and I knew that Michael would like to have it on, but I could not... I said, "Look at your magazines now, OK? He's a good boy!"

Mother was in the hallway. She looked at me in disbelief, "You mean you haven't even started to get ready yet? Now, you better shake a leg! We can't be late to the funeral!"

The casket dominates the front of the church. The portrait sits atop it enframed in a black wreath. Huge sprays of flowers are amassed on either side. The sun is streaming through the stained glass window in the front of the sanctuary, depicting in vivid colors a kind looking shepherd looking over his flock.

The casket will not be opened; the casket cannot be opened. Do not look at it: do not think about it. Listen to the music. Singing Sally is probably out in the woods or walking through the fields singing her heart out to. . .

Listen to the minister saying nice things about a nice boy; Dean would die if he. . .

"Yea, though I walk through the valley of the shadow of death... *"You wantta go for a quick gallumph?*

"Plucked out in the bloom of life . . ." Stupid truck driver! Goddamn idiot! How can anyone fall asleep while driving in a snow storm in the middle of the afternoon?

"Let not your heart be troubled: ye believe in God, believe. . ." *Don't be afraid—Believe me—Perfect—"*

"Thou foolish one, that which thou thyself sowest is not quickened, except it die; and that which thou sowest, thou sowest not the body that shall be, but a bare grain, it may chance of wheat or of some other kind; but God giveth it a body even as it pleased Him, and to each seed a body of it's own. . ." *—Seems like a lot of things point to it—Why, I'll bet your Grandma is watching us right now; like a guardian angel—Our spirits just shed the skin at the time of. . ."*

"And forgive us our trespasses, as we forgive. . ." *"Forgive and forget"* Goddamn drunken bastard! Why wasn't he killed instead of. . . *"Bitterness will tear you apart like a pack of wild dogs"*—"The quality of mercy is not strained"—Remember the good things—*"It was as though you were a gift from heaven."*

"Almighty God, giver of every good and perfect gift, the Strength of the weak, the Comfort of the sorrowful, the Friend of the lonely: Let not sorrow overwhelm Thy children, nor anguish of heart turn them from Thee. We praise Thee for Dean in whom Thy virtues shone so brightly. Receive our humble thanksgiving for the life of him whom we this day lay to rest. We thank Thee for the happiness and love his life has brought to us. And now that Thou hast called him from our side, help us to trust him to Thy care in the quiet confidence that knows no fear. . ."

Strength—Comfort—Friend—Dean—Happiness—Love—

My room was my haven. I did not want to see anyone or do anything or go anyplace. Days drug into weeks. Mother didn't say much; she was kind, considerate and solicitous. I did not dress other than to wrap a wool robe about myself for warmth. It is cold when love is snatched away. I sat in my chair or lay on my bed expending no energies, but exhausted; shedding no tears, but emotionally drained, afraid to read or listen to the radio, afraid of memories too painful to bear; unable to think beyond the moment.

Dad would come into my room and pat me on the shoulder consolingly and talk of men and women in history who had suffered terrible losses but had gone on to achieve great things rather than give in to defeat. He would elaborate on how, "Our own Abe Lincoln lost his first love, his true love, to death, and he met defeat and betrayal at the hands of his best friend and business partner. He knew grief and depression but he did not retreat. He was defeated repeatedly and even scorned and ridiculed but he kept trying and learned from his defeats and built on them. He did not give in to despair! He did become the greatest president this country has ever had—but he had no way of knowing what was in store for him when his young love died. You can't quit, Toot. You've already missed two weeks of school. You've got to eat; feed your body, feed your mind! You've . . . got to start living again."

I had no answer for him. I didn't care about ole Abe. I would stare at the wallpaper and follow the design about the room. I had nothing to say. Talking requires thinking. If I can keep my mind blank it won't hurt so much. The leaves are imperfectly matched in that corner over the door. I bet the paper hanger thought we'd never notice it. But it doesn't matter; who's to care anyway? I surely don't.

Dr. Matthews came blustering into my room, peering at me over his glasses. He held my wrist and took out his pocket watch as he had done dozens of times over the years. I listened to his wheezing and thought of how Grandma used to worry about the Doctor's health. He thumped me on the back and made me breath in and out and took my temperature and scolded me roundly. But I knew him too well to care.

There is always a bit of a thaw in mid-January; you can bank on it. The sun shines bright and the snow melts a little and the wind chill factor isn't quite so severe. It is a reprieve before the last of the hard winter weather sets in.

Mother brought the Sunday funnies in with the breakfast tray laughing about Dagwood and Blondie being so cute. I mumbled thanks and she offered to draw a bath. I declined.

She said, "Well, alright then, you just rest."

The food and the funnies lay untouched. I lay in bed staring at the ceiling, not thinking of anything, trying to go back to sleep. A hard knock on the door vibrated through the room. I did not answer. Alf called, "Toot? You awake?"

I turned over and pulled the covers over my head.

"Hey! Toot!"

He opened the door and stood rattling the change in his pocket. "Get up and get dressed! We're goin' huntin'!"

I murmured, "No, Alf."

He yanked the covers off me and yelled, "I said get up and get dressed! Or d'y want me to dress you?"

"Alf—no!"

"I'm not asking you; I'm telling you!"

His eyes were red-rimmed and bright and piercing. His voice was sharp, clipped and commanding. I said, "I don't feel like it."

"I know how you feel—Goddamn it! But you're not gonna lay in that bed another minute! Now get up or I'll drag you out by your heels! Goddamn it—I mean it! Get up!"

I sat up and held my head in my hands while Alf stood watching me closely. He grabbed the tray from the desk and set it on the bed ordering, "Eat that egg!"

I whimpered with distaste. He stood over me threateningly, "Eat it, Toot. Every bite of it or so help me I'll shove it down your throat."

He walked over to the window and stood looking out, rattling the change in his pockets. Every minute or so he'd look back at me to see if I was eating. When he was satisfied that I'd had sufficient he said, "Now get up and put your woolens on—we're goin out!"

Alf and I plodded through the very fields where Dean and I only three weeks before had so happily ridden the horses through a tangle of turns writing our names in the snow. It was cold and invigorating. He had bossed me so fiercely my ire was up and I was determined to show him—what? I was ashamed of—what? I was feeling guilty of—what?

The Browning Sweet Sixteen felt good in the crook of my arm. The hounds were trembling with excitement and restraint as they obediently matched our pace across the rough stubble in the snow-covered fields. I had no qualms about thinning out the pesky rabbits that wreaked damage and destruction to the crops, the new vegetation and the young trees in the woods. The challenge of matching wits with the clever creatures was stimulating. They had the advantage of a nearly impenetrable habitat and their keen senses warned them of our approach. They would run and hop in a zigzagging path and were a swift moving, unpredictable target. I had killed dozens of them over the years and was proud of the soft luxurious fur-coverings on the pillows in the study. We did not eat the meat but we gave it to those who did. Dad restricted the hunting privileges on our property to family and friends. Outsiders were strictly forbidden; but the game was freely given away to any one who wanted it.

Alf walked on my left and motioned me further to the right as we neared the blackberry briar bramble that stretched along the far west border between the field and the woods. It was the home and breeding place for countless cottontails. He signaled the hounds and they eagerly began their coursing.

I saw a cottontail about twenty yards ahead of me running for the bramble. I raised the shotgun, sighted, aimed and hesitated as the rabbit stopped and sat frozen with fright.

Alf said, "Take it!" and it bounded toward the thicket. "Fire! Damnit! Fire!"

I followed it in the sight as it turned to the left to jump into the bramble. Mechanically, I aimed and fired. The charge caught it in mid-air, just under its ears and it fell lifeless to the ground. Its head was cocked to one side and blood spilled out red in the snow. It never knew what hit it.

I stood momentarily transfixed, and then an over-powering, gut-wrenching seizure doubled me over and I vomited and retched and heaved and kecked and collapsed in pain and tears. Alf guided me away from the mess in the snow and held me as the scalding tears burned my cold cheeks. He patted me on the shoulders and urged me, "Let it go, Toot! Get rid of it! For Christsake, spit it out! Don't keep it inside! It'll rot your guts. God Almighty!"

He was crying too and cursing the powers that be for putting me through such hell. The taste in my mouth was vile and I was weak and spent. He wiped my face dry and comically tried to clean some of the mess from the front of my jacket. I cringed with embarrassment.

Alf said, "Don't be embarrassed—I've seen a hell of a lot worse, Toot! You feelin' better? Christ, you ought to! God, I feel like shit. I didn't mean to hurt you any more, Toot. I didn't even think about anything like this happening. I just wanted you to get out of the house! You can't just stay in your room. Life goes on; you've got to face up to it regardless of what it hands you."

He picked the shotguns up and brushed the snow from them with a soft curse. He whistled for the hounds and put an arm about my shoulder as we headed for home. He talked of his first hand experiences with pain and frustration at the brutal deaths of his close friends and others in his outfit during the war. He patted me consolingly on the shoulder and said, "I know a part of you died when Dean was killed and his death was senseless, but don't deny what you had with him! Hell—people live a lifetime without ever coming close to what you two had! I know it's painful for you, Toot. But you've got to remember and be glad for the memories! You've got to accept the fact that he's dead—but you can't give in to it! Ya feelin' better now?"

I nodded and tried to smile as I let him lead me across the uneven ground.

We heard the sweet clear voice and saw the lone figure of Mrs. Andrews, heavily bundled against the cold, walking toward us from the direction of the woods.

Alf said, "Here comes Freddie's Mom. Such a beautiful voice."

"Oh God, Alf! I hope she didn't see me . . . or hear me. Oh, I'm such a mess!"

Alf squeezed me on the arm, "She'll understand, Toot! Better than anyone."

We listened to the cheery lilting refrain. Alf said, "What is that? *Good King Wenceslas?*"

She was getting nearer us. The melody was familiar but the words— I strained to hear them.

"Through each wonder of fair days
God Himself expresses
Beauty follows all His ways
As the world He blesses
So as He renews the earth
Artist without rival
In His grace of glad new birth
We must seek revival."

We were within a few feet of her and she had dropped her voice to a soft humming.

Alf called, "Ello there! That's a pretty song!"

Mrs. Andrews nodded and strode steadily right up to us and looking directly at me said softly, "I sang it for you, Toot. I know you're grieving for Dean."

She looked up at the sky as though studying it, sighed tiredly and touched my arm. It seemed as though she had aged so much since the last time we had talked.

"Such a fine young man; always kind to me. So much like my Freddie . . ."

I said, "He was very fond of you, Mrs. Andrews."

She nodded and smiled. "He looked a lot like my Freddie. It just doesn't make any sense . . . There's comfort in the music, Toot!"

"Thank you, Mrs. Andrews."

She moved heavily a few steps away, then turned back to face us and said, "I've watched you both grow up. I love you both like my own."

Her face crumpled and she murmured, "I saw you writing your names in the snow! I'm sorry—truly sorry."

She stepped back and patted Alf on the arm,

"Take care of your sister", and walked quickly away.

Alf hurried me toward home as I cried tears of grief and mourning that seemed to wash away the last of my bitterness and resentment.

"Hurry up, Toot! We've got to get you home 'fore your eyelashes get icicles."

I breathed deeply of the cold January air and felt a great relief and a tranquility of heart and mind.

"Alf?"

"Yeah?"

"Thanks."

"You're OK, Toot."

18

🐦 BREAD ISN'T HEAVY

I started back to school the next day. The pressure from being behind in my classes and studies preoccupied my mind and spurred me on to whole-hearted efforts as 'college' again loomed as the most important goal in my life.

The March winds were blowing through the trees like the proverbial lion the night before Dad left to go back to his work 'up North'. He had been recuperating for three months and was still not well although he insisted he was 'fine and dandy.'

I was working in the study on an assignment. Encyclopedias were strewn about the library table and my papers were scattered about on the floor around Dad's desk in a semblance of order. The monstrous unabridged edition of the dictionary was propped up on Dad's drawing board. I was absorbed in my work and had not noticed him come in.

"Toot? You look like you're enjoying yourself!"

I looked up and saw Dad standing there with his vest open, his tie pulled down, his glasses pushed low on his nose, grinning like a FDR donkey and holding his hands mysteriously behind his back.

"Hi Dad. I didn't hear you come in. Am I in your way here?"

"No, no—not a'tall! I got all of my papers together this afternoon. What are you working on?"

"A dissertation on the League of Nations. Mr. Darian said it was a big joke! I hope to disprove him."

"You've got the material to do it—I don't want to interrupt your train of thought, but—"

"What'd you have in mind, Dad?"

He walked over to the fireplace and teasingly baited me by grinning mischievously and making a big to-do about keeping his hands hidden behind his back.

I said, "What 'cha got, Dad?", and padded across the room to him.

He chuckled, "Something old and practical, something old and precious."

He brought his hands forward to reveal Grandma's four-leaf clover brooch and her little Smith and Wesson, ivory handled revolver.

"Oh, Dad!"

"She wanted you to have them, Toot. They're yours."

He handed them to me carefully. I accepted them with a feeling of reverence and awe. I whispered, "Thank you, Dad. I'll treasure them always."

"I know you will, Toot. That's why I wanted you to have them— There's something else I'll mention now, just in case—Your Mother's been wanting everything put in her name so I've taken care of that."

"Dad! What do you mean?"

He made a production of filling his pipe, tamping it down, lighting it and blowing the smoke ceiling-ward. He said, "Oh, it isn't important, not in the overall scheme of things. I just did it to ease her mind, get her off my back. The house, the property, the bank accounts, the shares in the Co-op and the acreage out at Oaksville with the coal rights; it's all in her name now. So she won't have to worry about money or expenses."

"What are you going to do, Dad?"

He puffed on his pipe and watched the smoke swirl up above the mantel and move across the painting of Gethsemane as though it were a fog. He smiled whimsically, "I'm going back to work tomorrow. I've still got my job and some mighty fine pieces.

"I was going to open a checking account for you but your Mother was dead set against it. She promised me you'd have everything you need and then some. Just tell her what you want and she'll give it to you. She said you can open an account of your own when you go off to college but in the meantime it's drawing good interest."

"I'm going to miss you, Dad."

"And I'll miss you too, Toot—but I'll be back in a few weeks to check on things. You know how to get in touch with me if anything, unforeseen, comes up?"

"Yes, Dad."

His glance swept the room. He sighed and his eyes clouded over.

"I'll never understand it."

He puffed on his pipe and aromatic blue smoke encircled us. I inhaled deeply and smilingly sighed, "Ummmmm."

Dad grinned.

I said, "Sir Walter Raleigh?"

And he chuckled, "Yep! I let him out."

We both groaned and laughed at the reference to the dumb Prince Albert joke Josh had plagued him with at Christmas time. Mother came in talking, "Oh, there you are, Riley! I've been looking all over this house for you."

She looked about the room in consternation and gasped, "Why, Toot, what in the world are you doing with all of these books spread all over everything? Why, it looks like you've just taken over the whole room for your own. Do you think you can trust your memory to put those books back in. . ."

"She's working on a paper, Martha—"

"I'll put them up, Mother."

Dad tapped out his pipe on the grate, blew through the stem and put it in his pocket.

Mother waved her hand in front of her face, forced a cough and complained, "I'm not going to miss that pipe—Well, I see you gave her that anyway—Those are real diamonds! You'd better let me put it up for you before you lose it."

"I'll be very careful with it."

"Don't be loading that gun and I don't want to see it laying around anyplace. There's not a one of them that's good for anything but catching dust! That pin is worth something, though. Of course, you can't wear it. You're much too young for diamonds, but I had thought you could wear it for something old on your wedding gown—"

I turned away and Dad said, "Martha, for Christsake!"

"Well, I'm just saying it would have looked nice. . ."

Dad's voice had an edge to it that I'd never heard before, "Martha, I know you've got a good heart and a good mind. If you could only learn to bridle your tongue. . ."

Mother's tone sounded hurt as she shot back, "There you go with another one of your backhanded compliments. You just can't stop when you're ahead, can you? You just have to get your dander up and spoil everything! I know I don't count for anything in your estimation and you'd never give this hole a thought if it wasn't for the children and those precious guns of yours. But I've got the upper hand, Riley! Do you hear me? You'd better not forget it."

Mother flounced out of the room. Dad shook the grate and poked the logs and yanked the protective screening so hard it closed properly on the first yank.

He stood, wavered, clutched his chest and slowly straightened up, lifting his head high.

"Dad? Are you alright?"

He answered with short breaths, "Yes—yes—I'm fine. Think I'll go out—for a walk. Don't let her talk—bother you. She doesn't mean—any harm."

The next morning the skies overhead were leaden but the clouds in the eastern sky were tinted with vivid hues of orange and red and purple as the golden sun broke through with it's bright promise of dissipating the gloom and warming the crisp March, bone-chilling winds.

Breakfast was a hurried but elegant and delicious affair. Mother had prepared creamed chicken, fried potatoes, scrambled eggs with chives, tender golden brown biscuits and grapefruit cups.

The best china and silver were laid on a linen cloth and three jonquils lifted their bright yellow heads from the bud vase.

"Mother, this is so nice! Everything looks so good and the table is just beautiful!"

"Well, you know I always say if it looks good it's bound to taste better."

"I hadn't noticed the jonquils blooming yet."

"Those aren't jonquils. They're daffodils. I forced them!"

Alf had come running down the backstairs while we were talking. He grabbed a biscuit and teased, "Did you talk them out?"

Mother laughed and bustled about with the last minute preparations while explaining the process of 'forcing.'

Dad was pleased with the show of consideration. The food was delicious; seasoned to perfection, substantial but not heavy, balanced in colors and textures and teasing all the taste buds awake with little sighs of, "ummmm." Mother was a culinary artist and seemed to bask in the pleasure we received from her masterpiece. Dad was fluent in his expressions of appreciation and Mother giggled like a schoolgirl. The talk was pleasant and there was an underlying air of reluctance for it to end. Alf and I dallied over second and third cups of coffee and when the time came for us to "jump and run or you'll be late," we hurriedly said our good-byes and ran out on a stream of banalities, "Take care of yourself, Dad!"

"Don't overdo!"

"Have a good trip."

"Come back soon!"

"Take care!"

"Godspeed."

In the late afternoon as I was walking up our lane I noticed several daffodils with tight buds and thought it amazing that Mother had forced some to bloom.

I entered by the back door and saw, to my dismay, that everything was as it had been when I'd left early that morning. Food was dried in dishes on the table and pots and pans and utensils cluttered the stove and counter tops. Michael's radio was on upstairs, but no lights were on and it was nearly dark inside. I called, "Mother?"

There was no answer. I went through the first floor of the house; ran up the stairs calling for her, and realized that she was gone and that Michael was alone. He was sitting in his room on the floor listening to the radio and looking at his magazines.

"Michael? Do you know where Mother is?"

He grunted, "Uh."

"Did she go someplace?"

"Uh."

He had an unkempt look about him and a certain sulkiness that alarmed me and made me suspicious that he'd been alone for a long period of time. I said,

"Did you have your lunch?"

He stood up quickly and took practice steps back and forth in place as he did after sitting for a long period of time but did not say anything.

"Would you like to have some lunch now?"

"Uh."

"Is Michael a hungry boy?"

"Uh."

"Come on then. We'll get you something good, OK?

"Uhhh."

Michael had eaten and was sitting astraddle his chair watching me as I cleaned up the kitchen and began supper preparations when a taxi brought Mother home. She came in laden with packages and animated and talkative.

"Brrr—That wind is so cold it just cuts right through me! Did you walk home? I don't know how you stand it but then you're young and I know you don't notice the weather like I do."

Mother had to walk around Michael to dump her packages on the table.

"You shouldn't be sitting in that chair like that. You'll break the back."

Michael's eyes drooped and he jutted his jaw to one side as he lowered his head against the scolding tone. I said, "He's proud of that, Mother. It really takes some doing to get on the chair like that."

"Well, I know he likes something different once in a while but there's no point in tearing things up."

"He was looking mighty sad when I got home and he acted half-starved."

"Why, he looks alright to me. You're alright, aren't you, Honey— There's nothing the matter with him—I explained to him that I had to go shopping. He understands."

"You shouldn't leave him alone, Mother. There's all kinds of things that could happen and he wouldn't know how to handle them."

"Now, that's ridiculous! You're just letting your imagination run away with you. There's nothing going to happen here! Why, it's the same thing day in, day out. What could happen? I can't take him with me, can I? You're just making a mountain out of a molehill and I'm too tired to argue with you—You'd better turn that burner down before you scorch those potatoes and stink up the whole house."

Mother had thrown her coat over the back of a chair. Michael reached out, gingerly, touched it and chortled.

She said, "Well, now, somebody's glad to see me. I told you I'd bring you something good."

Mother pulled a new iron out of a sack and held it in front of Michael.

"See there? This one isn't as heavy as that old one and just wait until you see what the men are bringing out tomorrow—"

She turned to me as she continued with the patronizing tone of a benefactress, "You'd never guess if you had a dozen guesses! It's something that'll make our world so much easier than you could ever dream possible. Why, who would have thought they'd ever come up with anything like it? I'll tell you just like I told them at the store, I truly hope that whoever dreamed it up makes a million—I just can't understand why your Dad couldn't have thought of it. What with him being an engineer; of course, he's the one that told me about them, but. . ."

"For Pete's sake, Mother, what did you get?"

"Well, I'm trying to tell you—I bought us an automatic washer. I mean it does the whole stinking warsh all by itself. All you do is put it in and turn it on and forget about it. But that's only half of it—I bought an automatic dryer, too. You won't have to hang clothes up to dry anymore. They just spin round and round and get dry in the machine in no time."

"Well, it sounds great!"

Mother had been unloading her purchases as she talked. In addition to the iron she'd held aloft, there was a smaller iron designed for detail work, a rubber bottle with a sprinkler attachment, a cover for the ironing board that was supposed to reflect the heat, a small padded board on a stand for ironing sleeves, some personal sundries and for Michael, a sack of chocolate covered vanilla crèmes.

I asked, "What's all that ironing stuff for?"

"Well, now, I was just shopping and bought them while I was there. They'll come in handy."

"Did Dad get off early?"

"Oh, yes. He left right after you and Alf did."

"I wish he hadn't gone."

"Now, he knows his own mind! I learned a long time ago there's no point in me trying to persuade him or dissuade him once he's got his mind set on something. I know he's worried about all of the expenses but we'd have all the money we need and then some if he'd just sell some of those old guns, but, oh, no—He'd rather just have them about collecting dust than doing anybody any good! Why, if he'd a just sold some of those fancy guns of his so I could have found the right doctor that poor baby could have been cured and wouldn't be in the condition he's in today!"

"Mother! That's not fair! There is no cure for Mongoloidism! You know that! Dad has done everything humanely possible to help Michael David! And he gave you thousands of dollars for you to run around all over the country, to quacks that did nothing but hold their hands out for money! God, Mom—!"

"Now, it's alright, Honey—I know you're still upset and my, you are high-strung, but, really, you shouldn't talk to your Mother like that."

"I'm sorry, Mother. But please don't say anything else about Dad selling the guns. They have such a rich history and are so unique."

Mother gathered her things hastily and started to leave the room, hesitating to say, in terminating the subject, "You're getting to be as bad as your Dad about those guns and I don't like it! And you're wearing pants too much, too! It just isn't ladylike! Don't burn those steaks!"

Mother once again reigned over the house and the purse strings with an iron hand. Expenses continued to drain our 'resources'. She became obsessed with 'change' and with saving every possible dime. She demanded to know what I had had for lunch at school and how much it cost. She learned of a bakery where day-old bread was sold and insisted I walk there after school to buy bread.

"Bread isn't heavy and that bakery's only a few blocks from the school and you're young. It won't hurt you to do something to help with the expenses."

"Mother, it's the other direction from the school, and that's 'spose to be for poor people."

"We have to eat the same as they do. Now, I know you don't like it but it won't hurt you just to get a few loaves of bread. You can get three or four at a time and that way you'll only have to go once a week."

Alf had started using the 'blue, blue Hudson'. He would take me to school of the mornings but I would walk home afterwards rather than wait three hours for him to get off work. Sometimes friends would drive me home and stay for an hour of study or talk. We would usually work or visit undisturbed in the study.

English term papers were due before the dismissal for Easter Vacation. Elinor had been undecided on her topic and was frantic as the due date drew near and she had not even started. Wanda and I agreed to help her and the three of us huddled in the study reading and digesting the necessary material, chewing it over, discussing it, brain-storming, looking up references and seeking facts to substantiate some statement.

Elinor tended to clown and livened up the study sessions with wild antics that were hilarious but harmless. She had forgotten to write down the source for one of her quotes and was searching through the volumes in a near panic late one evening. I was typing up what had been written while Wanda was busily rewriting a segment of it. Mother had walked in and stood watching in consternation as Elinor flipped the pages of the encyclopedia she was holding, running her hands up and down the pages as one reading Braille might do, searching for the lost lines of factual material she so desperately needed. Discarded books were lying haphazardly on the floor as she pored over volume after volume looking for the elusive lines.

Mother's tone was angry and scolding and incredulous as she exclaimed in a sharp voice, "Well, I just can't believe my eyes! Elinor! We don't treat our books like that! You smudge the pages when you lick your finger! And that's so nasty! You shouldn't put your fingers in your mouth at all. Why—there's no telling where they've been! And it's much too hard on the books to hold them like that—you'll break their backs! Why, don't you know—Books are our friends! You must not thumb through them like that! That wrinkles the pages terribly and then they're not nice for the next one who wants to use them! Now, I just can't have it. You'd better go to the library to do your studying. They don't care how you mistreat their books. Why, as old as you are—licking your fingers!"

Mother stalked out of the study. Elinor's face was afire with embarrassment and humiliation. She looked as though she were tottering between crying or laughing. Wanda's face was red with restraint. Her eyes were shining with the merriment her lips were compressed to conceal; her cheeks were extended as she held her breath trying to make no sound until the door clicked behind Mother. She sprawled on the table shaking with laughter.

I felt trapped in a middle field of ironies. Mother's sentiments were right but her mode of expression had been wrong. Elinor's treatment of the books was wrong but she was trying so hard to be right. The ludicrous scolding—Wanda's giggles—I gave in to a spasm of hilarity. Elinor sputtered and collapsed in gales of laughter.

Mother heard us. The next morning I was told that I was not, under any circumstances, to invite anyone to the house for any reason. She refused to discuss it or to reconsider the matter. She claimed it was her home, her house, her decision; she would decide who was welcome and who was not.

Mother began doing ironings again and was in 'a stew' over the number of people who wanted them done. She worried about being unable to do all of them and regretted the money she was missing out on. She fretted over the long hot hours of 'nigger work' that no one appreciated. When Alf or I would try to reason with her about the unreasonableness of her worries or the unnecessary ironings she would be defensive and bellicose in blaming Dad, us children, and evil circumstances for her predicament. Alf would mutter a few choice phrases under his breath and walk out exasperated. I, too, tried to avoid the encounters. But it was difficult and made even more so when Mother decided to do her ironings in the dining room since we weren't using it anyway. She pushed the massive oak dining room table to one side of the room, removed a bulb from one of the sockets in the chandelier and strung an extension cord from it so she could have 'good light' for ironing. The ironing board was set up directly under the crystal chandelier. She used the dining room table for sprinkling the ironing and was oblivious to the water spots on the expensive table and chairs. The finished ironing was hung over the French doors that opened into the hallway, and there were words of reprisals if one of us so much as touched a finished product.

One day after a long grueling hour of jeremiad, Mother set the iron down on it's heel and said, "You can just thank your lucky stars, my dear, for your Mother! You may not know it now but you've always had the cream right off the top. Oh, I know, you've had a big disappointment, but we can't help that. God gives and God takes away, and I'll never understand it, but I'm talking about here at home. Why, you've had everything a girl could ever want and I'm the one who's given it to you, and, you know what—I'm not through yet! I've just been standing here all day ironing and it occurred to me, just like a blot right out of the blue—we ought to get a television. They've got a station in St. Louis and they pull it in pretty clear in town and I was thinking as high as our house is, why, we ought to get good reception. So, what do you think of that?"

"I don't know, Mother. I don't even know anyone around here who has one."

"Why—haven't you seen it at the hardware store? They have it right in the window."

"I have seen it as I was passing by, but I've never really watched it."

"Well, it'd be such good company for the baby. . ."

"Mother! Please don't call him that. He was doing quite well there for awhile, but now he's starting to act—babyish."

"It was that institution that ruined him. I should never have let you talk me into that. Oh, how I rue the day—poor baby! I do believe they mistreated him."

"Mother! He learned a lot there."

"That's a matter of opinion. But I've decided I'm going to make it up to him. I'm going to get a nice big television and put it right there, since we don't use this dining room anymore anyway. You can drag that big old green chair in here and he can sit right there and we'll watch television while I iron."

"Don't they cost a lot?"

"Sometimes you just don't count the cost! He'll enjoy it and you know how your Grandma always said, 'A merry heart is better than bitter medicine.'"

Late one rainy April night the police brought Alf home. He had missed a turn on the hard-road, skidded across the shoulder, plunged over an embankment and landed upside down in a cornfield. He was not badly hurt but he was drunk. The car was demolished. Mother said the car was not important and was thankful that Alf was not seriously hurt! I admired her attitude and her graciousness. She thanked the police for bringing him home and said she would talk with the farmer the next day and make the necessary arrangements about getting the car towed away, and make restitution for any damages, if there were any, to the plowed field. Alf was in a daze but insisted he didn't feel any pain and just wanted to go to bed.

The next morning at breakfast Alf was repentant and offered to pay for the car. He was bruised and scratched and had difficulty moving. Mother catered to him and tried to get him to stay home and rest for a few days. He insisted he was fine and could not afford to miss work. Mother said, "Well, it's up to you, Honey. You know how you feel. I think you ought to go to bed for a few days and get a good rest. You needn't worry about it being a bother to me, for, fact is, I'd enjoy your company. You don't know what it is not having a soul to talk to about intelligent things. Why, I just get so starved for a good conversation at times I can't see straight. But I wouldn't bother you—I know you don't want me meddlin' in your personal affairs, and I understand that. And if you feel you have to go to work then that's your business, but you've got to understand me on this! I don't give a hoot about that car; truth is it was too big to drive anyway. But I knelt by my bed last night and said a prayer of thanks that you weren't killed right out and, now listen, I know you don't want to hear this—but, I mean it! I don't want you to leave this house until you've given me your solemn oath that you'll never take another drink."

Alf balked; Mother nagged. He moved out the next day.

The Senior Prom was scheduled for the second Saturday in May. I had been working on the decorating committee and had accepted an invitation to attend with Bob Gardner, a casual acquaintance. I had not dated anyone since Dean's death, but I was enthused about going to the prom with Bob. I asked Mother if I should call Loralee or Marj about borrowing a gown, since the ones I had were for fall or winter. She said, "Oh, no, Honey. If you want to go we'll buy you a nice new one. Theirs would be too old looking for you and it'd just get crushed and wrinkled and mussed in the packing! We'll go shopping one of these days or you can look in the stores and see if you can find something with nice lines. Of course, you wouldn't want anything severe, but something nice for your age."

The week of the prom arrived. I asked again about going shopping for the gown. Mother was annoyed.

"Well, I know you need one. I know you've got to have one! But I can't afford anything right now. It seems like money's just going down the drain, but, if you'll just keep your britches on there's plenty of time to see about it. It's nothing to worry about, my dear. The lilies of the field don't worry about what they're going to wear."

"I've looked around the shops. There's hardly anything left."

"Oh, I'm sure you'll find something. If there's one thing you know how to do, it's to spend money. Why, I couldn't believe my eyes when I saw you pull in that driveway in that taxi this evening."

"There were three sacks of groceries, Mother. I couldn't possibly carry them all."

"You didn't have to get all of them at one time. My goodness—when are you going to learn to use your head for something besides a hat rack? And, something else, young lady! You had no business letting that strange man walk right into the house like that!"

"He was just helping me carry the groceries in."

"You gave him extra, didn't you? After I stand here ironing all day, trying to make ends meet, you just throw money around like you were some rich man's daughter!"

"Oh, come on, Mother! You tip people, don't you?"

"Now don't make fun of me! I show my appreciation, of course. But, a simple, 'Thank you' is sufficient. My—Your Grandma used to give money away like it was going out of style! But, then, it was her nature to be generous and she could afford it. I'm telling you though, those people get paid good wages for doing their jobs and it's foolish to pay for more than what you get."

Thursday afternoon after school, Wanda and Elinor and I went to practically every shop in town that carried formal wear. Elinor was in a tissy that I had 'only forty-eight hours to come up with something superb', and Wanda was trying to squeeze more hours into Saturday so we could make a quick trip to St. Louis to find something. They had each boughten a gown and accessories weeks before and could not understand why I had 'waited until the last minute'.

We did find an appropriate formal gown in one of the better shops. It fit me nicely and they were exuberant in their delight and relief that we had done it, we had found something, and it was really quite lovely. I asked Miss Mildred, the amused saleslady, to hold it for me, and hurried home to tell Mother.

She was enraged at my effrontery and worried about what the poor woman must think.

"Mother, you told me I could look for something. Miss Mildred didn't mind holding it for me. I told her I'd pick it up tomorrow. I think it fantastic that I found something so lovely at such a late date."

"Well, I just don't know. How do you think you're going to pay for it? Money sure doesn't grow on trees you know, although I sometimes think you children think it does. The way you stand up for Alf and him just drinking up every cent he makes. You think he's so perfect why don't you just see if he'd pay for it?"

"Mother, I haven't had any new clothes all year."

"Now, that isn't true! I bought you that nice black dress myself and you just wore it one time—It'll be the same thing with this formal. You'll just wear it one time and be done with it."

"It's a lovely simple gown, Mother, in a shade of soft yellow. I can wear it to Wanda's wedding—I'm to be a bridesmaid, you know. And I'm sure there will be dances at school next year."

"Oh, all of these high-falutin' plans of yours! That girl's so changeable there may not even be a wedding next month. You ought to know, if anyone does, that you can't count your eggs before they're hatched. I don't know why anyone in their right mind would want to graduate one day and get married the next. It's just jumpin' out of the pan into the fire."

"Mother, may I have the money for college now? You could call the bank in the morning and I could go by after school or during my lunch hour to sign any papers. Then I could get the dress myself."

"Now, if you'll just get off your high horse I'll see what I can do. There's no point in opening an account for you or even thinking about touching that money that's drawing good interest when you won't even need it for several months yet. I know I told you I'd get you a gown although I swear I must have had rocks in my head to promise such a ridiculous thing when I've got all of these other expenses to worry about. Why, you could have borrowed one from Loralee for nothing. I'll bet she has a closet hanging full of nice gowns. But it's too late to depend on her—What about that nice red one you have? It isn't too wintery, is it? Oh well, Saturday is soon enough to worry about it. Get him another bowl of ice cream and don't worry about it."

Mother woke me early Saturday morning and announced, "I've been studying on this prom business and I know you'll be disappointed but it can't be helped. My Papa always said that dancing is a tool of the devil and I'm thinking I'll be derelict in my duties if I let you go. You know as well as I do that all it'll be is dancing and that can lead to all kinds of things. No, now, the more I think of it, the more I am convinced in my own mind that you shouldn't go. It's just a lot of foolishness; a bunch of young people putting on airs and trying to act grown-up! Why, I'm telling you that can lead to all kinds of things."

"Mother, I've been dancing for years. You used to make me go to dancing class, remember? Bob and I are double dating. We have plans! You said it was alright two weeks ago. He'll be here at seven to pick me up. I must get the gown this morning."

"Didn't you hear me? Aren't you awake yet? I said, you're not going! And that's all there is to it!"

"Mother, it isn't fair. We have plans!"

"Plans can be changed, my dear. It won't hurt you to miss out this one time. Why, just think of all the things you've been in. I've watched you go running off to your fancy affairs time after time while I just have to sit here hemmed in by circumstances. You can't learn any younger that you can't always have everything your own way! But I'm not going to argue with you about it. I'm just not in a position to buy you a fancy gown for just one wearing and that florist wanted seventy-five cents just for a boutonniere. That's just one dinky little flower and I don't have that kind of money so you can just cancel that order."

"Mother, I'm going to call Dad. I'm sure he'll send me the money for the gown. I'll just charge it and then I can pay for it next week."

"You're not calling your Dad about anything! Haven't you heard a word I said? I swear, you're as bull-headed as he is! It just goes in one ear and right out the other! If Dean had meant anything at all to you, you wouldn't even be considering going out with someone else so soon after his tragic death. Why, it looks like you're fickle. It hasn't even been six months since he was laid to rest, and it's only been about five months to the day since you were carrying on like you didn't care if you lived or died. Why, if he had lived you'd be in the midst of making your wedding plans for next month and here you are having a fit to go dancing with someone else just like Dean never even existed!"

The bitter, acrid accusations whirled about my head in a red-orange fog. I lay back in my bed and pulled the covers up about me. I felt I was suffocating but I was so cold. Mother stood in the doorway talking on and on. I could hear the television and I thought, God, it isn't even seven o'clock and Michael's already watching his idiot box. There was a pause in the torturous voice and I kept my eyes closed hoping she would leave me alone. I felt her hand on my forehead.

"Do you have a fever? Why, you're as white as the sheet. There's not a drop of blood in your face! Maybe I should call Dr. Matthews—he said that neurasthenia could crop up again if we weren't careful."

I sat up and insisted, "I feel fine, Mother."

"Are you sure? Well, I hope so! There's a lot to be done today. I've got to go into town to do some shopping and this whole house needs a good going over. Now, if you feel like getting up out of that soft bed of yours, you can go call that young man and tell him you're not going tonight. Then call the florist as soon as they open and cancel that boutonniere!"

Bob did not understand why I could not go to the prom. He was very angry and peeved and went to great lengths to avoid speaking to me in the last weeks of school. Elinor and Wanda were the only ones who had any insight into my situation, but, even they could not understand why I could not reason with Mother. Bob was popular and well-liked. Several of his friends and some of our mutual friends showed their angry resentment to me for having broken our date at the last minute. I had no plausible explanation and the subject was a source of embarrassment and humiliation to me. The red-orange world of bafflement, frustration, disappointment and depression was my realm for the remainder of the last month of my Senior Year.

19

🌴 NO TIME LIKE THE PRESENT

June was hot and sultry and the occasional breeze was peppered with pesky oat-bugs. The tiny little black things floated on the breeze and got all over everything.

Mother alluded to the wedding that would never be as though it were a financial burden that she had escaped by heavenly intervention. Her words weighed heavily on my mind as they conjured up shattered dreams that were unthinkably painful. The melancholy was as draining and depressing as the heat and humidity were suffocating.

Then one day Mother surprised me with a lovely white dress that she implied she had bought for me for graduation. It was a designer dress of Swiss-polka-dot and fit me perfectly, as she had known it would. I noticed that it had cost three times more than the formal I had selected for the prom. When I commented on it she said,

"Oh, you can't compare the two. Besides, my dear, you're not 'spose to look a gift-horse in the mouth."

"It is lovely, Mother. It looks so cool and it feels exquisite!"

"Ummm, my! It's even prettier on you than I thought it would be. Honey, don't go near the graveyard in that. You'd revive the dead."

"Mother!"

Graduation Day dawned bright and sunny. Mother talked incessantly about how she regretted she could not attend the ceremony. I dreaded going alone for it was a family affair. I knew of no one else who was going without members of their family. The auditorium space was limited so the seating was carefully allocated according to a family's requirements.

307

I had only asked for two "family" seats and was mortified to think they would be unused.

I did my hair, tidied the house and tried to keep cool. The ceremony was in the evening. As the seemingly endless afternoon dragged on I was tempted to forget about going.

Late in the afternoon I heard a car pull into the lane. I didn't even bother to look out the window. I assumed it was one of Mother's customers coming about an ironing. But then a horn blared and a familiar voice called, "Anybody home? Hey, Toot!"

I looked out and saw Marj waving up to me. A surge of joy welled up within me. I called excitedly,

"Marj! I'll be right there!"

I flew down the stairs and through the house, calling to Mother and Michael as I ran.

"Marj is here! Mother, Marj is here! Michael! Come and see Marj!"

Mother continued with her ironing, but raised her voice to me. "Don't get that baby all excited! She can find her way in. She's no stranger and she's not company."

Marj was radiantly beautiful and looked cool in spite of the beastly heat. She was unloading a handsome set of luggage from the trunk of her car and called to me as I ran out to meet her.

"Congratulations, Graduate! We were all going to come but Steve had to work and Loralee isn't well, so, you'll have to settle for just little ole me."

"Oh, Marj, I'm so glad to see you."

"Well, don't get mushy. Loralee sent you the luggage. We put some things in the big bag that we thought you might like. But this is your present from me."

She handed me a small gift-wrapped box. The paper was white and thick and embossed with an intricate Chantilly design. The huge bow held a tiny gold mortarboard with a tiny gold chain for a tassel. I took great care in opening it as Marj stood impatiently urging me to hurry up. I was savoring the moment, but aware that Mother had not come out. I asked, "Marj? Maybe we should go inside for me to open it—?"

She said, "There's no time like the present—", and laughed, as she continued, "Oh, that's hilarious! I couldn't have planned it better. Hurry and open it so you'll see what I mean. No time like the present."

I lifted the lid of the box and revealed an oval-faced Bulova wrist watch with a yellow gold expansion bracelet.

"It's beautiful, Marj."

She beamed with pleasure and asked if I would prefer white gold.

"Oh, no, Marj. This is perfect. I love the watch and the luggage and I'm so glad you're here."

"I wouldn't miss your graduation, Toot. Didn't Mom tell you I was coming? Oh, Bull! She's getting to be as odd as a three-dollar bill. Come on, we better go in—Isn't this luggage beautiful? I told Loralee if you didn't like it I'd keep it myself."

"Oh, it's beautiful, Marj."

She laughed and looked at me questioningly. "You're beginning to sound like a broken record, Toot."

I grinned self-consciously. "Sorry. It's just things were so gloomy, but, now, you're here."

"Funny, Mom didn't tell you I was coming? What's she doing, ironing? Bull! That old bat thinks she's going to take 'it' with her, but I've got news for her. All she can take is her damned ironings!"

"Wait 'till you see the dining room."

"Alf told me it was full of chicken shit!"

We made our way to the backdoor carrying the lovely luggage and Marj's own overnight bag. It was the first time she had been home since Christmas. She looked much taller than her five feet, five inches, and much slimmer than her one hundred and ten pounds. She was wearing a dark blue sleeveless sheath of linen that was elegant in its simplicity. Her light brown hair was cut short and fluffy and her blue-green eyes sparkled with mischief. She edged her way in through the back door as I held it open for her. She whispered, "Where's Mom?"

"I think she's ironing—in the dining room."

Marj rolled her eyes and grimaced comically. She leaned toward me and whispered, "If she says, 'How de do, muh deah', I'll scream."

Mother was standing at the ironing board ironing and watching television as though she did not know anyone was there.

The ironing board was set up directly under the crystal chandelier. One candle-bulb had been replaced with a screw-in socket. The iron's electrical cord was plugged in there. It pulled the chandelier down on one side. An oscillating fan swept the room, and canned laughter filled the room as professional idiots performed their antics in some far off studio. Michael jostled excitedly up and down, his hands pushed deep into his lap, his eyes fixed in a stare at the one-eyed monster.

Marj breathed, "Shit!", and then called cheerily, "Hi, Mom! Hi there, Michael!"

Mother set the iron on its heel and turned to face us.

"Well, look who's here. How de do, muh deah!"

Marj screamed, "Ekkk! What happened to the dining room?"

Mother looked about her as though seeing it for the first time and then looked at me questioningly. I was weak with giggles but Mother's withering look dried them up in a hurry.

Mother said, "Why, there's nothing wrong with this dining room. What are you girls up to? I heard you giggling and. . ."

"Mother?" I said hurriedly, "Did you see the luggage? Isn't it lovely? Loralee and Steve sent it to me for a graduation gift! And look what Marj gave me!"

I held my arm up for her to see and admire the watch.

"A Bulova? That's nice. You be careful you don't over wind it. You'll break the mainspring. Did you drive down by yourself, Marjorie?"

"Nope! I've got a car full of men out there and they're all coming in to spend the night!"

Mother gave her a sidelong glance that held no mirth and said, "All you need is one."

Marj laughed with abandonment and then went over to Mother and gave her a big hug and kiss and stood with her arm around her shoulders and said in a stage whisper,

"I'll tell you what, Martha. Every time Mr. Right-for-me comes along and finds out what my pearl-of-great-price is going to cost him he hightails it to the hills! I guess I'm just doomed to be a damned old maid!"

"Pshaw! You haven't changed a bit! I don't think you'll ever grow up, Marjorie. Someday you'll find it isn't enough having everything you want if you don't have anyone to warm your feet on at night."

"Is that what you do with a man, Mother? You warm your feet on him—Chee, I think I'd rather wear socks!"

Michael David was sitting directly in front of the television seemingly unaware of the rest of us. Marjorie teased him about what he was watching and was surprised when he acted annoyed with her. She told him she had brought him something and fished around in her bag to find it. He watched as she unloaded many personal items before coming up with a crinkled sack with red and white stripes which she held out for him. He reached for it cautiously and then held it on his lap without offering to open it. Marj said, "Michael, look here! Open it!"

Mother said, "When he's watching one of his programs he doesn't want to be bothered about anything. Why, he's even gotten so he wants to eat his meals right there in front of that television. He even runs to the bathroom and back."

"Have to be thankful for little favors, huh?" Marj cracked.

She opened the sack for Michael and took out a mechanical, fat, fuzzy duck, with webbed feet and a head and bill that moved and quacked as it was pulled by a string. She pulled it across the floor and it waddled and bobbed and quacked. Michael grunted and got down on the floor with it. Marj showed him how to pull the string and he was fascinated with the results he got. Marj was satisfied that he liked it and patted him on the head saying, "Ah, life's little favors. It doesn't take much to make you happy, does it, boy?"

Michael babbled and we all laughed. Mother hung up the piece she had been working on and Marj asked her not to do anymore. Mother said, "Why, I can't stop now. I've several more pieces dampened down here."

Marj said, "They'll wait for you, Mom. Let's go out and have a nice dinner before the Graduation Ceremony, and then maybe we can hit a nightspot afterwards, if you insist."

"Oh, now, that's ridiculous! There's no place around here that would be appropriate for us to go to. But I don't plan on going anyplace anyway. You girls just go ahead and have a good time. I'll stay here with the baby and. . ."

"Good God, Mom! What baby?"

"Why—Michael, right there."

"That's no baby, Mom!"

"Oh, alright! Have it your way."

I asked, "Are you sure you don't want to come with us, Mother? You've plenty of time to get ready."

"No, now, I've told you I'd like to but there'll be lots of people there and no one's going to miss me. Besides, I've been to graduation ceremonies before and they're every one just the same. They're not even as important now as they used to be for everybody goes to high school nowadays and as hot as it is out here you can be sure that auditorium will be like a furnace. But it'll be nice enough for you, you're young, so, you go on now and get ready, we'll be alright here. We're used to it."

Marj asked me, "Do you want the luggage in your room, Toot?"

"Yes, please!"

She laughed, "Wait until you see some of the wild pajamas I brought you. They'll really liven up the dorm!"

Marj made the evening memorable. Alf met us at the school and all during the ceremony I could feel their presence. After the ceremony we went to a restaurant for dinner and just as we were about to order, a lovely brunette came up to our table. Alf introduced us to Sylvia, and moment's later four more of his friends walked in and headed straight for us. Marj laughed, "Toot? Do you understand now why we were seated at this big table?"

Alf stood and introduced Marj and Sylvia to Tom, Guy, Harold and Johnny. I knew them from the times they'd been in our home and they were my favorites. Alf asked, "Marj, have you ever had a blind date with two fellas at once? Now, Toot, you can take your choice of these ky-yoots, but sit here by me where I can watch you."

Sometime after ordering there was a bit of a lull in the conversation. I noticed Alf looking at me, beaming approval. Our eyes met and he leaned toward me and whispered, "You look lovely. D'ya like your dress?"

And in an instant I knew he was responsible for it. I said, "Oh yes, it's the most beautiful one I've ever had!"

He looked so proud and pleased. I asked, "Did you choose it, Alf?"

He laughed and shook his head, "That's not my department, Toot. I just gave Mom the money. She did the rest."

I leaned over and kissed him on the cheek,

"Thank you."

"I'm glad you like it."

Sylvia gave us a curious look, and Marj, sitting between two handsome men, suggested the kiss be passed around the table. Other graduates, with their families and friends were there. It was a festive, fun-filled evening.

Dew glistened on the grass and tiny droplets shone like jewels on the roses as Marj and I strolled through the back garden seeking momentary respite from the onslaught of tyrannical badgering from Mother. She was groveling in self-pity and was rife with resentment that she had not been included in "the partying". Marj had reminded her, "We asked you to come with us, Mom! Remember?"

"Oh, I know you asked me. But you didn't really want me to go. I'm used to being left out but I'll tell you it hurts when your own children go running off to have a good time and don't care whether you live or die. I know you think I'm just an old stick in the mud, but we could have had a good time right here at home, but, oh no, you had to go off to some fancy restaurant! I'll just bet you spent a pretty penny, too! You never could keep a coin in your pocket, even when you were a child. If you had a quarter you had to run to the store to spend it!"

Marj had tried to tease Mother out of her dark mood but had finally succumbed to the wheedling and asked with child-like innocence,

"What is that old axiom, Mom, about 'Silence is golden'? Isn't that based on a scripture? Isn't there a verse in Proverbs that says, 'Keep thy tongue from evil and thy lips from speaking guile'? Or is that in Psalms? I always get Psalms and Proverbs mixed up! That's what happens when one is made to memorize the scriptures. But I do remember the essence of one verse that claims 'Whoso keepeth his mouth and his tongue, keepeth his soul from troubles'."

Mother ignored the implication of Marj's remarks and worried, "No one listens to me or cares what I think about anything. I've tried to teach you children right from wrong and every one of you just throw it back in my face and do exactly as you please regardless of how it might hurt you. But, that's alright, I understand, you're young and you don't mean any harm, but, the day is coming when you'll wish you had shown more appreciation to the hand that feeds you."

Marj laughed, "That reminds me, Mom, do we get breakfast around here? Or do we have to go to some fancy restaurant?"

"Well, there's some puffed wheat and some corn flakes."

"God Almighty! Whatever happened to steak and eggs?"

"Well, I just assumed you girls wouldn't want anything heavy. You look like you've gained some weight, Marjorie, and you didn't even bother to tell me when you plan to leave and you're not helpless, muh deah."

"I'll be leaving in an hour or two, Mom. Toot? Let's go smell the roses!"

Marj picked up a stick and twirled away some eager spider's web from around the top of a rose bush. She bent over to inhale deeply of the sweet fragrance and exclaimed, "God! If only they could bottle that!"

The sun was shining brightly but there was mugginess in the air that forestalled any physical exertion. I had a lot of questions that I didn't know how to ask and I felt there were things Marj wanted to tell me if the opportunity presented itself.

"Marj, is Loralee alright now?"

"No, but she tries to act like she is. That Goddamned butcher really messed her up this last time and she's scared to death Steve's going to find out, but she's more afraid of having a monster for a baby."

"I don't see how she can keep it from him. Abortions, God! Did she go back to the same doctor in Chicago?"

"Ump umh. She told Steve she was going shopping. When she got there the Goddamned quack had raised his price. She'd been there twice before and he knew why she was getting them so he really stuck it to her. She's been hemorrhaging and having cramps for the last two weeks. Of course, that's really why they couldn't come for your graduation. Steve is worried sick about her and she's got a heavy guilt complex on top of everything else. Her doctor told her the other day she'll have to have a hysterectomy as soon as she's able to. So, at least, she won't have to worry about having any more abortions or . . . monsters."

"It is not hereditary!"

"I know, Toot. I know that's what they say, and, maybe if things had been different—but, for Christ sake—The way Mom shoves him down our throats, it's hard to be rational!"

"I know."

Marj succeeded in snapping off a half-opened red rose bud, which she checked carefully, flicking away the aphids that were clustered about the calyx with her long brightly polished fingernails.

"I don't want to reopen what must be a god-awful subject for you, Toot. You know we're all sorry as hell about Dean's accident."

"I know, Marj,"

"God, Toot! I've seen a lot of happy people and I've been there myself a few times, but, the two of you, at Christmas, God! it was wonderful just seeing you together. I know you must have gone through hell when he got killed like that! I cried for you. We all did! I wish I could have been here to help you."

"I knew about the . . . trip to Chicago. She told me at Christmas."

"Yes, she had delayed that one in order to come down here. And waiting until the first of the year would have been too hard on her. She had the appointment and couldn't put it off any longer. Steve called us at the hotel and told us what had happened. The next day, driving home, we stopped at a truck stop and cussed out some truckers!"

"Marj! You didn't!"

"We sure as hell did! One of the bastards said we were nuts. I told him it runs in the family and if I ever saw a drunken trucker on the road I'd chase him to hell and back to see he got what was coming to him! Actually, some of them were very sympathetic, and claimed they would help me."

"Marj, you are an idiot; A sweet, loveable idiot!"

"Don't get mushy! It's too hot. We had probably better go in before you know who . . . Hey, listen! Is that Sally? Singing Sally! Come on. . ."

Marj ran toward the far end of the lane heading for the woods. Dust covered her sandaled feet and my tennis shoes were brown with the filmy gritty grime. Marj ran ahead of me toward the sound of the sweet clear voice. Sweat was pouring from my brow, stinging my eyes, and my breath was coming in short gasps that hurt my lungs as I tried to keep up with her. I followed, stumbling over rocks and branches that she didn't even notice. I waved my hands before my face to disperse the gnats that hung in clouds in the patches of sunlight that pierced the shade of the tree-lined path. Marj skimmed over the ground like a young deer, fleet and nimble, as she pursued the lone figure of Singing Sally down in the clearing by the wide spot in the creek. I heard her calling, "Mrs. Andrews! Mrs. Andrews! It's me, Marjorie!"

I saw Mrs. Andrews embrace her, and I watched as Marj gave her the red rose bud. I stood in the shade trying to get my breath as they talked.

Presently, Marj moved toward me and as Mrs. Andrews's eyes followed her, they spotted me. I smiled and called,

"Good morning, Mrs. Andrews."

She smiled and nodded and Marj and I walked toward home.

"How can you run like that and not even show it?"

"Tennis, little one? It keeps one in shape!"

"I didn't know you knew Mrs. Andrews so well."

Marj didn't say anything for several minutes. Then, in a low voice, "One can never really know the private hell of another. There are so many screaming areas of discontent it is sometimes difficult to ascertain the basic needs or hungers from the frustrations and entanglements which we so unwittingly garb ourselves in. Yet, on any day of our life, we stand at some time in a situation where the honest and simple testimony to the goodness of God is greatly needed. Some have to go to church for it. Others see it in a sunset or a perfect flower or hear it in music or see it in a smile. Grandma used to say she could hear a more beautiful message in Sally's singing than she could hear in a month of Sunday Services. I wish the whole world could hear her sing! Freddie was so proud of her. He used to tell her she ought to be singing with the Met, for she had perfect pitch and a fantastic range. Of course, he had a good voice, too."

"Did you know him well?"

"We were good friends. We'd even dated a few times; nothing big or heavy, just good friends. I still have his letters."

Marj laughed and pushed me playfully, "Here I am preaching and it is much too hot for it! You know that time I went off the deep end and made you go to the altar?"

I started laughing in embarrassment at the memory and Marj was convulsed in giggles.

"God Almighty! Talk about a fanatical fool! I've no excuse. It was just, at the time, everything was so jumbled up. Freddie killed in the Pacific; Grandma, dying so suddenly; Dad and Mrs. Zimmerman carrying on, and that imbecile, the King of Nilesville, born on New Year's Day and everybody gossiping about him. And then, dear sweet Mom told me if I wanted to finish college I'd just have to work my way through while she sat on her big fat-assed bank account claiming she might need it for the Goddamned idiot."

"Is that why you quit school? She said you were bored."

"Mom has a way of justifying her decisions; contrary to fact! But, I've a good job and I like it—Oh, damn, I've ruined these scandals, and just look at my feet! Talk about idiots! Ohhh, look, wild violets. Let's take some to Mom! Maybe it'll sweeten the old bat up."

Marj selected the prettiest of the tiny blue-purple flowers and arranged them in a cheery nosegay. She broke a small ivy vine and tied it about the short stems to hold them in place and laughed about wishing she could find a poison ivy vine to use.

"I don't mean to be cynical, Toot. You 'member that great big scale Grandma used to talk about? Boy, I used to wish I could put her against my Philosophy Prof. She was so much more profound in comparison and I believe she was right. Everything is balanced; night and day, up and down, in and out; you can't be happy unless you've been sad; you've got to know hate to know love, you've got to have doubts before you can really feel hope and trust. You can't have roses without thorns or heaven without hell. But the choices are ours! How we balance the scales is up to us."

"I can't buy that, Marj. We're not really free to choose anything that matters. Things just happen. A no good drunk killed Dean. Loralee has had three abortions that I know of and I bet each one of those babies would have been perfect if, if only . . . I know she's scared, but it just isn't right, and Michael . . . Michael lives! God, it's so unfair. And Dad used to be so strong, but now . . . and Mother is so moody, so irrational. God, Marj, you can't imagine how she talks all the time. I get so tired of it."

"Now you listen to me, Toot. I know the way Mom plays Little Napoleon. She wants us to ask her permission before we take a pee. Oh, 'scuse me, I mean before we Number One. Now, whether you laugh or not at my crudity or the absurdity of the situation is your choice. It is your decision, Sweetie. You are the . . . Shhhh! Listen,"

Singing Sally's soul-stirring canticle of praise seemed to transform the woods into a cathedral. An awesome thrill tingled my spine as the hauntingly beautiful soprano voice sang as sweetly and as naturally as the wind in the trees.

". . . *When I in awesome wonder*
Consider all the worlds Thy hands have made,
I see the stars, I hear the rolling thunder,
Thy power throughout the universe displayed,
Then sings my soul, my Savior God to Thee;
How great Thou art, how great Thou art!
Then sings my soul, . . ."

Marj had tears glistening on her eyelashes as she stood listening, smiling, and gazing off into the distance. I felt my own heart 'strangely warmed' by the sweet vibrant strains that seemed at one with life and the universe and God.

> *"When through the woods and forest glades I wander*
> *And hear the birds sing sweetly in the trees;*
> *When I look down from lofty mountain grandeur*
> *And hear the brook and feel the gentle breeze;*
> *Then sings my soul, my Savior God to Thee;*
> *How great Thou art, How great Thou art!"*

The atmosphere about us seemed to be adorned with angel's wings; beautiful, but fragile and fluttery. I did not move or speak for fear of shattering the mystical moment. A cool breeze was rustling the leaves and making little ripples in the water as Marj and I stood on the grassy knoll by the creek. Occasionally a fish would surface for an insect and a lazy snake doctor circled above the reeds and seed-splitting cattails as though warning us away from the water's edge. Marj spoke, just barely breaking the silence with her softly modulated voice that trembled with emotion.

"We try so hard to be happy; anything to climb up on that great plateau of happiness. But we can never reach it, unless we learn to conquer our own unhappiness. Life is full of contradictions, and God knows, Toot, I don't understand it anymore than you do, but I know its hell without hope and trust and faith, in God! 'Member how Grandma used to tell us to think on beautiful things?"

"That was her favorite scripture."

"Yeah, Philippians; four, eight. Accentuate the positive, eliminate the negative, latch on . . ."

"Marj!"

"Same thing, Toot. Don't be so shocked. Grandma would have liked that song."

"It might be a similar thought but it somehow lacks the eloquence of King John's version: 'Whatsoever things are lovely . . .'"

"I concede, Graduate!"

Marj laughed and then sighed sadly, "Oh, this is so nice down here. Our own 'Walden's Pond'. But, we gotta go, Kid, back to reality."

Marj started hurriedly up the path, talking in short sentences paced with her long steps; waving a bee away from the nosegay; ducking as it dived for her hair; sprinting away from it with the agility of her athletic prowess and laughing when it chased me with fury before being attracted to the blooming blackberry brambles.

Marj waited for me at the edge of the lane. Together, we sauntered toward the house.

Marj said, "I'm so glad we came down here. Mrs. Andrew's song was hauntingly beautiful! I wish the whole world could hear her. But, it would be the same as it is here. Some would hear and understand; others would laugh and call her crazy."

"Marj—you are cynical!"

"Nope, not really. Just bracing myself to go see Mom."

We shed our shoes on the back porch and squeaked across the kitchen floor. Marj called, "Mom—brought you something!"

Mother came bustling in and gushed, "Oh, how pretty! Is that what you were up to? I saw you go running off down to the woods, but, my goodness, I didn't even think about you going down there to get violets for me. Why, there's lots of flowers right there in the back yard."

Mother took them in her hands and smelled them and exclaimed, "There's just no other posy quite as pleasing as a wild wood violet. Toot! Get that silver compote and put just the least amount of water in it. Oh, Marjorie, you can be so sweet when you put your mind to it!" Mother put the violets in the water and set them on the breakfast table. I said, "Marj, would you like a cheese omelet?"

"Sounds good. Do you have tomatoes and mangoes?"

"Um umph. Would you like some grits, too?"

Mother said, "Oh my, that does sound good, Honey. Michael's hungry. Make enough for all of us. He'll like that."

Marjorie gathered her things to leave shortly after our brunch. I thanked her for coming and for the gifts as we walked out to her car. She said, "That's OK, Sweetie. Gee, I'm glad you'll be going off to college in another two months. This is getting to be a real nut house. Sometimes I wonder if it really is haunted."

"You can't be serious."

"No? Well, maybe it isn't the house so much as Mom. She's getting weirder all the time. Be careful, Toot! Don't let her hurt you."

I laughed shortly, "Why, Mother wouldn't hurt anyone."

Marj got in her car and sat looking toward the house with an unreadable expression in her eyes. She fumbled in her purse for the leather key case, selected the right key, put it in the ignition, hesitated about turning it on, looked again toward the house, pushed the cigarette lighter in, fished in her bag for a cigarette, lighted it, and exhaled as though purifying her thoughts as well as her lungs.

"She's my Mom and I love her, but she's got a cruel streak that lashes out at every one of us. She just lives to put us on a fence and push us off and watch as we break into pieces so she can put us back together again and tell us how grateful we ought to be. She knows our weak spots and she knows how to knife us with her words where it hurts the most and how to twist things around until we either give up or run like hell! Don't give up, Toot!"

She closed the car door, and started the car. I said, "Be careful, Marj. Thanks again for everything."

"You, too!"

She smiled and waved, accelerated and the car started forward. She braked, backed up and said, "Memorize Psalms, twenty-seven, ten! That's twenty-seven ten, and don't hesitate to call me if you need me!"

I watched the car disappear in a swirl of dust as Marj drove off down the lane much as she had run through the woods. An emptiness settled about me and I turned, reluctantly, to go in the house. I heard Mother talking as I opened the door. "You shouldn't have detained her like that. She's got a long drive ahead of her and they say it's going to be bad weather. They've just forecast a severe thunder storm for us for later this afternoon. I knew we were in for it when that cool breeze started blowing. It seems there can't be any relief from the heat without one getting their pants scared off of them by thunder and lightening. What were you girls talking about all morning? Oh, I can imagine with her big important career and all of the executives she's hob-nobbing with, but, it'll all come to naught. Men that age are already married and settled down with nice families and she'll wake up one of these days and find she doesn't have a thing except some humdrum job. You just can't expect to get ahead in the business world if you don't have a college degree and she just didn't have the gumption to get one. You'd better damp-mop that kitchen floor. You girls ought to know better than to go tracking in dirt like that. Why, there's no excuse for it! Why did you go running off down there anyway?"

"We heard Mrs. Andrews singing."

"Crazy Sally? Why, you can hear her any time of the day or night. I'm surprised they haven't taken her off to Bedlam! You don't mean to tell me that you two great big girls went running off like that in that heat just to hear Crazy Sally?!"

"She was singing a beautiful song, Mother. It was one we had never heard before. You would have liked it, too. We were wishing everyone could hear her."

"That's absurd. I get tired of hearing her. Sometimes I think maybe I ought to put up a 'no trespassing' sign. She walks around over our land like it was her own."

"Aren't the violets lovely?"

"Oh, yes, they're very pretty. 'Course, they'll be gone by morning. Wild flowers don't last anytime. I'll tell you something though. I've just been standing here thinking about how you can read what people think of you by what they give you. She comes sailing in here so high and mighty and gives you a fancy wrist watch and luggage and clothes and what does she give me, her own Mother? A bunch of violets I could have gone out and picked myself!"

"Mother, you know the watch is for a graduation gift. The clothes are not new, and the luggage is from Steve and Loralee."

"Oh, I know, I know. It's easy to rationalize. But I can read between the lines."

Michael was glued to the television. His eyes were running and red and I could smell his sour sweat across the room. I said,

"Michael. Let's go sit outside on the porch for awhile in the nice breeze. I'll read to you, OK?"

He grunted and started to get up. Mother said, "Now, don't disturb him. He's watching his program. If you want to do something for him you can bring him a bowl of ice cream."

"He just ate, Mother. He had enough for three people."

"Well, since when do you care what he has to eat? He enjoys his eating and I'm not going to deprive him of that, his chief pleasure in life."

I was trying to clean his eyes and he was showing his resentment but tolerating it.

"Mother, I really think he ought to have glasses. Since he's been watching television all the time his eyes have gotten so much weaker and they've started matting again, terribly."

"Are you suggesting that I'm neglecting him? He just has a little cold. A lot of people have runny eyes when they get a cold. I wish you'd quit pestering him. You're blocking out the whole screen. Just because you don't like it, you don't want anyone else watching it either! Are you going to clean the kitchen up today? The day's half gone."

I stood in the doorway to the kitchen and ventured, "I really like the white dress, Mother."

"I knew you would."

"I didn't know Alf had paid for it."

"Oh? Well, he left it up to me to pick it out. I figure it doesn't matter where it comes from as long as you've got it."

"I'm surprised I didn't hear from Dad."

"Oh, well, I'd forgotten about it. Seems like there was a package the other day, it was just a small one."

"For me?"

"Well, that's what I'm saying! I think I carried it into the study."

I ran to the study and searched the room with my eyes. There was nothing that looked like a package any place about. I opened the top drawer of the desk, where the account books were kept. There was a small package addressed to me from Dad. I cut the string and read the postmark: May 10. It was more than a month since it had been mailed.

I tore the paper off and opened the cardboard box. There was a jeweler's ring box inside. I lifted it out, raised the lid and saw a beautiful birthstone ring with a most unusual setting. There were four topaz stones holding a diamond, all set in yellow gold. I slipped it on my finger next to the solitaire. It fit perfectly and the simplicity of the solitaire with the uniqueness of the birthstone ring was perfect for me. I opened the name-card that had been folded and pressed into the top of the ring box. Dad's bold, masculine writing stated in black ink, "Toot, Congratulations, Dad."

I was proud, pleased and relieved that Dad had remembered me. I admired the ring; tried it on my right hand, but liked the two together, best, on my left hand. I thought of friends I'd like to show it to and resentment began to gnaw at me. It must have been here at least two, maybe three, weeks. Why hadn't she given it to me? Did she really forget? She knew I had been checking the mail every day looking for something from Dad. This must have come while I was still in school.

It was getting dark from the gathering clouds. The breeze felt so good I dreaded having to close the windows and decided I would wait until the very last moment before the rain began.

I thought about Marj and wished she could have seen the ring. I wished I could have worn it last night for the dinner, as well as for the graduation ceremony. Alf would have liked it. If only Mother hadn't forgotten.

"Toot? Did you find it?"

"Yes, Mother. It was in the desk drawer. See? It is such a beautiful ring!"

"Good heavens—Another diamond? Why, you're only seventeen and you've got more diamonds than I had at thirty! I'm afraid you don't realize their value. You can't wear them around to do the house work and you must not wear them to do the dishes. Why, if you lost a diamond you'd never find it."

"Do you remember when it came, Mother?"

"I've no idea. But it just goes to reaffirm what I've suspected for a long time. Your Dad's been holding out on me. Now, that ring cost something! And he's been telling me that he sends me everything he makes except just for living expenses."

"Mother, I think Dad is very generous."

"Oh, indeed he is! Generous to a fault! While I'm doing ironings to make ends meet. But, no one cares about that."

"I meant generous with you, Mother. You don't have to do ironings. . ."

"It isn't your place to tell me what I have to do or don't have to do. You're just getting too cheeky for your own good, young lady! Here you are out with Marj for just a few hours and you get to actin' as independent as a hog on ice, and, if you think, for one min—"

I started laughing. Mother stopped in mid-sentence and stared at me. I said, "Mother, a hog on ice? Where did you ever learn such an expression?"

Mother grunted a grudging laugh. She seemed a bit uncertain whether she should indulge in the pleasure of the compliment. "Why, that's as old as the hills."

"What does it mean?"

"Why, it means, showing off or being difficult."

"Mother, I'm not showing off or being difficult, am I?"

Mother crossed her arms across her waist and stared at me. She cocked her head to one side and sighed audibly.

"Well! You'd better put those windows down. It's going to be raining cats and dogs before you can shake a stick at it! And the kitchen's waiting for you; Seems as though you girls can't fix anything without dirtyin' everything in there. Of course, Marj isn't one to offer to help but, you shouldn't be so inconsiderate as to leave those dirty dishes piled in the sink. You know I have to fix that poor baby something every time I turn around."

I pressed Dad's name-card back into the top of the ring box, and snapped it shut. Mother held out her hand and said, "I'll keep that for you. You don't need to be wearin' it around here."

I slipped it into the pocket of my skirt and assured her, smiling,

"I'll be very careful with it, Mother. I won't take a chance on losing it. I'll write Dad a letter after I have cleaned up the kitchen, and I'll go do that now. No time like the present."

Mother wore a worried expression and chewed on her lip nervously between mutterings of, "I knew he was holdin' out on me. There's no tellin' how much he's kept back or what he's done with it. But, I'm not goin' to stand for it. I'll fix him, and I'll just take Miss Smarty-Pants down a notch or two while I'm at it."

20

🕊 HOLD OFF AWHILE

Mother was terrified of thunder and lightening rainstorms. When they occurred during the night she would get up from her bed and dress fully; anticipating the worst and determined to not be caught unaware. She would stand at the window watching the lightening, exclaiming over the brightness, the intensity, and the proximity of it and shuddering with the inevitable roar, crackle, boom of the thunder.

She was wary, even of a gentle falling rain, because of its possible potential for growing into a terrible storm that might sweep her away into some unknown but oft-imagined horror.

I had watched and listened repeatedly in my childhood as Grandma or Dad would try to reassure her there was nothing for her to fear from the elements. On one occasion little Josh had lisped an adjuration with the solemnity and seriousness of a battlefront commander, while punctuating the air with an index finger: "*Ya gotta be brave, like me! Ya can't fly a kite with a metal srting!*"

We had laughed and repeated his admonition over the years as though it were sage advice. But Mother had continued to grow even more apprehensive, more fearful, and more irrational in her reactions to the storms. As the low rumbling thunder in the far-off distance began to permeate the thick walls of our home, Mother would begin pacing about the house, peering out the windows at the gathering clouds, going from floor to floor, from room to room, studying the sky from each direction, trying to judge when the storm would get to us. As the wind increased and the lightening darts broke through the darkening tumbling clouds causing sharp crackles of thunder, she would peek around the closed draperies as though drawn to the source of her fears by a morbid fascination for the spectacular phenomenon over which she had no control. On the rare occasions when piercing bright flashes of lightening, accompanied by loud crashes of thunder and seemingly sheets of wind-driven rain, assailed our haven, Mother would dash about, holding her hands over her ears, shrieking at each crash or crackle of thunder.

I had heard Grandma tell her many times the words that I now used to try to soothe her: *"Thunder can't hurt you; the danger's over by the time you hear the noise."*

Mother would rant and rave:

"You know there'll be another one! That lightening is the finger of God coming down to earth to punish the wayward."

"Now, Martha, you know better than that. The laws of the universe dictate the weather, lightening puts electricity in the air and makes things grow and, my goodness, you know how much we need the rain."

"I know how lightening kills and burns houses! Oh, just listen to that! That clap of thunder sounded like it hit right here in our yard! Oh, I just hate this house! Every time there's a storm, it's all around us. There's no escaping it!"

Grandma would sigh and offer to make a soothing cup of tea and murmur,

"Please don't worry so. It'll soon pass."

As the storm clouds moved away and the skies cleared, Mother would thank her lucky stars that she had survived that one and would wonder if the next one would have her number on it.

Now, Grandma was dead. Dad was living up North. Alf had his own house in town. Josh was living with Loralee and Steve, and Marj had her own interest's up-state. So, it was up to me to try to calm Mother during the storms. Michael sensed her anxiety and reacted in a like manner unless I could offset it.

I was awakened late one night by Mother shaking me and ordering,

"Get up! Get up and get dressed! We've got to go downstairs. You can't go out in the night in that flimsy gown! Hurry up and get dressed!"

She was holding a flashlight and was beside herself with fears. The electricity was blinking off and then on again. She went hurrying downstairs as a lightening flash penetrated the night sky. I lay on my bed watching as streaks of lightening shot fiery blue bolts that zigzagged from the churning air currents to the accompaniment of deafening blasts of thunder that rumbled and roared across the heavens and echoed through our house. Rain was wind driven in sheets that seemed to change directions at will, attacking us from all sides. I moaned, "Oh, God, not again."

I could hear Michael David whimpering and babbling in his room. My heart went out to him and with a feeling of pity that was stronger than the need for sleep; I pulled on a robe and went to his room. Mother had awakened him and had hurriedly dressed him. He was frightened and sleepy and sat huddled on the floor by his bed. I forced a bright cheery tone to my voice and held my face in a wide toothy grin as I crossed the room and sat down by him on the floor.

"Hi, Michael. That silly ole storm's OK, boy! It's just rain and that makes the pretty flowers grow. Yeah-yoo! It's OK, Honey Bunch. Michael's a nice big boy—sleepy boy, ummmm? Wanta sing a song? Lessee now; let's sing a song, about Boom, Boom, Boom."

Michael was beginning to relax. He raised his head and grunted, "Uhhh." I began singing a little ditty I had made up for him, patterned after action choruses and nursery rhymes that he was always amused by. I had showed him how to clap his hands for thunder, wiggle his fingers for rain, and wave his arms for lightening. So, as I sang, we both made the motions.

"When the hot air, hits the cold air
Then it goes Boom, Boom, Boom, Boom!
The lightening flashes, as thunder crashes
Making big Boom, Boom, Booms.
But it's alright, Luv!
Don't be afraid, Luv!
God planned it all, Luv!
When it goes Boom, Boom, Boom, Boom!
When the hot air, hits the cold air
Then it goes Boom, Boom, Boom, Boom!
The rain comes down, down, down,
Plip-plop, plip-plop, plop!
When it goes Boom, Boom, Boom, Boom!"

He began to chortle with delight and did not seem to be afraid of the noise without. Sometimes he would look toward the window at a cracking flash of lightening or at a particularly loud crash of thunder. I would roll my eyes and go, "Ohhhhhh". He would laugh and try to imitate me. I was still sitting on the floor with him when Mother came running back upstairs, calling for me.

"What on earth are you doing? Why didn't you bring him down? I told you to hurry downstairs!"

"It's alright, Mother. The storm's about over, now. I'll put Michael back to bed."

"You'll do no such thing! You don't know what's going to happen before morning. Why, a tornado could blow us away in a wink of the eye."

"Mother, we have never had a tornado around here."

"You just never can tell where they'll hit. They never strike the same place twice. There was one just south of here a few years back and it wiped out a whole section of town. My, the tales they told of that just made my skin crawl!"

"Did you check the barometer in the study?"

"Well, yes, of course I did, but I don't know if it's working or not. It could be broken."

Michael's eyes and actions were beginning to reflect her fears.

"I really think it is about over, Mother."

"Well, what do you know about it?"

"Would you like for me to put the tea kettle on for some tea?"

"Oh, just suit yourself. The electricity may not stay on long enough for it to get hot, but, if you want some, I'll have a cup with you."

I plodded down the back stairs to the kitchen thinking; one of these days I am going to start cussing not just bad words, but, colorful inventive phraseologies of truth that will hang in the air like a balloon in a cartoon or like the sword of Damocles. Each word will be as vivid and as colorful as a bold-faced zinnia and the atmosphere will be sweet and cheerful, even during a thunderstorm.

The next morning the sun rose bright and shone hot and heavy on the rain sodden countryside. A steamy mist was rising from the ground and the leaves on the trees shed their hoard of droplets as the branches swayed in a gently graceful waltz in the early morning breeze. The birds were singing cheerily and the katydids were calling from the woods.

I put the coffeepot on and went out to the front porch swing. I had heard Mother moving about upstairs. I dreaded the encounter. I knew from experience that she would be tired and cross and argumentative.

We had had a nasty scene when I had tried to keep her from giving Michael a big bowl of ice cream at three-thirty in the morning. She insisted on giving it to him and encouraged him to eat it all. He did, and promptly belched it back up. Mother had blamed me for addling him. Michael had been belligerent and had flailed his arms about wildly while coughing and sputtering.

The tea pot had broken when it was knocked to the floor. Hot tea had been strewn all across the newly waxed floor. Mother had been livid with rage and Michael had acted accordingly.

He fought us as we tried to change his clothes and wash his face. Mother fussed at him in scolding tones. He babbled back at her in anger.

I cleaned up the vomit and sopped up the spilled tea. I had the fleeting thought that I was a participant in a losing battle.

I had quit trying to appease Mother, for any words of encouragement incensed her temper. Michael was attuned to her state of mind and with the added frustration of the discomfort of vomiting he had regressed to howling and slobbering and scooting about on the floor. It took the two of us to get him back to bed. Mother had angrily threatened, "I'm not going to forget this, young lady!"

She had prevailed upon him to take additional pills for sleeping; bemoaning the cost of them, and scolding him when he would spit them back out. She had insisted I go to the kitchen for a spoonful of jelly, which she pushed the pills into and then coaxed him to swallow.

There was a sweet smell of honeysuckle and lilacs in the air and the cool breeze felt so good. The nightmare of the storm, both without and within, receded into the background as my mind dwelt on happier thoughts and memories of what might have been. The white Spirea that lined the fence between the lane and the pasture was cascading with long graceful boughs of tiny white flowers. The delicate white petals that had been beaten off in the storm were scattered about on the green grass and reminded one of snow flakes. Mother insisted on calling the Spirea bushes, bridal wreath, and frequently alluded to how lovely they would have been in the decorations for the wedding.

Had it only been six months? Dean . . . A lifetime ago. It was unthinkably painful. At times I wanted to run screaming in all directions at once. Other times I would not have been surprised if he had come riding up the lane, calling, "*Hey, Toot! Ya wantta take a quick galumph?*"

There had been other times when I would awaken from dreams of him—Dreams that seemed so real, so right; dreams that materialized into nothingness.

I heard Mother rattling pots and pans in the kitchen. God? Please don't let there be another storm? For crying out loud! Just let it rain easy, with no noise; no thunder or lightening. I am sure you can arrange that easier than I can reason with Mother! And God? Help me to keep from going bananas!

"Well, good morning, muh deah. Did you rest well?"

"Yes, Mother. And you?"

"Well, I just didn't get enough to amount to anything. But I'll be alright. I never did require much sleep or rest. I've known of people who'd go to bed with the chickens and then sleep half the day. But they were all fat and dull-witted. I never could stand to be around anyone like that. This coffee is delicious! Did you put salt in it?"

"No."

"Well, it's mighty good. I do enjoy a good cup of coffee first thing of the morning. That's one thing your Dad and I had in common. He's a good man, your Dad. He never once mistreated me or any of you children. He used to bring me presents all the time and when we were first married we went everywhere. Some people just talk about going and doing but not your Dad. Every time I'd say something about wanting to see someplace he'd take me to see it. Why, we went to Niagara Falls and the Grand Canyon. Then, one winter day I said something about going to Florida to get warm and he said, 'Well, let's *do it*' and we did. Umm umph! I just don't know what happened. Seems like everything went haywire after that poor baby was born in such pitiful condition. But, of course, he can't help that. But he sure ruined everything! Sometimes, like last night, I just don't know what to do with him. He's a lot stronger than I am. I don't know how much longer I'm going to be able to handle him."

"He can always be readmitted, Mother. It would be much easier on both of you."

"Well, I don't know. These tranquilizers have helped him a lot. But I think this last batch must be defective for they just don't seem to have much effect on him. Heaven knows, as much as they cost, we ought to get some good from them."

"Isn't it about time for Dr. Matthews to check him over again?"

"Well, yes, it's past time, but sometimes I think I know as much about it as he does. All he does is write another prescription and fuss about him gaining so much weight and charge me five dollars for the call."

"Shall I call the office after while and see if he can come out later today?"

"Well, alright. I guess we'd better. I'll tell you, the way he was acting last night scares me. I just can't manage him when he gets all riled up like that. Why, he weighs as much as I do and I just don't know how to deal with that fighting and carrying on. He bruised me here on my arm, see that?"

There was a long, mean looking black and blue bruise about the size of a dollar bill on the inside of Mother's right arm just about the wrist. "Good heavens, Mother, I didn't know you were hurt! That looks terrible. We had better have the doctor look at that, too."

"Oh, no, now, it'll be alright. It doesn't hurt that much, and Dr. Matthews might get the wrong idea. He's told me of things that could happen but he's also said that these children are usually docile and very obedient and it's just going to reflect on me if he finds out about him going so wild like that."

"Mother, maybe it's the medicine that upsets him. Or, maybe, waking him up in the middle of the night like that. . ."

"Oh, it's all my fault to hear you tell it! If you hadn't come running down here to make tea that teapot wouldn't have been broken. Why, I've used that teapot for twenty years, but I sure can't use it now."

"I'll get you another one, Mother."

"Why, there's no point in doing that. There's two others in there. My! You're getting so sensitive there's just no talking to you."

Mother went in the dining room and turned on the television. Within minutes she was talking to it as though the images on the screen were her own captive confidants. She bared her soul, bemoaning the faults of her ungrateful children, detailing her hard life and adventures in the school of hard knocks and portraying herself as the heroine who bravely faced the evils of life undaunted, carrying her cross proudly, persecuted by those who should be grateful, harassed and deserted by a husband who had never cared a snap for anyone or anything except guns, but, she knew God wouldn't give her more than she could bear and she was determined to stand the test of time with her head held high because it doesn't matter what people think since half the world doesn't know how the other half lives anyway.

Mother kept paper and pencil on the television for listing all of the new products that would make life easier for her. She bought them all and bewailed the expense.

Dr. Matthews had prescribed a stronger tranquilizer for Michael and had insisted that he be put on a diet, which he outlined thoroughly. Mother had the prescription filled and gave it to him regularly, but she rejected the diet adamantly, and argued, "Why, that's the only enjoyment he gets. He loves to eat and I'm sure he knows enough to know when to stop when he's had enough. How can I or anyone else know if he's satisfied or not? Why, the very idea! Telling me to take food away from that poor baby!"

Dad came home for a few days and packed some guns and books. Animosity hung in the air like a thick veil. He would come and go with no explanation. Mother refused to discuss him with the terse remark, "It's none of your concern!"

Michael David caught a summer cold and was very uncomfortable with it. Mother worried about him excessively but was busy with her ironings and could not get behind, "That electric meter won't stand still just because I need to stop for something else. I know he's heavy but you've got a good head and you can figure out how to handle him. It's messy work but that poor baby can't help himself. A lot of healthy people get diarrhea with a cold. It's just one of those things. They cough at one end and go at the other. But I've got to get this done and I can't afford to pay someone to come in here just to care for him when you're right here not doing anything anyway."

Alf called one afternoon to see if I would like to go to St. Louis to a ball game with him and several others. It sounded like fun and I wanted to go but Mother was in a tizzy so I told him Michael had a problem and I could not possibly leave. He said, "Awww, shit!"

"Alf, please! I'm up to my elbows in it."

"Has Doc been out?"

"Yes—four times."

"Well, feed him cheese! Are you all registered? Have you scheduled your classes?"

"Yes on both counts. I've got my room assignment, too. Second floor in Brafman Hall. Did you know I have a job in the office?"

"No, I didn't know that and I don't think you ought to have to bother with it. Who's idea was it? Mom's?"

"More or less."

"That figures! Well, I'll check with you later. Feed him cheese!"

"Have fun, Alf! And thanks anyway."

Michael liked cheese and I let him have all he wanted. By the end of the day he was better. The next day he was almost back to normal. I gave him eggs and cheese for breakfast, grilled cheese for lunch, and a big wedge of cheddar following supper. Perhaps the medicine finally took effect or maybe the bug had run its course. But, I thought the cheese had worked a miracle!

Michael had lost interest in trying to do any coordinating skills. He would grow sullen and sit with his hands in his lap and his head down whenever I would try to get him to string his beads or work with clay or look at pictures. All he wanted to do was watch television. Mother resented my 'interference' with him and insisted he was 'just fine' and 'content' and that it was 'cruel' to 'deny him his pleasures'.

He was fascinated with the television. He would sit in front of it all of his waking hours watching the moving talking figures and staring at the big black and white screen with total absorption. His little slanty red eyes would water and mat and he would growl and babble angrily if he saw the boric acid solution. Mother set a box of tissues by him and said he could dry his eyes himself; no point in pestering him about cleaning them if he didn't want it done.

His appetite for ice cream was insatiable. Mother would buy it by the gallons along with store-bought cookies, which were good enough 'since he doesn't know the difference any way'. He gained weight. It was harder for him to walk. He would sit down on the stairs and scoot up them or down them one at a time. And, more than not, he resorted to scooting across the floor on his bottom. He outgrew all of his clothes. Mother went shopping and bought men's sized jeans claiming he did not need any thing better since he never went anyplace and he did not know the difference anyway. She bought him wide, gaudy galluses and loud colored shirts. The effect was ludicrous and revolting, clownish and repugnant, laughable and grotesque. He did not know the difference. Mother would laugh and joke about the absurdities of his dress and tell him he ought to be in a side show or a circus and he would grin and babble with pleasure at the kind tone in her voice. I saw and heard and was haunted by the 'whys.'

I became aware as the summer days wore on that Mother was taking a keen interest in all that I did. I would frequently go riding in the early morning hours between five and six, before the cool wore off the day. Mother began getting up and dallying about the kitchen or the back porch and would try to detain me as she worried aloud about the possibility of a snake being in the grass someplace or on the path.

"Horses are afraid of snakes, you know. They'll shy if they come up on a snake and you could be thrown. Oh, I know, I know, you're experienced and you can ride as well as any man, but you don't have any business going out horseback riding all the time. Why, you could fall off and be killed and just lay there for who knows how long, before someone would chance upon you. But, there's worse things than death and you never know who you might run across out there on that road or down in those woods. You know that train track isn't very far away and there's all kinds of bums, even in this day and age, that would jus. . ."

"Mother, Mr. Swanson sometimes goes with me. The horses need to be exercised and I like helping him with them."

"Well, we'll just see about that! You don't have any business going out with him. That just isn't proper."

"Mother, for Pete's sake. He would have been my . . . why do you twist everything around?"

"It wouldn't be the first time an old man has taken a shine to a young girl, but I'm not going to sit on my hands and watch it going on."

"Mother, don't you dare do or say anything that would cause embarrassment to either Mr. or Mrs. Swanson. They are Dean's parents!"

"Well, I know that but. . ."

I had walked out of the house repulsed with her innuendoes and sick to heart that she could take such a simple pleasure and ruin it with her lewd imagination.

I usually cut through the pasture and the horses would follow me to the barn for the tack. I knew something was wrong when I saw both Ed and Ruth waiting for me in the barnyard. Ruth called, "Hi, Honey!"

"Good morning!"

"We've got a problem. Your mother just called."

I could feel my face flush with embarrassment and humiliation. Ruth walked up to me and put her arms around me and said, "It'll work out, Honey. We couldn't quite make heads or tails out of most of it, but Ed says he can talk to your Dad about it."

"I'm sorry! I don't know what's wrong with her."

Ed said, "Did she say anything to you about what she needs the pasture for? I've just no place else to put seven horses."

"The pasture? Why, no, she didn't even mention it."

He seemed baffled, "Umph! She told me I had to get the horses off today. Said she had to have it free. Something about having other plans for it."

I felt like a puppet. I could feel Mother pulling the strings. I said, "She just doesn't want me to go riding. I think it's her way of stopping me."

Ruth said, "I can't understand why she would object to something you enjoy so much! I used to love to watch you and Dean riding and jumping. Of course, he was really good, but, you could hold your own, and he was so proud of you. He claimed he taught you everything you knew and that was why you were so good."

I laughed, easy with the memory, and said, "That's true. I miss him so much, but, sometimes, when I am out riding, it seems like he's very near."

Tears filled Ruth's eyes and Ed said, "Yep! Me, too."

He gazed out across the pasture and shook his head and frowned, "I've been using that pasture ever since your folks moved there. Your Dad and I just shook hands on the agreement but we've both been happy with it. I just can't make heads or tails out of it. Martha said it was hers now and. . ."

I was relieved that Mother hadn't, apparently, talked to them in the same vein that she had talked to me. I tried to express more confidence than I felt.

"I'll go talk to Mother. Don't worry about the pasture. I really think it will be alright to leave the horses there. I'm sorry for all of the trouble."

Ed said, "It isn't your fault, Toot. Why would she mind you riding? You've been doin' it for years. Eleven years to be exact!"

"I don't know, Ed. I really don't know."

"Well, you know you're welcome to ride anytime you want to! Hell, Jinx is yours! Always has been, since the day he was born. I remember Martha. . ."

"Ed!" Ruth tried to stop him.

"Well, she did! Always meddlin'. Dean was upset because he'd promised you he'd call you and every time he'd call Martha would answer and tell him you were busy. Wouldn't even call you to the phone!"

"Ed—"

"You have any cold juice, Ruth?"

Ruth smiled, "Of course, I have."

Ed put his big arm around my shoulder and the other one around Ruth and guided us toward the house. He pulled us both close to him and said, "Let's go have some juice. And, then, Toot, if you want to, we'll go for a quick gallumph."

One of the hands yelled, "Hey, Ed! Where ya goin' with them pretty girls?"

"Get to work, boy!"

"You want those horses brought to the barn?"

"Hold off awhile!"

The sun was high when I left the Swanson's and cut across the pasture toward home. I expected Mother to be angry but she didn't seem to notice. I was hot and sweaty for we had ridden for miles over country roads and lanes and through the woods. I had rubbed Jinx down for the last time and had walked him to the Swanson's garden and pulled a carrot for him, just as Dean and I used to do. Jinx had followed me across the pasture and I stroked him for a few moments wondering if he knew it was a farewell. Perhaps it was just that my own emotions were in turmoil, but the strength and comfort and pure devotion that had radiated from Jinx fortified my soul and intensified my resolve. God help me.

I showered and shampooed my hair until it was squeaky clean. I donned a light sear-suckle sundress, set my hair, put my make-up on carefully and went downstairs to confront Mother.

She was busily ironing and engrossed in television. Michael was sitting in the big green chair in front of the television. It was blaring inanities and they were both concentrating on it. The temperature had climbed past ninety, but, Mother didn't seem to notice as she stood there ironing, with steam hissing up from the dampened clothes when she set the hot iron to them. I went to the kitchen to make some iced tea, salad and sandwiches. I knew I would have to meet Mother in her own time. I also knew the Swanson's were anxiously waiting to hear further as to the verdict on the pasture land.

I made chicken salad from left over remnants and stuffed it in big red tomatoes garnishing it with paprika and green pepper rounds. I spread butter on day old bread and sprinkled it with a sugar and cinnamon mixture and rolled it and toasted it in the oven and then dipped it in applesauce. I washed fresh mint for the iced tea and cut zinnias for the bud vase.

"Well, would you just looky here, Michael? Somebody's fixed us a nice lunch! My, my! Isn't it a wonder how one can be so thoughtful and considerate all at once? If I had a suspicious nature I'd think somebody was up to something. But that wouldn't be nice, would it? And I'm sure that wouldn't even enter your head since you were out galavantin' around all morning."

"Mother, I fix you lunch every day, don't I?"

"I'm not saying you don't."

The phone rang and Mother rushed to answer it before it could ring the second time.

"Hello? No— Isn't it a beautiful day— Oh, yes, it's hot alright. Alright. Oh, you're not disturbing me although I am just sitting down to eat after standing all morning slaving away at ironing. Alright. Bye."

"Who was that?"

"My! Isn't somebody inquisitive! I'm so hungry I could eat a horse. And speaking of horses, did you have a nice ride this morning?"

"Yes, I really did."

"Well, how nice. And did Mr. Swanson go with you?"

"Yes."

"Where did you go?"

"We rode down through the reserve to the lake."

"Why, you don't mean it! After I told you I didn't want you riding with him! That must be over ten miles down there . . . and you were gone all morning . . . without any regard to what people might think! Well, young lady! We'll just see about that! Did he tell you I told him I want that pasture cleared before dark?"

"Yes, Mrs. Swanson told me."

Mother looked as though she did not believe me. She ate in silence for a moment and then asked with wide eyes "Ruth told you?"

I nodded.

"Why, I purposefully talked to him."

"Mother, you don't really have any plans for that pasture, do you?"

"It's mine and I can do with it as I please without having to answer to you or anybody else."

"Dad has an understanding with Mr. Swanson about it."

"Your Dad has no say in anything! Can't you get that through your head? And I'm sick and tired of horses. I never did like them and ever since your Grandma got spooked out every time I look out there and see those horses I half expect to see a white one jump the fence!"

"That was just in Grandma's mind, Mother. They don't even have a white horse."

"I know that, but I know, too, it used to just make my blood curdle when you and Dean would come tearing up that lane and make those horses rear up on their hind legs and act like you were Gene Autry or somebody cute. Why, you could have fallen off and killed yourself right there on the spot!"

"Mother, please!"

"Oh, aren't we touchy? I'm just trying to get it through your thick skull I didn't like it! I told you time and again I didn't want you out riding. From the time you were knee-high to a grasshopper all you could think about was riding and hunting and I can't stand either one of them."

"Mother? Are you aware that the profit from the yield of their South Ten is in exchange for the use of the pasture?"

Mother chewed on her lips and looked thoughtful.

"Well, I knew there was some kind of an arrangement there. Your Dad isn't one to just give something away without getting something for it."

"You can check through the records. I doubt if you could do any better on it. If you used it for planting, well, it's too late this year and you'd have all the expense of hiring men and equipment and..."

"I'm not a farmer! I don't care about things like that."

"Mr. Swanson keeps it mowed and sowed, too."

"You know an awful lot about his business, don't you?"

"Ruth told me. It is fact, Mother."

"There's only one way I'll ever change my mind in regards to that pasture and that is for you to give me your solemn oath that you'll leave those horses alone and never get on another one again! Now, it's entirely up to you. It's your decision! You're so crazy about the Swanson's, going over there all the time. trying to act like you're one of the family, not giving a thought to how I'm inconvenienced. . ."

"I won't go riding any more this summer, Mother."

Mother looked at me suspiciously. She ate in silence. My stomach was aching and my head was swimming in a red-orange heat. I pushed away the memories of Dean and concentrated on fact; only three weeks until I leave for college. I can give up riding for three weeks. Maybe she'll forget about this by Christmas; if there is anything better than riding in the summer than it would be riding in the winter in the snow. Mother seemed to be reading my thoughts.

"You think I'm some kind of a dummy, don't you? You think just because you get good marks in school you can just skate circles all around me, don't you? Well, I've got news for you, young lady. I wasn't born yesterday, but I was born with all of my marbles! Nobody can put anything over on me, but nobody can accuse me of not being fair-minded either. I realize that if Dean hadn't been killed like that . . . such a terrible way to go! Now, listen to me! What I'm saying is, you may marry someday and then, I guess, what you do will be your business. But! You've got to promise me that as long as you're living in this house you won't ride another horse! Do you understand that?"

"Yes."

"Yes, what?"

"Yes, mam."

"Is that your final word then? Did you understand me?"

"I understand exactly what you have said, Mother."

"Well, alright then, now, that wasn't so difficult, was it? My, that salad was tasty, too. You seasoned it to perfection."

"Will you call Mr. Swanson now and tell him he can continue to use the pasture?"

"Oh, yes. I fully intend to do just that. You know, muh deah, you really do have a good head for business. You shouldn't waste so much time drawing; anyone can do that and the world is full of poor artists. But, not everyone is born knowing how to put two and two together!"

21

PSALMS: TWENTY-SEVEN TEN

The long hot summer days seemed to drag on endlessly. Mother's wheedling demands had extended from the house to the yard and gardens. We hadn't had rain for over two weeks now, so she insisted I draw water up from the old well out in back and carry buckets of water to the gardens that were out too far for the hoses to reach. It was hot and heavy and messy, dirty work. But, it made my mind think of times past, and the intriguing stories Grandma had told us about when she was a girl before all of the "modern conveniences".

There was always a bit of a breeze and I especially enjoyed the cacophony of the numerous songbirds that seemed to reside in the big old walnut tree and the apple and pear trees and the oak and maple trees. There was a *"Duke's mixture"*, as Grandma would say, of sparrows, house wrens, Dick Sessils, Orioles and barn swallows around the old barn that was showing signs of disrepair. The hummingbirds were such fun and so especially fascinating to me. Their bright colors showed so brilliantly against the blankets of yellow and white morning glory vines that covered the fences. I thought it amazing the way they could hover over the trumpet lilies and the heavily laden shrubs of Spirea. The Spirea, also . . . known as . . .Bridal Wreath—God. . .

Day after day I would hear Singing Sally walking through the fields and the woods singing her heart out and my heart went out to her with love and gratitude. It seemed her repertoire was endless. I was often amazed at the clarity with which I could hear and so clearly understand the words to the music. Her diction was better than even the pros I had heard on stage in St. Louis, or at the amphitheatre. Her singing and her

337

songs were constantly uplifting, thought provoking and always encouraging in some way. I got so I listened closely and I believed she had messages that were intended for me. I had never realized that the old familiar Christmas song, *Good King Wenceslas*, had verses that were all about Spring time and re-birth. Oh, God. I miss Dean so much. . .

> *"Spring has now unwrapped the flowers. Day is fast reviving,*
> *Life in all her growing powers, Toward the Light is striving!*
> *All the world with fills, Gold the green enhancing,*
> *Flowers make glee among the hills, And set the meadows dancing.*
>
> *Through each wonder of fair days, God Himself expresses.*
> *Beauty follows all His ways, As the world He blesses.*
> *So as He renews the earth, Artist without rival,*
> *In His Grace of glad new birth, we must seek revival.*
>
> *Praise the Maker, all ye Saints, He with glory girt you,*
> *He who skies and meadows paint, Fashioned all your virtue.*
> *Praise Him, Seers, Heroes, Kings: Heralds of perfection.*
> *Brothers, Praise Him for He brings, All to Resurrection."*

Grandma used to say Singing Sally's hymns meant more to her than a month of Sunday Sermons.

She had become such an intricate part of our lives; such a dear wonderful lady. *"Thank you God, that she told me that Dean loved me. Thank you that we had at least a few glorious months. Thank you God, for Mrs. Andrews. Please bless and care for her in a very wonderful way."*

Often the melancholy and grief for . . . what might have been . . . would tighten its' grip on my chest and the tears joined the sweat, until I braced myself with the cold water from the heavy buckets, in order to regain composure and be able to look ahead. *"Whatsoever things are beautiful . . . Think ye on these things." "Be of good courage, and He shall strengthen your heart, all ye that hope in the Lord."*

Since there was no one around I had started wearing my bathing suit under old shorts and a loose shirt so I could strip down to the bare essentials if I was hidden from view of the house. I was really developing muscles and I had the best tan I had ever had. It was really heavy and dirty work, but, I thought it preferable to being inside with all of the inane programs blaring out from the idiotic box constantly. The daily messes inside seemed insurmountable in themselves and were always left for me to clean up since I "hadn't done anything else all day, except loll about".

Periodically, Mother's loud piercing voice would cut through the quiet peaceful countryside calling for me to come quick, M.D. had had another accident!

It occurred to me one morning after the phone had rung, that I had not heard from Wanda or Kathryn or Almeda or anyone else in many days. Mother insisted on answering the telephone every time it rang and had asked me not to use it for any reason, because she paid the bill and it was hers alone to use. I walked down to the Swanson's and used their phone to ring Kathryn who enlightened me.

"Toot? Is that really you? Good God, we'd about decided you were either mad at us or being held incommunicado! Where have you been? Didn't you get any of our messages? God! Is your Mom weird! Every time I call she says you're not there and then starts talking about herself. You ought to hear some of the crap she told Almeda—all about diarrhea! We nearly died! Do you really have a new boyfriend? Your Mom told Wanda you were out riding with your new boyfriend and that he was old enough to be your father. Egad! How could you know any one that old. . . ?"

Dr. Matthews was sensitive and cognizant of my situation, but helpless to change things. He knew Mother and her obsessions and he made feeble jokes about there being no pills to cure one bent on martyrdom and/or revenge. He asked if there had been any significant changes. I told him of her rages and dark moods and how she had started trying to manipulate me and was suspicious of everything I did. He said there was nothing physically wrong with her and speculated that it was just her nature to be difficult. He encouraged me to hope for the best and suggested I try to make things as easy as possible for her and try to not upset her.

I found that if I could tune out the spiteful tirades, she would usually respond to some nicety in like manner. Other times she would stare at me suspiciously and mumble about me being too sweet for my own good.

I had gone to a movie one evening with Kathryn, Elinore and Mildred. It had been a spectacular and we were caught up in the beautiful and upbeat music and glamour on screen. Afterwards we had ridden around for awhile in Kathryn's new yellow convertible, with the top down, talking about our college plans and sororities and clothes for school. We stopped in a restaurant where several friends of ours had gathered for refreshments and talk. Two of the fellas, former classmates, joined us and then bummed a ride with us. We rode all over town stopping wherever friends were gathered or anything fun was going on. We had even stopped and parked on the downtown square at one point. The Hit Parade was on with all of our favorite songs. Kathryn turned the radio up loud and we were all dancing in the street. Others kept joining us; even adults, including the Sheriff and his wife.

It was quite late when we pulled up in our lane. It had been so much fun and we were all talking and laughing and singing with the music. Kathryn was driving and I was in the middle with Jack Bernard next to the door. It was necessary for Jack to step out of the car for me to get out. Kathryn's radio was blaring the popular, "Kiss me once and kiss me twice. . ." He gallantly walked me to the door as the others clowned and called bets as to whether he would get a good-night kiss. He yelled that he bet two bucks he would and to me, and everyone else, he comically begged, "Please, please, puh-leeese? Just a tiny little pecky kiss, please?"

We stood directly under the porch light, where all could see, and I laughingly planted a peck on his cheek. He whooped and jumped off the porch yelling, "I won—She kissed me—You owe me two bucks!"

We were all laughing and waving as they all loudly and happily drove off. I watched them for as far as I could see. It had been so much fun. When I walked in I saw Mother had been watching and was not amused.

"I just can't believe my eyes. Why, you would have been a married woman if Dean hadn't been killed and here you are selling kisses. That's cheap! Who was that? I didn't recognize him."

"Jack Bernard, Mother—His Dad's the mayor."

"Ohhhh. Are you dating him now?"

"No! I am not dating anyone! He's just a friend. We were just clowning."

"Well, it doesn't matter who he is, it just isn't nice for you to be carrying on like that. It makes you look like you're fickle. Here you tell me you're going to a movie with three girls and then a boy brings you home and gets paid to kiss you. Umm umph! You can't tell me Dean meant anything to you for if he had you wouldn't be running around—"

"Mother, I've asked you not to talk about Dean."

"Well, for heaven's sake! Aren't we touchy! I'll tell you what, and where, and when, and if, anytime I please. I am your Mother and you had better not forget it if you know what's good for you!"

"Would you like a glass of lemonade?"

"Oh, yes, Honey, please. That sounds good. Bring it out here on the porch and we can sit and swing and talk."

I carried the two tall tumblers of ice cold lemonade out to the front porch as the hall clock was striking twelve o'clock.

Mother took hers and eagerly sipped it exclaiming on how delicious it was. She talked in detail of some show she had seen on television and then mentioned she had had a note from Dad and that he would be home in a few days since his contract had not been renewed. The swing was squeaking and creaking and Mother's voice droned on and on. The tone was soft and melodic and I could barely keep my eyes open. It wasn't necessary to respond during her monologues. I had quit trying to turn the tide of words to ideas or current events; her thoughts, her talk, her world, revolved around her.

The new moon was a sliver of white in the night sky. Fireflies flickered above the lawn and a mockingbird was singing its fascinating repertoire from some tree top in the near sounding woods. Funny how they always seemed nearer at night. I could hear frogs croaking and once in a while, a singing voice that was very faint, very far away. Sally must be walking over on the far field tonight—or maybe the breeze is carrying her song in some other direction. I hoped there were appreciative ears to hear.

The creaking and motion of the swing was making me ill. I stood and stretched. Mother didn't seem to notice as she continued her diatribe, "Heaven knows it's just another week before you'll be expecting to go off to college and then what? That Josh has just got to come home! I know he doesn't want to for he likes the school up there and he likes being there with Steve and Loralee but enough is enough. I just can't do all of this work myself! Why, Honey, I don't know how I'm going to get by if you leave. I can't manage that baby as well as you do. I just don't have the time to work with him. You know, there are some things more important than college. A young girl doesn't need a college education just to get married and you know if Dean hadn't been killed the two of you would have been married and you would have been busy building your home—that would have been such a pretty place for a home—"

"Mother, please! Don't talk about him!"

"I just don't understand why you can't talk about him. I mean, it's just life—or death—it's part of living. Why, the two of you were so much in love and you acted like you thought the sun rose and set with him and then when he gets killed you try to act like he never existed; it just looks like you didn't really care at all. Can you explain that?"

"Finir par—la douleur, contre toute attente. . ."

"I don't understand a word of that gibberish!"

"I was just thinking, Mother. It is still very painful; for it to end in, such grief and suffering; without any warning; contrary to all expectations. . ."

"Well, that's just life! There's no guarantees on anything."

"The movie was really good, Mother. Would you like to go see it tomorrow night? I can watch Michael."

"Oh, I don't think so. I prefer stage shows. You know, I saw 'South Pacific' and one of Agatha Christie's who-dun-its and the Philharmonic. . ."

"When you took Michael to New York?"

"Why, yes, when else could I have? Since I was there, I thought I might as well make the trip worth while."

"Did you take him, too?"

"Oh, don't be ridiculous. He wouldn't have understood any of it."

"But, where did he stay while you went?"

"I was staying in a hotel. I just left him in the room. He was alright. I wasn't gone long and he had television to watch."

"It is so nice and cool out here, but I must get up early and practice my typing tomorrow."

"Is that job going to pay much?"

"It depends on the number of hours, but it will be around twenty or twenty-five dollars a week."

"Well, I guess every little bit will help. I've saved every penny that's come in from the Co-op. Your Grandma arranged that for you but I've been the one who had to manage it, although I don't expect any credit for it. I just don't know how I'm going to get by here at home, though, but, I guess, I'll manage. I always have."

"Do you know when Dad is getting in?"

"No, and I don't care. If he was worth his salt he'd pay your college expenses and I'm going to tell him just that!"

"Mother! Dad signed everything over to you! He even sends you everything he makes over his living expenses."

"Oh, he's so goody-goody to hear you tell it! The fact is he's never given me anything but hardship and grief. I've earned every cent I've got and I wouldn't have to be doing these ironings if he'd sell those guns! But, oh no, he can't part with them and you're just as bad as he is! Let me tell you it wasn't those guns that nursed you when you were little! But that's all the thanks I get! It just makes my blood boil to stand here and do some rich woman's ironing for two, maybe three dollars, if I'm lucky, and knowing all the time he's paying out insurance for a hundred thousand dollars worth of guns that aren't doing a thing but collecting dust. I could put that money to good use and then you whine around and say, 'Oh, please don't ask Daddy to sell the guns'—well, we'll just see about it when the time comes! You'll find out, sooner or later, he doesn't care a hoot where you're concerned. And here you are so high and mighty, always riding a high horse, standing up for him! You'll learn, muh deah, life's no bed of roses."

"Do you care for some more lemonade, Mother?"

"Oh, I don't believe so, Honey. Thank you so much! It was very nice and refreshing, but I think I've had sufficient."

"If you are ready to go to bed now, I will lock up and turn off the lights."

"You go ahead, Honey. I'm not sleepy."

"G'night."

"You'd better not turn the bedspread back, Honey. It's liable to be cool before morning and just a sheet won't be enough."

When Dad arrived home his haggard appearance was frightening. He insisted he was fine except that his contract had not been renewed and he thought he was too old to be competing with all of the young whippersnappers in the job market.

Mother worked all day in the kitchen preparing a sumptuous supper. Alf came out for the evening and we talked for hours after supper. Mother and I had carted all of the ironing gear to the basement and the dining room was once again in order except for the monstrous television and the big green chair that were pushed into one corner.

Dad asked me about the college curriculum and Mother worried about the "terrible slop" that they dished out at such fancy prices. Alf thought I should take a Liberal Arts program and Dad thought a Bachelor of Science Degree would carry more weight and Mother maintained her Degree had not helped her at all, and suggested that all a young lady really needs to worry about getting is a marriage license.

I mentioned that I had arranged to ride to the school with two ministerial students from town. Mother gushed how pleased she was that I was starting out in such good company and expounded on the wisdom of my choice of a small church-related school over the huge secular University. Alf rolled his eyes and raised his eyebrows comically,

"I don't know about that, Mom. Some of those do-gooders don't believe in smokin' or drinkin' or goin' to the movies, but they sure as hell like to roll the girls over in the bushes! That's the only entertainment they get."

Mother sniffed, "Alf!"

Dad chuckled, reached for another piece of pie, and said, "Toot—if it gets too rough for you there at that church school, you can always transfer to the University."

Mother looked concerned as she asked, "Alf? You are joking, aren't you? I mean, I know they're strict and don't approve of cards or anything, but, then, a little religion never hurt anyone! They do require courses in Old and New Testament but Marj liked it there. She really enjoyed her religious classes."

Mother laughed and shook her head and continued, "That girl is a paradox! Too bad she lost interest before she finished."

I remembered Marj telling me to look something up—what was it— "Twenty-seven ten."

They all looked at me. I giggled self-consciously and explained,

"I just remembered something Marj had told me to look up. I had forgotten about it until you mentioned her religion classes."

Alf looked thoughtful and puffed on his cigar as he gazed off into the distance. Later as he was leaving, he put his arm around my shoulder and said he wanted to show me his new car. Then as we were walking out about, he asked me, "Psalms? Psalms twenty-seven ten?"

"Yes, do you know it?"

"Look it up, Toot. Hope ya won't need it, but it's a good one to know. Ya might want to expand it a bit. Maybe more like Psalms 27:10 to14."

We could hear Mother's voice coming through the open window as she chided M.D. over something. Alf looked toward the window, sighed and sadly shook his head. "Well, maybe, with Dad being here, I'm hopin'. . . Surely, everything will be alright. Hope ya don't get anymore shit, kid."

He gave me a big brother sideways hug and said, "Welp, Toot. Guess I'm a hell-uf-a poor example. But, ya know, ya can always call me, if ya need anything. Hear me?"

Mother and Dad were talking pleasantly on the front porch. I put Michael to bed and carried the supper leavings and dirty dishes to the kitchen. God—it was good to get that crappy ironing mess out of the dining room. Now, if only I could get Mother to quit doing them. I tidied the kitchen and put the flatware back in the silver case. The windows were up and a nice cool breeze was blowing the curtains, billowing them out into the room. Faintly, very faintly, I could hear Singing Sally out in the fields. I went out in back to listen to the clear melodious voice.

A sudden yearning gripped me and I ran down our lane toward the woods. The late august moon was riding high and darkness seeped from the low places afoot. Some small creature scurried from my path as I climbed through the fence and made my way along the edge of the corn field toward her, calling, "Mrs. Andrews! Mrs. Andrews—it's me, Toot."

She stood waiting for me.

"What are you doing out here this time of night, Child?"

"I wanted to see you! I'll be leaving day after tomorrow for college— I'm going to miss you."

"Why, how very sweet of you; I appreciate that more than I can say—I'm going to miss you too, but I know you'll enjoy your studies."

Mrs. Andrews hugged me tight and kissed me on the cheek, just like Grandma used to. She said, "Don't be anxious about being out on your own, child. Remember, God cares for the little sparrows, how much more He cares for you."

"Mrs. Andrews? Did you know . . . Dean and I . . . we were going to ask you . . . to sing at our wedding."

"That would have been a pleasure. I know how much he loved you and I watched you both grow up. Dean always told me that you were "his girl" and he was so proud of you. I grieve for Dean just as I grieve for my Freddie. But you, my Child, must keep going! God has a special plan for you."

"Thank you, Mrs. Andrews, for everything. I'll see you at Thanksgiving. G'nite."

"I'll look forward to seeing you then. G'nite, Child—Watch your footing now."

The cacophony of night sounds was all about me in its orderly discord. The stars were shining brightly and the milky-way cut it's swath across the night sky. The breeze was deliciously cool. As I started up our lane, I could hear Mrs. Andrews singing of the majesty of God's universe.

Packing had been such fun. I was excited and enthused about going to college and living in a dormitory. My classes sounded interesting and challenging and I was in awe of campus life and all that it entailed. Marj had given me her black and orange Freshman Beanie and I had been wearing it around the house all day. I thought it such fun for my College Colors to be the same as my High School Colors.

We were leaving early the next morning and I had everything done except for going to the bank to open a checking account. Mother had put me off from day to day for one reason or another but this was my last chance to get it done. After lunch, I dressed for town in a light brown, sleeveless linen sheath that had a matching jacket. I pinned Grandma's four-leaf clover pin on my lapel and put on my graduation watch and the lovely ring that Dad had given me along with the solitaire.

Mother opened the door to my room and stood there staring at me. She was chewing on her lips and had her arms folded tightly across her waist. She looked all about my room and I followed her gaze. My luggage, that Steve and Loralee had given me for graduation, and my portable typewriter were stacked neatly on one side, ready to be carried down and loaded in the car. Old clothes, including a black dress, worn only one time, and an assortment of scuffed shoes were in paper bags for the 'needy'. The desk drawers were organized and nearly cleaned out for the first time in years. Mother looked at the sketches and paintings on the walls without comment and then picked up a tennis racket that was laying on the bed and placed it back in the closet on a shelf.

I had stacked some books and study supplies on the chair near the door. Mother bent over to look through them and then straightened, put her hands on her hips and cocked her head to one side and said in soothing tones, "Honey—I've got some bad news for you. Now, it isn't the end of the world, but—uh—well-lah, it's just that . . . you can't start college now!"

I sat down on the edge of my bed. Mother's eyes were unduly bright, hard and piercing; her voice was plaintive, mollifying and conciliatory. I had heard her use the same tone, the same voice so many times with Michael when her words did not match the kindness in her tones. She was saying,

"Now, I understand. I know you're disappointed, but it just can't be helped. You've got to learn you just can't have every little thing you want. Now, I'm sorry, but, you'll get over it in time. Time heals all wounds and you'll soon forget all about it just like you forgot Dean. It'll hurt for awhile but one can live without. . ."

"Mother! Why? Why can't I go? You've said it was alright! Is it money? I only need three hundred and fifty dollars, now. You said Grandma left money for me! I know there's over fifty thousand in the Co-op alone. It is my money. Why can't I have it?"

"Now that's neither here nor there, but it's nothing for you to get all upset about. You know I wouldn't deny you a thing under the sun and there is absolutely nothing that you will ever need as long as I have anything to say about it. But, right now, I just don't have that kind of money and here you are wanting to go open a checking account and you don't have any experience with that kind of money. . ."

"Mother, you know I already have all of my classes scheduled. I have a job lined up in the office. My room has been designated and my "Big Sister" has been assigned to me. I've plans to leave early in the morning. Bill and Chuck are picking me up. . ."

"I know, I know all that, but don't you hear what I'm saying? You're not going! I can't afford it now. So, you can just put it out of your mind. Think of someone else for a change, instead of just what you want to do. You know as well as I do that I need help with that poor baby. Here he's been so sick this summer and all of the medicines are so expensive. You know how many times we had to call the doctor. Why, you even called him when it wasn't necessary but I had to pay for the visit anyway. Nothing's free or easy and you might as well learn it now as. . ."

"Mother, why are you doing this to me?"

"Why! The very idea! Just look at yourself. You don't look to me like you're wanting for anything. You have everything anyone in their right mind could want, and I work from sun-up to sun-down to make it possible, but I just can't do anymore than I'm doing."

"I only need three hun. . ."

"I know that! But that's just a drop in the bucket, for next year you'll need more and it just goes on and on and here I don't know how long that baby's going to live. Why, he may outlive me and what then? Now, I've told you I'm sorry and there's no use in belaboring it. In a few days you'll have forgotten all about. . ."

Her voice droned on and on. She had become very animated and I had the terrible thought—God! She's enjoying this! I said, "Does Dad know?"

"Humph! A fat lot he cares about anything. If I've told you once, I've told you time and time again he doesn't care about anything but his old guns. He just bought another one this morning and he's flat cleaned out—spent his last cent on it and him without a job. I told him he ought to be selling them instead of buying them. . ."

Mother laughed and wobbled her finger at me and talked of how she had warned me. . .

It seemed everything was pressing in on me; the heat, the voice, the red-orange world. I walked to the window; no breeze, no relief, no abatement. Jinx moved away from the other horses and seemed to be looking toward me. He neighed and shook his head and took a few steps in place . . . I could hear the sounds emanating from the idiot box and M.D. snorting at some canned laughter. I crossed the room and hesitated only briefly before leaving Mother standing there, alone, in my room, talking, talking, talking.

The stairs were steeper than usual but I clung to the railing. I would not fall; I must see Dad. I called, "Dad—Dad—Dad?"

He answered me from the study. A huge fan was oscillating on it's raised axis. I stood in front of it for a moment until my head cleared. Dad was sitting in a big leather chair in front of the big impressive gun cabinet; his new piece across his knees, and an oily flannel cloth in his hand.

"Dad?"

"Come 'ere, Toot. You gotta see this! It's an old Mason Russell and it's worth ten times or more what I got it for. Look at the silver tooling on that barrel. Why, it's a work of art; a thing of beauty . . . and, it's yours, Toot."

"Dad?"

"Oh, it needs a bit of work but I'll clean it up. It's yours, Toot! God knows . . . I wish. . ."

"Mother says I can't go. . ."

Dad stared off into the distance. I stood waiting. He sighed and began rubbing on the elaborately carved stock.

Admiration and respect for the fine piece . . . love and pity for Dad. . . frustration and disillusionment and the painfully sharp shattering of my dreams, my plans, my careful preparations . . . forced my query out over my constricted throat in a low, barely audible voice, "Is it true, Dad?"

He nodded sadly, and, then shook his head and sighed,

"Don't be too hard on her, Toot. She's all mixed up. I tried to reason with her—but, I can't reach her—Everything's in her name! I wish I hadn't done it but I thought it would ease her mind. I've never kept anything back from her. I didn't pay money for this piece; I took it as payment on a debt. God! I don't know what's wrong with . . . I had no idea . . . there's just no reasoning. . ."

My head was spinning. My legs were rubbery. My eyes were seeing through a dark, red-orange mist. I could hear voices as though they were far away: Dad's voice, Mother's voice, Michael David's voice, babbling, babbling. I was walking through the hallway to the stairs. Michael was scooting down the stairs blubbering and grinning moronically. I waited for him. There was not room for both of us.

It was hard to breathe. I had seen Dad's eyes; so full of worry and alarm—or was it hopelessness? I heard Mother's whining, wheedling, apologetic voice, but her eyes belied her words!

Grandma's sincere, guileless, melodic voice sounded in my mind and her advice from over the years rolled over me in waves that were cool and refreshing and revitalizing—*Don't make rash judgments. Take time to think things through just as you take time to aim for a sure and accurate shot—Trust your instincts*! *God speaks in a small voice—harness your emotions: use them, but control them. Relax, relax, don't tighten your mouth or wrinkle your brow. Keep your countenance calm. Relax—don't be bitter; forgive and forget—Trust in God, but do the best you can. God helps those who help themselves.*

I had made my way up the stairs and down the hall to my room. Think good thoughts—Such a happy home—No, the truth—Such a nice big house. I looked about my room—My room! Mother was gone. I hadn't seen her on the stairs or in the hallway. I closed the door and tried to think calmly. I walked over to the night table, straightened the green, stiffly starched, crocheted doily that stood up like a clown's ruffle around the base of the brass lamp, opened the drawer and closed my hand over the ivory handle of Grandma's little thirty-eight. Comfort and confidence flowed over me. Dad's Thompson Chain Reference Bible was open on the desk. I turned to Psalms, chapter twenty-seven, verse ten, and read, "When my Father and my Mother forsake me, then the Lord will take me up."

I dropped the revolver into my purse and gathered up everything I could carry and walked down the stairs.

The door to the study was open and I could hear the fan whirring out it's superficial comfort. Mother was in the dining room standing at the ironing board that she had set back up under the beautiful crystal chandelier. She was talking to the television. Michael David was sitting on the floor in front of it, staring up at it intently through red runny eyes, his jaw jutted out, chewing on his tongue.

I walked through the kitchen, past the breakfast nook that was still cluttered with the luncheon remains, and out the door; out into the fresh air, out into the sunshine.

A cool breeze wafted up from the direction of the East woods that bordered the pasture. It was carrying a familiar, clear, sweet voice that was singing, *"His eye is on the sparrow and I know He watches me. . ."*

I breathed deeply and looked out over the yard and gardens, rich in bloom; the fields of crops, the peaceful woods, the pasture where Jinx, "my Jinx", was swishing his tail and contentedly grazing with the other horses. . .

I started walking down the dusty lane to the graveled road. Hot tears stung my eyes. My chest felt so heavy I could only gasp for breath as the sobs tore from my innermost being. I didn't know what to do or where to go or how . . . Why was Mother so mean? Why is she so irrational? Why is she so obsessed with Michael David? Why did Dad give her control of everything? Oh, Dad, Why do you have to be so sick? Why can't it be like it used to be? God, we used to be so happy. We were happy when Grandma was here. We were so happy before Michael David. Why did he have to. . . ?

Aunt Katie always says, it was having to care for him that caused Grandma to have a heart attack. God, why did you let Dean die? He was so good, so perfect in every way, so highly qualified as an engineer and as an agrobiologist . . . Why, God? Why . . . and Michael David lives on . . . just ruining every ones lives . . . and he neither knows . . . nor cares.

Jinx saw me and came running toward the fence expecting. . . Oh, if only . . . how I wish I . . . could go for one last *"galumph."* Dean . . . *"We could get married and both of us go to school."*

My mind was racing in reverse. Memories. Dad saying, *"Of course, God cares about sparrows. That's why he made worms . . . to feed the sparrows. Besides, your Grandma told me God watches over the sparrows and you and me, too, and I believe it. Yes, Sirre, Toot. Why, I'd bet my bottom dollar on it."*

And the way Alf hugged me and said, *"Ya might want to expand it a bit. I'd suggest bits of Psalms 27:10 through 14. It's good to know."* *"When my Father and my mother forsake me, then the Lord will take me up . . . Teach me Thy way, O Lord, and lead me in a plain path . . . Wait on the Lord. Be of good courage, and He shall strengthen thine heart."*

I could hear Mrs. Andrews' voice much clearer now and I saw her in the distance at the edge of the pasteur. Her beautiful soprano voice was singing what seemed to be a happy, lilting hymn: *"God be with you till we meet again. By His councils guide, uphold you, With His sheep securely fold you, God be with you till we meet again. Till we meet, till we meet. Till we meet in God's time someday. Till we meet, till we meet, God be with you till we meet again . . . 'Neath His wings protecting hide you, Daily manna still provide you . . . When life's perils thick confound you, Put His arms unfailing round you. . ."*

I knew she was singing it for me and it gave me such a comfort, an assurance, a security that seemed to envelope me and somehow empower me.

The luggage was heavy and my purse was bulky and my shoes were not made for walking, but, I felt light and free and capable of whatever I have to do and my mind began to sing, *"Remember the good."* *"Forgive and forget."* *"God, guns and Grandma, that's all I really need."* *"Life's tapestry must have dark threads as well as the bright."* God works in *Mysterious ways His wonders to perform."* *"His eye is on the sparrow, How much more He cares for you."* *"Ya know, ya can always call me, if ya need anything. Hear me?"*

22

🦃 EPILOGUE - OLIVIA

D r. Olivia Mason, tall, slim and elegant in her tailored classic attire, threw the applicant's resume on her desk, pushed back her long light brown hair, removed her reading glasses and laying them on top of the resume, let her gaze and thought sweep across the luxurious penthouse office that was one of the badges of her success. She rose, and, like one in a dream, walked across the deeply piled carpeting as though drawn to the window in anticipation, or perhaps, escape; escape from memories that hurt anew.

That name . . . his name. Oh God, the memories a name can conjure up.

When one has a responsible and respected position and a demanding and fulfilling career, there is little time for memories. But, in the dark of night they creep into the dreams and sometimes on the street or even in the aisle of the Concorde there will appear a familiar figure or one will hear a voice or laugh, so like one out of the past, and then the memories well up and vie for consciousness.

Sociologists argue over the question of heredity versus environmental influences in trying to understand and explain how what constitutes memories affects, molds, motivates an individual and we are each an argument in favor of or in support of one concept or the other. But, if we were to balance those memories on the scale of life it would undoubtedly fall heavier on environment.

One wonders if it is some trick of the mind that the Almighty is amused to inflict upon us mortals or is it just a quirk of nature that certain memories are so vivid they play upon the retina in color and are complete with sounds and scents and every nerve end in our body is attuned and taut with memory.

The years come, the years go. Just as pennies make dollars, minutes make days, days make years. Time has a freaky way of clouding the memory, especially if one helps it along. Happy memories stand out like shiny coppers, while the majority, the discolored, the tarnished, the slightly bent, recedes into the background.

She straightened the small but brilliant solitaire on the ring finger of her left hand, where it had been placed so many years ago; a sad, bittersweet symbol of the bright promises that had been snatched so tragically from her.

She fingered the unique brooch on her lapel and smiled with the memories of the many lapels and collars it had adorned, and she remembered the story . . . Her Grandfather saying, *"Probably the only Christmas Tree in the world that has a four leaf clover on it."*

She glanced at the cabinet where her purse lay and thoughts of the little ivory handled 38, Grandma's little "Lady's" gun, caused her to shake her head and ponder. Why do I carry it . . . If God looks after the sparrows . . . Yet, it is not from necessity. But rather, just, that it provides me with a sense of security and a warm feeling of being protected and cared for. . . And, the solitaire . . . The unfulfilled promises. So, Mother was right, I wear my socks at night, when I sleep, if my feet are cold . . . And, yet . . .

I have traveled the misty isles and stayed in a castle on the bonny, bonny banks of Loch Lomond. I stood alone on the grassy banks of the loch and I could hear my Grandma telling me again the legend of the old ballad, and I felt, again, the thrill of the encounter and the pride in my heritage.

A few days later I stood with a group of friends gazing up at the Eiffel Tower. It was our first day in France. We were all gay and excited about being in Paris and being able to actually see with our own eyes the scenes familiar from years of history lessons.

Thoughts of home were buried deep and were as far removed as the innocence of childhood. A hacking cough caught my attention and I turned to see an elderly, slightly stooped American man in a rather seedy dark blue suit and old gray hat, standing alone on the edge of the crowd, puffing on a pipe. He saw me looking at him and he tipped his hat and politely drawled, "How de do, Miss!", and gesturing toward the spectacular tower with the stem of his pipe, he marveled, "Ain't that somethin'?"

Tears clouded my vision. I nodded my head and smiled with the memory of another old man: Dear sweet Mr. Aiken, our hired hand and friend who had gone off to fight the war the only way he could; working in the ammunition factories. Oh God! The hours I had spent playing the music box he had given me when I had the measles. A leaning tower that went round and round to the melancholy tune of *Fur Elise*. This old gentleman seemed so like him. . .

"Yes sir," I said, letting my gaze sweep over the tower and back to him.

"It's really somethin'!"

In Carmarthen, Wales, I listened to the musical tongue of the indigenous people and I was enthralled to find a monument to one of my ancestors, the great teacher and preacher who was actually jailed for practicing his faith and defying his peers by using the Sunday services to teach the masses to read and write.

London, the city of many sights, where I rode in an open carriage through the downtown streets, saw delightful shows and toured the museums and inns and abbeys and grand old Cathedrals.

It was in a small village out from Cambridge: I had stopped to browse in a small quaint shop. A full grown, grossly over-weight Mongoloid girl of indeterminate age came rushing down the aisle at me, babbling incoherently, excitedly chewing on her tongue and flailing her double-jointed arms about wildly. I tried to give her room but she hit me on the head and knocked me against the counter. A thin, colorless aged woman rushed up. She grabbed the girl's hand and pressed a peppermint stick into it, loudly ordering, " 'Ere! 'Ere! Eat yer sweet!"

Turning back to me, she sweetly explained, "I couldn't give 'er the sweet 'till I paid for it, ye know? Please forgive 'er. She didn't mean to 'urt ye. She's just not 'erself, ye know?'"

"It's alright, Mam. I understand. I had a little brother who had. . . Down Syndrome."

A look of astonishment flashed across her face and then melted into instant kinship and warm empathy.

"Ye don't mean it! Down Syndrome? A Mongoloid? Why, I say now, wot a shame, and I'm sorry, Madam, but . . . yer American? I can't thank ye enough fur tellin' me."

She grasped my hand in a tight grip as tears filled her eyes and rolled down her cheeks. Her chin quivered and her mouth worked wordlessly as her early-aged lined face crinkled. She sniffed, and wiped her eyes and nose and shook her head and grasped my hand and murmured, "Thank ye, Madam. Thank ye fur telling me. Bless ye", and deftly guided the becalmed girl, who was sucking on the penny candy stick, toward the exit.

How many times have I seen the defiant look in their eyes . . . change to one of friendship . . . Once they know . . . that . . . I, too, have been there.

Oh God! Have I ever been there. . .

In the receiving office, Kaye, Dr. Mason's personal secretary, was watching the handsome self-assured young man closely. He had unbuttoned his dark blue suit coat and looked with ennui through the magazines on the end table. She was still a little puzzled over Dr. Mason asking her to go to the store for a dozen naval oranges. Kaye had told her they were out of season, but Dr. Mason had insisted that she wanted the best that could be found: A dozen of the biggest, juiciest, orangeiest oranges in Chicago. And then she had added, "And a little basket to put them in and don't forget some napkins: Big, red, country napkins . . . and a knife."

Kaye had asked, "Why do you want a knife?"

"To peel the oranges."

At exactly 9:30 Kaye nodded to the receptionist, who, in turn, told the young man, "You may go in now."

His heart seemed to be beating rapidly and his hand felt sweaty on the doorknob. All of his life he had heard stories about Dr. Mason. Stories of how she had excelled in school and had since become the foremost psychologist in her field, stories of her Mother's peculiar "eccentricities", and stories of his Uncle Dean waiting for "His girl" to grow up. He had seen her photos from over the years: As she had looked as a young girl and recent ones of her in newspapers and in Time magazine.

But apprehension filled him as he opened the door and entered the prestigious office. The room was dominated by a huge mahogany desk that shone with the lustre and patina of much care. The few items on the top of the desk were in careless disarray. For the first few seconds he thought he must be alone in the room. Then he saw her, standing at the window, looking out, seemingly lost in thought. He was afraid to make a move and his voice seemed to be caught in his throat. She became aware of him, and, as though she were embarrassed to be caught in the act of peering into the distance, she busied herself in a self-conscious attempt to straighten the perfectly hung draperies.

Then, she turned to face him. With a composed smile of greeting she approached this young blond Adonis with the ruddy good looks and the nearly perfect resume.

"*My God!*" she thought, "*how very like Dean he looks.*"

Aloud she said, as she grasped his hand, "Dean, I am so pleased to meet you. Your family are all dear friends of mine. And, as you must know, your Uncle Dean and I were to have been married, but fate stepped in."

"Yes Mam, I know, and, I'm so sorry. Grandma and Grandpa talk about you all the time. I'm really happy to meet you at last. All through school it has been my dream to intern with you."

Dr. Mason looked at him keenly and felt the strength of his character. The handshake was brief and proper . . . But the bonding . . . She leaned toward him and took his arm as she said, "And that you shall, Dean. Come, sit down, tell me about yourself, and please call me Olyvia."

With a new found ease and peace of mind, Olyvia ushered the young candidate toward the comfortable seating arrangement that looked out over Lake Michigan. She rang the receptionist to bring in coffee and as she busied herself putting him at his ease, her thoughts raced and in her mind she could hear Singing Sally's hauntingly beautiful soprano voice . . . *"His eye is on the Sparrow and I know he watches me."*

She forced herself back to the present and listened intently as he talked of growing up downstate. He answered her inquires of family and friends and they talked of Schools and Seminars and some of the better Hospitals with their Departments of Neurology, Pharmacology and Experimental Therapeutics. They talked of the great strides Medical Science had made and the possible promises in store as it continues to evolve. They discussed the new screening tests for the many women of high risk and about the exciting progress Scientists are making in the Down Syndrome Critical Region in regard to the discovery of the tripling of some genes suspected of being another factor along with Trisomy 21.

And then Olivia reached for an orange, spread a napkin on her lap, picked up a slim ivory handled knife, and said, "Dean, your Uncle and I used to love oranges for a snack. Would you like an orange?"

He leaned forward, chose a big thick-skinned orange and laughed, "I thought you'd never ask."

The security guards were turning off the lights and locking up the auditorium as Dr. Mason and her staff mingled with the few remaining guests in the adjoining Banquet Room. It had been the culmination of the most productive two years they could ever have dared to dream of.

The main speaker for the banquet was still busily autographing his latest published work for eager buyers. It was a 'how-to' on caring for infants and children with Trisomy 21, formerly known as Down Syndrome. Even that name had been a misnomer from the beginning, but that's what it had been called for over a hundred years. Dr. Down, with the limited knowledge of his day, had concluded that the condition was a throw-back to the earlier mongoloid race, and it was amazing how prevalent such opinions reined even in recent years among medical people.

Olivia had been so impressed with the manuals that she had instructed there to be hundreds of copies available. When she had first received her complimentary copy of it, she had marveled over the clarity and explicitness and was heard to sigh, "God, if only we had had something like this."

Now, she glanced about the room, saw Dean, her brilliant young associate, gathering his papers and materials. She was so proud of him. He had given such an outstanding clinical and decisively, even a brilliantly enlightening presentation on the merits of a new test, chorianic villus sampling, that can be done much earlier in a pregnancy than the amniocentesis. Never again must an expectant parent have to suffer through doubts and fears and suspicions over whether or not one's baby will be normal.

Thoughts of Loralee flashed through her mind from so long ago. Oh God, the waste, the abortions, the damn needless abortions; done out of fear and dread of the horrors of what might be! Loralee and Steve had finally adopted three precious children and had worked so hard at giving them every advantage that a loving, caring, happy home life can offer.

Oh God, I wish Dad and Mother could have lived to know of all of the advances we have made. I wish I could have saved them from the grief and heartache and blame and guilt that consumed their very lives. God, we've helped so many to understand their choices.

Kaye was running across the room calling her name. Olivia broke from the melancholy reverie and assumed a smile as Kaye rushed up waving airline tickets.

"You're all set. I had the airlines deliver your tickets so you wouldn't have to bother so early in the morning. Are you sure you'll have time for this? You have to be in D.C. to speak before Congress at 10 o'clock Monday morning."

"Not to worry, Kaye. I can't miss my niece's graduation. Did you get the gift?"

"Yes ma'am, and the paper cost almost as much as the watch! Oh, not really, but it's like you requested. Snow White and heavily embossed with a tiny mortarboard and a gold tassel on the bow. I put it in your briefcase."

Olivia checked the time on her own watch and thought of the Bulova Marj had given her on her high school graduation, so long ago. She smiled at Kaye and said, "Thank you so much. Marj will. . ."

"Oh, speaking of Marj, she called earlier, said not to disturb you, but to tell you Josh will meet you at the airport and Alf and his family are getting in tonight so everyone will be there for the graduation, and Marj said she's going to really surprise you with your favorite cream puffs. Oh God! I didn't say that."

Olivia laughed, "It's alright, Kaye. I'd be more surprised if she didn't have them. What was the final tally on the attendees?"

"Twelve hundred and eighty-five. Twenty-two from England; Ten from France; Twelve from Germany; Fifteen from Russia; Five from China; Three from Japan and Seven from Australia. And every State and major University represented. Best one ever. Everyone said so."

"Yes, everyone seemed to think it was most beneficial. You have all done a super job. Kaye, I know you must be exhausted, what with the tight scheduling and everyone looking to you for everything from toothbrushes to lost briefcases. Take next week off and treat yourself to a good rest-up."

Kaye beamed, "Oh, thank you. Actually, I'm alright. A bit tired, and I really found it hard to read some of our guests, but, then I heard Dean kinda quietly whispering that song he's always singing about, *His Eye Is On The Sparrow and I know He watches Me*. So I really tried to connect with some of the most difficult ones and I really think it helped. I figure anything I can do to help anyone just automatically helps everyone."

Olivia smiled and inclined her head as she said, "Thank you kindly, Kaye. I'm much obliged."

AUTHOR'S NOTE

There have been so many families, from everyplace that I have lived, that had a child or adult with Trisomy 21, commonly called a Down Syndrome, although in the 1940's, the doctors referred to them as mongoloid idiots.

I know personally of the tremendous drain on the lives, emotions, physical and mental health, and the debilitating of the monies, savings and plans for the future of many of the family members, who had no warning that they would have a baby with Down Syndrome. I encountered them with their heartbreaking stories and pleas for help in the corn belt of central Illinois as I was lecturing with the Home Bureau: in Oklahoma when I was a member and President of a Garden Club: a winner in a Horticultural Show as well as the State Chairman: in Louisiana I was speaking to a large group and corrected a rather pitiful spoiled child who then popped his glass eye out and handed it to me, for Pete's sake. I had never chosen to be so identified with those who needed "someone" to understand what they were going through. It isn't easy.

My husband was a Methodist Minister and an Air Force Chaplain. I was his helpmate, best friend, choir director, sound board, cheer leader and the back-seater on our Bicycle-Built-For-Two. We were both reared in Mt. Vernon, Illinois, and were friends forever, but, never dated until college days.

We had 19 homes from Virginia to California, the Upper Peninsula of Michigan to Louisiana, Oklahoma, Colorado and three year tours each in Japan and England. Vietnam was a bitter heartbreak many times over, with Samsun, up on the Black Sea across from Russia, the "best kept secret" as it should have been. Our logo/motto for the Air Force was "PEACE IS OUR PROFESSION". It was my privilege, on one occasion, to be asked to represent the 500 members of our Officer's Wives Club to speak on our motto against a young fiery Tom Brokaw. (Luv'em)

I was also first runner-up two years in a row for Air force Wife of the Year, due to many projects I had worked on as well as Children Have A Potential. Later, I received The Good Neighbor Award from Sir John

Wedgewood, in England, for my lecturing and "enlivening" the British Women's Institute for three years. (We had lots of fun and lots of laughs. There was a lady who had a Down Syndrome daughter I wrote about in Chapter 22. I visited with them many times while I lived there.)

I was a contributing reporter over the years for several little community newspapers, the military papers as well as the *Pioneer*, the *Stars and Stripes*, the Officers Wives Clubs, the Chapel Periodicals, including *The Solidarity*, *The Rebeccas'* and the *Protestant Women Of The Chapel*. I also served several times in various positions in a political club including President of a Political Business and Professional Club for four years, and was a County Chairman for a State Senatorial Candidate. I was an Arlington Lady at the Arlington National Cemetery for four years. Currently, I am serving as Chaplain for the Colorado Federation of Republican Women.

I have freely used artistic license, particularly in the last chapter, and rather grandiose embellishment that dictates the manuscript be fiction. I really wanted . . . a happy ending.

MaryLou Vaughn

COMMENTS ON THE MANUSCRIPT
FROM FAMILY MEMBERS

I first started writing this in the sixties on the old Smith-Corona portable typewriter that my Dad had given me years earlier for my sixteenth birthday. I talked with the members of our family about me working on a manuscript, shared parts and reminisced with them and asked for their input.

I will enclose some of their comments on my writing and our shared experiences. Their comments were as varied as they were. One refused to discuss it or even talk about it.

"It's a hell of a book, Toot. Only one who has been there can write that." *BeaLee-An older sister*

"I can't believe we lived through all that shit . . . for nothing." *Wendell-My little brother*

"Leave it alone, Toot. Just leave it alone." *John-An older brother*

"I'm glad I got to see what you have written. I forgot how happy we were . . . until he . . . That's why _____ broke our engagement. It should never have happened. 'It' should never have been born." *Audrey-An older sister*

"You children just never did understand. _____ is just like an albatross around my neck, and that's the way it is, whether you like it or not." *Mother*

"Mom wanted him buried there with her and Dad, so I bought the plot and everything's ready. He's 65 now and they still just keep him alive. Mom wanted a tombstone for him, so, it's just waitin' . . ." *Gordon-My little brother*

"You kids were so happy and so much fun. Mama loved you all so much and if ever she had a pet, it was you. Everybody loved it when you all would come out to the farm. We wouldn't have anything 'cept for your Dad, and look what happened to him after _____ was born and then your Mother went bananas. We all knew Mama killed herself tryin' to clean and care for that idiot and he never even knew anything." *Edith-an Aunt*

"I finished the book last night and I wanted more. You could have had a sequel. I enjoyed the book very much and glad you had a happy ending. As I said, I didn't know your Dad that well and only remember seeing him a few times. I remember Aunt ____ doing ironing for people. I remember ____ and that he was put in the ____ and that he was taken out. Kind of lost track of everyone . . ." *A cousin: Barbara, 'Bobby'*

I wrote this manuscript in stages, with emphasize on different thoughts and influential happenings in our family. I first "finished" it in 1980 and began submitting it to well known publishing companies. There were several who just rejected it with no comment. There were three publishers who were very complimentary on my writing, but they did not believe that the reading public would be receptive to a Down Syndrome child.

One publisher's assistant called me repeatedly asking about the many "details" on Down Syndrome, and telling me how interested the Editor was in having it published. She had many questions pertaining to the various stages and abilities of those whom I had known. Then I received the manuscript with a reject.

Later, I learned that a TV program starring a grown Down Syndrome man was on Television. When I tried to call the assistant, I was told she was not available. That particular "program" only ran for three months. I never saw it.

The manuscript was in "mothballs" for years. In 2008 I began submitting it again, and received numerous rejections . . . but, with complementary remarks on my writing.

I first learned in 1989 that 1 out of 800 births were babies with Down Syndrome, or more properly called, Trisomy 21. I read in 2009 that the stats are now 1 out of 625.

I understand that the subject is disconcerting to those who have not had similar experiences. I do hope that you will learn from it and experience a kinship with the very real characters that I grew up with, and am thankful for and love more than I can ever say. I do hope you will read it, like it, and pass it on.

MLV

LIST OF SONGS, PLAYS, AND STORIES
MENTIONED IN THIS BOOK

America the Beautiful, written by Katharine Lee Bates, 1835.

At the Bar, variable lyrics sung to the tune of *At the Cross* by Isaac Watts and Ralph E. Hudson

Dona nobis pacem, (Latin: *Grant us peace*) is a phrase in the *Agnus Dei* section of the Roman Catholic mass. It was set as a separate, final movement in Bach's Mass in B Minor.

Fur Elise, Ludwig van Beethoven, 1810-1812

Give of Your Best to the Master, Words: Howard Grose, 1902.

His Eye is on the Sparrow, lyricist Civilla D. Martin and composer Charles H. Gabriel, 1905.

How Great Thou Art, lyrics by Carl Gustav Boberg (1859–1940).

I Know Whom I Have Believed, Words by Daniel W. Whittle, 1883.

Jesus Loves Me, Written by Anna B. Warner, first Published in 1860.

Joy To The World, Words by English hymn writer Isaac Watts, first published in 1719.

Kiss Me Once, Kiss Me Twice, Lyrics from the song *It's Been A Long Time,* Popularized in 1945 by Bing Crosby. It was written by Sammy Cahn & Jule Styne.

Loch Lomond is a well-known traditional Scottish song (Roud No. 9598). It was first published in 1841 in *Vocal Melodies of Scotland.*

Londonderry Air, Written by Rory O'Cahan, The Lyrics of *Danny Boy* are often set to this tune.

My Country, Tis Of Thee, Samuel Francis Smith,1831.

Nearer, My God, to Thee is a 19th century Christian hymn by Sarah Flower Adams.

Now Is the Hour, is a popular song, though often described as a traditional Mâori song. It is usually credited to Clement Scott, Maewa Kaihau & Dorothy Stewart. 1913.

Nuns Luncheon, from the short story collection *Mortal Coils,* a collection of five short fictional pieces written by Aldous Huxley in 1922.

Oh Freddie Boy Is actually *Danny Boy,* written by Frederick Weatherly and usually set to the tune of the *Londonderry Air.*

Peg o' My Heart, Written by London-born playwright, John Hartley Manners 1870–1928.

When Freddie Comes Home Again, is actually *When Johnny Comes Marching Home Again,* with the lyrics changed. American Civil War song, original lyrics written by Irish-American bandleader Patrick Gilmore.

White Christmas, Irving Berlin, 1940.

Made in the USA
Charleston, SC
02 September 2010